LOVE OF THOL

BOOK 3 IN THE THOL SERIES

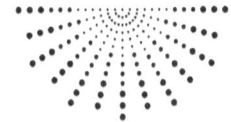

DAWN GREENFIELD IRELAND

ARTISTIC
ORIGINS

CONTENTS

Love of Thol (Book 3) by Dawn Greenfield Ireland

Published by Artistic Origins Inc.

The cover was designed by yours truly, me, the author via an image from an AI program

The paperback cover was put together by Brandon White www.victorylaurel.com

Map of Thol: Cartography by Scott K. Leslie www.theadventurerspack.com

Glossary of Thol by https://www.fiverr.com/ayshaarias

The egg icon for my scene break was created by

Interior layout by Dawn Greenfield Ireland (changes made 10/29/2022, 6/26/2024, 3/31/2026

ISBN 978-1-940385-22-8 (eBook)

ISBN 978-1-940385-23-5 (paperback)

BISAC YAF056030

Dawn Greenfield Ireland

Artistic Origins Inc.

www.degreenfield.com

Publisher's Note: This is a work of fiction. Names, characters, places, and incidents are a product of the author's imagination. Locales and public names are sometimes used for atmospheric purposes. Any resemblance to actual people, living or dead, or to businesses, companies, events, institutions, or locales is completely coincidental.

This book may contain references to specific commercial products, process or service by trade name, trademark, manufacturer, or otherwise, specific brand-name products and/or trade names of products, which are trademarks or registered trademarks and/or trade names, and these are property of their

Please visit my website and leave a review: www.degreenfield.com and sign up for my newsletter and get the latest news before the public.

❀ Formatted with Vellum

Nonfiction	
The Puppy Baby Book	Mastering Your Money (2022)
Puppy Adoption and Beyond	Writers Preparation Handbook
Mastering Your Money (2008)	What's Breaking Your Budget

Online Classes	
Writers Preparation Handbook	How to Format Word Docs Like A Pro

Cozy Mysteries	Sci-Fi-Fantasy
The Alcott Family Adventures	**The Thol Series**
Hot Chocolate	Prophecy of Thol
Bitter Chocolate	Gifts From Thol
Spicy Chocolate	Love of Thol
Nutty Chocolate	King of Thol
Katz' Cat Series	Earth Calling Thol
Katz' Cat	**Sci-Fi Romance Adventure**
Bill Hill's Pills	Forced Dreams
The Detectives	**Dystopian**
The Pact	The Last Dog
	Texmexzona

Books by my Alter Ego ~ DG Ireland
Bonded Shapeshifter Billionaire Series
Bonded
Tothars
Tilted
Unforeseen
Connected

Need A Notebook?
See my 54 themed notebooks on my website www.degreenfield.com/notebooks

Screenplays formatted as books	
Plan B (Dark Comedy)	Where's Ralphie? (Family Comedy)
The God Child (Action Adventure)	Standing Dead (Drama/Tragedy)
The Far Corner (Sci-Fi/Psychological/Creatures)	

Screenplays as TV Episodes	
Hot Chocolate ~ Episode 1	Prophecy of Thol ~ Episode 1
Bonded ~ Episode 1	

See my screenplays and awards on my website: degreenfield.com **Filmfreeway, ISA Network**

ACKNOWLEDGMENTS

The cover was designed by yours truly, me, the author who struggled and stumbled all through the AI cover creation.

The paperback cover was put together by my eldest son, Brandon White www.victorylaurel.com

I wanted a map of Thol, but I'm not even capable of stick figures. Thank you Scott K. Leslie www.theadventurerspack.com the cartographer who tackled the Map of Thol.

The glossary for the Thol book series was created by Ayshaarias from Canada. Man oh man, that gal had her work cut out for her, and she did a fabulous job. Many thanks that I found her! https://www.fiverr.com/ayshaarias

Creatures, creatures, creatures... A hearty thanks to Alex Gravalis (Fiverr.com) for Ghury, the Egrom creature; AskOrbin (Fiverr.com) for my diwal dog; and my son George White for Jakla Bosakin. The borjo creature was created by me via an AI program. YAY me for figuring this out!

Love, hugs and a great big Thank You to Joseph Thompson for saving me from myself. Joe tweaked my baseball dialog and plays to make sure I didn't embarrass myself. I just don't have a sports gene and need all the help I can get in that department.

CHAPTER ONE

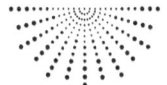

*T*hree months had passed since D'laine and Trakon were married by the Visionary in a breathtaking Tholian ceremony. Brian and Jamie complained bitterly to anyone who would listen about all the kissing going on. D'laine and Trakon were caught kissing down every corridor, around every column in the palace and down practically every alleyway in the kingdom.

Both towheaded boys vowed they would never kiss a girl, and definitely would not be kissing a girl every time they turned around. They were, what D'laine claimed, up-and-coming heartbreakers. Even here on Thol, they turned girls' heads.

"When you're in love, you do a lot of kissing," Lee told his sons. The forty-six-year-old blond engineer found himself engaged in the same activity anytime he was with Ethaderia, queen Kitry's cousin. "You're eleven years old. Just wait a couple of years, Brian. I expect you might be kissing girls within the next year or so."

"You're crazy, Dad!" Brian said. He picked at one of the pockets on his futuristic-looking, nearly indestructible blue and black jumpsuit that resembled an Earth superhero costume.

"You look pretty interested in Yucovia." Lee raised his eyebrows at Brian.

He glared at his father and stomped out of Lee's suite, affronted.

"Why'd you say that, daddy? Brian's not going to be kissing Yucovia!" Jamie said, defending his brother. He stomped out the door and ran to catch up with Brian. At seven, Jamie had even less interest in kissing girls than his brother.

Lee chuckled. "Please let me be able to recall this conversation down the road." He relaxed back in his chair. He liked the comfortable clothing the citizens of Thol wore. They made the material from the silk the hosks spun, and the sap from the agrin trees, which made the material self-healing. His one-piece suit was gray and black. It breathed and kept him cool.

D'laine knocked on the open door. "Hi daddy. What's wrong with Brian and Jamie? They looked mad."

Pup, D'laine's tamed diwal dog, made himself at home and wandered, sniffing around Lee's suite, looking for any crumbs or forgotten scraps of food.

"We were having a conversation about kissing—something they commented about—that you and Trakon engage in kissing at every chance you get. I told Brian I expect him to be kissing girls anytime in the near future. He swore that would never happen," Lee said. "What are you up to today?"

"Ethaderia and I are going to the market. Do you need anything?" D'laine asked. She did not look like a deadly warrior in her two-toned gray suit, but one point of her finger and a channeled thought, and her opponent would be toast.

Lee had his laptop from Earth on his desk. "No, I'm trying to link up with Ben and Victor's laptops."

"How are you going to do that?" D'laine asked. "It's not like there's an interdimensional network."

"While that may be true, think about it. How does wireless work? There's a device—the wireless router—that uses radio waves. We just need the right transmitter and receiver," Lee said.

"Yeah, but this wireless isn't going through the walls of the palace, daddy. It's going through a portal to another dimension," D'laine said. She raised her eyebrows in challenge.

"Ben and Victor are working on their end. Stanley and I will discuss this with the Egroms to see if we can tweak something," Lee said.

"Good luck with that. I'm going downstairs to get Ethaderia," D'laine said. Pup jumped to his feet and joined D'laine. They walked down one flight of stairs and entered the small salon where Kitry and her cousin were talking. "I'm ready."

"Are you sure you don't want to come with us?" Ethaderia asked Kitry.

"You two go and have fun. I'm going over to the nursery," Kitry said. "It's counting day." The queen had her hair in her signature chignon with spiral streams hanging loose. She and her cousin wore the domestic outfits similar to saris.

D'laine remembered when she first arrived in Ebscalon. Trakon had explained the communal hatching centers. She had a difficult time getting her head around the idea that Tholian women did not have live births—they passed eggs like a bird. She supposed she would find out how she would give birth one of these days.

Ethaderia and D'laine left the palace and wandered over to the marketplace. It was crowded with Tholian humans from different kingdoms, along with Plotals, and some lesser creatures of Thol, like D'laine's Safri friend Bok-Tor.

As the women and the dog wandered through the market, they noticed different booths contained replicas of D'laine's wedding dress. There was also jewelry depicting Buffy, the diwal dogs, and D'laine riding Lulu, her pakow.

D'laine spied Stanley with a woman at a booth. They looked seriously interested in each other.

"Ethaderia, who is that woman with Stanley?" D'laine nodded in the direction where the scientist and the mysterious woman stood.

"Oh, that looks like Treikie," Ethaderia said. "She's a scientist."

"A scientist! I hope they are a good match. Stanley needs someone who can keep up with him, brain-wise," D'laine said.

"Treikie would be good for him. She's challenged, socially," Ethaderia said.

"What do you mean?"

"All she talks about are scientific things. It's as if nothing else in the world is relevant," Ethaderia said.

"That sounds just like Stanley! Oh, I hope this works out. Stanley has tried so hard to find a girlfriend, but after an hour with him, the women seem to lock themselves in their rooms," D'laine said.

"Let's see how they act when we approach," Ethaderia said.

"Is that a wise idea?" D'laine asked. She didn't want to chase off a potential match for her scientist friend.

Ethaderia latched her hand through D'laine's arm and steered her toward the two scientists.

"Hello, Treikie!" Ethaderia called out.

The woman turned her face away from Stanley and noticed Ethaderia and D'laine approaching. She smiled widely.

Stanley appeared nervous. "Hi D'laine. Hi Ethaderia. D'laine, have you met Treikie?"

"Hi Stanley. No, how nice to meet you, Treikie," D'laine said.

After he introduced the woman, they chatted for several minutes about all the replicas of D'laine, Trakon and everything else in the marketplace. Ethaderia made excuses, and she and D'laine left the potential love interests to themselves.

"The last woman Stanley tried to get involved with giggled all the time. I'll bet that scared him far away," D'laine said.

"Treikie would be a great match for him. They could spend hours talking about scientific things and never get bored."

"While that sounds fascinating, there's no romance in your theory. They can only go so far with all that talking before it falls apart. They have to find something beyond their careers," Ethaderia said. "They need to share their favorite colors, food, interests other than work-related—all those things that glue a relationship together."

D'laine pulled Ethaderia to a stop. "You and my father make a wonderful couple. Are you going to marry him?"

Ethaderia cast down her eyes. "We have discussed marriage." She raised her eyes and met D'laine's questioning head on. "We love each other. I hope you and Brian approve. It would mean the three of them moving to my quarters. Jamie has already interviewed me as a potential mother and he approves."

D'laine pulled Ethaderia into a hug. "Oh, yes! I so approve of you as mother material, and I'm sure Brian would as well. You're not mean like that Queen Kansing."

"I don't know what my cousin was thinking when she introduced your father to Kansing! I'm glad we got that straightened out without a war," Ethaderia said.

"You and my father make a beautiful couple with your contrasting skin and hair color," D'laine said.

Ethaderia had the customary black hair of Thol, dark sparkling eyes, a heart-shaped face and skin the color of copper-highlighted tan. She stood a few inches taller than D'laine.

They stopped at a booth that sold yarn, material, beads and trinkets. Ethaderia made her choices, paid, and requested the packages be delivered to her house. They wandered the marketplace.

CHAPTER TWO

*B*en Joplin sat in his office at Rice University and took in the room. He had spent a good many years as the head of the physics department. He glanced at the paperwork on his desk. At sixty-two, and a widower with no children, the retirement package lured him. Ben knew what he wanted to do —emigrate to Thol and live among the Kudaja.

A knock sounded on his office door. Ben looked up and recognized Al Jordan, the reporter he had talked to over a year ago about D'laine's disappearance. Ben stood.

"Al! What brings you to my office?" Ben asked.

"Hello, Doctor Joplin. I'm doing a story on the Jacksons," Al said. "It's the one-year anniversary of the disappearance of the entire family. There's heavy speculation on the web that they joined D'laine, wherever she went."

Ben nodded. "While that might seem reasonable, perhaps they just moved and are keeping a low-profile existence?" Ben figured Al wouldn't swallow that line, but it was the best he could do.

"Nah. Lee willed his property to his housekeeper, so this disappearance was planned," Al said. "I spoke with Rosa and her husband this morning and they've kept Lee's office as a shrine, so I doubt the family moved somewhere else."

"Sounds as if you have more information than I do, Al," Ben said. "What else have you come up with?"

"When we first spoke, after D'laine disappeared, I mentioned a wormhole through to another dimension. I'm wondering if the Jackson family had some unique connection with wherever D'laine went," Al said.

"So, you believe she came back and got her family and they returned to this other place?" Ben asked. It concerned him about the reporter's curiosity. What if he, Ben, passed over to the other side? Would the reporter latch onto his disappearance? Get the military involved?

"That's the only logical explanation I could come up with," Al asked. He practically drooled with the thought of this wormhole theory.

Ben picked up the retirement papers on his desk. "Al, I'll be retiring and moving within the next several weeks. Please don't get it in your head I've "gone over" to the Jackson's paradise, or wherever they're living."

"You think it's a paradise?" Al asked.

"Surely, they wouldn't move to a harsh, dangerous world, you don't think?" Ben said. "Lee would be too concerned of danger for his young sons to even consider that aspect."

Al hemmed and hawed in consideration. "Yeah, that makes sense. Where are you going when you leave here?"

"I'm looking at travel trailers. I want to see the entire USA, then Central and South America and beyond," Ben said. That was the only logical explanation to tell the reporter so he wouldn't jump to the conclusion he vanished into thin air. He contemplated spinning a story about his death and running an obit in the Houston paper to stop the trail. He'd decided he better talk to Victor about it.

"Wow. That sounds like a great retirement. What was the

name of the guy Victor and Stanley worked for out in California?" Al asked.

"Dr. Joe Paxton at the Whitting Institute. Victor Bennett still
works there. We talk every once in a while," Ben said.

Al stood. He stretched out his hand and shook Ben's hand.
"Well, thanks for taking the time to talk with me. If I don't see
you before you leave the university, have a wonderful
retirement."

"Thanks, Al. Good luck with the story," Ben said.

The reporter left. Ben returned to his desk. He picked up a
pen and signed the documents. He made up his mind. Adventure called, and while he was not doting in his old age, he
wanted many years to explore the place he wanted to call his
new home.

BEN PICKED UP THE PHONE AND CALLED VICTOR. HE LISTENED TO
the ringing three times, waiting for voicemail to kick in when
Victor answered.

"Victor, it's Ben. Do you have a minute?" Ben asked.

"Hey, Ben. Everything okay on your end?" Victor asked.

"Wanted to give you a heads up on something—actually a
couple of things. First up, remember that reporter that did the
original story on D'laine's disappearance?" Ben asked.

"Yeah, why?" Victor asked.

"He just left here. He plans to contact you and your boss.
He's doing a follow-up story on the one-year anniversary of the
entire Jackson family's disappearance," Ben said.

"I'll let Dr. Paxton know. He's not going to be happy about
that," Victor said. "He's still filling out paperwork about Stanley's disappearance. What's the other thing you wanted to talk
about?"

"I've put in for retirement, Victor," Ben said. "I want to

contact Lee and find out if the Kudaja will accept me living there."

Victor groaned. "Kara and I have discussed this in great detail, but I bet you'd go at the first opportunity."

"I'm not getting any younger, Victor. I want to have my chance exploring that world. I haven't made up my mind what to do with the condo and my possessions," Ben said.

"Can't you take some of your favorite things with you? Sell or donate the rest," Victor said.

"I told that reporter I was buying a travel trailer and would be traveling full time," Ben said. "I think that's the best plan. Buy the trailer, sort through things, sell the condo and come your way. I'll sign the vehicles over to you."

"I'm at a loss for words," Victor said. "I'm excited and sad at the same time. Kara and I are still talking about it. Hopefully, once you get settled, we'll make another trip and stay longer."

"Remember, there's the ten-year time lag," Ben said. "I don't know if it's reversible, but we're aging here rapidly compared to aging on Thol."

They ended their call. Ben picked up the papers on his desk and walked briskly to the HR department. He was so ready to move on with his life.

CHAPTER THREE

*L*ee and Stanley sat in Lee's suite in deep discussion about communicating with Victor and Ben.

"I think we need to develop a form of radio frequency device," Lee said. He sketched ideas on a sheet of paper made from hosk silk and agrin tree leaves that was soft and durable. He tapped his writing instrument, similar to a ballpoint pen on Earth.

Stanley stared off into space, his super-brain making connections and qualifying thoughts and contingencies. His odd-shaped head, rounder than his original skull, had reshaped when Greg Claymore changed some structures in Stanley's brain. Luckily, he didn't have to wear the restricting helmet. The scientist's brain would incapacitate anyone without the old helmet. He was eternally grateful for the cure.

Claymore lived on the other side of Thol with the Oolarooloo people, and had traveled back and forth between Thol and Earth more than once. Lee, Stanley, Victor and Ben had studied everything they could about the man.

Stanley held up a hand. "I've got it."

Lee looked away from his project. He had pulled his drawing up into a 3-D diagram and studied it. "What do you mean?"

"I'm going to focus my complete brain power on Victor's cellphone number. It can't hurt, right?" Stanley said.

Lee shrugged. "Give it a try. What do we have to lose? It could be as simple as the power of your thought."

Stanley closed his eyes. He focused on Victor's phone number in the vast contacts list stored in his head. He thought hard about the connection. About the phone ringing. Suddenly, there was a static change and Victor's voice answered in Stanley's head.

"Hello?" Victor said. "Who's calling?" He sounded angry.

"Victor! It's Stanley!"

"Stan? Where are you? Did you return to Earth?" Victor said. He shot out of the chair in his home office.

"I'm home, on Thol. Lee's with me. We've been working on ways to contact you and Ben through RF frequency, but I figured I'd try my brain," Stanley said.

"Wow! That super brain of yours knows no ends!" Victor said.

"I'm learning new applications every day," Stanley said.

"Listen, I talked to Ben the other day. He's retiring from Rice and wants to live with the Kudaja. Can you ask them if he'd be welcome?" Victor said. "We're aging here, as you know. Ben's sixty-two and wants a life."

"I'll talk to Lee. We'll fly out and visit the Kudaja. I'll bet they'd welcome him," Stanley said. "Lee said we'll have to coordinate with D'laine for when Ben comes. That part is pretty easy—I think we're old pros at it."

"How can I get in touch with you?" Victor asked. "The only thing I know that works is the connection through D'laine."

Stanley relayed the question.

"Lee said that until we get things fine-tuned, D'laine's connection will have to do," Stanley said. "This is strange. Lee can't hear the whole conversation, just what I say to you, but I can hear everything in my head. Lee said we'll talk to Ghury. He may be able to figure something out."

"Gosh, I miss all of you. How's Buffy doing?" Victor asked.

"She's doing good." Stanley said. He talked to Lee. "He's asking about Buffy."

"Tell him I'm positive Buffy's age is reversing," Lee said. "She seems more active and energetic, and her face appears to be younger. This could be a serious indication of Thol regeneration."

Stanley passed the information along to Victor.

"Have either of you noticed any changes in yourselves?" Victor asked.

"I don't seem to be any different," Stanley said. "However, with the changes in my brain, I'm not sure. What about you, Lee? Have you noticed any changes in yourself?"

"Not really, but to be honest, I haven't focused on that part of myself," Lee said.

"We'll keep an eye on Buffy and will let you know if we experience any changes," Stanley said. "I think I'd better end this communication experiment for now. My head's getting twitchy."

"I'm so glad this worked out," Victor said. "I'll call Ben and tell him about the Tholian phone service. Take care, Stan."

Stanley blinked hard. He felt the connection disengage. "Wow! That's something I never would have expected." He stood. "Let's go take a look at Buffy and tell everyone about our successful experiment."

LEE AND STANLEY WALKED DOWN THE STAIRS TO THE FIRST FLOOR of the palace. The dogs were nowhere around. They walked to the front archway and stood outside.

"Buffy!" Lee called. He reached out with his mind and called to D'laine. *Is Buffy with you?*

No. She's probably with Pup and Chatter. Why? Is something wrong? D'laine asked.

Just looking for her, Lee said. He turned to Stanley. "Not sure where she is. D'laine said she's probably with Pup and Chatter."

"Why don't we walk over to Trakon's shop? She could be over there," Stanley said.

They headed off in that direction. They found Hexlon and the men working on one of several crestriders. The entire fleet was being fitted with the crystals so the ships could fly at night. The experimental ships worked flawlessly once the crystals had been shaped and aligned as Stanley and Lee suggested.

Soon, a team would teach other kingdoms how to upgrade their ships. Before long, they would be back to where their planet was, technologically, before the Great War of Taylon.

"Hey, Hexlon, is Trakon around?" Pup and Chatter were curled up on an old sofa cushion on the floor.

"Yeah, he's in the office," Hexlon said.

The guys smirked.

Lee and Stanley headed for the door in the back of the shop.

"Wonder where Buffy is," Stanley said.

Lee opened the door. Trakon and D'laine were wrapped around each other in a smoldering kiss. Lee cleared his throat. "Sorry to interrupt."

Now that they were married, they no longer sprang apart from the guilt of being caught. Trakon ended the kiss. They smooched once, quickly, then turned to Lee and Stanley.

"What's up?" D'laine asked.

"We saw Pup and Chatter, but we don't know where Buffy is," Lee said.

"Have you checked with Brian and Jamie?" Trakon said.

"What's going on?" D'laine asked. "It's unusual for you to be worried about Buffy."

"We were talking to Victor, and your father mentioned that he thought Buffy was regenerating," Stanley said.

"What?" D'laine shrieked. "You talked to Victor? How in the world did you do that?"

"What do you mean, Buffy's regenerating?" Trakon asked.

Lee held up a hand. "Stanley's big brain connected to Victor's cellphone. We don't know how it works, only that it does."

"We want to check Buffy over. Her face seemed like it looked younger," Stanley said. "Oh, and Ben wants to immigrate to the Kudaja forest. Do you think they'd let him live there?"

Both Trakon and D'laine were dumbfounded over the two subjects.

D'laine called out to her brother. *Brian, Jamie, is Buffy with you?*

Yeah, Jamie sent.

Where are you? We want to check out Buffy, D'laine sent.

We'll be right there. Where are you? Jamie asked.

We're at the shop.

"I'm not sure where they are, but they're on their way," D'laine said. "Sounds suspicious to me when they get secretive."

"Can't you do that thing and find where they are?" Stanley asked.

D'laine got quiet and let her eyes go soft. She saw Brian and Jamie running with Buffy. "I'm not sure where they were, all I see is they're on the way. Looks like they were near the ball field."

"There's nothing over there they could get into," Trakon said.

"That's what you think," Lee said. He shook his head. He knew his boys.

They walked out of the office into the shop just as the boys and Buffy arrived. The diwal dogs bounded around Buffy and the boys.

Lee eyed the boys. They squirmed.

Buffy ran up to D'laine expecting a scratch or two. Pup and

Chatter didn't want to be left out, so D'laine ended up giving each of them a scratch.

Lee squatted. "Come here, girl."

Buffy joyfully trotted to him, flopped down on the floor and waited for a belly rub.

Lee rubbed her tummy while he looked her over.

Stanley got on his knees and ran a hand over her body. He didn't pick up anything wrong.

They studied her face. She did look younger.

D'laine joined them on the floor. She focused on the family dog. She held her hands over the dog. One by Buffy's head, one by her rear end. D'laine closed her eyes.

She detected the buzzing of blood flowing in veins.

She heard a strong heartbeat.

There was no indication of any cancer or disease. Overall, Buffy was in great shape.

D'laine opened her eyes. "Huh. It's like she's a young dog inside. There's none of the age-related problems I expected. No arthritis, nothing wrong whatsoever."

Lee and Stanley stared at Buffy. This was crucial information. If a dog could rejuvenate, what about human Earthlings?

"Let's keep an eye on her," Lee said. "This is a significant finding."

"We're off to visit Herish and Meeri in a little while. We'll ask about Ben," Trakon said. "Since Herish is the heir apparent, we'll ask if he can give permission for Ben to live there. Maybe his father and a committee has to approve something like that."

TRAKON STEERED THE CRESTRIDER TO THE EDGE OF THE TREES and landed the craft. He and D'laine hopped down to the ground just as Herish and Meeri walked out of the forest into the open.

"There you are!" Meeri said. She ran up to D'laine, and they hugged.

Trakon and Herish grasped arms in the Tholian customary greeting. Trakon grabbed Herish's hand and shook it.

"That's how they greet on Earth," Trakon said. "It's a lot friendlier."

"Yeah, I like that," Herish said, giving Trakon's hand another shake.

The foursome walked through the trees into the dense forest. After a good twenty yards, they rounded a tree and climbed the stairs affixed to the gigantic agrin tree, into the canopy. They walked the boardwalk for quite a distance until they came to the marketplace where a crowd of Kudaja bargained with shopkeepers.

D'laine loved the Kudaja village in the trees. The structures were breathtaking. The boardwalk a work of art. She enjoyed the marketplaces where haggling between buyer and seller was interesting to watch. Sometimes the parties became a little heated, but she wondered if that was a show to get or keep a price of an object.

They passed through the shops and approached the palace. They walked around to Herish and Meeri's suite. An attendant brought a platter of finger-food, plates and napkins, while another attendant brought a pitcher of kahl and goblets.

The men dug into the food while Meeri poured the kahl.

"I swear you'd think they never had regular meals," Meeri said.

D'laine snorted a laugh. "Back on Earth, we would have to prepare our own food. I don't think I could keep Trakon's stomach full."

Meeri's eyes opened wide. "You had to cook your own food?"

"Yes, not everyone is privileged and lives in a palace with staff at their beck and call," D'laine said. "My family were working people. We had a housekeeper that cooked and cleaned, but she didn't wait on us."

"They have food delivery," Trakon said. "You'd love pizza and chocolate! I miss those things. And wine!"

D'laine nudged her shoulder into Trakon's. "I had to cut him off from our wine. He became boisterous after just a few sips."

"What is wine made from?" Herish asked.

"Grapes," D'laine said. "There are many different varieties of grapes that make different types and flavors of wine."

They munched on the food. Trakon brought up Ben's request.

"I don't see any problem with Ben living here. We can ask my father before you have to head back," Herish said.

"He loves the forest, and likes the idea of living in the trees," D'laine said.

"I wonder what his earthly gift will be," Meeri said. "You Earthlings seem to bring special abilities when you settle here."

"Hey, how's Stanley doing without his helmet?" Herish asked.

D'laine's face lit up. "I think he has a girlfriend!"

"How come you didn't tell me?" Trakon asked.

"I just found out today," D'laine said. "I saw him in the marketplace and he was with this woman that Ethaderia recognized. Her name is Treikie, and she's a scientist. I hope this works out. Stanley is not the best at socializing."

"Treikie Soluvia? I know her!" Trakon said. "She is very much like Stanley—all brainy babbling and not knowing when to stop and have fun."

They spent the next couple of hours talking about their new lives. When Trakon and D'laine were ready to head back to Ebscalon, they all went in search of King Cagmondoore. They found him conducting business similar to how Jor-Dan did with petitions from the people.

"Father, do you remember Ben, the Earthling you met at D'laine and Trakon's wedding?" Herish asked his father.

"Yes, he was one of the scientists, wasn't he?" the king asked.

"That's right. He would like to live here among the Kudaja," Herish said. "Can we grant him permission, or do we have to have a meeting with your advisors?"

King Cagmondoore rubbed his chin. "No one has ever approached us about living among us. I would think we would all enjoy having Ben live here."

"Can I tell him you will accept him then?" D'laine asked. "He fell in love with your forest home."

"Yes, please tell him to come when he is ready," the king said. "I will have a place prepared for him."

They left the palace. Herish and Meeri walked Trakon and D'laine back to their crestrider.

"It's getting close to dark," Herish said. "You don't have to worry about the ship failing?"

"Not anymore," Trakon said. "The upgrades with the new crystal solar collectors and batteries work perfectly. The Egroms helped with the crystals. They had to shape them the way Stanley and Lee suggested. Now everything works at night!"

They made their goodbyes and D'laine and Trakon boarded the crestrider and headed for home.

CHAPTER FOUR

*J*or-Dan, Marrak the documentarian, and the rest of the king's advisors sat in the throne room and listened to petitions from the citizens. La'gar'ish, Jor-Dan's trusty diwal dog, lay at his feet, snoozing quietly.

A long line of petitioners stretched past the doorway and wound around the inside wall of the large room. People munched on food stored in the pockets of their clothes. They understood they would be there a while, so they came prepared.

Brian sat between the king and the documentarian. He took it upon himself to learn these proceedings with the people so he would understand the government of Ebscalon.

Not every eleven-year-old boy would be interested in hearing the petitions, but since he needed something to occupy himself with, this was a good start. Brian was sure his father and the queen would be happy that he wasn't running through the kingdom getting into scrapes.

Two farmers were arguing as they approached the king. They hit their chests with their fists in the customary greeting of the king.

"King Jor-Dan. I'm Ulf and this is Quag. We share a well, but

Quag, here, has been using a lot of water for his gardens. I'm afraid the well will run dry."

Quag sputtered under his breath. "Listen here, I'm not using any more water than I have for the past thirty paths. I can't figure out what's wrong with Ulf. He's being unreasonable."

Jor-Dan stared at the farmers. He let out a snort. "Tell me what you are here for. Since you share your well, and you have not petitioned me about any problems in the past paths, what do each of you expect to gain by this audience?"

Marrak looked through his books stored in his communicator. He searched for the farmers names, but didn't find any record of them. "There have been no petitions or audiences from either of these farmers."

"I want Quag to stop using so much water!" Ulf said. He almost hollered.

Quag looked to the king and Marrak with imploring eyes. It was obvious he didn't understand what was going on with Ulf. They had been sharing the well for paths without any problems.

Brian scrunched his face. "Ulf, has your head been hurting?"

The farmer looked at Brian for a long moment. "Yeah. How'd you know?"

"Jor-Dan, it might be a good idea if D'laine looked at Ulf's head. He could have a brain tumor or some condition that is causing him to make accusations," Brian said.

Jor-Dan nodded acknowledgment. "That's a superb idea, Brian. There could be some physical condition that's beyond what we can see."

Marrak hit his communicator and called to D'laine. "Would you be able to come to the throne room and help a petitioner?" He listened. "D'laine will be here shortly." He addressed the farmers. "Please wait on the bench."

The farmers moved over to the bench and the next petitioner approached, fist to chest.

D'laine entered the room. Brian ran over to her. He

explained the odd behavior and introduced his sister to the farmers.

"Ulf, how long have you had these headaches?" D'laine asked.

The farmer though for a moment. "I'm not sure."

Quag harrumphed. "We've been fighting about the well for two months. We've never had any problems before then."

"Okay. Ulf, I'm going to scan your head. It won't hurt. You tell me if you feel odd, okay?" D'laine ran one hand around an inch from Ulf's face, and the other hand over the top of his head and down to the back of his neck. She let her eyes relax as she looked inside. As Brian suspected, and she concluded, a tumor was causing the problem.

"I found the problem," D'laine said. "Brian, can you find a bucket or something that won't burn from acid?"

Brian ran over to Dannin, at the end of the table. "Where can I find a sturdy bucket that won't be missed?"

Dannin got up. He and Brian left the room and returned shortly with something that looked like a lidded metal trash can. Brian placed it on the floor by his sister.

Jor-Dan and the advisors gathered nearby to watch the procedure.

"Okay, Quag, please move a safe distance away. Ulf, I want you to lie down on the bench." D'laine retrieved her crystals out of her pouch. She looked to Brian and Dannin. "I'll require some wet cloths to wipe my hands with. They're going into the bucket when I'm finished with them."

Dannin and Brian ran out of the room and returned with two wrung out cloths.

"I'll be doing trance work, so when I ask for something, step forward and do as I ask," D'laine said. "But in the meantime, step over there where Quag is. Stay out of the way unless I call you."

"Okay, got it," Brian said. He and Dannin moved over to where Quag stood.

"Ulf, this will feel strange, but everything will be okay. My work will not hurt you in any way, just stay as still as you can, okay?" D'laine said.

Ulf nodded. He seemed confused.

D'laine picked up the bucket and moved to the other side of the bench. This was the side where she detected the mass growing in Ulf's head. She placed a crystal on Ulf's forehead in the third eye position. She then ran her hands several inches over the top of his head, and the left temple.

Her right hand plunged through Ulf's temple. She ripped out a vile, throbbing mass and flung it into the can. "Cloth!"

Brian hurried over to his sister with a wet cloth.

D'laine wiped her hand as thoroughly as possible then cast the cloth into the bucket. "Close the lid!"

Brian closed the lid on the trash can.

D'laine scanned Ulf's head. She removed the crystal from his forehead. "Come!"

Dannin hurried over and retrieved the crystal.

"Move back!" D'laine said as she pointed to where the others waited.

She bent over the farmer looking straight into his skull. She stood straight, held her hand out. "Crystal!"

Dannin returned with the crystal.

"Back!"

He hurried away and watched the proceedings, fascinated.

D'laine moved slightly. She pushed the can with her foot to reposition it. She plunged her right hand into Ulf's skull over his left eyebrow. "Open the can!"

Dannin held Brian back. "Stay here!" He rushed forward and removed the lid. The tumor sizzled and spit from the bottom of the can.

D'laine pulled another mass out of the farmer's head and flung it into the can. "Cloth!"

Dannin covered the can. He turned to leave, but D'laine's clean hand thrust out and grabbed his arm. "Stay."

Brian ran forward with the cloth.

"Should we get more cloths?" he asked.

"One more," D'laine said. Her voice sounded strange, distant.

Brian ran from the room. He returned with another wrung out wet cloth.

D'laine wiggled her fingers into Ulf's head and pulled out some tendrils.

Dannin opened the can, and D'laine tossed the gore inside.

D'laine ran her hands above the farmer's head. She walked around to the top of his head, bent down and looked closely. She stood. "Cloth!"

Brian placed the wet cloth in her hands. She wiped her hand thoroughly. Dannin reached to take the cloth.

"No!" D'laine stated. She tossed the cloth in the can. She removed the crystal from Ulf's forehead. In a few seconds she came out of her trance. "Ulf, how do you feel?"

The farmer blinked. "Where am I? What happened?"

Quag came forward. "We're at the palace. We came to petition the king about the well."

"What's wrong with the well? Did it run dry, or something?" Ulf asked.

"There's nothing wrong with your well," Brian said. "You had a tumor growing in your head and it made you think there was a problem with the well and you were arguing with Quag."

Jor-Dan was amazed at what his daughter-in-law did. "This was remarkable, D'laine."

"One of my many gifts," she said.

Ulf sat up. "Quag and I don't have any problems. We've been neighbors and friends for a long time."

Quag helped Ulf stand. He grasped D'laine's arm in thankfulness. "I can't thank you enough for saving my friend."

D'laine lifted the lid of the can. "This is what was wrong."

She showed them the growth. "That was crowding out your thought-processing abilities, Ulf. I removed it. You shouldn't have any more problems, but if you do, I'll help you again."

DANNIN, BRIAN AND D'LAINE WALKED THROUGH THE CITY GATES to the field. Dannin carried the trash container that held the tumor. They walked far away from the populace and stopped. Dannin set the can on the moss-covered ground.

"Stand back. I haven't done this before, so I'm not sure if this will work," D'laine said. She pointed to the can with intense focus. Something like a storm cloud shrouded the can. Then it was gone.

"Where'd it go?" Brian asked.

"I thought it destroyed, so it didn't go anywhere. I think it evaporated," D'laine said.

They returned to the palace. D'laine climbed the stairs to her and Trakon's living quarters. Brian and Dannin took their places at the table and the petitions resumed.

"Everything taken care of?" Jor-Dan asked. The king and his advisors were amazed at the healing procedure D'laine had performed on the farmer.

A man in an unfamiliar black and brown uniform approached the table. The first thing Brian noticed, that stood his hair on end, was the man did not perform the respectful greeting of his fist to his chest to the king.

Suddenly, La'gar'ish was on his feet and literally pushed Jor-Dan's chair back as his deadly teeth clattered their warning of attack.

The man whipped out a long blade and thrust it into Marrak's chest.

Screams and shouts erupted from the petitioners and the

advisors. The guards swarmed the man and rustled him to the floor. He never uttered a word.

Jor-Dan clung to La'gar'ish's collar to keep him from attacking the assailant. "La'gar'ish, calm!"

The dog stopped struggling against Jor-Dan.

The advisors and more guards swarmed around the king, protecting him.

"D'laine! Come quick!" Brian screamed into his communicator.

The advisors grabbed Marrak and laid him on the floor.

"Remove the attacker to a holding cell!" Jor-Dan barked to the guards.

The guards hauled the man away.

"We have to stop the bleeding!" Jor-Dan tore a strip of cloth from the hem of his tunic and knelt beside Marrak. He held the cloth over the wound, around the knife and applied pressure.

"Has anyone called for D'laine or the Visionary?" Jor-Dan asked.

D'laine rushed into the room. She gasped when she saw Marrak on the floor covered in blood, a knife sticking out of his heart. "Stanley!" She called out to the scientist using The Voice.

Stanley, Lee and Trakon rushed into the room, followed by Kitry and Ethaderia. Chatter and Pup circled the room, teeth clacking, sniffing for the attacker.

"Oh, no!" Kitry wailed. Then her eyes took in Jor-Dan, covered in blood. She was about to react when he shook his head.

"Not my blood."

"Stanley, I need you to get Marrak outside on top of some dirt," D'laine said.

"Move back!" Trakon bellowed at the crowd.

Guards moved in to control the people who wanted to get a better view.

Stanley focused on Marrak. He stretched his arm out in

front of him and the dying documentarian levitated several feet off the floor. He walked out the door, the levitated body steady in front of him.

D'laine, the dogs and everyone else followed as Stanley left the palace. He stopped in the courtyard and looked around. He spotted a large garden area and headed that way. Stanley gently lowered Marrak onto the ground.

"I remember Greg Claymore telling me that there would be times when I would have to sink my feet into the soil to perform a difficult healing." D'laine pressed a button on each of her boots and they deflated. She stood, barefoot in the dirt.

D'laine pressed the button on Marrak's uniform, deflating the suit. She tossed the blood-soaked cloth aside that the king had applied to the wound. She ripped the suit, so she had access to the wound. Taking in a deep breath, D'laine pulled the knife out of Marrak's chest. Then she placed her hands on the wound.

Her hands were covered in blood. She grounded herself by moving her feet in the soil until they were covered in dirt. D'laine closed her eyes. She felt her hands getting warm.

"Look at that!" Lee exclaimed.

They could see a golden glow surrounding D'laine's hands and Marrak's skin underneath. The blood stopped flowing from the wound.

Marrak's suit tried to repair itself.

"Brian, go get a bath towel. We have to get Marrak's suit off," Lee said. He approached Marrak and D'laine. Trakon joined him. "Let's try to get this suit off him so it doesn't interfere with the healing."

They eased the suit down and released the documentarian's arms from the loosened sleeves. By the time Brian returned with the towel, they had removed the suit. Lee covered Marrak with the towel.

"This will most likely be better for the healing," Lee said. "His body is on top of the soil with no barrier."

"I hope she can save him," Jor-Dan said. Marrak was like a son to him.

Kitry put her arm around her husband. "It will be okay. Our daughter-in-law performs miracles."

The Visionary and his two acolytes, Ekal and Rettu, stood on the sidelines watching the healing.

"The Golden Girl of Ebscalon has merged with the essence of Thol," the Visionary claimed. "She is pulling her love of Thol out of the ground to heal this man."

D'laine stood still, eyes closed. She didn't move an inch. Her chest barely rose with breath she took in or released.

Marrak didn't seem to be breathing at all.

Brian fussed, silently. He liked Marrak and didn't want him to die.

Lee hugged his son to him. "He'll pull through. There's not much your sister can't do."

Trakon hovered nearby. He always worried when D'laine used her profound abilities. He feared something going wrong and her getting hurt, or damaged in some way. He wasn't sure he could survive without his wife. Their love had grown over time and distance from when D'laine was in a coma. When she had briefly returned to Earth after conquering the robots, his heart shattered.

Now, he watched with trepidation, as D'laine was healing Marrak. She was performing deep work. She had never tried to bring someone back from death. Trakon wasn't sure if Marrak had still been alive when D'laine started the healing process.

Jamie and Buffy ran up to the crowd. Pup and Chatter met them. Jamie squeezed in between people. Once they saw the dogs, people scattered apart letting them through. No one ultimately trusted the diwal dogs.

"What happened?" Jamie asked. He approached his father and brother.

"I'm not sure," Lee said.

Jor-Dan shook his head. "We were listening to petitions and this man in a uniform I didn't recognize, stabbed Marrak through the heart."

Jamie gasped. "How come?"

"We aren't sure. We will question him once Marrak is out of danger," Jor-Dan said.

"Why would anyone want to hurt Marrak?" Brian asked. "It doesn't make any sense.

HOURS PASSED WITHOUT D'LAINE MOVING. ONLY A HANDFUL OF people remained on watch, waiting for a sign that Marrak would survive the attack.

"Let's go talk to the warrior who attacked Marrak," Trakon said.

Jor-Dan pulled his eyes away from the healing process and focused on his son. "Okay. We need to sort out this attack."

Trakon, Jor-Dan, Lee, Stanley, Brian, Jamie and the dogs returned to the palace. La'gar'ish stayed tight against Jor-Dan's legs.

Trakon led them down a back hallway to a door. They descended two stair levels to what only could be construed as a jail.

A wall of cells greeted them. The attacker was in the middle cell. He was curled up on the cold, stone floor instead of on the cot.

The dogs went wild. Teeth clacked a deafening staccato while the dogs growled at the warrior. They clawed through the bars of the cell trying to get at the man.

"Jamie! Call off the dogs," Jor-Dan said.

Jamie stared at the dogs, silently.

Pup turned his head and stared at Jamie.

"Huh. Pup said this isn't a man. He's something else, but he didn't know what," Jamie said.

"But of course, it's a man. He's right here in front of us," Trakon said.

Jamie got closer to the bars. "No, it's not a man. He's cloaked his real form and has taken this form to trick us."

Brian stared at the man on the floor of the cell. "Whoa! I just had a vision of something!"

"Spit it out, son," Lee said. "We haven't got all day."

Brian focused on the man again. Creatures scrambled around on all fours. Their backs were up in an arch and they were covered with brown and black hair. He projected his visuals to the others.

"What are those?" Trakon asked. "I've never seen those creatures before. Are they from Thol or another place?"

"I don't know," Brian said. "I didn't detect a portal, so this is Thol. The creatures were just there."

"Can you talk to him, Jamie?" Lee asked.

Jamie stared at the creature man. *Why did you attack?*

The man didn't respond.

Jamie tried again. *Who are you and where did you come from?*

The creature made eye contact with Jamie. *I Fod.*

"He says he's Fod. I'm not sure if that's his name, his kind, or where he comes from," Jamie said. He wandered away and returned with a bowl of water. He slid it under the bars. "He won't be able to use the faucet, so he needs water and food the way he's used to eating and drinking."

"Good observation, son," Lee said.

Stanley patted Jamie on the shoulder. "Let me look inside his mind. I should be able to sort this out." He studied the man creature for several long moments. He let loose a deep breath. "Let's go upstairs, shall we?" He made eye contact with Jor-Dan, then Trakon.

They took the hint that Stanley didn't want to discuss what

he discovered in front of the man. Everyone returned to the main floor in the palace and they settled into the small salon.

"His kind are called Fod. It's unknown if he, himself has a name, but they're from Mount Aguberro. I think they got confused when they sent this creature on this mission," Stanley said.

"What do you mean?" Jor-Dan asked. "What were they confused about?"

"Marrak is a documentarian. The Fod wrongly thought Marrak was the one who tried to steal a scroll from the cave Maldi Amadal visited. Get it: scroll means documentarian to them," Stanley said. "There's some type of magic in those mountains that transformed this Fod into this man. He can't talk like a human. He doesn't have that capability. He can only communicate as his animal form, and in a simple language of pictures in his head."

Trakon shook his head. "Let me see if I understand this. This Fod creature came here to punish whoever was in the cave. Is that right?"

Stanley bobbed his head. "More or less. I'm not sure punish is the correct term. He struck Marrak a deadly blow with a knife straight into his heart. So, theoretically, he was sent as an assassin to make sure no one returned to the cave containing all the scrolls and priceless antiques."

"It sounds like his kind are the sentinels of the caves," Lee said.

"What do we do with him?" Jor-Dan asked. "He needs to understand that his kind made a terrible mistake."

They stood in silent thought pondering the problem. The creature wasn't a murderer. He was protecting the holy cave and the priceless contents.

"Let's go see how D'laine is doing with Marrak." Trakon turned to the door and left the salon.

CHAPTER FIVE

itry, Ethaderia, the advisors and several guards remained outside watching D'laine and Marrak. Trakon was several steps ahead of his father, their group and the dogs. He didn't see any change. He rubbed his hand across his face in frustration. "No difference?"

Kitry kissed his cheek. "We will have to be patient, son."

The majordomo and a line of kitchen workers approached with bowls of food. Four men carried a table. Others carried chairs.

"It has been too long since you have had nourishment," the majordomo said.

The table was prepared. Plates, silverware, napkins, goblets and food were laid out.

"Sit. Eat," the majordomo said.

Everyone sat at the table and picked at their food. Trakon rested his chin in his hands while the staff removed the food. They left the goblets and pitchers of water.

"Why is it taking so long?" Jamie whined.

"The knife was thrust into Marrak's heart, so there was a lot of damage," Lee said. "This is much better than a hospital and surgery back home."

"Healing on Earth is barbaric compared to this," Stanley said. "I'm grateful that D'laine let me return to Thol with her."

"How do your people heal on Earth?" Kitry asked.

Lee pondered the question. "Earth has doctors and hospitals for the sick, but they don't heal. Surgeons operate on patients and remove body parts, organs and diseased things."

"There are some healers, but they don't have the capability to do what D'laine does," Stanley said. "Many times, people come out of a hospital sicker than when they entered it."

Kitry and Ethaderia exchanged shocked expressions.

"Why is your planet so far behind?" Ethaderia asked.

"You don't know the half of it," Lee said. "If we were to return to Earth to share our knowledge and new capabilities with the world, the government would arrest us. They would prod us, poke and experiment upon us, and the military would want to use our powers to overcome other nations, or places if they could access a portal. This is why I'll never return to Earth, willingly."

Everyone sprang to their feet when Marrak pulled in a deep, shaky breath.

D'laine opened her eyes, but kept her hands in place. "I've brought him back, but there is much more healing to be done."

"We're so grateful, D'laine," Jor-Dan said. "I'd be quite lost without Marrak."

Trakon grabbed a goblet of water and held it to D'laine's lips. She took a long drink.

"Thanks. I needed that," she said.

"Do you need food or anything?" Trakon asked.

She shook her head. "I'll be able to release him in a little while. I've repaired his heart. It's beating strong. His arteries are functioning properly."

"What's left?" Stanley asked.

"I'm calming the shock to his body," D'laine said. "It's not every day you get killed and restored. That's hard on the body, mind and soul."

After several more minutes, D'laine removed her hand from the documentarian's heart, and stepped back. "Stanley, think you can move Marrak to his apartment?"

"Sure. Where does he live?" Stanley asked. He held out his hand and raised Marrak off the ground.

"I'll show you," Brian said. He ran ahead of Stanley.

They entered the palace. Brian led Stanley and the procession down half a dozen corridors to a door on the main floor. He opened the door for Stanley. Kitry and Ethaderia turned down the bedding and Stanley settled Marrak onto his bed. They covered him with the top sheet.

D'laine and Trakon entered the apartment. "He'll sleep for several hours, possibly even a day before he wakes fully."

"We can take turns watching over him," Kitry said.

"No, I'll ask Twum. She likes Marrak," D'laine said.

As everyone sat in the salon discussing the Fod, one of the palace guards interrupted. "Treikie Soluveia has arrived."

Stanley sprang to his feet. "Oh, no! I forgot!"

Treikie entered the room. After a moment of perusing all in attendance, her eyes latched onto Stanley. They met each other halfway across the room.

"I waited for you, but worried something happened," Treikie said.

"I'm so sorry! I've ruined your lunch," Stanley said. He took her hands in his. "We had this situation…"

"I heard rumors of the documentarian being attacked." She looked Stanley over to make sure he was not hurt. "I wanted to make sure you were not harmed."

Lee cleared his throat.

Stanley turned to the sound and realized the entire roomful of people were staring at him and Treikie. "Oh, I'm sorry." He maneuvered Treikie slightly and made introductions.

"I know your father," Jor-Dan said. "How is he doing?"

Treikie tapped her fist to her heart. "He is doing well, King Jor-Dan. He'll be happy to hear you remembered him."

Stanley stopped in front of Lee and Ethaderia.

"Are you keeping Stanley out of trouble?" Lee asked.

Stanley blushed.

Treikie chuckled. "We keep each other out of trouble. Our minds are very similar."

"You obviously didn't meet him when he had to wear the helmet," Lee said.

She squeezed Stanley's hand. "No, but I saw him on several occasions and wondered about it."

Pup jumped to his feet and his three layers of teeth extended and clacked. He rushed from the room with Chatter, La'gar'ish and Buffy on his heels.

Trakon took off after the dogs. "Guards! With me!" Three of the palace guards fell in behind their prince, laser weapons drawn and ready.

D'laine and the rest of the family followed. They headed to the doorway that led to the jail. She held up a hand when they reached the doorway that Trakon and the guards passed through.

"Only warriors past this point. Jor-Dan, you and Kitry need to return to the salon. We can't have anything happen to you," D'laine said.

Jor-Dan nodded. "I will escort my queen and everyone else back. We'll wait to hear what is happening."

D'laine, Trakon, her father, Stanley and the guards hurried through the door and down the stairway.

The Fod had transformed back to its animal form. It was a

strange-looking creature. D'laine reasoned that if she bent over with her hands on the floor and her butt in the air, she would be the same shape as the animal in the cell.

It made a *crik crik crik* sound as it stood on the cot, as far away from the diwal dogs as it could get.

DOWN! D'laine bellowed using The Voice. The three diwals, Buffy and the Fod fell to their bellies.

"Huh. The Fod understood your command," Trakon said.

"What are we going to do with this creature?" Lee asked. "We can't hold it responsible for the attack. It's an animal."

The Fod jumped to its feet and stared at Lee. It made a series of crik's.

"Huh," Trakon said. "It seems to recognize you, Lee."

Lee raised his eyebrows. "I can't imagine why. The closest I've been to the mountains was when we brought Brian to the Oolarooloo from the ragapunga attack."

They all stared at the creature.

"If we let it go, we will have to make sure the dogs don't go after it," Trakon said. He opened an empty cell. "Pup, Chatter, La'gar'ish, in here. Buffy, you too. Come on!"

The dogs reluctantly entered the cell. Trakon closed the door, and it automatically locked. Pup grumbled at being locked up. Chatter made bitter clacking with his teeth. La'gar'ish and Buffy flopped on the cot and groomed themselves.

"Stanley, would you be able to step out of Ebscalon far enough away with the Fod and set it free?" D'laine asked.

"Yeah, I can do that," Stanley said. "I don't think I can get it back to the mountains unless I have Ghury or Adrum direct me."

"Make sure you notice which direction it takes," Lee said. "I don't remember where those mountains are from the Egrom lessons."

"The Raagor mountains are a portion of the Aguberro, but the cave where Maldi climbed to is far to the east," Trakon said.

"I remember how to get to the Oolarooloo," Stanley said. "Should I take him there?"

"That would get him closer to home, and we wouldn't have to worry about the dogs trying to track him," D'laine said.

"Okay, we have a plan," Trakon said. "Latch on to him and I'll unlock the door."

Stanley levitated the Fod. It made frantic cricking sounds, but at a higher frequency because it was scared.

Trakon tapped his communicator and unlocked the cell door.

Stanley maneuvered the Fod out of the cell. Pup's teeth clacked like crazy in full attack mode.

"Pup! Enough!" D'laine yelled.

The dog was in a frenzy trying to get to the Fod.

STOP! D'laine commanded. She angled her hand in a down command and Pup complied, reluctantly.

Stanley stepped the Fod out of the jail. They vanished.

"Lee, go open the door. I'm going to let the dogs loose," Trakon said.

Lee opened the door and jogged up the stairs. Trakon and D'laine waited.

"Door's open. The coast is clear," Lee said.

Trakon tapped his program and unlocked the cell door. As soon as he opened the cell, Pup and Chatter sprinted up the stairs. Lee took to the stairs to see what the dogs would do. He ran to the palace entrance. He found Pup and Chatter standing in the courtyard, noses to the air. They were confused. There was no scent of Stanley or the Fod.

Pup walked a few feet, turned in different directions sniffing the air, then sat.

"They're gone, Pup. Come inside," Lee coaxed. He returned to the salon.

La'gar'ish and Buffy didn't seem interested in putting in the effort. They leisurely trotted up the two flights of stairs to the main floor.

La'gar'ish led Buffy to the salon where he joined his king. The dog took full responsibility for his job protecting Jor-Dan. Buffy wiggled over to Jamie and Brian.

Trakon and D'laine entered the salon.

"You've released the Fod?" Jor-Dan asked.

They explained that Stanley stepped to the Oolarooloo location where he would release the animal, and should be back momentarily.

Treikie fidgeted. "Perhaps I should go home."

"You don't have to run off," Kitry said. "Please stay for dinner. Stanley will be back shortly."

STANLEY STEPPED INTO THE OOLAROOLOO VILLAGE WITH THE Fod. Oogo spotted them and approached Stanley.

"What is this?" Oogo asked. He studied the Fod.

"It's called a Fod, and it's from the Aguberro mountain. Do you think if I let it go here it can find its way back home?" Stanley asked.

Oogo pointed to the east. "The Aguberro is far away over there."

"Can someone take me there, or get me closer? I don't have any reference to get there by myself," Stanley said.

More of the villagers came forward. They gawked at the Fod held in the air. Greg Claymore came out of the forest. He spotted Stanley and the animal and joined his villagers.

"Hi Stanley, what's this Fod doing here?" Greg asked.

"You're familiar with the Fod's? Can you help me get this one back to the base of his mountain?" Stanley asked.

"Sure. I've been all over the Aguberro's. I made it up to the

Crest of Ingosaquille," Greg said. "Did this one go all the way to Ebscalon?"

Stanley explained what happened and how D'laine healed Marrak.

The Fod made criking sounds and struggled to be free.

Greg placed his hand on Stanley's shoulder. "I'll guide you."

With a blink, they were gone. In another blink, they returned, minus the Fod.

Greg studied Stanley's face and head. "Let me do more work on your head."

He led Stanley over to a stool and had him sit. Greg walked around Stanley, examining his head. "Show me an image of you from when you first arrived on Thol, before the helmet."

Stanley projected the image from when D'laine brought him through the portal with her family.

Greg nodded. "Got it." He held his hands on each side of Stanley's head as he gazed on the image in his head. Greg stepped in front of Stanley and looked at his face. "Almost there. Do you feel any different?"

"Nope, everything seems the same to me," Stanley said.

Greg placed his hands on Stanley's head again. There was a tiny pop.

"What was that?" Stanley asked. He was mildly freaked out about his brain and the shape of his head.

"Adjusting bones. Don't worry, your brain power won't hurt anyone. It's in there but in a chamber that won't cause any harm," Greg said. "Let's test it out."

He called Oogo over. The elder stood in front of Stanley.

"His head looks more normal," Oogo said.

"You don't notice anything pulling on your brain?" Greg asked the village elder.

"No, everything in my head is fine," Oogo said.

Stanley stood. He rubbed his hands down his head, over his face, then the sides of his head where his ears were. "My face feels like it was back then—longer instead of round. Do I look okay?"

Greg trotted to his hut under the tree canopy. He returned with a mirror and held it up for Stanley.

The scientist examined himself. "This makes me feel so much better. I have a girlfriend now and I was a little worried about not looking my best. I hope she likes what I originally looked like."

Greg patted Stanley's shoulder. "Not to worry. You're back together again."

"Thanks for guiding me to the mountain. I should be able to get there on my own if I ever need to return," Stanley said. "Goodbye, Oogo. It was nice seeing you again." He waved, then stepped into the palace salon.

"Stan!" Lee called out. "Did you see Greg? Your face looks like it's back to normal."

"Yeah, Greg made more adjustments. It sure is nice to look normal again," Stanley said.

Treikie approached Stanley. She ran her hands down the side of his face and over his ears. "Oh, you look so handsome!"

Stanley beamed with pride. "This is what I used to look like before I came to Thol and my brain expanded. There was one point where I really looked like a freak."

"Did the Fod make it home okay?" D'laine asked.

"Greg guided me to Mount Aguberro. He's been all over the mountain. Borjos are all over the place! And there must be hundreds of caves," Stanley said. "I set the Fod on the ground and I can now understand their unusual posture. That thing took off up the mountain as if it were one gigantic staircase."

Stanley projected a vision of the Fod scurrying up the mountain, the borjos flying all over the place, and the many caves visible in the mountainside.

"Father! We can bring some borjos back to Ebscalon!" Trakon said.

"Where would we keep them? Ekka has a tower, but there's only a few more and we can't be sure if borjos would share their spaces or not," Jor-Dan said.

"We could build nesting places for them on the tallest buildings." Trakon was eager to fly on the back of a borjo whenever he wanted. Ekka was the protector of Ebscalon. Trakon rode him every once in a while, but the borjo had claimed Jamie and preferred his human above all others.

"I'll talk to Ekka," Jamie said. "I'll see what he thinks about this plan."

"Hurry back, son. Supper is almost ready," Lee said.

Jamie hurried out of the salon and out of the palace. He ran full throttle to Ekka's tower and climbed the stairs. Ekka was on his nest of gauze and looked up when Jamie entered his tower. Jamie threw his arms around the borjos neck.

"Hi Ekka. I love you so much!"

The borjo rubbed his face against Jamie's head.

"Trakon wants to go to the mountains and bring back some borjos. Would that be okay? You would still be the protector of the kingdom, and you'd be in charge of all the borjos to make sure they behaved." Jamie listened.

"Trakon wants to build nests on top of the tall buildings." Jamie listened to his borjos silent comments. "Okay, I've got to get back home. We'll go for a flight later, okay?" He hugged his gigantic dragon-like pet, then took to the stairs.

Jamie ran back to the palace, stopped in the public restroom and washed his hands and face. He pulled a comb out of a pocket in his Tholian suit and tamed his hair, then proceeded to the dining room.

He slipped into his chair. "Ekka likes the plan. He'll be the boss of all the borjos and make sure they behave." Jamie turned to Trakon. "Ekka likes the idea of you building nests. He said the wild borjos would appreciate having a place to sleep out of the elements. They get tired of the rain and being all wet."

"What do you say, father? You said we had to get through the wedding. We checked that off the list," Trakon said.

"It would be great excitement to have the freedom to ride a borjo whenever we wanted," Jor-Dan said, his eyes lighting up. He would never forget the time he flew with Jamie on Ekka.

"There are other benefits to having borjos in Ebscalon," Trakon said. "If anything attacks us, borjos would be the first line of defense. All it might take is to have them fly over the kingdom and come home to roost. We have Ekka and the diwal dogs. I think we would be the best defended kingdom on Thol."

"Remember, they would need to fly far away to feed. We can't have them hungry and eyeing the population or the pakows," Kitry said. "Where would they go to eat?"

"Perhaps we should only bring back two or three," Lee said.

After a week and two turns, Marrak appeared in the throne room ready to get back to work. Jor-Dan and his advisors were on their feet visibly examining him.

"You look well," Jor-Dan said, as he looked over the documentarian. "How do you feel?"

"It's hard to explain," Marrak said. "I thought I died when that man attacked me. Twum took care of me, even though all I did for a long time was sleep."

Jor-Dan coaxed Marrak to sit. "You did die. D'laine brought you back and healed you."

CHAPTER SIX

*S*everal turns later, at breakfast, D'laine felt a little twinge in her gut. She patted her stomach and hoped she wasn't coming down with the Tholian version of a stomach virus. Since living on Thol, she rarely experienced being ill.

Kitry was chatting about the nursery and the latest counting she did.

"Can I go with you?" D'laine asked. She wanted to see how the eggs were kept in the many stages until they hatched.

"Why, yes! I will show you the future children of Ebscalon. Perhaps one of these days, you will have an egg for the nursery," Kitry said.

They finished up breakfast. Kitry and D'laine walked to the communal hatching center building that was near the Visionary's temple. Women warriors guarded the building. Kitry led D'laine inside. D'laine looked around in wonderment. There were rows of nests filled with gauze.

"This is the incoming room," Kitry said. She walked over to a desk where an attendant sat. "When a woman brings in her egg, it is logged into the journal and assigned a nest location. As the egg grows, we monitor it to make sure all is well inside."

D'laine's eyes wandered the room. "Can I walk around?"

"Of course. As you can see, there are attendants, so if you have questions, they will do their best to answer you," Kitry said. "I'll be in this room, over here." She pointed to a door.

D'laine walked over to the nesting area. There were small eggs, the size of a chicken's egg, then various sizes. She spotted a huge egg and walked over to it. An attendant was close by, arranging gauze around an egg in a nest.

"Is this the largest egg here?" D'laine asked.

"Oh, no. This egg is in its second year. I'll show you one that will hatch within the next few turns," the woman said. She led D'laine through another doorway to a room that contained eggs with shells between two to three feet in diameter.

"Oh, my goodness!" D'laine said.

The attendant showed her a very large egg that had a shadow crack in its shell. "This little one will hatch soon."

"What happens when they hatch? Does the mother come to collect her child?"

"Not right away. We take them to the acclimation room," the attendant said. "Even though our children are fully developed and have all the knowledge they need to live productive lives, we teach them how to feed and dress themselves. They also need a little help socializing, especially the Youngmen."

D'laine lay her hand on the egg. She sensed a movement inside. A small hand rested against hers from inside the shell. "Oh! I felt his little hand!"

"It's best not to do that, otherwise he may bond with you and think you're his mother," the attendant said.

D'laine whipped her hand away from the shell. "Oh, no. I wouldn't want to cause any confusion. I don't think his mother would appreciate me stealing her child!"

The attendant giggled. "Any mother would be thrilled to have the princess claim her egg."

"Thanks for showing me around," D'laine said. She returned to the incoming room and headed to the door where Kitry was. She slipped inside and was stunned at the scene before her.

There were around a dozen boys and girls in various stages of undress. Kitry and the attendants were schooling the children on dressing themselves. The children had choices. Boys could choose either the short-sleeved, short pant legged suits, or more domestic pants and tunics. Most Youngmen chose the short-sleeved version over the traditional long sleeves and long legs.

The girls chose either a warrior suit, or the sari-type of dress that domestic women and girls wore.

Kitry looked up. "Hi D'laine. Are you learning about our process?"

"It's amazing. Tell me what is happening here. I can see these children are getting dressed, but what makes them choose their outfits?"

"They already know what function they will serve in society," Kitry said. "So, the boys will either be Youngmen—future warriors and guards, or they will work with their parents, or in another form they decide upon. The girls have the same choices. As soon as they see the clothing, they understand their function in life. They just need help learning how to dress."

She watched a little girl with a pixie-like face with curly black hair. She wanted both a sari and a jumpsuit.

"Kitry, this little girl wants both outfits. What does that mean?" D'laine asked.

Kitry finished with the little boy, inflating his boots, then turned to the little girl in question.

"She's a warrior. But since they wear both outfits, depending on the situation, sometimes a little one can't decide what to wear first," Kitry said. She knelt down by the little girl. "Why don't you wear the warrior outfit? Then your mother will know your function and she will also provide you with dresses for informal occasions."

The little girl smiled, showing two dimples.

"They don't talk?" D'laine asked.

"Not yet. That's the next phase which comes within a week or two. Then, like all mothers, you wish they would be quiet for a little while." Kitry smiled mischievously.

"Did Trakon talk a lot after he was hatched?" D'laine asked.

"Your husband would barely stop talking to let anyone sleep!" Kitry chuckled. "I would read to him thinking it would help him wind down, but it did just the opposite. He kept asking questions over and over! I'm grateful he is an intelligent man, but he was a challenge for the first several months until he more or less understood limitations."

"That is so funny. I wonder what our children will be like. I'm still not sure how my body would process pregnancy," D'laine said.

"Only time will tell," Kitry said.

There was a fuss that an attendant rushed to. Two Youngmen wanted the same suit. The woman sat them down and handed each a suit of identical colors. That seemed to settle them. They set about learning how to dress themselves.

"This is so fascinating," D'laine said. "I forgot to ask earlier, but do the eggs have to be turned, or do they stay in the same position?"

"No, they don't get turned. It is best to let them be," Kitry said. "Occasionally, an egg becomes unviable and withers. It is very sad for the parents."

"Oh, no! What causes that?"

"Nature takes its course. We rarely see birth defects in our society, and I think it's a blessing," Kitry said.

D'LAINE LEFT THE NURSERY AND RETURNED TO THE PALACE. SHE climbed the stairs to return to her suite, but decided to continue to ascend to the top floor. She couldn't recall going higher than Stanley's suite. She reached the top floor and started to explore. There were four doors per corridor that were empty suites.

At the back corridor there was a door at the end of the hall. D'laine opened the door and discovered a sunny stairway. She climbed the stairs to a turret room. Cobwebs hung from the ceiling and corners of the room. She walked to one of the open windows and looked out. She had a view of the entire city and beyond. There was a dusty game board on a small rickety table with two short stools, and a small, carved crestrider toy. D'laine smiled as she picked up the toy ship and grinned. Trakon must have played in this room as a child.

The room was about the same size as Ekka's tower room. She looked around and decided to claim the room. It would be her secret place. She descended the stairs and entered her suite. D'laine sat on a lounge chair and thought about how to proceed. She wasn't aware of where cleaning products were stored. How would she clean up the place?

There was no way she could reach the ceiling to whack down the cobwebs, even with a regular eight-foot ladder. She huffed, determining she would need Trakon's help. She called out to him.

Where are you?

At the shop, but I'll be back in a hour for lunch, he sent.

Okay, I'll see you then. I want to talk to you about a secret project. You can't blab about it, not even to Herish.

That's some secret, Trakon sent.

Ten minutes later, Trakon entered their suite, Chatter and Pup on his heels. He flopped on the lounge beside D'laine. He gathered her in his arms and pulled her in for a steamy kiss.

"I figured you wouldn't wait," she teased.

"Well, when you tell me it's this big secret, I'm not about to wait," Trakon said. "Come on, tell me what this is all about."

"You know that turret room at the top of the palace?" D'laine asked.

"My old hiding place?" Trakon chuckled. "How'd you find it?"

"I realized I've never explored the tower. The highest floor I'd been to was to go to Stanley's place. I love the turret room," she said. "Can you help me clean it? Even though it's open to the elements, it's dusty."

Trakon stood and grabbed her hand. "Come on, let's go take a look at the place, and you can tell me what you want to use it for."

They climbed the stairs to the turret room; the dogs rushing ahead of them. Trakon walked to one of the windows and leaned out. "I used to love this room. I'd play up here for hours."

Pup stretched up beside Trakon and had his front paws on the ledge. He couldn't see out the opening. He used his claws to scrabble up the wall to lift his head to see out. The diwal dog sniffed the air, then slid down the wall to the floor.

"Who did you play games with?" D'laine asked. She pointed to the game board on the kid-sized table.

Trakon stared at the old game and smiled nostalgically. "Kyo, Dannin's younger brother. We used to be best friends."

The dogs had their noses to the floor. They explored every inch of the space.

"You're not friends anymore?" D'laine asked.

"We grew apart. Being a prince, I was privileged in so many ways. I think he felt he wasn't good enough to be my friend as we grew older," Trakon said.

D'laine detected the sadness in his voice. She hugged him. "I'm sorry you had to experience that. Why don't you reach out to him? He might want to resume your friendship, especially if he's married."

"Maybe," Trakon said. "So, what do you want to do with this room?"

D'laine chewed on her bottom lip. She placed one of her hands on her stomach. "I want this to be our nursery room."

Trakon stared at her in silence, eyes huge. He closed the space and grasped her face. "You're pregnant?"

D'laine scrunched her face. "I think so. I had this twinge…"

He rocked her in his arms. "Oh, D'laine!" He stepped back and looked at the room with renewed interest.

"I don't want to tell anyone," D'laine said. "It's best to keep this a secret, so no one is disappointed in case my body rejects the egg."

"That won't happen, but we will keep it a secret. I promise," Trakon said. He swatted at some cobwebs, then headed to the door. "I'll be right back."

Chatter ran down the stairs after his person.

Trakon was mystified why she had chosen this room and not the guarded chamber where the eggs of Escalon's future lie.

She couldn't explain why it was so important, but a strong instinctive urge drove her to seek this room and prepare it. She wanted no one to know until a later time.

Trakon and Chatter returned several minutes later. Trakon had a wooden pole in one hand and a piece of cloth in the other. He wrapped the cloth around the pole and tackled the cobwebs.

Two days later, after supper, D'laine noticed Trakon was fidgety in their suite. He kept glancing at the window every few minutes.

"What's wrong with you?" D'laine asked. "Why can't you sit still and read your book?"

Trakon huffed. "I'm waiting for it to get dark. I've got a surprise to show you, but I can't go get it until the suns set."

As he spoke, one of the suns set. The other required at least another fifteen minutes.

"Be right back. Meet me upstairs," Trakon said. He took off out the door, Chatter on his heels.

D'laine got up and walked to the window. She saw Trakon and Chatter running toward the workshop area. "Come on, Pup." D'laine and Pup climbed the stairs quietly. She opened the door to the turret room and Pup launched himself up the stairs. He started on a sniffing expedition, then tried to see out the windows.

"Looks like I need to get Trakon to make you a step-up for each window," D'laine said.

She heard the door open and walked to the top of the stairs. Chatter romped up the stairs and explored the room, nose to the floor.

Trakon carried something in each hand, but she couldn't figure out what it was.

"What do I need to make Pup?" he asked.

"He's not tall enough to see out the windows. I told him you could make him a step-up for each window," D'laine said. "What is that?"

Trakon placed the wooden slats on the floor, along with a gigantic wooden bowl. He took the slats and put them together. They made a stand for the bowl.

"Oh, Trakon, it's beautiful! Did you make this?" D'laine asked.

"Yes. I need to go get some gauze from the hosk building. Want to come with me?"

"Yes!" she said.

They left the turret room with Pup and Chatter on their heels. Instead of going to the main floor and the front of the palace, Trakon led D'laine down a corridor on the second floor. He quietly opened a door that exited to a side door on the ground floor. The dogs shot out into a garden area.

Trakon put his finger to his lips. D'laine nodded. They crept away from the palace and through streets and alleyways to the hosk building.

Make the dogs wait here. I don't want the hosks thinking they're going to be slaughtered! Trakon sent.

D'laine nodded, turned to Pup and Chatter and gave the stay command with her hand. Then she followed Trakon inside the building. She heard the soft breathing of the sleeping hosks.

Trakon quietly moved through the room to the area where the gauze was made. He grabbed a cloth sack and stuffed it with gauze, then handed it to D'laine. He stuffed another one and waved her back the way they came. They left the building, closing the door with barely an audible click of the lock.

They jogged the same route back to the palace with the dogs between them. When they got to the garden area, they heard voices. Trakon held out his hand to make D'laine stop. Chatter's teeth clacked once. D'laine shook her head at Chatter and used a hand signal to make him lie down.

Trakon tried to peek around the corner without being seen. A man and a woman talked in low voices, then kissed. Trakon sent D'laine a visual.

She slammed her hand across her mouth. *Who is it, do you recognize them?*

I think its kitchen people, Trakon sent.

Why would kitchen people be here in the garden at this time of night? D'laine sent.

Trakon shrugged. He set their sacks on the ground to wait.

After listening to giggles and more smooching, the secret lovers walked to the other end of the garden and disappeared.

They picked up their sacks and D'laine motioned for the dogs to get up. They made their way to the door and returned to the turret room.

"I wonder who that was?" D'laine asked.

"Doesn't make any difference," Trakon said. "They weren't

doing anything bad, just sneaking around to be together. Thank Thol they didn't do anything else!"

Trakon emptied his sack of gauze into the large wooden bowl. He grabbed D'laine's sack and added more to the bowl. He stood back and looked at his handiwork.

D'laine grabbed his hand and held it as they gazed at where their future child would grow.

CHAPTER SEVEN

$\mathcal{B}$en's calendar on his office wall sported fat, black Xs. His last day was circled, highlighted and had lines surrounding it, like the sun. Tomorrow couldn't come soon enough as far as he was concerned. He had sold his condo and was living in the travel trailer. He had shipped boxes and a few pieces of furniture he really loved, to a storage unit that Victor had access to. He didn't know how he would get those things to his new living quarters on Thol, but he figured he'd deal with that in time.

He checked his watch. It was five-thirty. He headed over to the Rice Cinema on campus where a retirement party was being held in his honor. Ben had already met with the Dean, who told him to stay long enough to receive everyone's blessings. Since he decided not to start his drive across the wide state of Texas until the morning, he calmed himself.

"Hey, Doctor Joplin!" several students called out. "Ready to explore?"

"You bet!" Ben called out. He reached the cinema door ahead of a group of five and slipped inside.

A huge retirement banner hung from the ceiling. Students

holding trays of hors d'oeuvres walked among the throng of attendees. People from his department swarmed Ben as soon as they saw him. There was a lot of backslapping, hugging, and a few tears among his peers.

They presented Ben with a beautiful, round, personalized, crystal retirement plaque. There were way too many speeches, but the party finally ended. He slipped away with the black box his award came in, and headed across the parking lot to his travel trailer where he would spend the night.

After tossing and turning in the small bed, he got up, dressed and climbed behind the wheel and started the vehicle. He plugged his phone into the docking system and enabled his mapping program. He dug a bottle of water out of the cooler on the front passenger floor, worked the cap open and stuck the bottle in the cup holder. Then, he started on his journey. Ben maneuvered the vehicle through streets and finally merged onto Interstate 10.

According to his mapping program, it would take him ten hours and thirty-nine minutes to drive the seven-hundred forty-five miles from Houston to El Paso. Then, an additional twelve and a half hours to drive the eight-hundred two miles to Los Angeles. It wasn't easy to leave Texas. Whether you drove east or west, it was time-consuming, especially if there was road construction.

Ben found NPR on the radio and settled in, listening to the current content. He grabbed a plastic bag of mixed nuts from the passenger seat and chomped down on a few. Five hours later, he pulled into a Walmart parking lot, locked up, and took a nap in his tiny bed.

THREE DAYS LATER, BEN TOOTED THE HORN AS HE PULLED UP alongside the curb in front of Victor's house. The front door opened. Victor and Kara emerged with welcoming smiles. A few minutes later, Darren charged out the door. Ben got out of the vehicle, stretched and was enveloped into a group hug.

"You made it!" Victor said.

"That's some undertaking, let me tell you!" Ben said.

"Did you have any problems along the way?" Kara asked.

"There were a couple of big traffic accidents, then a detour that got me lost for around forty-five minutes, but nothing I couldn't get around. I can't tell you how annoying it is when your mapping system keeps telling you to take the next left. I ended up in a neighborhood following the directions to no avail. I finally found someone to tell me how to get back on I-10. Mr. Alvarez got in his car and guided me through this gigantic maze of the neighborhood and back to the freeway," Ben said.

"What a kind gesture," Kara said. "See, humanity holds surprises."

"Need help bringing anything inside?" Victor asked.

"Yeah, I brought a cooler of steaks, chicken and ribs from the condo. I figured you could use them, unless you've suddenly turned vegan," Ben said.

"Not in this lifetime," Victor said.

Ben opened the door to the travel trailer. Victor went inside, saw the cooler and hauled it out.

"Let's go inside," Victor said. He carried the cooler to the house with the others following him.

They settled in the kitchen, and Victor and Kara unloaded the cooler.

"Wow! This is very generous, Ben," Kara said.

"I used up as much as I could over the past couple of weeks, but I buy from a farm Co-op, so there's a lot of packaged cuts. Glad you can use the food. I'm looking forward to natural living on Thol," he said.

"Do you still have that communicator from the Egroms?" Victor asked.

Ben bent his ear forward. "Seems odd they took all yours, but not mine."

Victor shook his head. "You're forgetting that Egrom woo-woo stuff, Ben. They most likely had a mental X on a calendar as to when you'd be returning."

VICTOR, KARA, DARREN AND BEN STOOD ON THE SAND AT Coronado Beach. It was an emotional moment for Victor. He was losing the last of his team from so long ago. How he wished it were his family crossing over. Maybe they'd get to that decision someday, but he knew it would have to be soon, due to the ten to one equation of aging. If they didn't decide soon, he and Kara would be in their dotage and Darren might be Victor's age.

Ben had a large, sturdy package strapped to his back. They said their last goodbyes, and Ben stepped forward. He vanished from the Earth plane into Thol.

HE WAS GREETED BY THE JACKSONS, STANLEY, THE BRAMSTONE'S and the Cagmondoore's. They all hugged and talked, then climbed aboard the large crestrider and flew to Ebscalon. They decided Ben would spend a few turns at the palace before permanently moving to the Kudaja forest.

BEN SLIPPED THE HEAVY BAG OFF HIS SHOULDERS AND SET IT ON A table and tore into it. He pulled out two large pizza boxes, still warm, and handed them to Trakon.

Trakon's eyes lit up. "Pizza! You brought me pizza!" He put the boxes down and grabbed Ben in a hug, then turned to Herish and Meeri. "Wait until you taste this Earth food!" He mentally called for plates and napkins, and the kitchen staff delivered them. Trakon tore the boxes open, grabbed a slice of the pie and bit into it. He groaned with delight.

"Don't be a pig… uh, og," D'laine said.

Herish, Meeri and the rest of the group dug into the pizza. Herish's eyes widened.

"I like this Earth food!" Herish said.

Jor-Dan grunted his appreciation. "This is delicious."

"Save one piece so your cook can figure out how to make this," Meeri said, as she licked sauce off her fingers.

Ben pulled out the rest of his bounty. He spread things out on the table. "I tried to focus on plants and trees that grow some of the food we love, that would thrive here." He pointed to the clear plastic bags. "Tomatoes, a pecan tree, and… drum roll… cocoa bean pods."

D'laine's face lit up. "You brought chocolate seeds!" She turned a wild, happy face to Trakon. "We can grow a tree that we can eventually use the beans to make chocolate!"

Trakon stared at the pods. "Oh, Ben! This is worth all the moss of Thol!"

Ben produced several bags of different varieties of chocolate goodies.

Trakon tore into a bag, unwrapped a treat and popped it into his mouth. He passed the bag to Herish. "Try one of these."

Herish dug a candy out, unwrapped it and took a cautionary bite. "Oh, My Thol! Meeri, taste this!"

When everyone had sampled the chocolate and calmed down, Ben explained how to grow the cocoa beans.

"Cocoa beans grow in pods on trees of the Theobroma cacao species. They're beautiful trees, and we shouldn't have any problem growing them here. They require a fairly constant, hot growing temperature, high humidity and a lot of rainfall all year round," Ben explained.

"Thol should be a good place to produce a crop successfully," Lee said.

"The tomato plants are an heirloom variety. I made sure that everything I brought would not be GMO," Ben said.

"What's GMO?" Kitry asked.

"Genetically modified organism," Stanley said.

The Tholians appeared skeptical.

"Why would anyone want to change a food plant?" Jor-Dan asked.

"The population of Earth is at a peak, and there's not enough food to go around. The government decided to tweak plants for more yield, but a lot of people in the United States, where we come from, avoid anything that has been modified," Lee said.

"We should talk to Drusta," D'laine said.

"Who's that?" Lee asked.

"He's the Egrom elder who has a close connection to plants," D'laine said.

"Why don't we plan to go there tomorrow?" Trakon said.

"Can we bring Chacoodi back with us?" Brian pleaded. Chacoodi was an Egrom boy who Brian and Jamie liked to play with. They had many adventures together, including making the first baseball and bat.

"We'll see," Lee said.

Kitry controlled her face from smiling. She knew good and well that they would have the Egrom boy for a sleep-over.

"Oh, I almost forgot!" Ben said. "Kara has all but one text book ready to send."

Lee rubbed his hands together. "That's fabulous!"

Brian and Jamie scowled. They were going to be stuck with homeschooled lessons as soon as the books arrived. Brian didn't see the need to learn all the Earth education. He would never return to his former home if he had his way. Thol was everything a kid could ever dream of.

Herish and Meeri stood. "We're going to head back home," Herish said. "We'll see you in a few turns, Ben. Thanks so much for the pizza and chocolate."

They shook hands in the Earth style. Trakon and D'laine walked their friends outside.

AFTER BREAKFAST, TRAKON FLEW THEM TO THE EGROM VILLAGE. They left the dogs behind with Jor-Dan. Trakon landed the ship and they walked across the moss. They were met by Ghury, Kestrum and Adrum. Chacoodi ran up to Brian and Jamie like a wild boy. Kestrum silently scolded him, and Chacoodi stopped abruptly. He behaved like a good Egrom child.

"Welcome home, Ben," Ghury said.

Ben's face lit up. "Home." He looked around, nodded, and smiled. "Feels good to be here." He was wearing the same type jumpsuit that Lee and Stanley wore. It wasn't a warrior's suit, but very similar.

Drusta came out of his mushroom house and approached the group. "You have need of my plant expertise?"

Ben showed the Egrom the plants he had brought from Earth.

"These plants should all grow on Thol," Drusta said. He picked up the bag of pods. "Plant these pods three mushrooms apart. They will grow very large here—larger than the normal size on Earth, and require plenty of space between trees." He picked up the bag with the tomato starters. "These tomato plants will thrive here. Don't plant them near a building. This nut tree may produce its own forest, so be careful where you plant it."

Ghury met Ben's eyes. "Would you like to stay here for your

lessons? When you visited last, you weren't here long enough to require learning about Thol."

Ben glanced over to Lee. "Is that okay with you? Can you inform Herish I won't be moving to my new place right away?"

"Shouldn't be any problem," Lee said. "You're going to enjoy the lessons!"

"Someone should plant these," Ben said. He handed the bags of pods, seeds and starter plants to Lee.

They said their goodbyes, leaving behind Ben and taking Chacoodi with them.

ONE MONTH LATER, BEN JOINED THE KUDAJA. HERISH AND MEERI showed Ben his living quarters in one of the giant agrin trees. It was larger than his condo back in Houston, and the view was so much more beautiful—dappled light through the tree branches. They showed him where the large eating hall was located. Ben supposed it was very much like a cafeteria, or perhaps a better match would be a large hall from a Viking longhouse.

After a tour of the walkway above the forest floor, they returned to Ben's house.

"I wish I had remembered to bring my work journal with me," he said.

"Will D'laine help with transporting your belongings?" Meeri asked. She and Herish were familiar with D'laine's powers.

Before Ben answered, a worn leather journal stuffed with pieces of papers, plopped down on the table in front of him.

"What the…!" Ben stared at the book. He picked it up. "It's my journal! It was in storage. How is this possible?"

"Maybe that's your gift!" Herish exclaimed. "Try something else! Let's experiment."

"I'm trying to determine what I should try to bring over,"

Ben said. "My computer and iPad are in a box in the storage unit. I'll send for that."

Almost as soon as the words left his mouth, the box appeared with a thump on the floor.

"Do you have a knife to cut through this tape?" Ben asked.

Herish pulled his pocketknife out of a pocket and slit the tape.

Ben dug into the box. Sure enough, it was the correct box. He wiped his hand down his face. "I'm like a wizard or something! This is amazing! I wonder if it works both ways?"

"Is there something you can send Victor!" Meeri all but screeched with excitement.

"I should write him a note and tell him what's happening!" Ben looked around his living quarters. "Is there any paper here?"

Meeri rushed over to a desk and pulled out a piece of paper and a writing instrument.

Ben wrote a note.

Victor, this is Ben. You'll never guess what my gift is. I'm like Harry Potter without the wand!! I materialized my journal, then my box of computer equipment here! I'll wait for several minutes. You can write a reply and I'll think this paper back to me.

They waited patiently, then Ben thought the note back.

You're a wizard? You'll be able to bring everything in the storage unit over there? Once you do that, I'll cancel the contract so your bank account isn't debited. – Victor.

They all stared at the note. Since neither Herish nor Meeri read English, Ben translated, giddy.

"I can't wait to tell Lee and Stanley about this gift of mine!" Ben said. "I have several boxes of books back home. Who can I contact here to build me two or three bookcases? And, how do I pay for them? I have plenty of Earth money, but that won't do me any good here."

"I'll send someone about the bookcases. You are now a

contributing member of our society. You will earn your way of life here in all the things you do to help the forest and our people," Herish explained.

Ben rubbed his hands together. "I can't wait. As soon as they deliver the bookcases, I'll bring my things over. I have a few pieces of furniture, cooking utensils and linens, and the books." He glanced around. "This house doesn't have a kitchen—a place to cook meals?"

"Our ancestors determined it would be safer to have one place for food preparation, beside the palace kitchen. All it would take is one careless act to set the forest on fire," Meeri said.

"Oh! I hadn't considered that disaster," Ben said.

CHAPTER EIGHT

*W*hen Herish and Meeri left, Ben explored his quarters. The bed looked to be a queen or king bed. He figured he'd ask Kara if she wanted his Earth bed linens, because he remembered how comfortable the hosk silk-spun sheets felt against his skin.

The smart closet fascinated him. Not needing a washing machine or dryer was a little bizarre. Those machines were the only option of cleaning clothes, sheets and towels back home, besides dry cleaning. The smart closet cleaned and repaired the clothing. The material that combined the hosk-spun gauze and the agrin tree sap made material nearly indestructible. Ben remembered how Trakon, Lee and D'laine had demonstrated the healing properties of the cloth.

The forest people dressed similar to the legendary Robin Hood of Sherwood Forest. At first, Ben balked over what seemed like tights. But he set aside his embarrassment when he contemplated about the uniforms all the Jacksons and Ciertrons wore. They had explained how the material kept them cool.

The loose shirt had built-in communicating tools. He would have to study the communicator to make sure he understood how to hail someone if he were in trouble or needed help of any kind. He wondered how he would communicate with Lee and Stanley. He studied the menu. He would have to learn what everything was before he fiddled around.

There must be an address book in here somewhere, he determined.

Since there were no entertainment electronics—no movies, TV, computers, iPads—nothing whatsoever, he would have to figure out how to spend his time. He couldn't get his head around what people did for entertainment on Thol. He'd have to talk with his fellow Earthlings about this subject before he made a fool out of himself.

It was a huge change from leaving his position at the university to having no set schedule. His time had been filled with tasks or extracurricular activities that filled his workdays and weekends for years and years.

There was a bathroom in his unit that was bigger than the kitchen in his condo. It contained a toilet, a smaller bathing pool than what was in Lee's suite, and what he determined was a shower stall. He didn't understand the plumbing. How was the water heated? There wasn't a hot water heater anywhere as far as he could tell. Where did the waste go? He had questions piling up in his head.

Ben sat down in the living area. He got up and walked to the desk and fished out a piece of paper. He sat at the desk and wrote a note to Lee. He focused on Lee and the paper vanished. He chuckled as he considered Lee and Stanley's response. D'laine's as well. He didn't think the Tholians would understand the concept of Harry Potter or anything magical. Egroms were the closest things to magical beings. Of course, D'laine was a close second. Who would have thought a normal Earth teenager was practically a revered deity on another world?

He waited around ten minutes then materialized the paper to his hand. Sure enough, Lee had responded. Ben determined

Lee hadn't finished writing, so he returned the paper with a note saying he'd wait another ten minutes before retrieving it again.

Within moments, his communicator pinged. Lee wanted to talk to him.

"You materialized a box of your stuff?" Lee all but roared through the communicator device. Ben heard the smile on Lee's face.

"First, I thought my journal here, then I figured what the heck. Herish is sending someone to build bookcases for me, then I'll bring everything I have in storage and Victor can shut that down," Ben said.

"Better watch out… Herish and Trakon may have you materializing pizza," Lee joked.

"Unless Victor or Kara ordered it, I wouldn't be able to pay for it," Ben said. "I'm not stealing food for those two."

Ben and Lee laughed over different scenarios. Then Ben got serious. "Just think, Lee. I could theoretically check out books from any library and return them. I can bring over other things as well."

"I'd like to communicate with Rosa and Erik," Lee said. "Now, you have made this possible. I also have to take into consideration the ten to one ratio with aging. I may have D'laine bring me back to the house so we can plan what to do with the house and property. Let's face it, in four or five Tholian years, they could be dead."

"I know. I want to push Victor and Kara to emigrate before it's too late for them," Ben said.

"I understand Kara's fears," Lee said. "Outside the walls of Ebscalon, and your elevated city is a wild, dangerous world. We are only familiar with a fraction of Thol and what lives here, even with the Egrom movies. And, truthfully, I don't feel comfortable enough to explore further out. We've already experienced some pretty scary animal life here."

They ended their talk and Ben turned the sheet of paper over and started a list of what he should materialize. Scientific books, journals, magazines and the likes were at the top of the list. He would share them with Lee and Stanley. He started a list of equipment and nixed that idea. They didn't need cameras. They had the capability of snapping a picture or video with their brain and downloading it to their communicator. He didn't truly understand how that worked, but he was happy to have the amazing ability.

Brian was the portal detector. D'laine was their transporter between realms. Now, with his newfound magical ability, he would be able to conjure things from Earth. He didn't need a stove or any other appliance. Didn't need a vehicle. Crestriders, borjos and pakows were all anyone would require on Thol, and they were the best modes of transportation around. He couldn't wait to fly on the back of a borjo! All he needed was a wizard's outfit!

There was a tap on the door. Ben opened the door to two guys who carried a large bookcase between them.

"Prince Herish said you needed bookcases, BenJoplin," one man said.

"Oh, come in, come in!" Ben said. "You can call me Ben."

"Where would you like this, BenJoplin? And, do you need one or two more?" the other man asked.

"Against this wall would be perfect. There's room for two more." Ben pointed to the wall near the desk.

The men stood the bookcase against the wall. "We'll be right back."

They returned with two more units and set them up.

Ben ran his hand across a shelf. "Did you make these? They're beautiful. Works of art in wood."

"Yes, we make furniture. Do you need us to make you anything?" the other man asked.

Ben looked around his space. "I don't think so, but once I get settled, I'll let you know. What are your names?"

"I'm Corl, and this is Gafn. Contact us if you need help with anything," Corl said.

After the men left, Ben got quiet. He focused on the storage unit. Within a blink, twenty boxes appeared in front of the bookcases. "This is just too cool!" He determined the boxes were too close to the bookcases for him to unpack them. Within a scratch of a second, the whole lot stood three feet back from the shelves.

"I sure could teach Hollywood a thing or two." Ben chuckled at his accomplishment. "Let's see how magical I can get." He focused on the boxes and within another split second, the bookcases were filled with books, binders, stacks of papers and a few knickknacks. He then focused on breaking down and stacking the boxes. Then he returned them to the storage unit back on Earth.

He brought the rest of the boxes and sifted through them. He returned all the linens to the storage unit with a note to Kara. Next, he brought the few pieces of furniture to see if he still wanted them. He kept the coffee table and his recliner. He returned a chest of drawers. He had no use for it here.

Ben wrote a lengthy letter to Victor and Kara. He told them about his Tholian gift, that he emptied the storage unit of everything he wanted, and they could donate anything they didn't want for themselves. He made a point of the ten to one ratio of time and implored them to give serious consideration about emigrating.

He reminded them that Lee's two sons were thrilled here, and Darren would have a truly liberating life. Ben reminded them of the healing capabilities on the planet. He signed off by telling them he would use his magic to deliver their answer to his letter the next day. He explained if he received the letter and determined it was incomplete, he would send it back.

"That's the best I can do," Ben said out loud. "I hope they make a decision soon."

He sent his letter, then opened the door and tried to remember how to get to the dining hall.

"WELCOME, BENJOPLIN! I AM UNI. LET ME SHOW YOU WHERE TO start," the Kudaja man said. He walked Ben to the large tables of food, and fetched a tray for him. "The utensils are at the other end. Why don't you try a small portion of things that appeal to your eyes and nose? We know you aren't familiar with our foods yet. When you're finished with your choices, please join me and my friends." He pointed to the table where a group of men and women sat. They raised their arms and waved at Ben.

"Thank you, Uni. I'll join you shortly," Ben said. He wondered why everyone called him by his full name, crammed together. It almost sounded like Benjamin. He took Uni's advice and placed a sampling of different foods on his plate. Mostly everything looked and smelled good, making his mouth water.

Ben joined Uni and his group at their table. They left a place for him at the end of the table. He settled in and sampled the food. It was delicious.

"I can teach you how to ride a borjo," Borg said. "Crestrider, too."

"I would love that! Those are two skills I want to learn," Ben said. "I appreciate you all taking your time to make me feel at home."

"Earth differs greatly from Thol, doesn't it?" a woman asked.

"There's no comparison," Ben said. "The air, water and soil are so polluted back home. Plus, it is very crowded. I don't miss it at all."

"Why didn't you settle in Ebscalon where your friends are?" someone asked.

"I fell in love with your forest living," Ben said. "As soon as I discovered your village in the trees, it called to my heart."

They finished their meal and Ben tagged along with Borg to where the borjos stayed. A male borjo fluttered out of the trees and landed on the clearing floor.

"Looks like you have a borjo," Borg said. "This is Aob. He has chosen you."

Ben looked surprised. "Really? I didn't expect to be chosen so quickly. This is exciting."

"Borjos don't waste time making decisions," Borg said. "Aob is a middle-aged borjo, approximately eighty paths old. He will make sure you are well protected while on his back. He wants to learn as much about you as you do about him."

Aob lowered his head and nudged Ben.

"He wants you to stroke his face and snout," Borg said.

Ben ran his hand over the borjos velvety nose, across his face and down his neck. "You're a good boy, Aob. Thank you for choosing me."

Aob huffed.

"He wants to take you for a ride," Borg said. "You can tell him where to go, what you want to see, when to turn in what direction. I don't know if you can mind-talk with him or not. I know that young boy at Ebscalon communicates directly with most of the animals he comes in contact with, but you're new here and might not have those skills."

"Where do I hold on? There's no bridle or reins like for horses on Earth," Ben said. He conjured a picture of a horse, saddle, bridle and reins to Borg.

"We don't use those things on a borjo, only on pakows. All you need to do is sit on his back and hold onto the fuzzy layers here." Borg ruffled the fuzzy dark jewel-toned layers above the wings.

Aob hunkered down for Ben to mount. He flung his leg across the borjos back and grabbed the fuzzy fur. "Please go slow, Aob! Once I'm used to flying on your back, we can go faster."

Aob huffed once. He spread his wings, and they took to the sky. Ben's eyes were all over the place. It amazed him seeing the forest, plains and mountains while gliding through the air. The canopy of trees was so thick there was absolutely no sign of the Kudaja village, or where the Egroms lived close by.

"We can go back now, Aob," Ben told the borjo. "We'll fly every day! Thank you for such a wonderful ride."

They landed and Aob returned to the top of the tree he called home. Borg approached.

"Well, how was your first borjo ride?"

"Amazing! Aob is a good borjo. I may fly to Ebscalon tomorrow to see my friends," Ben said.

Borg led the way back to Ben's house and said goodbye. Ben walked inside and looked around. He tapped his communicator and called Lee.

"Hi Lee. If I were to manifest a coffee maker and coffee, how would I power it? I really miss coffee," Ben said.

"We've got that figured out," Lee said. He explained about a solar-powered battery pack and how they were using them to charge their laptops, and D'laine's iPad. "Maybe you should conjure up some coffee beans so we can grow our own."

"I'll see if Kara can buy me a coffee maker. Do you want one? Also, what brand and flavor of coffee do you like?"

They discussed the various devices, coffees and made their decisions.

"I'll come visit you tomorrow. I have a borjo," Ben said.

"I'd better tell Jamie so he can make sure Ekka doesn't get territorial," Lee said. "We can show you the solar-powered battery packs and how they work with our laptops."

"If you, Stanley or D'laine think of anything you want from back home, let me know. I'm going to have to figure out how to order things and where they should go in the event that Kara and Victor can't buy things for us," Ben said.

CHAPTER NINE

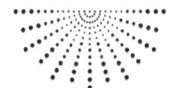

*B*en flew Aob to Ebscalon. It was a delightful journey that lasted less than thirty minutes. They landed in the courtyard where Lee told him to. Lee, Stanley, and D'laine waited outside the palace and greeted him.

"Should Aob wait here, or can he fly away and I'll call him back when it's time for me to go home?" Ben asked.

D'laine approached the borjo and patted his neck. "He said he'll go hunt. You can call him when you're ready to go home."

"Can I talk to him like that… in my head?" Ben asked.

"Try it," D'laine said.

Aob, can you hear me?

Ben saw a picture in his head.

Is that you, Aob? That picture in my head?

Aob nudged Ben.

Go hunt, or nap.

The borjo spread his wings and leapt into the air. He flew over the moss fields and headed toward the woods.

"He seems to talk with pictures," Ben said.

"Let's go inside," Lee said.

Stanley stared at Ben. "You look like the Kudaja. Are those clothes comfortable? Do they keep you cool?"

"They're like your suits. The way the material breathes and keeps me cool is so bizarre," Ben said.

They walked up the stairs to Lee's suite and piled in. They showed him how they powered their Earth equipment. Ben studied the solar battery pack.

"I want to see this wizardry in action," D'laine said.

"Can you think of anything you want from your old room?" Ben asked.

"My crystals and amethysts!" D'laine explained where they were.

In the snap of a finger, Ben materialized four crystals and two large amethysts.

"Oh, my god! Thank you so much, Ben!" D'laine said. She snatched up the minerals and quartz crystals, one by one.

Everyone stared at Ben. His gift was powerful.

"I need to put a caretaker in place for my house and property," Lee said.

"When we were there, Rosa and Erik looked to be in their forties," Stanley said. "By now, they're in their fifties, and at the end of the path they will be in their sixties."

"That means caretakers will have to be reconsidered often," Lee said. "I thought we could use my address as the place to deliver anything we ordered, but I can now see we're going to be limited. What we're comfortable with now, such as Amazon and ordering things from the Internet, we may not have anyone to do that for us in another couple of years."

"We'd better get what we want immediately," Stanley said. "There may not be coffee makers before long, which will be ten or twenty years from now on Earth."

"I'll ask Kara to search where we can buy organic coffee tree plants," Ben said. "I can send her my debit card."

Lee looked thoughtful. "I wonder how long our bank accounts and debit or credit cards will work?"

They all groaned.

"Why don't we bring some of our cash here?" Stanley asked.

"That would only work until our bills were too old as payment," Ben said. "They could be phased out for another source."

"We just need to let it all go," D'laine said. "We can get coffee and coffee makers, but when those devices wear out, we'll be right back to where we started. We should figure out how to manufacture something as a replacement."

"I can transport the school books," Ben said.

They left it at that while they all muddled over the money and other issues that came up.

THE DISCOMFORT BEGAN AS D'LAINE FINISHED HER MORNING meal while listening to one of Jamie's humorous stories. She winced in pain and placed a hand on her stomach, trying to quell the spasms. D'laine cautiously moved her eyes to the others in the room to see if anyone had noticed. Evidently, they hadn't because no one seemed to be the least concerned, as they were all still engrossed with either their meal or their conversations. She thought it was gas, because by the time the meal was finished and everyone went their separate ways, there were no more pains.

D'laine headed to the library. She was perusing the library shelves, when she felt a hard twinge below her navel. She gasped and staggered half a step. Another twinge slammed her. This was definitely not gas! She hurried from the room and took to the stairs. She barely made it to the turret room when she was so overcome with the pain she could hardly focus.,

Trakon!

D'laine had guarded her secret well. She knew it was time for the egg to pass. She hadn't told her father, or anyone other than Trakon, wanting to keep the knowledge limited to herself and her husband for fear of something going wrong. She spent hours in private thought and meditating about the Tholian birthing process. She simply couldn't imagine her body changing from a live birth to laying an egg.

Another wicked pain jolted her.

Wave after wave of pain rocked her body. She forced her pain inward. D'laine screamed out telepathically to Trakon, babbling for him to come to her, and not to tell anyone.

Amid a discussion about a herd of wild pakows which were too close to the pens, Trakon flinched as D'laine's painful scream entered his mind. His eyes blanked for a moment.

"I need to attend to something, but I'll be back shortly," he blurted.

"Young love," one man said.

The rest of the attendees snickered and made snide comments.

Trakon hastily left the group, silently communicating with D'laine. He staggered momentarily from the pain that was being transferred to him through her sharing. Sweat broke out on his forehead as he hastened to her. At one point, blinded by the pain, he took a wrong turn on the way to the private turret room. He retraced his steps down the corridor until he was on the right path again.

D'laine rocked back and forth in severe pain while on top of the pile of gauze beside the vessel that would hold the egg.

Trakon staggered into the room and ran to her side.

"Help me out of my suit." Her voice was shaky with pain.

Trakon pressed the various buttons to deflate her suit. He pushed the loose material and helped her pull her arms out of the suit. Then he slid the uniform down the trunk of her body.

"Would you rather stand, or lie back so I can pull the rest of the suit off you?" he asked.

"Stand!" She gasped out.

Trakon helped her to a standing position. "Hold my shoulders or back so you don't fall."

He eased the suit down her legs. He picked up one foot, then the other and tossed the suit aside. Trakon settled D'laine's naked body down onto the pile of gauze on the floor. He grabbed a length of the material and wrapped it around her shoulders. It covered her like a large shawl.

Trakon knelt down in back of her and took her in his arms. He followed the rhythm of her rocking. He bit his lip as he felt helpless. He hoped her body wouldn't reject the birthing process. He didn't want anything to damage the egg, but he didn't want to take a chance with her well-being, either. An egg was replaceable, but she was not.

"Something must be wrong! The women of Thol do not experience this pain," Trakon exclaimed.

He didn't know what to do.

After what seemed an infinite amount of time, a wavering apparition of Ghury appeared before them.

"Do not fear, the pain will pass. Everything is normal. Your body will adjust accordingly." The Egrom's huge form vanished silently, without a trace.

Moments later, an egg passed. D'laine grabbed Trakon's arm hard enough to crush bones. She breathed through the pain.

"The egg!" D'laine lifted her torso slightly to show the bloodied egg, the size of a jumbo chicken's egg on the gauze.

Trakon pulled his knife out of his suit and cut a piece of gauze. He wiped the blood off the egg and held it preciously.

"Our child, D'laine!" He held it for a moment. D'laine ran her hand across the brown shell. Trakon placed the egg on the gauze in the growing vessel.

Another wracking pain hit D'laine. She thought she was

being torn in half. "Trakon!" She rocked back and forth, breathing hard.

"There must be something wrong! You shouldn't have any more pain!" Trakon was near to panicking.

Within moments, another egg passed onto the bloody gauze beneath D'laine.

"Two eggs? Impossible! Improbable!" Trakon sputtered. He wiped the second egg and placed it gently in the nest. The shell was a lighter color than the first egg.

D'laine shakily rose off the nest with Trakon's help. They stood there, silently looking down upon the fruit of their love and passion.

Trakon wrapped his arms around her. He held her tightly and showered little kisses along her neck and shoulder.

"Are two eggs uncommon?" D'laine asked.

"I have never heard of any woman passing two eggs before," Trakon said. "I'll have to check our histories to be sure."

"Looks like you'll have to make another vessel and stand," D'laine said. She walked to the window and scanned the beautiful horizon admiring all that she saw.

D'laine glanced down to the ground and noticed a familiar figure. Sitting on a woven gauze mat, arms and face lifted toward the heavens, the Visionary chanted softly.

"We cannot keep secrets from him," Trakon said, worried.

"It will be okay," D'laine said. "Now, help me get dressed."

TRAKON HELPED D'LAINE DOWN THE STAIRS TO THEIR SUITE. He curled up behind her on the huge bed, spooning her. He ran his fingers through her white-blonde hair.

"We need to tell our families about our eggs," Trakon said.

"That's fine. I didn't want to make an announcement until

we knew everything would be okay," she said. "Let's wait until after dinner."

D'laine drifted off into a deep sleep. Trakon stared into space with the worry of a new father. He slipped out of bed without waking D'laine and headed to the door. The dogs were on his heels. They left the room and Trakon headed to the turret room.

The dogs galloped up the stairs, Trakon on their heels. He stood over the vessel that held both the eggs. Pup sniffed the eggs. He licked them, then looked up at Trakon.

"Those are our children, Pup. Protect them!" Trakon said.

Trakon gathered the bloody gauze from the floor. He wasn't sure where to dispose of it, but rolled it into a ball so no one would suspect anything if they saw him with the bundle.

Pup didn't want to leave the room.

"Come!" Trakon said, forcefully. The dog refused to obey him. "I'm shutting the door downstairs. You won't be able to leave the room, Pup. Come on!"

The dog stayed by the vessel. Trakon knew it was too dangerous to even attempt to pick him up and carry him out of the room. He shook his head in frustration, left the diwal dog and returned to the suite to check on D'laine.

She was just stirring, when he and Chatter entered the bedroom. D'laine sat up in bed. She noticed the bundle tucked under Trakon's arm.

"Why don't you put that in the smart closet?" she suggested.

"Do you think it will clean it? I was going to take it out to the field and burn it," Trakon said.

"The smart closet will get it clean," D'laine said. "Where's Pup?"

"He won't leave the turret room. I'm not sure what to do—I don't want to leave the door open," Trakon said.

"Cut a dog-door into the door. We have them on Earth. A dog pushes the door with its head, and they can come and go as they please," D'laine explained. She shared a mind picture of Buffy going in and out of the house back home.

"That's clever. I can cut a door like that for him," Trakon said. "I'm going over to the wood shop to make another vessel and stand. I'll be back in time for dinner."

"I'm going to rest for a bit more," D'laine said. "I'm exhausted and sore all over."

He bent over her and kissed her forehead.

TRAKON AND D'LAINE WERE FIDGETY THROUGH DINNER, AND IT had not escaped the notice of everyone at the table. When they all retired to the salon, the evening chatting continued. The young couple's hands were clasped tightly as they sat on a sofa.

Lee set his eyes on his daughter and son-in-law. "Okay, I can't stand it anymore. What's going on? You two look like you've done something wrong and are afraid of getting caught."

Stanley snickered. "They're married. There's not anything they could do now that would get them in trouble."

"Well?" Kitry arched her eyebrows.

"We have an announcement," Trakon said. He pulled D'laine to her feet. "D'laine has given birth to two eggs!"

"What?" that word was in stereo as everyone clambered to their feet and rushed the couple.

D'laine survived crushing hugs and kisses. Trakon was thumped on the back and had his hand shook by all.

"Wait, did you say TWO eggs?" Kitry sucked in a breath.

"Yes," D'laine said.

"When?" Lee asked.

"This morning," Trakon said.

"Where are your eggs?" Jor-Dan asked. "Your heirs will have to be protected."

"Pup won't leave the nesting vessel," Trakon said. "I didn't know we would have two eggs, so I have to make another vessel."

"They're in the turret room, upstairs," D'laine said.

"Show us!" Lee said.

D'laine and Trakon led the family up the stairs, down corridors to the door to the turret room. They led the way up the stairs.

Pup was on guard duty. He stood, teeth clacking. He sniffed the air, determined there were no enemies, then flopped on the floor.

Everyone gathered around the nesting vessel and looked down on the eggs.

"This was the first." Trakon rubbed the darker shell.

"It's beyond my comprehension that the eggs grow and expand to hold a baby," Lee said.

"Daddy, have Ethaderia take you over to the nursery building so you can see all the stages. It's quite remarkable," D'laine said.

"Thol changed your physiology," Stanley said. "I don't understand it, but here's proof right in front of us."

"Two eggs are rare," Kitry said.

"How rare?" Lee asked.

"Extremely," Kitry said. "For as long as I've been queen, I've never heard of a woman having two eggs. We need to ask the Visionary about this."

"You are not transporting the eggs to the nursery?" Jor-Dan asked.

"No. I want them to grow here," D'laine said. "I was drawn to this room. It seems very important that they do not leave here."

"We will station guards… one up here, another outside the door," Jor-Dan said.

"Son, did you make this beautiful stand and vessel?" Kitry asked Trakon.

Trakon nodded. "I need to make another so they each have

their own resting place as the shells grow. I'm also going to make a dog door for Pup. He won't leave the room."

"A dog door?" Jor-Dan asked.

"Good idea," Lee said. He showed everyone what Buffy's dog door looked like in the kitchen back home on Earth and how she used it.

Jor-Dan stared at Buffy's door. "That is quite clever."

"The dog can be locked inside or outside," Lee said.

Three women warriors started up the stairs.

Pup was on his feet, teeth clacking a dangerous cadence at the intrusion of the strangers.

The family members yelped in fright and backed to the other side of the room.

D'laine grabbed Pup by his oily scruff and restrained him. *PUP, DOWN!* she bellowed using The Voice. Once she had him under control, she unhandled him.

"Come up the stairs slowly and enter the room. The dog needs to detect your scent," D'laine called out.

The three women entered the room, cautious, weapons drawn.

"Jor-Dan, Pup will need to meet any change of the guard," D'laine said. "He's much more sensitive and protective now. He understands these are our children, and he takes his job very seriously, like La'gar'ish."

D'laine led Pup to the three women warriors. "Let him smell your hand. Just hold it out. Don't touch him. He will take the initiative."

Pup sniffed each outstretched hand, a couple of them, shaky. He gave each a little lick then wagged his tail.

Everyone breathed a sigh of relief as Pup returned to his station by the nesting vessel. The women holstered their laser weapons.

"I want one of you in this room at all times, another on the stairs, and another downstairs on the outside of the door," Jor-

Dan said. "When the dog is in residence, he won't let any strangers near the eggs. We will introduce him to your shift replacements as soon as possible. We don't want accidents."

"A word of caution," Trakon said. "If someone were to get past the guard's downstairs, whoever is upstairs in this room should let Pup do his job. Stay out of the way, or you'll be dead within moments. You've seen diwal dogs take down a pakow. When diwals are in bloodlust, their common sense no longer exists. Guard the eggs. If someone manages to kill the dog, then you will protect my children."

"Yes, of course, Prince Trakon," the lead woman said.

CHAPTER TEN

*T*here were four shifts of warrior women guarding the passageway to the turret room, the stairwell, and the room itself. The royal eggs were well protected by Ciertrons and Pup, the fierce diwal dog. The only time Pup's teeth clacked a warning was when someone came near the downstairs door that he didn't recognize. They decided to have two warriors in the room at all times. They scanned the area through the open windows with their eyes and their Tholian telepathic sight.

For the first month, D'laine rarely left the palace. She visited the turret room throughout the day and night, sometimes taking a nap by the vessels. Her maternal instincts were in high gear and her hormones raged from the wholly different pregnancy and birthing process. A week after the first month, she calmed significantly.

Trakon breathed a sigh of relief. While he was every bit the protective father and husband, he recognized that his wife had gone overboard with her emotions. There were several instances where he mentally tiptoed around her. He never knew what would set off her ferocious emotions.

An announcement was sent to all the kingdoms, and an

event was being planned for the next month. Meeri and Herish were the first to visit and see the eggs prior to the party.

"I can't believe you birthed two eggs!" Meeri said. She wrapped an arm across D'laine's shoulders. "I've been searching archives and I can't find any instances of twin eggs!"

Like all men, Herish thumped Trakon on the back hard enough to displace his footing.

"The book paid off!" Herish said.

Meeri bashed Herish, then glared at him. "Control your bad manners, husband!"

D'laine was grateful that Tholians did not smoke cigars. She didn't think she could tolerate that celebratory notion.

"I don't know how you beat us in the baby department," Herish complained. "We married before you. We should have been first having eggs."

"It will happen when it happens," Meeri spat. She slugged Herish in the arm, not appreciating him pointing out any possible flaws in their joining.

"Ow!" Herish said. He rubbed his arm and scowled at his wife.

"Why don't we go downstairs and have some refreshments?" D'laine suggested. She didn't want her best friends to wallow over not being the first to produce eggs.

"Good idea," Meeri said. "It's not good to be in close quarters to your eggs if I'm going to have to tear into my husband over his behavior."

D'laine patted Meeri's back as they walked down the stairs. They made their way to the salon.

The majordomo provided finger food and drinks.

"Thank you so much," D'laine said. "Do you provide for the guards in the turret room?"

"Yes, princess. I've made sure they have meals, drinks and tidbits between meals," the majordomo said.

"Be sure not to send anyone the dog doesn't already know," Trakon warned.

"I have notified my staff of the consequences," the major-domo said. "No one wants that kind of an incident."

When the majordomo left the room, they resumed their conversations.

"How are you going to present the royal eggs to the event next month?" Meeri asked.

"I don't know what's planned," D'laine said. She looked askance to Trakon.

"We definitely won't have anyone going near the turret room," he said. "I'm sure my parents plan to have visuals only. Pup would go berserk if any of those people approached the stairs."

"Yeah, let's not start a war over a diwal dog devouring a guest," Herish joked.

Meeri elbowed Herish in the side.

"What is the matter with you today?" Herish glared at Meeri. She let out a little huff of anger.

"How's Ben getting along?" D'laine asked.

"He's been very helpful," Herish said. "He's helped moved some heavy equipment with his gift. He can even reposition things with just a thought. It's amazing to see his gift in action."

Trakon looked thoughtful for a moment. "I wonder if he can do that with people. Maybe he could bring Victor and his family here and return them with just a thought!"

"That sure would make things easier," D'laine said. "My father, Stanley and Ben worry that Victor and Kara will let too much time go by before they make their decision to emigrate to Thol. That ten to one ratio of time is rather harsh on the Earth side. Darren was in between Brian and Jamie's age, but now he'll be much older, so he won't be that wild boy Kara worried so much about."

"Ben didn't seem to have aged from when he was first here," Trakon pointed out.

D'laine thought it through. "You're right. Ben didn't seem to have aged an entire decade. Let's ask my father and Stanley."

"I'll contact Ben. Let's ask him about this," Trakon said.

Within moments, Ben appeared. "Congratulations on your new family status."

"Thanks, Ben," D'laine said. She studied his face and clothes.

Lee and Stanley entered the salon. Everyone greeted each other.

"We were discussing the time difference between our two dimensions," Trakon said. "Then we realized something significant." He swung his focus to Ben. "Ben doesn't seem to have aged from when he first visited."

Everyone studied Ben as if he were under a microscope.

"Huh. You're right," Stanley said. "How is that possible? Look at how Victor aged and all the events in his life that changed in that brief span of time from when we first arrived here."

"That's inconceivable according to the laws of physics," Lee said. He studied his friend. "Now that I think about it, you don't appear any older than when I met you and Victor when D'laine first disappeared."

"What's going on?" Ben said. "I'm only a year older, and according to that ratio Stan worked out, I should be in my seventies, and should look that age also."

"Victor aged a decade, had a wife and family in the one year of Tholian time," Lee said. "Buffy aged significantly, remember?"

"You're right, but remember, Buffy now seems to look younger," D'laine said.

"Something else we wondered about, which I think Ben just proved," Trakon said, "is maybe he can bring people here and return them."

Meeri and Herish watched and listened to the interplay.

"Why don't you experiment," Meeri said. "Why not bring your friends here right now?"

Everyone looked at each other.

Lee called out to Brian and Jamie. *If you want to see Darren, come to the salon room right now. He'll only be here for a little while.*

"That's a good idea. I can send Victor a note," Ben said.

Stanley smirked, then waved a hand at that. "I'll call him on my interdimensional telephone network provided by my super brain." Stanley focused on Victor's cellphone... hard. "Victor? It's Stanley. We want to try a little experiment with Ben's new gift." He listened a while. "Is Kara and Darren nearby? Okay, hold hands. Ben's going to try to bring you here for a fast visit then he'll return you."

Brian, Jamie, Buffy and Chatter rushed into the room. The boys looked around the room.

"Where's Darren?" Brian asked.

"He'll be here in a minute, or less," Lee said.

Stanley gave the thumbs up, but held a finger up to have Ben wait.

"Are you ready?" Stanley nodded to Ben. "Okay, here goes."

Within a flicker of a moment, the Bennett's appeared in the salon.

There was a ruckus of happy greetings.

Victor approached Ben. "Look at you! Kara, don't you think Ben could be a double for Robin Hood?"

Kara approached and hugged Ben. "You look wonderful, Ben."

The Tholians studied the visitors.

"How old are you, Darren?" Lee asked.

"I just turned nine!" Darren said.

"How is that possible?" Stanley said. "There must be some algorithms we haven't taken into consideration."

The boys escaped to a corner of the room and shared stories of what they had done since the last time they saw each other.

"Don't disappear," Lee warned. "They can only stay a little while."

They had the same discussion with Victor that they had amongst themselves. None of the scientists had any explanation why Ben hadn't aged. They didn't understand why Darren had only aged one year, and why Victor's life had changed so abruptly in the short span of a time. None of it made sense.

Kara, D'laine and Meeri huddled, then the women left the room. D'laine led them to the turret room, and she showed Kara the eggs, with Pup's approval.

"Everyone says two eggs are not common," D'laine told Kara.

"Was it painful?" Kara asked. "They're nowhere near the size of a newborn, but it seems to me it would be painful to have an egg pass through."

"It was very painful. I thought I would accidentally break Trakon's arm, I gripped him so tight, and I mind-shared the pain without knowing it," D'laine said.

"The pain-sharing is something we do," Meeri said. "But the pain is minimal for Tholian women. I'll bet it was different for you because your body changed."

Kara stared at the eggs in the twin vessels. "D'laine, how long does it take for the baby to be born... hatched?"

"The shell will expand for three years, then the baby will crack the shell—actually not a baby, but a small, fully matured boy or girl," D'laine said. "It's still confusing to me."

"That seems a little sad to me," Kara said. "Not being able to hold your baby and watch it grow."

"We'd better get back downstairs," Meeri said. "Isn't there a point where you have to return so you don't age?"

"Let's go," Kara said.

STANLEY WAS COUNTING DOWN TIME IN HIS HEAD. "OKAY, WE need to get you back home, otherwise people will think you've been kidnapped or something."

"If we moved here, what would we do?" Kara asked.

"You could do or learn anything you wanted," Ben said.

"The first month you'll stay with the Egroms. They'll teach you about Thol and you'll acclimate to this environment," D'laine said. "Then your gifts will come through."

Brian heard his sister and piped up. "My gift didn't come through right away, remember?"

D'laine rolled her eyes. "Okay, I'll amend that—your gift may take a while to come through. That might reveal what you focus on for a future."

"The most difficult thing you'll face is back home in the preparation to move," Ben said.

Jor-Dan and Kitry entered the salon.

"Hello, Victor, Kara..." Jor-Dan looked around the room until he noticed the boys. "And Darren!"

Kitry grasped Kara's hands. "How are you, dear? Are you still well?"

"Yes, D'laine completely healed me. I've never felt better... so vibrant, full of energy."

"I'm so happy to hear that," Kitry said.

"Where would we live if we moved here?" Victor asked.

"Well, here in the palace, of course," Jor-Dan said. "We have many empty suites. Or, if you prefer, you could live in a house in the kingdom."

"I think you should consider the palace for the first several months. It may take time until you are comfortable with your new environment," Lee said.

Kara turned to Ben. "You would help us bring whatever we want here?"

"Yes! My wizardry is amazing. You wouldn't need Earth

clothing—unless you want to keep some favorite things, but they would not be appropriate here," Ben said.

"Ben had all his things in the storage unit, remember?" Victor asked Kara. "We could put everything we wanted to bring with us in the small room where he stayed when you were sick, and he would poof it here."

"You would be the last of our original team," Lee said, thoughtful. "Everyone who was involved with the investigation of D'laine's disappearance would have vanished from Earth."

"That seems significant," Victor said.

"You can bet Al Jordon, that reporter for the Houston newspaper, will have a fit. He'll be putting together stories, but he'll never be able to solve the mystery," Ben said.

"The hardest thing is saying goodbye to those you love. Family, friends, neighbors... on the other hand, I never looked back," Lee said. "Victor, you'd better make sure you don't leave any documentation behind about Thol. If, for some weird reason the government got involved with your disappearance, it could get scary."

Victor and Kara's eyes locked on each other. Then Kara turned her attention to Darren. "I want a better life for our son. Earth is becoming more and more violent, and I worry for his future. I know this is the right decision, but I don't want to tell Darren our plans until we are ready to go."

Victor nodded. "Better get those schoolbooks ready to ship." Victor and Kara hugged fiercely. They had finally made the decision.

"Okay. I'll check in with you periodically," Stanley said. "You can let us know your plans."

"You ready to go back home?" Ben asked.

The boys groaned.

"I don't want to go back home!" Darren complained.

"Be happy that you got the chance to visit Brian and Jamie,"

Victor said. "Come on, we have to go home. We've been gone for a few days by now."

Kara grabbed one of Darren's hands, and Victor grabbed the other.

"Thanks for the free interdimensional travel," Victor said. *See you soon*, he mouthed.

Ben stared at the Bennett's. Within a flash, they were gone.

"I'm glad Kara made the decision," Lee said.

"I agree. It would have been iffy if Victor had strong-armed the decision," Stanley said. "This way, Kara will be comfortable with the process, and leaving everything behind."

Jor-Dan appeared thoughtful. "It seems significant that everyone involved in D'laine's disappearance will have vanished from your home world. I just can't connect what that means."

Lee flopped onto a chair and drilled his fingers on his thigh. "It seems to me that we are all supposed to BE here, for whatever reason."

"I wonder if this has anything to do with the prophecy?" Trakon asked. "We're pretty sure that involves just D'laine and me though."

"Who knows," Stanley said. "I suspect the Egroms are holding back information, but I don't know why they would. What could our immigrating here mean in the scheme of things?"

CHAPTER ELEVEN

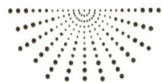

*V*ictor, Kara and Darren returned home in the middle of their living room. Victor looked Kara and Darren over, searching for a clue of any noticeable aging. Not finding anything, he sighed a relief. "Looks like we haven't aged."

"Aw, why couldn't we stay longer?" Darren sulked, missing his new friends.

Kara gave Victor one of those parent stink eyes warning him not to say anything.

"Thol is very dangerous outside of its kingdom cities, Darren," Kara said. "You'll have to be satisfied with short visits."

Darren shuffled to his bedroom to pout.

Victor checked his cellphone and discovered three missed calls, one from the Houston reporter. He placed it on speaker so Kara could listen.

"What do you think? Should we do this Skype interview?" he asked.

"Yes. Then we can wipe our hands of him. He most likely will drop everything after his follow-up article," Kara said.

"Yeah, until he gets wind of our disappearance," Victor said. "I want to stage it so we leave a fully cooked meal on the table."

Kara swatted him. "That would be a nice touch of drama. Let's clear out the spare room since that will be our storage room for everything we want to bring with us. I feel bad about abandoning things I would like to give to people, or donate."

"How are we going to handle our finances, the property, things like that?" Victor said.

"Bank accounts and our investments need to be included in some sort of living trust so they are not abandoned," Kara said. "Should we do a new will? What if Darren wants to return to Earth when he's grown?"

"The only ones who know about Thol, other than our core group, are Lee's housekeeper and her husband," Victor said. "I suppose we could find someone to appoint—someone still young, but trustworthy, and who understands the science, somewhat."

"We don't know anyone like that. I wouldn't feel comfortable with any of your colleagues, Victor. They are ladder climbers and want to publish," Kara said. "Why don't we look at that reporter a little more closely? Ben told us that Al Jordan believed in other worlds and dimensions."

Victor stared at Kara as if she had lost her mind. "Hon, he'd blow the lid off this can of worms."

"No, he wouldn't! He'd examine the science behind the whole thing. I think he'd be a good choice. We could even arrange for him to live here. The house is paid off. Surely, he'd be able to pay utilities, taxes and the rest," Kara said.

"Let me think about it," Victor said. "I want to talk to Ben, Lee and Stan about this before we make any solid decisions."

Victor walked to his office and wrote a note. "When Stanley calls, we'll see what he and the others have to say. I'd better return these phone calls."

"I'm going to go get the mail. Be right back," Kara said.

DARREN TOOK OFF TO HIS FRIEND BOBBY'S HOUSE, A FEW HOUSES down the street. As soon as he was out of sight, Kara and Victor emptied the spare room. They dismantled the bed, carried everything out to the garage, and Kara stuffed the sheets into the hamper.

"What do we really need to bring with us?" Victor asked. "I mean, besides my computer, the scientific equipment I own, and my files?"

"Our books, some of Darren's things—if they are in pristine condition, they may be worth quite a lot of money when he's our age or older," Kara said. "If he returned to Earth for any reason, he would have our money, and might get a little nest egg from some of his things. I want to bring my earrings. I'm not sure if women on Thol wear them or not, but I love my earrings."

Victor gave her a look. He snuggled up to her and kissed her neck.

"The first thing that can go in the room is the box of school books you gathered," Victor said. He went into the study and grabbed the box and brought it to the spare room. "How are we going to get boxes without alerting someone we were moving?"

"Don't get them close to home," Kara said. "Wear a ballcap, sunglasses—you know, make a disguise that isn't too fake to attract attention. Let's make a list of supplies."

VICTOR RETURNED FROM THE BOX STORE WITH TWENTY BOOK boxes. He parked the car in the garage, then carried a package of tape inside the house along with a couple of boxes.

"Are we moving?" Darren asked, in a panic.

"No, we're going to paint my bookcases. We're going to pack up everything on the shelves so nothing gets damaged."

"Oh, okay," Darren said, as he raced back outside and down the street.

Victor's cellphone rang. "Hon! Stanley's calling!"

Kara raced into Victor's office. He put the call on speaker and they discussed what to do about their property and holdings, and the reporter.

"I think Al Jordan is a good choice," Ben said. "He's keen on science, and science fiction."

"I liked him," Lee chimed in. "He's not so full of himself that he misses the human experience in his research and writing. Why don't you tell him he can write a novel about what we tell him? He can't divulge any facts in an article, but he could profit from writing a science fiction story. We can even show him pictures of our world and some of the creatures."

"Oh, that's a good idea," Kara said. "The school books are ready to go. They're in the spare room, where you stayed, Ben."

"Oh, okay. I'll bring them over," Ben said.

"That's where we'll put everything that's coming with us," Victor said. "Can anyone think of anything important we should pack?"

"Bring a pizza. My son-in-law is driving the chef crazy with mimicking his favorite food. Hopefully, the tomato plants will yield fruit soon," Lee said. "How about grabbing the plants that make up Italian seasoning—oregano, parsley, and whatever else they put in the jar? We can grow our own for the tomato sauce."

Everyone chuckled about Trakon's obsession.

"Okay, we're going to invite Al Jordan over and lay it all out for him. Can you send pictures to my phone?" Victor felt sure the reporter would jump at the chance to be involved in the Tholian ruse.

They ended the call. Kara and Victor stared at each other, then hugged tightly. They had made a huge decision to emigrate to another dimensional world that no Earthling knew about. Then they made another monumental decision to involve someone who could turn their tale into a media circus for his own gain.

"Call the reporter," Kara said. "Do it now. He'll have to make arrangements to travel here, and I want to leave as soon as possible."

AL JORDAN CLIMBED OUT OF HIS RENTAL VEHICLE IN VICTOR'S driveway. He grabbed his weekender bag, walked up the driveway and rang the bell. Kara opened the door.

"Al? Welcome to our home. Come in," she said.

"Thanks for having me, Mrs. Bennett," Al said.

"Why don't you stash your bag in the spare bedroom. Victor's on the phone, but will be off shortly," Kara said. "Would you like some iced tea?"

Kara showed Al to the spare room which she once used as a hospice for her brain cancer before D'laine healed her. Al deposited his bag on the bed, dug into a side pocket and pulled out his notepad and a couple of pens, and his recorder. Then they went to the kitchen.

Victor joined them and greeted the reporter. "Glad you could make it, Al. We've got a lot to talk about."

After shaking hands, they sat and sipped tea with fresh mint.

"I can't tell you how much I appreciate you taking the time to talk to me about your experience with the Jackson case," Al said.

Victor and Kara shared a knowing look.

"Al, what we're going to talk about can't be printed in the newspaper," Victor said.

The reporter sputtered his disbelief. He had traveled across the country for the exclusive interview. He couldn't believe what he heard.

Victor held up a hand, and Kara patted the reporter on the

arm. "What you can do, though, is write a best-selling novel. We're going to give you details, and pictures of where our friends are now living. In exchange, we have to request a service from you."

Al's mouth was still hanging open when the story unfolded. They talked for hours. Anytime Darren came back home, the subject was side-stepped. When Darren went back out to play with Bobby, they picked up without a hitch.

"This is Jakla Bosakin, the commander of the Plotal army," Kara said. "And this is a pakow."

"They look huge, both of them," Al said.

"Plotals and Egroms range about seven to eight feet tall. Pakows remind me of wooly mammoths, but they have these strange eyes," Victor said.

"Will I be able to visit there sometime?" Al pleaded with his entire body.

Victor and Kara exchanged a glance.

"That's not our decision," Victor said.

Al nodded. He understood. He was grateful for the tremendous gift that had been bestowed upon him. While the world, his friends and colleagues would fuss over the novel, he, and no one else on Earth, would know it was a far cry from a make-believe story.

Over the next two days, more information unfolded. They also worked out a system for unexpected communication changes. If Al had to change cellphone service providers and couldn't keep his same phone number, he would be able to write a note and leave it in the small room. Ben would bring the note over and they would reestablish communication.

"When are you leaving?" Al asked.

"When you leave here to return to Houston. You can be part of the ruse," Victor said. "You can call several times, different times of the day and night for several days, and start a panic that something happened. Have the police come check on the house —that sort of thing."

Kara explained how they would leave the food on the table, and how all of Victor's books and things would be gone as well, which would be a mystery. Darren had told Bobby about the bookcases being painted and things being packed up.

"We'll check in with you periodically to find out if everything we set up is working," Victor said.

Al hung his head for a minute. "I don't know what to say. This is awesome and overwhelming at the same time."

Victor thumped Al on the back. "You'll be able to write your assignment for the newspaper. Let everything unfold. Write the book, Al."

Darren ran inside. The front door slammed shut. He ran to his room, then ran to the living room where his parents and their guest sat. "Mom, I can't find my superheroes! They're all gone!"

"We'll look for them later, Darren. Al is getting ready to go back to Houston, so come say goodbye," Kara said. She got up, went to the kitchen and attended food on the stove. She could barely contain her excitement.

"Are you coming back again?" Darren asked Al.

"I suspect I will return to your lovely house in the very near future," Al said.

"Okay! I'll see you later, then," Darren said. With that, he ran outside, superheroes forgotten.

Victor and Kara walked Al out the door to his rental car. They walked back into the house when Al's vehicle disappeared down the street.

Kara put the bowls of food on the table. She double checked that the stove was turned off. She looked around her neat kitchen, then she joined Victor in the spare room.

Victor was changing clothes. He eased the Ciertron suit up his body, pulled on the boots, then pressed the inflating button at his wrists and cuffs. Kara changed. They each held the tiny voice translator that Ben had sent to the spot in back of their ear, and it settled into place.

"Okay, we're ready. Call Darren to come home for supper," Victor said.

Kara grabbed her cellphone and called Bobby's mother. Under ten minutes later, the front door opened and slammed closed.

"In here, Darren," Victor called out.

They heard the toilet flush, then Darren came down the hall and stopped, open-mouthed, when he saw his parents and the contents of the room.

"Where'd you get those? Can I wear one?" he asked.

"Here's yours," Kara said. "Come change." Kara folded Victor's clothes, then hers, placing their shoes on top of their clothes.

Victor helped Darren with the suit and showed him how to inflate it. Then he pressed the translator device in place and laughed as it settled behind his ear.

"Wow! This is so cool. Can I show Bobby?"

"Just stay here for a minute," Victor said. "I'm expecting an important call."

"What's all this stuff? I thought this was dad's books?" Darren asked. He looked around. "Hey! There's my superheroes!"

Victor's cellphone rang. "We're ready," he said to the caller.

"Let's hold hands," Kara said.

Darren seemed confused, but held his parents' hands.

In the next moment, they materialized in their new home on Thol.

CHAPTER TWELVE

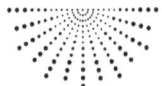

*T*he Bennett's and their boxes materialized in their new suite in the palace. Lee, Ben, Stanley, D'laine, her brothers and her husband were there.

"You made it!" Lee said.

"That's quite a trick, Ben," Victor said. He looked around, all boxes accounted for.

"Everything is okay with Al?" Ben asked.

"That was a good decision," Kara said. "He's sincere and is grateful for the opportunity."

Darren was in a state of shock. "Are we going to live here?"

"Yeah, you'll love it. Want to help us at the baseball park? There's a game tonight between the Plotals and Egroms!" Brian said.

"Plotals are those big alligator men, right?" Darren asked.

"Uh huh. They can't use their tails, though. That's cheating," Jamie explained.

"You get back here for dinner in two chacks," Lee said.

"What's a chack?" Darren asked.

"An hour, so we have to be back and wash up for dinner before everyone sits down. Those are the rules," Jamie said.

"Darren, you can go, but you make sure you're back here like Mr. Jackson said," Victor said.

"What about Bobby? I was supposed to help him with his paper route," Darren said.

Kara shrugged. "Here's the choices. You can live here and have an incredible life, or we can go back home and you can help Bobby with his paper route, go to school, things like that. I know you would have wanted to say goodbye to your best friend, but your father and I thought it would be best if we just disappeared."

Darren's eyes tracked from his mother to his father. He was still having somewhat of a difficult time with the abrupt change in life plans.

Pup, Buffy and Chatter romped into the room. The dogs sniffed the newcomers. The diwal dogs recognized the scents and competed with Buffy with their licking campaign.

Darren scratched Pup's head. He looked at his mom and smiled. "I like it here better."

The boys and dogs hurried from the suite, down the stairs and out of the palace. They ran through the city to the gates of the kingdom, and over to the baseball diamond.

"When you go to stay with the Egroms for your training, you'll meet Chacoodi, our best friend," Brian said.

"He's an Egrom boy," Jamie said. "He can do all sorts of things."

"What sort of training did you get?" Darren asked.

"It's so cool. You'll sit with one of the Egroms in his mushroom house, and they show you movies in your head!" Jamie said.

"Wow," Darren said. He looked around the baseball field. "What do we have to do here?"

"We have to set things up. The bases, the bats, gloves—simple stuff," Brian said. "Since the two teams are really big creature people, the bats and gloves are huge. We have two sets of everything. One for regular people like the Ciertrons and Kudaja, and then these for the creature people."

Brian showed Darren the enormous gloves. The boys pulled the equipment out of the storage building. When everything was set up to Brian's satisfaction, they ran over to the pakow pens and climbed up on the fence.

Jugdaak, the pakow attendant, rode up on a pakow. "Do you want to ride?"

"Can we?" Darren almost fell off the fence he was so excited.

"Yeah, let's go for a ride," Jamie said.

Jugdaak saddled up three pakows and led them outside the corral to the boys.

Jamie instructed Darren on pakow handling, mounting and riding.

Darren looked his pakow in the eye. "Please let me ride you."

The pakow knelt. Darren climbed up the huge leg the same way Jamie and Brian mounted. He flopped down into the saddle and grabbed the saddle horn.

"Hold the reins," Brian said. "You really don't need them, because you can talk to the pakow in your head. Let's go. We'll go slow."

They took off and rode over the field of amber-colored moss. Hosks scattered out of the path of the pakows.

"Let's play with the hosks," Jamie said. He asked his pakow to stop.

Brian stopped close by, but Darren's pakow kept running.

"Darren! Tell your pakow to come back here!" Brian yelled.

It didn't look like the pakow would stop. Brian and Jamie raced their pakows to catch up with Darren's mount.

Jamie scowled at the pakow. *You stop when you're told to stop! Now come on, turn around!*

Darren was a little shook up. "He wouldn't stop. I pulled on the reins and I talked to him, but he wouldn't listen!"

"I told him he was bad," Jamie said. "I'd better tell Jugdaak he needs more training."

Brian tapped his communicator and checked the time. "We'd better get back home, or we'll be in trouble."

They turned back and rode to the pakow pens, dismounted and handed the reins over to the attendant.

"This guy needs more training. He wouldn't stop when Darren told him to," Jamie said.

Jugdaak scowled at the pakow. He knew better than to argue with Jamie. The kid had conversations with animals.

"I'll come see you tomorrow," Jamie said. "Maybe there's some problem we don't know about."

"Okay," Jugdaak said. "See you tomorrow."

The boys returned to the palace and headed to the common restroom to get cleaned up.

"Don't tell my mom and dad about the pakow," Darren said. "They'll freak out."

"It will be our secret," Brian said.

They walked to the dining salon and discovered they had beat the adults. Within moments, everyone took their places at the table. Ethaderia and Treikie were in attendance and introductions were made.

"Did you have fun?" D'laine asked Darren.

"Yes! I can't wait to see this baseball game tonight!" Darren said.

"This will be the first game between the Plotals and Egroms," Lee said. "I'm not sure if either can play against regular Tholian humans. They would be so mismatched due to their size and strength. We'll see how this game goes."

"Guess we showed up at the right time." Victor rubbed his hands together.

"Tomorrow morning, I'll fly you to the Egrom village," Trakon said

"As long as none of you have a dangerous brain, you should

have a great learning experience." Stanley cringed slightly at the memories of his first experiences and the crisis that unfolded. He would be forever grateful to Greg Claymore for aligning his brain and skull so he wasn't stuck wearing a helmet for the rest of his life.

After dinner they locked the dogs in D'laine and Trakon's suite and followed people over to the baseball diamond. The stadium seating had expanded to accommodate kingdom-wide attendance. It had also been imperative that the seating be engineered to support the extreme weight of Egroms and Plotals in attendance.

Jakla spotted the royals and their entourage and waved a small group of Plotals to accompany him.

"King Jor-Dan, Queen Kitry, may I present my mate, Neska; my son Cadj, and my daughter Fazi," Jakla said.

"Welcome to Ebscalon! It is so nice to meet you," Kitry said.

"I didn't realize you had a family," D'laine said. "It goes to show you how little we know of each other."

"We know all about you!" Cadj said. "You saved my father from the robots!"

Jakla's tail pod opened a pinch, and he whacked his son on the butt. Cadj, jumped and scowled at his father.

"Act civilized," Neska said to her son. She turned to D'laine. "He's very excited to meet you, Princess D'laine. His father regales us with all your stories."

Neska was a smaller, more refined version of her mate. She had the same mottled green scales, but her skin was a brighter mauve, and her mohawk scales were curly instead of the straight spikes on the male's heads. Her eyes were more golden than her husband's bright yellow eyes with the streak of brown down the middle.

"Jakla, you remember our Earth friends who were here for our wedding, don't you?" D'laine asked. "This is Victor, his wife Kara and their son Darren."

Jakla greeted them with the traditional Tholian gripping of forearms. "Yes, I remember when you arrived. My tribe worried there was a portal breach, and the robots had returned. Welcome back to Thol. Are you visiting again?"

"Hello, Mr. Bosakin. It's nice to see you again," Kara said. "We have left our home planet behind to live a better life here."

"It will be nice to get to know you, and to have our children learn about other cultures," Neska said.

"We'd better take our seats. Won't you join us, Neska?" Kitry asked.

"We would be honored," Neska said. She and Jakla rubbed their tails together in affection.

"I'd better go join my team," Jakla said. "We're going to beat the Egroms!"

Chacoodi ran yelling up to Brian and Jamie. He was so excited to see his human friends again.

D'laine called them over and introduced the boys and Chacoodi to Jakla's children.

Brian, Jamie, Darren, Chacoodi and Cadj took off running around the field. Fazi felt left out. Neska rubbed her tail along Fazi's tail.

"They're boys. They don't think girls are interesting play-mates," Neska said.

"I don't care," Fazi said.

Both D'laine and Neska knew Fazi had her feelings hurt, but there wasn't much they could do about it. The boys were running wild. They wouldn't settle down until the game started. D'laine called out to her brothers.

The game will start soon. Come back over here and don't be rude and ignore Fazi just because she's a girl!

She heard some grumbling, but the boys headed back to the

stadium seating and sat in the middle of the bleachers to have a good view. It was interesting seeing three Earth boys, an Egrom boy and a Plotal boy sitting together having fun.

Lee slipped his umpire shirt over his head. He called all players to the middle of the field. "Let's go over the rules to refresh everyone's memories."

There were some silent grumbles among the two teams.

Those Plotals don't stand a chance.

Egroms can't run as fast as we can.

They can't use their tails.

They'd better not step to the bases!

"This is going to be an honest game. Here are some reminders."

1. You can't use any powers you possess to play this game.
2. You will all use your legs to run. No beaming yourself anywhere.
3. Use your hands to hold the large bats we created for you.
4. You will use the bat—and nothing else—to hit the ball.
5. You will not help the ball go where you want it to.
6. No brawling.

"We are here to have fun. This may be a new concept for you and your team, but play by the rules."

The teams separated. The Plotals took to the field. The baseball gloves were enormous, specifically designed for their very large, scaly hands.

Jakla walked to the pitcher's mound. He tossed the ball in the air and caught it in his glove. He waited for Lee to call the game to begin.

"Play ball!" Lee said.

Jakla stared at the youngish Egrom holding the bat. He wound up as the game holographic movies taught him, then released the ball. It sped to the batter faster than any pitchers ball on Earth.

The Egrom's eyes clocked the ball's approach. He swung the bat and connected with the ball. It soared into the air. The Egrom tossed the bat to the ground, churning up dirt, then he took off running toward first base.

Victor leaned toward Jor-Dan. "That play is called a short fly ball."

"Short fly ball?" Jor-Dan asked.

"Yes. Sports has its own terminology," Victor explained.

Lee watched the players to make sure no one cheated.

The ball fell to the ground and a Plotal outfielder ran and snatched it up. He saw the Egrom player had rounded first base, thinking about taking second, but the Plotal outfielder cut him off with a throw to second. That stopped the Egrom's plan to try to steal a base.

The crowd cheered and jeered players as the game continued. The Egroms had scored one home run. Next up were the Plotals.

Jakla grabbed the bat and tested the weight in his large hands. He looked over other bats and chose one he liked better.

"Look, your father is first for our team," Neska said. She was excited to witness her mate take part in the new game.

Fazi watched the field. She liked the game.

The Egrom pitcher nodded to Jakla. He wound up and let the ball go.

Lee could tell it was a superfast ball, faster than what Jakla threw.

The resounding crack of the bat connecting with the ball

sounded like an explosion. Lee expected to see the bat splinter, but it held fast.

Kara cheered for Jakla. She remembered how civil he was to her when they had first visited Thol for D'laine and Trakon's wedding.

Jakla threw the bat to the ground and took off running, his tail straight out behind him, his pod closed. He barely made it to first base when the Egrom caught the ball.

Lee called him safe. There were grumblings in the Egrom camp.

"His foot touched the base pad on the ground before the ball was caught," Lee explained for all to understand. "If someone gets to the base before the ball, they are safe. Do you need me to show you a visual?"

There were grumbles and heckling from the team and spectators, so Lee projected the visual with the focus on Jakla's foot, the base, and the ball being caught seconds later.

Ghury and the elders sat in the stadium silently watching the game.

We will have to talk to our young players about being good sports, Adrum sent to the elders.

The Egrom elders nodded.

The Plotals scored two home runs.

The game continued with no fights between the teams. The Egroms won the game with a six to five score. Not many spectators cheered. Lee determined they'd have to be coached in team sportsmanship, maybe watch the holographic videos again to see how people in the stadium cheered for their team. Neither the Plotals nor Egroms brought food or trinkets to be sold. That was another thing they would have to learn. But maybe on Thol, that wasn't important to the teams or the spectators.

The Earthlings didn't choose sides. They cheered for both the Plotals and Egroms to keep the peace. All in all, everyone had fun. The stadium emptied, and spectators surrounded their chosen team.

Jor-Dan approached Jakla. "This is quite an interesting sport, don't you agree?"

"Yes, we like this game. We will have to practice more to beat those Egroms next time," Jakla said.

"You were excellent," Jor-Dan said. "If I were younger, I'd try to play."

Kitry shook her head. "I don't understand why everyone thinks this is such a good game. You hit the ball and run in a big square, with everyone yelling at you!"

Jor-Dan patted her on the shoulder. "It's fun yelling—cheering your teammate on to success."

Kitry shook her head again and walked toward the scientists. Jor-Dan sighed.

Jakla roared out a laugh. "Perhaps queen Kitry and Neska would make good game companions. It appears Kara enjoys the game."

Ghury and the elders approached them.

"You are fine with the outcome of this game?" Ghury asked Jakla.

Jakla let out a snuffled sound through his snout. "Yes. We like this game. We will practice more."

The Egroms nodded. They didn't want war over this new sport.

Adrum approached Victor. "We will take you to our village now, if you are ready to learn about Thol."

"Kara?" Victor hollered for his wife. "Do you want to go to the Egrom village tonight?"

Kara walked over to Victor with D'laine at her side.

"This would be such a wonderful cultural experience," Kara said. "Sure, let me get Darren. He already has an Egrom play-mate, so he won't be bored."

CHAPTER THIRTEEN

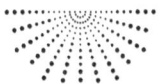

*E*xcept for the game, days passed since the new expectant parents had left the city's confines. They wanted to stay close to the eggs to make sure that everything was perfect in the private hatching room.

D'laine sat on the gauze beside the two nesting vessels in the tower. She stroked the egg shells while she daydreamed, with Pup snuggled beside her.

The guards gave her space when she visited her unborn children by slipping into the stairwell, but keeping a vigil with their keen senses.

The door opened at the foot of the stairs. Keeshi and Amoroso, the warrior women, jumped into high alert.

"Identify yourself!" Keeshi sounded formidable.

Chatter rushed up the stairs, tail wagging and butt wiggling. He sniffed the vessels and the eggs. He and Pup started on a sniffing campaign.

"Just me," Trakon called out, as he jogged up the stairs and entered the turret room. He sank to the floor beside D'laine, took her in his arms and kissed her.

Pup wiggled into the space between them. "Pup, go lie down!" Trakon nudged the diwal dog.

The dog grumbled. He got up and trotted to one of the windows and jumped up on his bench. Chatter tried to hop up on the same bench, but Pup didn't want to share. He looked around and sniffed the air. Pup glanced out each of the open areas and repeated his sniffing, Chatter following his lead. When they were satisfied that all was safe in the kingdom, Pup walked over to his plump gauze bed and flopped down. He let out a sigh and snoozed, one ear perched up. Chatter sat down, his tail wagging on the floor. It didn't take much to make him happy.

Trakon silently rubbed a finger over the shell of each egg. He kissed D'laine on the forehead. "Let's go for a ride. We need a change of scenery."

"That would be nice," D'laine said. She bent and kissed each egg, then let Trakon pull her to her feet.

Time was the main factor now, as they waited for the embryos to grow within the shells. They were uncertain of the development of the babies. No one knew if the eggs would develop slowly within the shell over the next three years, or if they would develop as an Earthling embryo and "be ready" at the end of the nine-month duration. No one could tell at this point—even Ghury seemed unable to decide the course that nature would take, or he was skirting the issue until stronger signs appeared.

They entered the stairwell, Chatter following Trakon.

"We'll be back later tonight," Trakon said.

The warriors tapped their chests.

"No one will harm your unborn," Keeshi growled.

The women warriors returned to the turret room, circling the large room, looking out the windows, similar to Pup.

TRAKON AND D'LAINE LEFT THE TURRET AND DESCENDED TO THE lower levels, finally leaving the palace. D'laine's pet waited impatiently at the pakow holding pen. Lulu sniffed the air and bellowed loudly as she picked up D'laine's scent.

D'laine patted Lulu's leg, and the pakow lowered her muzzle for the kiss she expected.

"What a good girl. My Lulu," D'laine said. She rubbed the pakows snout and tickled her ears.

Lulu was like a giant, overgrown puppy. She was always happy to see her human. The ritual completed, D'laine climbed up Lulu's front leg to her back and settled into the saddle.

Trakon mounted his pakow, then signaled for the attendant to open the gate. "D'laine, you have ruined that pakow. She is so spoiled," Trakon griped.

"Maybe, but she'll do anything I ask of her," she chided.

"That's true," he admitted.

Chatter took off across the field. He looked over his shoulder to make sure the pakows were following him.

Lulu was tired of being penned up. D'laine had to restrain her from charging out of the pen, possibly running over someone. As soon as they were out of the confining gates, she guided the animal north and let her run to her heart's content.

The pakows six legs thundered across the moss. Hosks scattered. A resting par took to the air and flapped its scarlet wings. Chatter had his fill and headed back to the city.

D'laine and Trakon were an uncommon sight in the contrast between them. Dark and light, day and night. D'laine stood out wherever she was because of her beautiful golden tanned skin, and long white-gold hair, which was currently blowing in the wind. She was quite a sight to behold.

After riding for about two hours, the beasts slowed to a comfortable pace. The prince and princess had enjoyed the much-needed romp away from prying eyes and the restrictions of the palace.

Off in the distance stood a cluster of trees. They steered towards them to rest the animals and have a bite to eat. D'laine took in the beautiful scenery and the clean, flashing sky. She noticed something in the sky off in the distance to the left of the trees and pointed to it.

"What is that?" she asked.

Trakon shielded his eyes with his hand. "Just a par." He kept tracking the air-borne creature, but upon a closer look with the gap closing, he wasn't sure.

"That isn't a par; what is it?" he asked. "I'm not sure I've ever seen a creature like that."

Whatever it was, they watched it glide through the air, flapping large wings that were colored like light through stain glassed windows. They were closer to the oasis, and the creature was high over the tops of the trees.

"Too big for a par; not an insect. This creature looks like a combination of bird and beast. I don't know where it comes from or what it is," Trakon said.

"It looks like a butterfly from my world, but it can't be because they are only this big." D'laine held her thumb and her index finger in a "C" shape to show the size. "This looks like a man with a butterfly's wings. Thol doesn't have a history of these creatures? Where do you think it came from?"

"I haven't studied this species. Of course, many things have become extinct as our world changes, but we have documented all those creatures so that future generations will know about them. We need to get a better look," Trakon said.

They watched as the creature disappeared over the treetops and vanished from sight.

"Do you think it's a new species that might have evolved from something secreted away?" D'laine asked.

"That's possible. Let's return tomorrow morning to see if we can catch a better glimpse of it. Maybe we can follow it back to its nest," Trakon said.

THE FOLLOWING DAY WAS A REPLAY OF THE PREVIOUS DAY. THEY couldn't follow the creature's flight through the small thicket of trees, and by the time they rode around them, the creature had vanished from sight.

Frustrated, Trakon jumped down from his mount. "We should have taken a ship out here! It's our own fault for losing the thing." He ranted for a few minutes.

"Trakon, if we saw it twice in one week, we can return in a ship tomorrow," D'laine snapped. "It's not the end of the world!"

They headed back to the palace, Trakon grumbling all the way.

The next morning, they flew out to the copse of trees in a two-man crestrider. As they waited at the edge of the thicket, it was obvious that the creature was not going to make an appearance.

"Want to spend the night?" D'laine asked.

Trakon looked around. The ship was already packed with enough provisions for a week, so they had no reason to return to the city. Their unborn children were safe with the women warrior guards, Pup, and their families who would make many trips to the turret room.

"Sure." Trakon tapped his communicator. "Father, D'laine and I are going to spend the night on the plains so we can try to catch a glimpse of that creature again."

"Stay safe. All is well at the palace. I'll let everyone know," Jor-Dan said.

They gathered wood for a fire. After their sparse meal of roots, seeds and dried meat, they spread their bedding out around the fire and made themselves comfortable. The sun rested on the horizon. The two moons would be overhead soon.

"This reminds me of when we met," D'laine said.

119

Trakon wound his arms around her and pulled her in for a kiss. "I'll be forever grateful for being stranded with you."

D'laine swept her fingers through his black hair as she stared into his dark eyes. "I wonder where this prophecy came from. When I was in the coma, after the accident that killed my mother, my father and I were convinced that the dreams began then. I just don't have any way to prove that's when they started."

"When would that have been?" Trakon asked.

"Remember the ten to one ratio," D'laine said. "I've been here for two Earth years—completed paths. Somehow that doesn't equate correctly—I've got to ask my father and Stanley about that ratio. That would make it twenty years, but I haven't reached twenty yet. It's all so confusing."

"I began having dreams that didn't make much sense," Trakon said. "I clearly saw you, but you were younger. It was all a mix of images I didn't understand at that time. Since my trip to your world, I understand it a little better. I saw all the ground vehicles, and now I know that I witnessed the accident that claimed your mother's life. I never told my parents about those dreams."

"I wonder what role our children will have in this prophecy," D'laine said.

"We'll do everything we can to keep them safe! The entire kingdom is looking forward to their emerging day," Trakon said. He kissed her deeply as the sun disappeared and darkness fell upon them.

D'LAINE CAREFULLY DISENTANGLED HERSELF FROM TRAKON. IT amazed her that the blinding light of the flashing sky didn't bother her anymore. She tried to remember when she had become acclimated, but lost the thought quickly as she gazed into the sky and noticed a speck approaching from a distance.

"Trakon! Wake up! The creature has returned!" D'laine yelled.

They jumped up, threw their bedding onto the ship and clambered aboard. Within moments the ship was airborne, racing towards the speck that was now within range for them to get a real good look. Except for the manlike body, the creature looked like a giant monarch butterfly. The intricately patterned wings were brilliant orange and black when the sun shone through, and two long antennae were atop the creature's head. They watched the graceful flight of the butterfly-like being.

The creature was adept at evasive flight. It gave the ship's pilot a real workout. Its speed was not like its insect cousin from Earth, which would have been considered slow and meandering. This flying thing could outrun the ship and out guess each maneuver that Trakon implemented.

A squadron of Kudaja on their borjos buzzed around the crestrider.

"What are you doing out here?" Herish yelled.

D'laine pointed to the creature. "We want to find out what that is."

Herish and his team watched the butterfly-being.

"Where did it come from?" Herish asked. He landed his borjo on the ship's railing and dismounted. He morphed to full-size.

"We've been tracking it for a few turns, but today we are going to find out where it comes from," Trakon said.

"I've never seen that type of creature before," Herish said.

Trakon steered the ship to the best of his ability. He had the reputation as the best navigator of the air fleet, but he decided he was not quite good enough for this sleek, graceful creature. It could fly circles around them any turn of the week.

They all observed as the creature flew straight up into the

sky, away from its pursuers. Trakon hovered the crestrider to determine what the thing was going to do.

It was almost as if the creature were flying directly into the sun when it suddenly took a nosedive. It was heading straight for the ship at a reckless speed.

Trakon used evasive flight patterns. He nimbly handled the controls, now being the hunted instead of the hunter.

The creature closed in on them quickly.

Trakon, D'laine and Herish stood on the deck of the ship watching, horrified, as the insect-man swooped down, causing them all to duck. Before anyone knew what had happened, D'laine was jerked right up into the air, screaming.

"D'laine!" Trakon and Herish yelled.

Herish yelled to his squadron. "Morph and follow that thing!"

Borjos and Kudaja morphed into their full-sizes. The borjos pursued the creature. Their powerful wings displaced air which helped the borjos fly at great speeds.

Trakon jumped into action once he recovered from his initial shock. He grabbed the controls and forced the ship to leap forward as he kept an eye on the creature. He wasn't gaining on the insect-man, but he wasn't losing sight of it either. He bashed the communicator on his chest. "The princess has been abducted! Send the fleet!" Trakon gave his coordinates and turned tracking on for the fleet to find the ship. He shared an image of the creature for all to see.

MILES WHIZZED BY AS THE CREATURE CONTINUED ITS FLIGHT, NOT seeming to tire from the distance or from its burden. They were heading in a northerly direction. The cold, frigid mountains loomed ahead in the distance. No temperature change was apparent as of yet, but Trakon and Herish were puzzled over the direction the insect-man was taking. They couldn't understand what sanctuary it was seeking.

"Why is that thing heading up to the mountains?" Trakon asked.

"It doesn't make much sense. It isn't wearing any protective clothing," Herish said.

They both knew that the creature would not survive in the cold mountain climate. For that matter, hardly anything could survive there except for the Raagor and their chuns.

The frigid temperatures left everything barren with no hope for survival to anything that tried to climb its slopes. Yet the creature kept on in the direction of the snow-capped mountains, as if its life depended on reaching that destination.

Thol, being mostly a tropical world, had not taught its inhabitants how to survive in any other climate. It was preposterous for the snow-capped mountains to even exist in the tropical setting where temperatures soared hotter than any Earth location. No one knew what the mountains held because they had never been fully explored, or if they had, no one lived long enough to record any information. Forever a mystery, they remained virgin territory, even to the tough Plotals.

THE INSECT-MAN FOLLOWED THE TOWERING MOUNTAINSIDE AND began a steady climb in altitude. The Kudaja that pursued on borjos were just out of range of the creature.

Trakon steered the ship and tried to keep up, being cautious of the uncharted territory.

Trakon and Herish noticed the borjos up ahead. Soon, the Ebscalon fleet caught up with them and spread out in a V flight pattern, similar to geese and ducks on Earth, with Trakon's crestrider in the lead.

The temperature was noticeably cooler now as they

approached the base of the formidable mountain slopes. The insect-man kept onward, steadily climbing, keeping just outside of the fog that surrounded the cold slopes looming ahead. The atmosphere thinned as they climbed higher and higher.

Trakon's hands clenched tightly on the flight controls. His eyes never swayed from the pair up ahead of him. Fear edged his heart when he thought of the creature tiring and releasing its captive.

"How is it possible for this insect thing to survive in the cold?" Herish asked. He rubbed his hands up and down his arms. While his clothing breathed for the extreme heat and humidity of the planet, the cold penetrated the clothes.

"I don't understand it," Trakon said. He looked around the desolate mountain. "The Raagor are up here somewhere. Probably those Fods, as well."

"What's a Fod?" Herish asked.

Trakon shared a mental image of the creature. "They guard the caves in the Aguberro mountains. One attacked our documentarian."

Herish stared at the image. "What an odd-looking creature."

The butterfly man was on a steady course ahead of them.

Trakon's communicator crackled. "Prince Bramstone!" A flight lieutenant called out. "Use extreme caution. This is unchartered territory. The kingdoms of Ebscalon and Kudajara cannot have their heirs killed in pursuit of the princess!"

Trakon fumed. He bashed his communicator. "Klaxjor, do you think for one minute I would not pursue this creature to rescue my wife? Do you forget that she is the Golden Girl of Ebscalon, the mother of my children, and the warrior woman who saved us—and Thol—from the robots?"

"I did not mean to be discourteous, Prince Trakon, I felt I should caution you about the peril, not just for you, but for the kingdoms," the lieutenant said.

Herish laid his hand on Trakon's arm. "He means well. I

understand his caution. Should we fall back and let the fleet take the lead?"

Trakon shook his head. "I have to go after her. She's the love of my life, Herish. I'd never forgive myself if I fell back and they lost her."

Herish nodded, grim-faced. "I'd do the same if it were Meeri."

The higher they climbed, the denser the fog became. Within seconds, Trakon lost sight of his quarry and realized that the creature had entered the fog just ahead of him. He braced himself for the unknown as he steered the crestrider into the thick, cold fog, slowing his speed, searching for a sight of D'laine and her captor.

The Kudaja flying their borjos flew back and flanked the crestrider. One of Herish's team tapped his chest. "Prince Herish, the air is too thin. Our borjos don't have a problem, but we do. Breathing is difficult because we can't acclimate flying in. It may be best to continue on foot."

A crestrider approached them. Lieutenant Klaxjor's ship gently bumped Trakon's ship. "We need to retreat to a lower elevation before we succumbed to elevation sickness. It won't do your princess any good if you get killed. We can hike in. That will allow our bodies to acclimate so we don't pass out."

Trakon squinted his eyes while stretching his body forward, and spotted the creature and D'laine in the distance. As he watched the insect-man climb higher in his flight, he noticed that D'laine's head slumped forward toward her chest.

"The thin air has affected D'laine," Trakon said. "It looks like she's passed out."

"It's too dangerous to fly," Herish said.

Suddenly, the fog swallowed the insect-man and D'laine, as the creature disappeared between twin ragged mountain peaks. Not rational of their predicament, or their safety, Trakon sped up the vessel and climbed after the two.

"Prince Trakon!" the lieutenant yelled.

Trakon suddenly cleared the same peak that his prey had disappeared around. He regretted his action instantly as he found himself suddenly overcome with a dizziness that was impossible to shake.

"We're going down! Brace yourself," Trakon warned. He barely got the words out of his mouth when Herish succumbed to the thin atmosphere and slid to the floor.

CHAPTER FOURTEEN

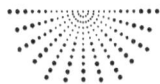

*T*he ghostly fog was replaced with a lush tropical haven of a hidden valley, secretly nestled between the snowcaps of the mountain. Overcome with the pressure of the incredible height and lack of oxygen, Trakon crumbled to the floor of the ship, his hand dragging across the control panel. As the ship glided haphazardly through the sky, the creature circled back around to investigate the trouble.

Spared from smashing into the sheer rocky cliffs, the ship and crew luckily escaped death. The ship skirted the tops of the trees and smashed through layers upon layers of branches until the ship crashed softly on the ground. Nothing moved in the vessel, the two bodies sprawled about, entangled limb by limb, with a trickle of blood glaring out from the floor of the ship.

THE CREATURE DESCENDED IN A SLOW SPIRAL AND THEN LANDED on a ledge outside of a huge cave. As the insect-man lowered D'laine gently onto the ledge, he stilled his wings and folded them against his body. He picked up his captive and carried her into the cave and placed her on the floor. He backed off about five foots, and rested on the ground a conservative distance away from his captive. He moved his head slowly from side to side. He observed that the woman who lay in front of him was stirring. He got to his feet.

D'laine slowly regained her senses. She got to her knees and turned slowly in the shadowy cave, trying to get her bearings. Huge sack-type things hung from the roof toward the entrance of the cave. She turned around slowly to take in her surroundings. She nearly screamed at the figure blocking the entrance of the cave.

Dark brownish-black and unclothed, unless his wings were considered body coverings, she recognized the creature as the insect-man. She assumed that he was the one she had observed over the past few days.

He had a head and trunk of a man, including two well-formed legs. Two muscular arms did not protrude from his shoulders, but from waist level at his sides. Two antennae with rounded knobs at the ends graced the top of his dark head, which was void of any hair. Aside from the insect features, he had all the normal facial features of a man.

They stared at each other in silence. D'laine was sure he was sizing up the situation, as she was. He was curious; she was frightened. She decided to try to communicate with him since he wasn't making any effort. She wanted to find out why he had abducted her from the ship.

D'laine concentrated as she sifted through his mind for intelligence, and didn't find any speech patterns. Not letting that stop her, she tried another approach through sign language, pointing first to herself then to him. The creature just stood there, head moving in the same pattern, not making any intelligent gestures at all.

D'laine got to her feet.

The creature's wings spread slightly open. They began to move slowly as if gauging her movements to see what he needed to do.

She took a chance and moved toward him.

He moved back, stretching his wings across the opening of the cave, his meaning clear: she was not to leave the cave.

D'laine tried another tactic. She turned around and moved toward the cluster of sacks hanging from the roof of the cave. That didn't seem to bother him, so she decided to check them out. She ran her hands over the rough surface of one of the sacks, then she turned and tried for the mouth of the cave again.

His mighty wings spread to cover the expanse of the opening. There was no way to get around him other than to go through him. She didn't want to hurt him since he had shown no hostility at this point.

"Out!" she said, pointing to the doorway.

She tried telepathy again and failed. The creature clearly had no compatible intelligence, and she couldn't understand what he wanted with her. She continued with verbal and sign communicating techniques, pushing her hands to the side, trying to make him understand that she wanted out of the cave. Finally, she stepped forward, grabbed him by the arms, swung him aside and stood looking out in amazement at the lush, tropical area that lay before her.

Never had she gazed upon such beauty! Blossoming flowers and plants in all colors and sizes stood everywhere, with trees and shrubberies in abundance. The floor of the valley did not hold the moss, as all other areas of Thol. Instead, it had real, thick, green grass, the same as her homeland on Earth! Spellbound at what she saw, the beauty of the secret valley took her breath away. The mystery of the grass befuddled her mind into a reeling mass of confusion.

THE TREES WERE SMALLER THAN THE GIANTS ON THE OTHER SIDE of the mountains, and more like the species on Earth. All this, hidden by the frigid facade of the mountains! D'laine forgot her companion in the cave. She wondered if any other human being had ever set foot in this valley. She decided that she was the first, otherwise she was positive Adrum's movies would have shown this scene.

Trakon had never mentioned this place, and she doubted if the wandering Safris had ever climbed those rugged cliffs. Perhaps the Egroms knew of these creatures' existence, but since she never saw them in any of Adrum's movies, she didn't think so. How could they have lived here unnoticed, she wondered?

Instantly, her thoughts drifted to the ship and her companions.

Trakon! Can you hear me? she called telepathically.

D'laine listened intently for a response. She didn't hear anything except for the swaying of foliage in the light breeze, and the flapping of her keeper's wings, showing his agitation. She turned to face him and stood in a position to allow the light to illuminate more of his features so she could study him.

As she stared at him, she decided that she had been wrong about his features. He was not devoid of hair. What she had assumed was skin, was actually a fine fuzz, so similar to the insects of Earth.

She looked around the inner walls of the cave and tried to estimate how many sacks were hanging from the roof. D'laine made a rough guess, between twenty and thirty. The cave was quite large, or so she thought, since she couldn't detect the depth because of lack of light towards the rear of the cavern. She moved about, gingerly, wanting to explore the prison. She kept to the right side of the cave, and walked for several feet, when she heard the increased flapping of his wings.

D'laine turned to face him and tried to understand what was upsetting him. Still looking at him, she backed up a few inches at a time, testing him. His wings continued fluttering until she came to a stop, then he was still. It was obvious that he didn't want her to go toward the rear of the cave.

As she observed his actions, she noticed his antenna moving. D'laine looked around. She wanted to see if he was communicating with someone or something. Aside from the sacks, they were alone. The movements kept up a steady pace for several minutes, and then he stopped and resumed his guarding stance.

A sound resembling pebbles dropping to the ground and bouncing drew her attention to the rear of the cave. D'laine strained her eyes to make visual contact with whatever made the scuffling noise. She only saw dark, empty space. As she crouched to get a better look, she discovered the source of the noise. Another butterfly creature crawled out of what appeared to be a smaller inner cavern inside the rear of the cave. This explained the void at the rear of the cave caused by the inner dwelling.

As the creature stood, D'laine was surprised to come face to face with an exquisite female of the race. She had a delicate heart-shaped face with doll-like features: feathery eyebrows finely shaped into a curve; almond-shaped eyes covered with long, black, feathery lashes; a tapering nose and a small heart-shaped mouth with tiny, delicate lips. Smaller than the male, she had an air of femininity about her.

D'laine smiled at the china-doll creature standing before her. She received a smile in return, showing two dimples in the butterfly's delicate cheeks. The lady's antennae moved in silent communication with her partner.

D'laine wanted to talk to these creatures. She was curious to find out what they wanted with her and where they came from.

Neither Trakon nor Herish recalled seeing similar creatures in the skies of Thol.

What a beautiful race, she thought, as she watched the two creatures talking back and forth for a few minutes in their silent communication using their twitching antennae. Caught off guard, she jumped when the silence was broken by the female.

"I am Noona," she said, softly, "and this is my mate, Tetonie. We think we are the last of the Sagritols. The others have never emerged from inside the pupa sacks, as you can see. We fear that our brothers and sisters will never breathe the air or spread their wings in flight, and our race will end with us."

"I know it was wrong for us to bring you here against your will," Tetonie interrupted, apologetically. "But I determined you were different from the others of your city, and we thought perhaps you could help us."

Stunned from hearing the verbal communication, D'laine hesitated before finding speech. "You can talk? Why didn't you answer me before?" she asked Tetonie.

"It was important for me to see what your reactions would be to being here," he said.

"Well, that's ridiculous! I don't enjoy being abducted," she said, defensively.

"I'm sorry. I have little experience at life, and the need for seeking outside help is not an instinctive pattern," he apologized once more.

"When did you and your mate emerge from your sacks?" D'laine asked, softening.

"We first opened our wings nearly ten turns ago," Noona replied. "The others should have followed, but didn't. We have tried prodding the sacks, but there aren't any movements from within. We have just about accepted the fact that we are the last of our people. There used to be thousands of Sagritols in the skies of Thol, but as the years passed, the eggs grew fewer and fewer until this last hatching, which only produced us. The survivors of our race. You must help us find out what is wrong."

"Noona, I don't know what I could possibly do, but I promise that I'll try. Do not give up hope. There has to be a simple explanation, and if I can't discover what it is, I will ask the Egroms. They know about all life forms and their knowledge is vast. I am sure that between the Egroms knowledge and my own, we will come up with a solution," D'laine told the distressed creatures.

"Tetonie, I would like you to go in search of the ship and lead my companions here. They are probably still searching for me and we may need their help. Please don't lock me out of your mind. I want to communicate with you," D'laine said to the male.

"The craft was acting strange when I last saw it," he said, nodding his understanding. "I will try to find it again."

"What do you mean? Did it crash?" D'laine asked.

"Perhaps it did. Your companions seemed to be sleeping. I thought that to be strange," he said, confused.

"Oh, no! I'll bet it was because of the high altitude," D'laine said. "Did you see fire or smoke coming from the ship, or from the area where it disappeared through the trees?"

Tetonie thought for several seconds. "No, I did not."

D'laine studied him. "Tetonie, do you know what fire and smoke are?"

"No, but there wasn't anything strange in the sky, so I'm sure I did not see those things," he said.

"For the love of Thol, do you need to learn the basics! You'd better get going if you're going to find them," D'laine said.

The three walked to the edge of the cave. D'laine watched as Tetonie spread his wings, catching a gentle breeze that lifted him up off the ledge of the cave. He soared up over the valley, his mighty wings carrying him in an elegant ballet in the sky.

Such a majestic sight could never be duplicated by another

creature of any world. D'laine vowed to herself that she would help these beautiful, graceful creatures to the best of her ability. The universe would mourn at the loss of such natural beauty; *I will find a solution!*

In his search for the ship, Tetonie followed the same flight pattern he had taken when he returned to the valley with D'laine. Not finding any sign of the ship, he retraced his flight and looked towards the ground, in case they continued the journey on foot.

Tetonie widened his area of search. He found nothing, and headed back toward the mountain slopes to resume his search in that direction. The fog made visual contact with the ground difficult, forcing him to fly lower and make continual sweeps of each area.

The Sagritol was convinced that the ship was not in the cold fog of the mountain. He climbed higher in flight, heading towards the twin peaks where he had entered the hidden valley. He began a spiraling flight over the treetops, swooping lower when the landscape allowed. As he approached an area where tree branches were hanging down, broken, he slowed to investigate the source of the damage.

Nestled in between a clump of trees on the grassy floor of the valley, lay the ship. At his vantage point, he saw no movement around the area, so he decided to land and investigate, making sure the two aboard the ship were alive. He coasted downward, steadily surveying the ship for signs of life. He spotted the unconscious occupants on the floor of the vessel, as well as a trickle of blood. He landed with ease a few feet away from the ship, hurried over and climbed aboard.

Neither the Ciertron nor the Kudaja stirred. Tetonie decided to take a chance and bring them back to the cave one at a time, so that D'laine could take care of their wounds. It would be difficult taking off from the ship, he thought, but he could do it.

He grasped Trakon by his upper arms. Tetonie lifted off the

ship and fluttered precariously through the trees until he was high enough where he could fully spread his wings and speed up his flight. He called ahead to D'laine and alerted her that he was returning with her injured mate.

As he flew over the valley towards the cave, he saw the two women standing at its mouth. Approaching the cave, Tetonie called out and instructed the women to be ready to grab his burden, so that he could return for the other victim back at the ship.

D'laine and Noona managed to support Trakon's weight between themselves with some difficulty. Noona's wings hampered a comfortable position for one of Trakon's arms to rest across her back.

They dragged Trakon to the interior of the cave and laid him out on the floor. Both women huddled over him, taking inventory of his wounds. They discovered a small gash across his forehead, where he probably struck his head when he fell to the floor of the ship. Not an alarming sight, but Noona went to fetch water and a soft leaf, so that D'laine could clean the wound. As D'laine mopped his brow, Trakon was just coming around, when Tetonie returned with a wide-eyed Herish.

Tetonie set the panicky Kudaja down to the ground, then fluttered down, himself. Not wasting a minute, Herish scampered out of the Sagritol's way. He was not happy with his journey to the cave by the unknown creature.

Happy to see D'laine unharmed, Herish scurried over to her side.

"You okay, D'laine?" Herish asked.

"Yeah, everything's fine."

Trakon was up on one elbow, holding his forehead with his free hand.

"Trakon, lie back down so I can attend to your wound. It's minor and will only take a minute," D'laine said.

Reluctantly following orders, Trakon eased back and

watched as D'laine put her fingertips over the gash, closed her eyes, and concentrated on the wound.

Within seconds, Trakon felt a tingling sensation, followed by warmth around the area on his forehead. When D'laine opened her eyes and removed her hand, he felt the spot which still held a trace of the warmth, and could feel no wound, at all.

Amazed, Noona gasped at what she had witnessed. She and Tetonie stared at each other in bewilderment. They could hardly believe what they had just seen.

"Oh, D'laine! You have the power! I know you will be able to help us now," she exclaimed.

"Noona, I don't know what we can do, and I hate the thought of disappointing you," D'laine said.

She briefly explained the problem to Trakon and Herish.

"Can't you probe the sacks to pick up any life signs?" Trakon asked.

"That's what I plan to do. If I don't detect anything, we can ask Ghury to come here. He would know what they needed," D'laine replied, as she moved to the closest sack hanging from the roof of the cave.

She ran her hands over the rough surface and felt all around the outside of the sack, not knowing what she was searching for, exactly. D'laine closed her eyes and continued probing, this time using the powers of her mind to guide her. She detected a weak life force from within, stopped and concentrated on it for a minute, before opening her eyes, then moved on to another sack. She moved from sack to sack, detecting the same weak signal.

"Tetonie, where were your sacks when you and Noona emerged?" she asked.

"We were over here," he indicated to two spots close to the mouth of the cave.

"I'm positive the problem is these sacks are too far away from the sun for them to finish developing into mature adults.

The life force inside is very weak, but we can probably still save them if we move them outside, directly into the sunlight. There are too many sacks for us to move them to the front of the cave; the crowding would block off the light to the unfortunate sacks at the rear," D'laine told the Sagritols.

"Can't we tie them to the trees?" Herish asked.

"I don't see why not," Noona replied, turning to Tetonie. "If there is any chance of saving our people, please let us try!"

CHAPTER FIFTEEN

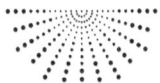

*T*hey heard faint calls in the distance by a multitude of voices.

"Prince Trakon! Princess D'laine! Prince Herish!"

Trakon walked to the edge of the cave. Herish and D'laine joined him.

"Do you hear that?" Trakon said. "The search party is close by." He tapped his communicator. "We are here, in a cave. We will have the male Sagritol show you the way." He turned to the insect man. "Tetonie, can you lead our people here? They can help us with the sacks."

"Yes, I will show them the way," Tetonie said. He took to the air and headed in the direction of the search party.

Trakon tapped his communicator. "Do not shoot at the insect-man. He is not a threat. He and his mate required our help."

"Understood," Klaxjor said. "We see him."

The men on the ground waved at the Sagritol. He dipped down closer to the search party of Ciertrons and Kudaja.

THE LAST OF THE KUDAJA CLIMBED OVER THE LEDGE OF THE CAVE. The Ciertrons and Kudaja studied the Sagritols, and the sacks that hung from the roof of the cave.

Trakon hefted one of the sacks, judging the weight. "We really need a ship to carry the sacks, and to hover where we can hang them from the trees."

A debate ensued between the Ciertrons and the Kudaja.

"I feel acclimated enough to fly a ship here," Klaxjor said. "We can load five sacks at a time and get them strung up."

"What are we going to use to tie them with?" D'laine asked. "These trees don't have the vines that are readily available on the agrin trees."

"If you take us back to where we entered the valley, we can summon our borjos and get the vines," Herish said. "Like Klaxjor said, I feel acclimated to the thin air here so we should be safe."

"Try summoning the borjos from here. I'm sure they will be within range to hear you," D'laine said. "If not, I can summon them."

EVERYONE AGREED TO THE PLAN. HERISH AND HIS TEAM CALLED out to their borjos. In a few minutes, the sky was filled with the Kudaja rides, plus a few wild borjos. The Kudaja gave Klaxjor and four Ciertrons a lift to the ships.

The wild borjos seemed intrigued with D'laine, Trakon, the Sagritols and the sacks. They flew near the cave, dipped down and spied on them, then landed on the mountainside. One very large borjo landed on the ledge and folded in his wings. He waddled inside the cave a few steps and snuffed in a breath.

D'laine approached him and stroked his snout. *Do not blow fire or smoke here. You will damage the unborn inside the sacks.*

He nudged her in understanding.

Protect the Sagritols and these sacks.

The borjo snorted.

Noona and Tetonie timidly looked upon the large borjo.

"They want to fly with you," D'laine said.

Noona and Tetonie communicated silently, their antennae twitching.

"We will fly with them," Tetonie said.

The large borjo turned around and leapt out of the cave and took to the air.

The Sagritols walked to the edge of the cave and watched the borjos gliding through the air. They lifted off their ledge. Their large, delicate-looking wings carried them into the sky.

Trakon and D'laine watched from the cave.

"Look how beautiful these two species are dominating the sky!" D'laine said.

Several minutes later, the crestriders flew into view. The borjos and Sagritols flew around the ships. It was an amazing sight, something no one else would ever experience.

Trakon shielded his eyes as he watched the ballet playing out in the sky. His eyes lowered, and he saw someone approaching on foot. "Who's that?"

D'laine stretched her neck as she shielded her eyes. "Is that Bok-Tor?"

"Either Bok-Tor, or another Safri," Trakon said.

The Kudaja returned with the vines, and the group began their work. Being the smallest, Noona had the task of cutting the sacks from the roof of the cave, as it was relatively easy for her to flutter in the air like a hummingbird.

There was a clatter at the cave's ledge, and the Safri scurried into the cave.

"Hello, Bok-Tor! What are you doing way up here?" D'laine said.

"Safri's are wanderers. I had to run away from an og. He wasn't friendly at all," Bok-Tor said. He fluttered his tiny wings as he joined D'laine on the sidelines.

Ciertrons and Kudaja caught the sacks. They brought them to the edge of the cave where they loaded them on a ship. A pilot flew the sacks to where Trakon, Herish and Klaxjor sat perched in trees with strips of agrin vines handy. They secured the sacks to sturdy branches.

They worked as a team and moved the twenty-two sacks outside, filling branches on five trees, which made an amazing sight. Noona entered the cave and returned with a large wooden bowl filled with various fruits, and an urn containing water.

"Oh, how wonderful," D'laine said, taking the bowl from Noona.

"A well-deserved repast after such hard work," Noona said, smiling.

"I DON'T KNOW HOW WE WILL EVER BE ABLE TO THANK YOU FOR what you have done here today," Noona said to the group as they ate. "I hope this solves the dwindling numbers of our kind. In the future, we will be wiser. Hopefully we will be able to build up the numbers of our race to the size of the colonies that were alive in past paths. If only our people had realized that they were unintentionally killing themselves."

"We need to find out why the sacks were hidden in the cave instead of hanging on the trees. It seems they should be out in the sun through the development stages. There must have been a good reason for one of your people to do that, don't you think?" Trakon asked.

"On Earth, butterfly pupa hang from flowers and trees, in

LOVE OF THOL

the sunlight, not in caves. Does your species migrate to another location each year, Noona?" D'laine asked.

"No, this valley is our home. There may be others somewhere else, but I don't think so," she said.

"Do you recall any enemies that could have preyed upon your ancestors? On Earth, birds eat our small butterfly insects, but you have to understand that they are only this big," she said. She held her fingers to show the size of the butterfly's back home.

Neither Noona nor Tetonie knew the answer. D'laine seemed to think there must be a hidden clue someplace, but it would take time to find it.

"I would like to see you fly later," Bok-Tor said. "If only my wings were big and graceful as yours are. I want to fly through the sky!"

"What happened to your wings? They are tiny and useless to you," Tetonie said, spreading one of Bok-Tor's little wings wide.

"We used to fly many thousands of paths ago, but then we developed longer legs and bigger hooves, and we discovered that we could run awfully fast. I guess as the paths go by, we'll lose even these pitiful things," Bok-Tor said, sadly as he fluttered his tiny wings.

After they finished their meal, the Kudaja and their borjos flew out of the valley, and through the twin peaks. The Ciertrons boarded their crestriders.

"Do you want to return to Ebscalon, Bok-Tor?" D'laine asked.

"No, I will walk around and explore this region some more," the Safri said.

"We'll come back in another ten turns to check on the progress of your people," Trakon promised. "If there are any problems, or if you need anything, come to us for help." He explained where Ebscalon was in conjunction to where Tetonie had found them.

They bid their farewells with promises to keep their knowledge of the valley in the mountains a secret.

THE JOURNEY BACK TO EBSCALON WENT SMOOTHLY WITH NO interruptions or problems; the ships hummed through the air, riding the currents smoothly.

"So much beautiful, untouched land," D'laine said as they travelled. "Do you think any of the kingdoms will build here, Trakon?"

"No. We've already experienced that. Our society has learned a valuable lesson in that what we have is precious and we should not abuse it. It's up to us to keep the world in balance," he said seriously.

They were happy to be back within the walls of the city. Jor-Dan, Victor, Stanley, Lee and Ghury greeted them in the plaza outside of the hanger.

Chatter romped up to Trakon and sniffed him all over. Every once in a while, his teeth clacked, but not aggressive for attacking. It was more of a curiosity, like he couldn't figure out what the scent on his person was from.

Trakon scratched the diwal's rump. "You smell a new scent, but you won't be visiting the Sagritols anytime soon."

"You handled yourself well," Ghury silently praised as he nodded to D'laine. "The Sagritols will survive. Instinct guided you in your decision and I could not have done any more for them."

D'laine rested her hand on one of his furry, white arms. "You amaze me, Ghury, you seem to always be with me, silently guiding me, yet I feel that one day, I will be guide you. I don't know where I get that crazy notion from!"

The ancient Egrom looked deep within her eyes without communicating. He nodded his understanding but would not comment on her strange statement. His eyes seemed to look into the depths of her soul, but he wouldn't share the thoughts that were passing on the locked sided of his brilliant mind.

"Were you aware of the Sagritols existence?" she asked.

"It has been many, many paths since I have even thought of them, so tucked away are they in their valley. I am surprised the male ventured out through the frigid cold of the mountains where he could have easily died from exposure," Ghury said.

"Why were the sacks hanging in the caves? What happened to the masses that Noona spoke of?" D'laine asked. "And why are certain things in that valley similar to earth?"

"Many thousands of paths ago, large flying creatures called Xidilots, which were similar to your eagles of earth, hunted and persecuted the Sagritols. The Xidilots, now extinct, raided the Sagritols when the eggs were freshly encased and hung on the trees. There were no adult Sagritols left to protect them. You see, after the eggs are encased in their protective sack, the adult dies, their life span being only between twenty to thirty paths."

"With no one to protect the young, the Xidilots would raid the sacks, rip them open and eat the undeveloped young inside. The Sagritols must have learned of this plundering and took the precautions of hiding the sacks in the cave, tricking the Xidilots into thinking they had left the valley. Now that the creatures are extinct, the Sagritols need not worry about hiding their unborn in the cave," Ghury explained.

"The wild borjos will help protect them," Trakon said.

"Yes, it was good to have the borjos come through the mountain peaks," Ghury said.

"What about the grass and trees that look to be from earth?" D'laine asked, defensively.

Lee and Stanley perked up.

"You found grass and trees?" Lee asked.

"Yes! I couldn't believe it," D'laine said. "I think it's Bermuda grass, but I'm not sure." She shared a picture of the valley.

"That's Saint Augustine grass," Stanley said. "Are those oak trees?"

"Looks like it, but they sure look small compared to the agrin trees," Lee said.

"Are they from earth, or are your earth trees and grass from Thol? My guess is that at one time, eons ago, a portal must have lined up in the valley. There are no other places on Thol where those exact duplicates exist," Ghury explained. "And to satisfy your longing, the answer is no, there are no others from Earth secreted away from you."

What was the true homeland of the trees and grass? It was something to think about at a later time. D'laine left the men to their talk. She knew they would entertain each other for a long time, sharing stories. She sauntered into the palace and headed for the turret room that housed the eggs. She smiled as she entered the room and the tender scene before her filled her heart with happiness. A doting grandparent, Kitry sat on the floor before the raised nests, a loving smile on her face as she gazed at her future grandchildren, nestled within their shells.

Kitry looked up as D'laine entered the room.

Pup leapt from his bed and hopped around D'laine in the doorway, making half whines and half yips. Then he started a sniffing campaign.

"Okay, Pup. Settle down now," D'laine said.

Kitry held out her hand to her daughter-in-law, beckoning D'laine to join her on the floor.

D'laine took the outstretched hand and settled down beside Kitry. Pup snuggled against D'laine, resting his head on her thigh. The princess reached out and caressed the eggs in front of her. They had grown in size, and were now the size of a football, showing great progress.

"I can't wait to see my grandchildren," Kitry confessed. "Whether they are boys or girls, or one of each, they will be beautiful children."

"I wonder which one of us they will take after?" D'laine said.

"Both of you, of course. They will take the best of both," Kitry said, proudly.

"Has anything happened of any importance during the past two days?" D'laine asked.

"Not one solitary thing," Kitry told her. "Ghury, your father, Jor-Dan, Victor, and Stanley have been discussing the learning processes. They are devising a plan to educate the three boys."

"My brothers have turned into wild boys, without going to school for several hours every day," D'laine said. "I hope Ghury and Adrum can help my father with their education. Kara wants Darren to continue his education as well."

Jor-Dan loved the Egrom dearly and spent hours with him when he visited. He showed him every corner of the city and they debated every subject either could think worth debating.

Kitry rose from her spot on the floor, and bid D'laine goodbye. "I will leave you alone with your children so you can have a moment of peace by yourself," she said as she left the room, nodding to the guards.

D'laine scooted closer to the nest, reached out and placed a hand on each egg. She hummed a song from her childhood. Then, she gently picked an egg up and rested it on her lap. She rocked it back and forth still humming to establish a closer connection to her child. She missed the natural process which would have had her carrying the embryo within her. She thought these children would not bond with her in the same sense she had bonded with her mother.

Pup licked the egg.

Deep in thought over the seriousness of the subject, she didn't hear when the door opened and Trakon climbed the stairs and entered the room. He sat down beside her, put one arm across her shoulders, and placed his other hand on the surface of the shell.

"The child grows within," he said. "The time will go by fast and soon we will have our sons or daughters with us, D'laine."

Sentimental, she placed the egg back on the nest and picked up the second egg and repeated the process.

She rested her head on Trakon's shoulder. After a few minutes, they left the room, hand in hand, leaving the fruit of their love behind to grow and mature.

CHAPTER SIXTEEN

*D*arren and Chacoodi ran on the outskirts of the Egrom village. They ducked in and out of the forest in their quest for adventure. A tiny Kudaja girl slid down a vine and landed on her feet in front of the two boys. She morphed to full size.

"Can I play with you?" she asked.

"Sure," Chacoodi said. "I'm Chacoodi and this is Darren."

"I'm Vila," the girl said. She looked like a tiny version of Meera with a little oval face where two huge dimples formed in her cheeks.

They took off running in and out of the trees, gleefully yelling. After twenty minutes, Vila stopped her companions. "I have to return home. My mother wants me to gather agrin vines. I had fun."

Darren stepped up to Vila. "Can you play tomorrow? I have lessons with the Egroms in the morning, but maybe we can play later?"

"Maybe we can ride your borjo!" Chacoodi exclaimed. He loved flying with Brian and Jamie on Ekka. It was exciting to have the wind ruffle his white fur.

"Yes! I'll call out to you when I can get away," Vila said.

They all waved goodbye. The boys returned to the village.

VICTOR WAS IN DEEP DISCUSSION WITH ADRUM. HE HAD experienced some disconcerting visions and didn't know if he was okay or not.

"I think I can see into the future," Victor said. "I'm not quite sure though."

"Can you determine something simple we can test? Something that might happen within, say, a hour?" Adrum asked.

Victor softened his eyes. He stared ahead, out of Adrum's mushroom house. "Kestrum is going to scold the boys."

"That's too generic. She is always scolding Chacoodi," Adrum said. "Try to find something more specific."

Victor focused. His face turned serious. "Swezek is sick. He's going to fall."

Adrum showed concern. "Egroms rarely get sick. Are you sure? When is this supposed to happen?"

Victor jumped to his feet. "Now!" He rushed out of the mushroom, Adrum on his heels.

Swezek was in a cluster with Drusta, Bensol and Ditol, having a silent conversation. Suddenly, the elder Egrom dropped to the moss.

The Egrom community came alive with loud chirping and grunting, voicing their concern in their language.

Ghury stepped back from Ebscalon and joined the elders around their fallen companion. "It is time?"

"I saw that he was sick," Victor said. He was out of sorts with what was happening.

Kara's fingers were on her lips as she took in the situation's seriousness. Kestrum patted her on the shoulder.

"All life cycles eventually end," Kestrum said.

Chacoodi and Darren ran to catch up with the Egrom crowd to find out what happened. Chacoodi shared information with Darren. "Swezek is one of the ancients, and his time has come to pass on."

More Egroms appeared out of nowhere. Thousands of Egroms, more than those that lived in Ghury's village.

"He's dying?" Darren asked, startled.

Chacoodi nodded. "He has stayed past his allotted time."

Darren's eyebrows knitted. "What do you mean?"

"Our species lives for a thousand paths. Swezek has stayed for two extra paths," Chacoodi said.

"Wow! That's old!" Darren said.

A crestrider thumped to the ground. D'laine sprinted from the craft followed by her father and Trakon. Stanley stepped to the Egrom village from Ebscalon.

"There is nothing we can do for Swezek?" D'laine asked Ghury.

"No. Swezek must give up his form. He will join the others who have gone on before him. We will choose his replacement," Ghury said.

D'laine thought about what he said: *He must give up his form.* She didn't understand what he meant, but figured she should wait until a later time to ask more questions.

The seven remaining elders surrounded Swezek: Ghury, Adrum, Drusta, Bensol, Ditol, Absadul and Trabet.

The humans stayed off to the side where they could watch the Egrom ceremony.

All Egroms held their four hands out, facing Swezek. The old Egrom's body turned transparent. Thousands of tiny dots of light, similar to dust motes, rose up into the sky. In just a few minutes, all that was left was an impression in the moss. Within a split minute, the moss lifted, and all that was Swezek was gone.

D'LAINE WAS OUT OF SORTS WITH THE EGROM'S PASSING. SHE withdrew into herself and thought heavily on what Ghury said. *He must give up his form.* She replayed the disintegration of Swezek's body over and over in her head. Finally, she determined that the Egrom's soul had joined his ancestors.

The Bennett's training had completed, and they were back in Ebscalon. Darren grumbled about not having a special talent. Kara's hadn't shown up either, but, as she reminded her son, she wasn't sitting around whining about it.

Victor spent a lot of time with the Visionary in the temple. After his prediction about Swezek, they determined that he needed guidance and training to hone his skills.

BRIAN, JAMIE AND DARREN RODE PAKOWS ACROSS THE PLAINS OF moss heading toward Ta'Byu'Vohon to visit Cadj. They promised Kara they would not ignore Fazi.

They arrived at Jakla's city. Unlike Ebscalon, there were no gates. The Plotals figured they didn't need gates to hold out an enemy. Since they were fierce, warring creatures, the Plotals would welcome trouble and deal with it on their doorstep. Still, when the boys rode into the city, they were stopped by guards.

"What business do you have here?" A Plotal guard asked. There was no welcoming in his tone.

"We're here to see Commander Bosakin's children," Brian said. He showed no fear or discomfort to the guard.

The Plotal snuffed. "You may leave your pakows over there with the attendant." He pointed to his left where a pen had been constructed for visiting pakows. "I will contact the commander's children."

They rode over to the pen and dismounted. The attendant led the beasts into the pen.

"We'll be back in a couple of hours," Jamie said. "Can you give our pakows some water?"

"We have a water trough in the pen," the attendant said.

"Thank you," Jamie said. "They're very good pakows."

The attendant grunted.

The boys wandered back over to where the guard was. Cadj and Fazi ran over to greet them.

"Welcome to our new home!" Fazi said.

"We'll show you around," Cadj said. "Our father is working with the architects in developing our city."

"Everything is so big," Darren said.

"Adult Plotals are big," Fazi said. "So, we need big places to live and meet."

"What are those tents for?" Brian asked. There was a sea of tents sprawled across the field in the distance.

"Plotal families and soldiers live in those tents while they wait for the construction to be finished. Want to see our tent?" Cadj asked.

"Yeah!" Jamie said. "I've never been in a big tent before."

They ran around construction crews and piles of building materials until they were amid the tents. Cadj and Fazi led the boys to the largest, most colorful tent. Cadj held the flap, while Fazi ushered the boys inside.

The interior was similar to the Arabian Nights story. Plush carpets on the floor. Gauze hung from the peak of the tent in various places to create rooms. Everything was oversized for the large Plotal forms. The boys' eyes were wide with awe, as Cadj and Fazi showed them around the beautiful tent home.

Neska came around a sheet of gauze. "Welcome to our home, boys! Are you hungry?"

All the children chorused a "Yes!"

"Come into the dining salon," Neska said. Her tail pod opened and the deadly barbs clicked together.

Within moments, two female Plotals entered the room with trays of food and drinks.

Brian noticed three smaller drinking vessels for their smaller human hands.

"My mother would encourage this cultural experience," Darren said.

Neska chuckled, which sounded something like a prolonged cough. "Yes, your mother is a wise woman and I can see that she would welcome this experience."

Brian and Jamie recognized some of the bite-sized food, and guided Darren.

"These are vegetables," Jamie said, as he pointed to two of the platters. "This looks like roasted par, and I think that's sidel."

"Very good," Neska said. "You can try anything you want. If you don't like something, just leave it on your plate. We have adopted a pack of diwal dogs and they get table scraps."

Neska was happy to see the boys including Fazi in their conversations and interactions. After the meal, the boys and Fazi thanked Neska. Then they went to the side of the tent where their beds were, separated by gauze curtains.

Both rooms contained large platform beds. Cadj's bed had a pile of colorful gauze at the foot of the bed. Fazi's bed was neat with her gauze covers draped nicely across the foot of the bed.

Each room held a closet with vests, tunics and boots. Fazi's held scarves, and the same items Cadj had. There was headgear in Cadj's room that was similar to his father's helmet.

Jamie noticed some carved toys in Cadj's room. A pakow, diwal, even a crestrider. "Oh, cool! You have toys!"

Cadj picked up the crestrider and ran around his room with it in his hand.

"We haven't met many Ciertron children, only Youngmen. They don't play with anything but weapons," Brian said.

Fazi ran to her room and returned with a Plotal girl doll. "I have toys as well. I even have a toy laser!"

"Who makes these?" Darren studied the toys.

"There are craftsmen that carve our toys out of agrin wood," Cadj said. "It is a very hard wood, and the toys rarely break."

They walked outside.

"We should go home now," Brian said. "We didn't tell anyone where we were going, and we don't want to get into trouble."

Cadj and Fazi walked the boys toward the pakow pen. Two non-human hands appeared out of thin air and grabbed Jamie. He screamed as something tugged him toward a portal.

Guards came running. Jakla ran across the construction site, laser buzzing.

"Don't let the intruder get away!" Jakla roared.

Darren shoved his hands out in front of him. An electrical voltage leapt from his fingers to each of the hands that held Jamie captive. They heard an agonizing wail, and Jamie was released.

An Egrom stepped to their location. Before he could act, Brian closed the portal and sealed it.

Jamie fell to the ground, dazed. He sat up and shook his head. The Egrom and Jakla looked him over to make sure he was okay.

"You are not hurt?" Jakla asked.

"No," Jamie said. "I don't know what happened, or who that was."

"That creature was aware you could talk to animals," the Egrom said. "I don't understand why he wanted you, but they won't be able to breech Thol again. Brian permanently sealed that doorway."

Brian beamed satisfaction for a job well done. His skills were very useful. "Darren, you're just like my sister! She's sort of like a walking weapon."

The Egrom and Jakla snorted.

"You will need training so you don't kill someone who shouldn't be killed," the Egrom said. "I will discuss this with Ghury and the elders. They will know how to proceed."

"We'd better go home or we'll get into trouble," Brian said.

They gathered up their pakows and romped across the fields until Ebscalon was in sight.

"We'd better tell everyone we were out riding," Brian said.

"We could say we were looking for Oggy," Jamie said.

"Why don't we say we were looking for a place to build a fort!" Darren said.

"Yeah!" Brian said.

They rode to the pakow pen, turned their beasts over to Jugdaak, the attendant, and ran through the gates.

"Let's go to the marketplace and look around," Brian said.

Jamie and Darren followed Brian into the crowded and noisy bargaining place, filled with open area shops and stalls packed with merchandise. After spending time browsing with no intent of purchasing anything, they left the marketplace and headed toward the palace.

"Want to come to my room?" Darren asked. "My mom brought my superhero toys."

Jamie's eyes lit up. "Toys! Let's go!"

The boys trotted over to the palace and went inside. They thundered up the stairs and entered the Bennett's suite. Neither Victor or Kara were there, so Darren brought his friends to his room.

Darren's superhero toys were lined up on a shelf. Jamie and Brian each grabbed one of the figures and looked them over.

"You have the numbered action figures, not those fakes," Brian said.

"My mom said they'd be worth something when I'm older," Darren said.

"Yeah, back on Earth," Jamie said. "Are you going to go back to Earth?"

Darren shook his head. "Nah, I'd rather live on Thol."

"Me too," Jamie said.

"Same here," Brian said. His communicator beeped. "That's my fifteen minute warning. We'd better get cleaned up and down to the dining salon."

They headed to Darren's bathroom, washed their hands and faces, and combed their hair. When they were presentable, they headed out of the suite and down the stairs. They were the first to arrive at the dining salon.

Kitry and Ethaderia entered, followed by D'laine, then Lee, Stanley, Trakon, Victor and Jor-Dan. Kara and Treikie were the last and hurried to their places.

The majordomo silently summoned the waitstaff. After everyone made their choices, eating and dinner conversation began.

"I find it interesting, the contrast between the Egroms and the other races of Thol," Victor said.

"Not all Tholians have or use technology," Trakon said. "The Raagor Ice People and the Oolarooloo live off the land."

"What about the Plotals? They're building that vast city," Stanley said. "They have technology, don't they?"

"Their tent cities didn't have technology, but they have and use communication tools, and laser weaponry," Jor-Dan said. "Once they complete their build-out, I'm sure they will have smart closets and the whole works."

Kitry focused on the boys. "The three of you were gone for quite a bit. What did you do today?"

With straight faces, they spilled their stories.

"We were searching for Oggy, but we couldn't find him," Jamie said.

"We took a ride in the meadow," Brian said.

"We're trying to find a place where we can build a fort!" Darren said.

Kara stared at the three boys. She drilled her eyes into her son. "You are all telling lies!"

All eyes were on Kara. She shook her head. "I felt a tingling at the back of my head. Instinct tells me those are outright lies."

The boys started talking all at once.

"We rode to Ta'Byu'Vohon!" Brian said.

"We played with Cadj and Fazi," Jamie said.

"Mrs. Commander Bosakin gave us lunch," Darren said.

The adults' eyes swung over to Kara, waiting for verification. She nodded. "That was the truth."

"Did anything interesting happen while you were there?" Lee said. His eyes drilled into his boys.

Brian, Darren and Jamie looked at each other. They didn't know if they should mention the portal incident. They all vehemently shook their heads.

"Lies!" Kara said.

"What happened?" Trakon said. "The longer you delay telling the truth, the worse it gets for you."

Jamie huffed out his irritation. "Okay! A portal opened and these hands—paws, actually, grabbed me and tried to pull me through."

"Yeah, Jakla and some guards came running, but Darren saved Jamie!" Brian looked at his sister. "He has powers just like yours, D'laine! It was like lightning bolts coming out of his hands!"

"That creature let Jamie go, and Brian closed and sealed the portal just as an Egrom got there," Darren said.

"That's what Jakla told me," Lee said. He huffed his displeasure at his son's indiscretions.

Kitry slyly looked the boys over. "I believe the kitchen staff could use some help after dinner."

The adults smiled.

The majordomo nodded in Kitry's direction. "We always welcome additional help with the cleanup."

"Perhaps all that work, and the weight of those lies, will make you so tired that you should go to bed early," Victor said.

The boys sank down in their chairs. Jamie, especially, who had first-hand experience of the horrors of washing dishes in the palace kitchen. Stacks and stacks of dishes, along with pots and pans and greasy water. They all moaned.

"Now, Kara, tell us about this lie detector you seem to have," Stanley asked.

"I'm not sure how it works, but this must be my gift," she said.

"Let's try it out. I ran forty miles today," Trakon said.

"Lie," Kara said.

"Treikie and I discovered how to build a ship to go to the moons," Stanley said.

"Lie."

"The eggs in the hatching building were dancing," Kitry said.

"Lie."

"I asked Ethaderia to marry me today," Lee said.

Ethaderia blushed and smiled widely.

Everyone waited for Kara's declaration that a lie was spoken, but none was forthcoming.

"Is that true?" D'laine all but screamed. She got out of her chair, ran around the table and threw her arms around her father, then Ethaderia. "Congratulations!"

CHAPTER SEVENTEEN

*T*he boys had a torturous couple of hours doing the dishes and cleaning up the kitchen and dining salon. After they finished, the kitchen staff presented them with a Tholian pudding dessert.

"You did a very good job," the majordomo said. "My staff appreciated the night off."

Brian, Jamie and Darren grumbled as they ate their pudding.

Biggan, D'laine's old guard who kept her and Trakon from getting into trouble before their wedding, appeared in the kitchen doorway. "Someone told me these young men were so tired they needed to be escorted to their suites for an early night in. Otherwise they might not find their way."

Brian slammed his fist on the table. "I will never lie again!"

Jamie glared at his brother. "It's your fault! You're the one who told us we'd better not tell where we were."

"Doesn't matter now, that's over and done with," Darren said. "From now on, we don't make things up."

They left the kitchen and climbed the stairs with Biggan on their heels.

JAMIE JERKED AWAKE IN THE MIDDLE OF THE NIGHT. HE ROLLED onto his back and laid there, wondering what had disturbed him. Everything was quiet. He rolled onto his right side and snuggled down into the soft gauze bed linens. His eyelids fluttered shut and he let out a soft yawn. He caught himself before he stuck his thumb in his mouth. He hadn't sucked his thumb in years. He mentally whacked himself.

He was right on the slope to dreamland when a screech rolled around inside his head. Jamie popped up in bed. "Ekka?"

He heard an agonizing noise from his borjo. "Ekka! What's wrong?" Jamie flung his feet over the side of the large bed and hit the floor running. He didn't bother with a robe or slippers. He was out of his room and out of the palace, running for Ekka's tower. He flew up the stairs and was aghast at what he saw.

Ekka was on his side. His stomach was distended as if a buffalo were inside.

Jamie rushed to his borjo and placed his hand on the creature's nose. It was dry and cracked. "What's wrong, boy?"

The borjo made awful pain-ridden sounds from deep in his gut. It surprised Jamie that people didn't come running from all the racket.

He placed his hand on the borjos distended stomach. Ekka released a painful moan.

"Did you eat something bad?" Jamie asked. He silently called out to his sister. *D'laine! Ekka's sick! He's very, very sick. Can you help him?*

Several minutes passed, then Jamie heard two sets of feet on the stairs. Trakon and D'laine entered the turret.

Ekka mewled in pain. Jamie thought the borjos stomach seemed to be more distended than when he first arrived.

D'laine and Trakon noticed the bulging abdomen.

"Do you know what he ate?" D'laine asked her brother.

"I don't know. Let me ask him," Jamie said. Ekka, what did you eat?

The borjo coughed as if he would vomit. He shared a vision with Jamie of him swooping down and snatching up an animal, flying to another location with the animal in tow and then eating it.

Jamie shared the vision with D'laine and Trakon.

"What is that?" D'laine asked.

"Oh, no! That's a queper. They're poisonous!" Trakon said.

"Jamie, go run to the Visionary's temple. Tell him your borjo ate a queper and find out if he knows if there's an antidote," D'laine said.

Jamie was on his feet and flying down the stairs.

Trakon shook his head. "I'm not sure he can survive. Queper's are extremely toxic, and the poison has most likely spread throughout his body."

"Oh, no. We have to find a way to save this borjo," D'laine said. She rubbed her hand over Ekka's face.

Jamie's stomping feet zoomed up the stairs, followed by the silent Visionary. The old man approached the borjo. He carried two vials. Jamie carried a bowl.

The Visionary poured the vials into the bowl. "Jamie, instruct your borjo to drink this liquid. Every drop, no matter how bad it tastes."

"Okay," Jamie said. He held the bowl under the borjos head. "Ekka, you have to drink all of this or you will die."

The borjo groaned in pain.

"Lift your head up. Open your mouth. I will pour this into your mouth. You need to swallow all of it."

Ekka tilted his head. Jamie reached up, but he was too short.

Trakon moved in and lifted Jamie.

Jamie tilted the bowl into the borjos opened mouth. He

tapped the bottom of the bowl to make sure the borjo swallowed every ounce of the liquid.

Trakon lowered Jamie to the floor.

"He will either recover with the help of the formula, or he will perish," the Visionary said. "If he has shown no progress by morning, I will mix more formula and we will administer another dosage. Because of his size, he may not have received enough to force the poison out of his system."

Jamie wiped his eyes as his tears rushed down his cheeks.

EVERYONE WAS GETTING SETTLED IN THE DINING SALON FOR breakfast. Lee noticed Jamie, D'laine and Trakon missing. He turned to Brian. "Where's your brother?"

Brian shrugged. "He wasn't in his room."

"Has anyone seen D'laine and Trakon this morning?" Lee asked.

"I know D'laine sometimes goes upstairs to the turret room to spend a little time checking in on her eggs," Kitry said.

"I guess they'll show up soon," Lee said.

The majordomo and the kitchen staff arrived with food and drinks. They placed bowls and platters on the table.

When Jamie still didn't show up, Lee became concerned. He tapped his communicator. "Jamie? Where are you? Why aren't you at breakfast?"

Jamie answered. He was crying, sniveling and hiccupping. "Ekka's dying. We've been with him all night."

Chairs scraped back and people scrambled to their feet and rushed out the door. Lee led the runners to Ekka's tower, and they all plowed up the stairs.

"What happened?" Lee asked. He looked at the writhing animal; saw the distended stomach.

"He ate a queper," Trakon said.

"Oh, no." Jor-Dan lowered his head and closed his eyes.

"What's a queper?" Lee and Stanley both asked.

"A poisonous animal. You can touch them with no harm, but everything on the inside is a toxic poison," Jor-Dan said.

The Visionary came up the stairs and entered the room. He carried more vials. He stooped beside Jamie and Ekka. "I have mixed five times the amount of formula we would normally give a pakow. The first dose hasn't been effective."

"Five times? Is that safe?" Kitry asked.

The Visionary shrugged. "At this point it makes no difference. This will either neutralize the poison, or he will die." He emptied the vials in the bowl.

Trakon lifted Jamie, and they repeated the process from the middle of the night.

The borjo wallowed in pain. His eyes were glazed over. The skin on his snout appeared cracked and drier than before.

Jamie sniveled as he rubbed his hand over the top of the borjos head.

Kara approached D'laine. "Can you pull the poison out of him like you did my tumor?"

All eyes were on D'laine.

D'laine warily looked at the borjo. "I can try, but he may burn the tower down. I don't know what to expect."

Jamie pleaded with his eyes. "Please, D'laine! He's in a lot of pain."

Trakon stepped up. "We'll need a large container for the animal and any poisonous toxins you remove."

"Don't forget the wet cloths for her hands," Stanley said. He remembered what they witnessed at Victor's house when D'laine removed Kara's tumor.

"Anything else you require?" Jor-Dan asked.

D'laine shook her head. "This should be everything."

"Have a bowl of water on hand for the borjo to drink," the Visionary said.

Trakon, Lee, Stanley and Victor scattered out of the tower.

Jamie patted Ekka's front leg. "D'laine will remove the bad stuff in your belly. Please don't burn down the building with us in it."

Ekka huffed at Jamie.

Stomping feet climbed the stairs. Trakon and Victor hauled a large metal container into the room. Lee followed with the lid. Shortly thereafter, Stanley returned with a metal bowl of warm water and a pile of gauze cloths.

They looked everything over.

"This should do it," Trakon said. "Looks like everything we had at your house, Victor."

"Drinking water!" Jamie said. He leapt to his feet, raced down the stairs and returned shortly with a large bowl of water. He set the bowl on the floor, out of the way.

D'laine approached the pitiful beast. She placed her hands on the top of his head and looked deeply into his eyes. "Ekka, I'm going to remove the queper from your stomach. It may feel strange, but it will not hurt you any more than what you are going through right now. Lay down and be still."

The borjo flopped back on his side, belly extended.

"Trakon, I may need you to help me pull the queper out. I don't know how heavy it is," D'laine said. "Keep your sleeves in place to protect your arms. If your hands get burnt, I'll heal them."

D'laine looked about her. "Trakon, stand here." She showed where. "Bring the container here so we don't trip over it."

Once everything was in place, D'laine placed both hands on Ekka's belly. She took three deep breaths. Her eyes softened as she focused on the task. She plunged her hands into the borjos belly, elbow deep.

Ekka mewled in pain.

D'laine braced her feet on the floor, knees slightly bent as she grabbed the queper's hooves and pulled.

Two hooves appeared, sticking out of Ekka's belly, slimy with stomach acid. Trakon grabbed them and pulled.

"D'laine, let me get in there and help Trakon," Victor said. "This isn't a small animal."

D'laine stepped out of the way and Victor grabbed hold of a third hoof as it appeared.

Ekka groaned in pain.

"It's almost over," Jamie said. "I know it hurts, but they have to pull that queper out of your guts."

Lee and Stanley moved the container closer as they judged where the queper would land once it was fully removed from the borjos stomach.

Trakon nodded to Victor. "Ready? We should only need one last pull."

"Ready," Victor said.

They braced their feet on the floor. Trakon counted down. "Three, two, one. PULL!"

What was left of the queper popped out of Ekka's stomach and landed in the container. There wasn't any brown hair left on the animal. Chunks of the queper had been dissolved from the potent stomach acid.

Ekka let out a loud sound that seemed a lot like a sigh of relief.

Stanley, Jor-Dan, Kitry and Brian were busy wetting and wringing cloths and handing them to D'laine, Trakon and Victor.

"Throw the used cloths in the container. They have stomach acid and poison on them. This will all have to be burnt," D'laine said. She wiped down her sleeves, in between her fingers, and tried to clean the goop from her fingernails.

"This is disgusting," Trakon said, as he cleaned up.

"Reminds me of when my grandfather had to assist with the birth of a calf that was trying to be born breech," Victor said.

D'laine moved to in front of Ekka's stomach, which was

back to its normal size. She ran her hands over his belly. "I'm sure his stomach acid will break down any poison left in his system."

The Visionary nodded. "He should heal now that you have removed the animal." He stared at D'laine in awe.

"Will the smart closet be able to clean our clothes, or should we throw them out?" D'laine asked.

All eyes fell to Kitry. "This is unprecedented. Put them in your closet and monitor the progress."

D'laine, Trakon and Victor finished cleaning their hands and arms. They all stared at the huge container with the sizzling animal inside.

Lee flopped the lid onto the container.

"This will be very difficult to carry down the stairs," Trakon said.

Stanley waved a hand. "Not a problem for Mr. Levitator. Where do you want this?"

Trakon looked to his father for advice.

"You need to take this far outside the city," Jor-Dan said.

"D'laine, can you evaporite this like the Egroms did to the robots?" Trakon asked.

"Oh, maybe I can do this right here," D'laine said. She looked over to the Visionary. "I don't have to worry about this action creating a hole in the floor, do I?"

"I don't believe so," the Visionary said. "Focus on the container, not on anything else."

Everyone moved out of the way.

D'laine held out a hand in front of her. She had a hard focus on the container. Then it was gone.

Everyone let out a collective gasp.

"I can't get used to my daughter being a super powerful woman," Lee said.

"You should have seen her when we battled the robots," Jor-

Dan said. "She is a formidable warrior, and you want her on your good side."

Trakon draped an arm across D'laine's shoulders. "That's my girl!"

Ekka snuggled down into his bed of gauze, exhausted from his ordeal.

Jamie dragged the bowl of water closer to Ekka. "Take a drink when you're thirsty."

"Come on, son. He needs to rest so he can recover," Lee said.

Jamie rubbed his hand over Ekka's face. "I'll see you later, Ekka."

Kitry shooed everyone out of the tower. "You need to get out of those filthy clothes immediately."

Everyone clomped down the stairs and returned to the palace.

CHAPTER EIGHTEEN

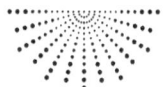

D'laine and Trakon entered their suite. Chatter was lying on his dog bed, on his back, feet in the air. He flopped over and stood, nose sniffing the air. He circled his people.

Trakon lowered an arm to the diwal. "This is what you smell."

The dog took a sniff and backed away. He seemed to know it was bad.

"Poison," D'laine said.

The dog returned to his bed and plopped down.

Trakon and D'laine hung their grungy suits in the smart closet, away from the other clothing that hung nearby. The arms of D'laine's suit were soaked with slime. Trakon's suit was a little better—he didn't have to reach inside Ekka's belly. He just had to grab ahold of the queper's hooves and pull.

"This will be the ultimate test of this technology," Trakon said. He pressed a button to enhance the cleaning process.

They headed to the bathing pool and walked down the stairs into the steaming water.

"I feel so filthy," D'laine said. "Make sure you scrub your fingers and fingernails."

They scrubbed their bodies from top to bottom, then climbed out of the pool and dried off. D'laine wrapped a towel around her hair.

"I'm exhausted." She stifled a yawn.

"Why don't we take a nap. We've been up for hours and haven't even had breakfast," Trakon said. "I'm more tired than hungry right now."

D'laine unwrapped her waist-long hair, bent over and towel dried it as much as possible, then ran a comb through the damp tresses. They walked to the bedroom and climbed into bed and snuggled each other. Within a few minutes, they were deep asleep.

Two hours later, Trakon and D'laine entered the dining salon, with Chatter on their heels. Jamie was exiting the kitchen with a plate of food. Trakon looked over Jamie's plate and saw breakfast food. He strolled into the kitchen, but the majordomo shooed him out.

"Why does Jamie get to go help himself to breakfast and I can't?" Trakon asked the man.

"We will bring out plates for you and the princess," the majordomo said. "Jamie is much more familiar with the kitchen than you, my prince."

D'laine snorted. "Guess you never helped with the dishes?"

Trakon glared at her. "There are other things far worse than kitchen duty."

"Like what?" D'laine asked. She was curious about what Kitry and Jor-Dan did to punish their son.

"Do you have any idea how much comes out of the rear end of a pakow?" Trakon grumbled with memories of his punishments. "Or, how many nuggets an adult male hosk seems to expel?"

Jamie raised his eyebrows. "I'll take kitchen duty any day." He shoveled scrambled par eggs into his mouth.

One by one, the family members entered the dining salon for lunch and took their places at the table.

"After we finish eating, I want to go look at the garden," D'laine said. "Ben's plants and trees should be growing."

"I'm eager to see if they do well in this soil," Lee said.

They finished eating and everyone headed to the rear gate of the city. The guards opened one side of the gate. As they stepped through the gate, a wild sight shocked them. A pecan tree, double the size of a normal tree on Earth, was heavy with nuts. Pecans looked to be about the size of a peach. The tomato plant vined across the moss for a good twenty feet or more, with fruit that ranged in size between a grapefruit and a pumpkin.

"These tomatoes are enormous. I wonder if they taste the same as tomatoes from Earth," Lee said. He pulled a pocketknife out of his suit and grabbed a tomato. He cut a wedge of the fruit and sampled. His eyes widened. "Oh, this is so much better!" He sliced wedges and handed them out.

Kitry and Jor-Dan hesitated, then nibbled.

"Oh! This is delicious! Let's take some back to the cook," Kitry said.

D'laine looked around, disappointed. "I guess the cocoa pods didn't take."

Stanley looked at the nearby forest. "Uh, D'laine, we have a forest of chocolate trees!"

Trakon jumped around, excited to have a supply of chocolate, even if it was in the raw form and he couldn't pluck and eat it yet.

"I'll try to find a book about processing raw cocoa into chocolate," D'laine said.

"We can see if Al can find something, then Ben can zap it here," Lee said. "I'm going to find a box and pick some tomatoes and pecans for Ben." He headed back through the gate.

Kitry and Jor-Dan each carried tomatoes to bring to the cook. Stanley, Victor, Kara, D'laine and Trakon stayed behind.

"Let's crack some nuts and see if they're any good," Stanley said. He stomped on a fallen nut and cracked the shell. He sat down, picked the pieces of shell away from the nutmeat and popped a handful into his mouth. "Tastes just like pecans from back home!"

Everyone stomped on nuts. D'laine offered a piece of nutmeat to Trakon. He popped it into his mouth and chewed.

"This is good. What are they again?" Trakon asked.

"They're pecan nuts," D'laine said. "We add them to cookie batter, make them into pies, or just eat them like we're doing right now."

Stanley picked a nut off the ground that was still in the husk and showed it to Trakon. "When you see one of these, the nut inside isn't ripe yet. The husk should be open, or the brown nut can be on the ground."

"Kara, do you have measuring cups and spoons back home?" D'laine asked.

"Yes, why?" Kara asked.

"The cook will most likely need something to go by for recipe conversions until he can improvise with Tholian measures," D'laine said. "I want to send for some cookbooks. I'll be able to translate them into Tholian."

"You can do that?" Kara asked.

"Yes, and you should be able to translate also. It's sort of built in from the Egrom training. If you have problems with something not working, Ghury will tweak your learning center," D'laine said. "At first, I couldn't read Tholian, but everyone else could. Ghury fixed the problem."

Lee returned with a box. "How are the pecans?"

Stanley picked up a smashed nut and gave it to Lee. "They're fabulous! And I'm glad they're bigger than the ones back home."

Lee loaded up the box with tomatoes and pecans. He nudged Stanley. "Want to go visit Ben? You too, Victor."

"That sounds like a good idea," Victor said. He turned to Kara. "Do you mind? We won't be gone long."

"Tell Ben I said hello, and how happy we are for this incredible crop!" Kara said.

Lee, Victor and Stanley headed through the back gate, and wandered through the city until they reached the crestrider checkout building.

"I reserved one for us," Stanley said.

"When did you do that?" Victor asked. "I didn't see you working your communicator."

Stanley tapped the side of his head. "I can do most things through my noggin."

"Show-off," Lee said. "The rest of us are stuck with doing things manually."

"Already contacted Ben to let him know we're on the way," Stanley said.

A worker flew their reserved ship around and landed it in the open area.

"Thanks," Stanley said. "We should be back in a couple of hours."

"No problem," the worker said, as he jumped to the ground.

Stanley pushed the button that lowered the stairs. The men walked up the stairs, and Stanley took to the controls. He pressed the button that tucked the escalator back into place, then the ship lifted into the air. He steered the crestrider over the city toward the Cember Forest.

Victor couldn't keep a straight face. The technology on Thol delighted him to no end. He loved flying through the air without hundreds of similar vehicles crowding him. Every once in a while, he thought about his life back on Earth—the traffic, population, inconveniences of ground travel. It quickly made him realize that even though his life had been cozy in California, nothing compared to the complete freedom that was life on Thol.

He knew that he would have to settle down and find some constructive work, otherwise, he may go stir crazy. But he was sure he would be spending a lot of time with the Visionary. He was fascinated with the covered dome under the open skylight in the temple. Who would have guessed he could see the future?

And look at Ben—he was a wizard! All of his friends had incredible talents. Who would have imagined Darren would be a protector? He wasn't surprised that Kara was a human lie detector. She always knew when he fibbed, or when Darren tried to pull a fast one over on them.

Lee was watching Victor. "You look like you're having a good time in your head."

Victor laughed. "I was just thinking about the turn of events. Look at us! I can't get over how fortunate we are. I know it's a terrible thing to say this, but am I ever so glad that D'laine was pulled through that portal!"

Lee nodded, a solemn expression crossing over his face. "Trust me, I understand. It was a dark period for me, especially after everything that happened five years previous with losing Lori in the accident." He released a sigh. "What we have here is beyond anything I've ever considered, even with working at NASA for so many years. And being so privileged from all of my patents. I will never consider going back. I'll be forever grateful for D'laine returning to get us."

They were all silent, lost in their thoughts.

"I wish I hadn't gone around hurting people when I first arrived." Stanley shook his head from the memory. "Who would have guessed a brain and skull could expand?"

Victor was thoughtful. "I'm not surprised, Stan. You're beyond most people's intelligence, and it seems appropriate that your IQ would increase due to the Tholian effect on your brain. I hope there's enough here to keep you from getting bored."

Stanley tapped his head. "I've been working on some things, so I seriously doubt if I'll get bored. I'm considering spending some time with the Egroms in their village. I want to absorb their ways, and also want to get to the bottom of this quirky business where they don't explain everything, or answer all questions. I'm positive I can safely get into their brains without hurting anyone anymore."

"Is everything okay with Treikie?" Lee asked.

Stanley smiled. "She's a gift! I never have to worry about her not understanding me. I can't tell you how nice it is to have a girlfriend who is a brilliant scientist."

The ship approached the Cember Forest. They noticed Ben standing out in the open. He waved at them, and pointed to where they should land the ship.

Lee grabbed the box of produce. Stanley landed the ship and Victor pushed the button that lowered the escalator stairs. There were a few thumps on backs and greetings.

"Present for you," Lee said. He handed the box off to Ben.

"Are those tomatoes?" Ben asked, incredulous. "What are these?"

"Pecans!" Victor said. "You've got to come to the garden. You would not believe how these tomatoes vined."

Stanley let out a snort. "Never mind the tomatoes. You should see the size of the pecan tree! And the chocolate pods turned into a forest, just like Drusta said."

They walked into the forest, then over to one of the trees which had stairs to the overhead boardwalk. Ben led the way, and they were soon at his new home.

"I'm still not used to not having a kitchen," Ben said. He explained how things worked in the Kudaja city. "This bartering system works so well."

"So, let's see some of this wizarding talent," Victor said.

"Is there anything you left behind that would be helpful here?" Ben asked.

They all contemplated for a moment.

"Yeah, Kara's measuring cups, measuring spoons, cookbooks and her recipe binders," Victor said. "D'laine's going to translate them into Tholian, so that the cook can try out some recipes using tomatoes and nuts. We will also need a book that will explain how to make chocolate from the raw product."

"I wonder if Al is at the house right now?" Stanley said. He used his brain to connect with Al's cellphone. It rang four times before the reporter picked up. "Al? This is Stanley Daigle. Are you at Victor's house right now?" He listened for a few minutes. "Would you be able to go to the kitchen and see if you can find Kara's measuring cups and spoons?"

"Tell him the measuring cups are in the cabinet to the left of the stove, and the spoons are in the third drawer down below that counter space."

Stanley passed the message to Al.

"Found them," Al said. "Anything else?"

Stanley told him about the cookbooks and binders.

"Give me a minute. I'll grab a box," Al said.

"When you're finished, put everything in that small bedroom. That's the place Ben can lock onto and bring them over," Stanley said. "Has anyone asked about the Bennett's?"

"It's been a circus off and on. I've met Darren's friend Bobby. He's convinced the aliens beamed them up. There's a missing persons bulletin out for the whole family. It was clever of Kara to prepare a meal. And since nothing was out of place, with no obvious struggle, violence or anything, the authorities will be scratching their heads for decades," Al said.

Stanley heard a thump.

"I just put the box of books in the little room. The measuring cups and spoons will be on top of it—the box is full," Al said.

"Okay, stand back," Stanley said.

With only a thought, Ben brought everything over. Lee, Victor and Stanley could hardly believe what they saw.

"It's gone!" Al exclaimed.

"It's here!" Stanley said.

Al could hear the smile in Stanley's voice.

"Hey, ask Al how the book is coming along," Victor said.

Stanley asked the reporter.

"I have a solid outline," Al said. "I'm going to start writing this weekend."

Stanley passed along the information.

"I can't wait to read it," Lee said.

They rounded up the conversation and Stanley closed the connection.

"We forgot to ask about the chocolate process," Lee said.

"No problem," Ben said. He went over to the desk and grabbed a sheet of paper and the writing instrument. He wrote out a note. With a blink, it was gone. "I sent it to the kitchen counter. He'll see it eventually," Ben said.

D'LAINE AND TRAKON SAT ON A LOW SOFA THEY HAD HAULED UP the stairs—actually, Trakon and Dannin did the hauling while she did the supervising. They each sat with an egg cuddled in their laps, rubbing the shells with their fingers. Pup was curled beside D'laine, his chin on her thigh. Every once in a while, he stretched his neck and licked the shell.

The expectant parents appeared blissful, soaking up the quiet time.

"I wonder if any other husbands have sat with their eggs," Trakon said. "Seems to me they leave these things up to the women, which I now know is a huge mistake."

D'laine turned to face him. "It's a cultural thing with your people. I'll bet that over the centuries—a century is one hundred completed paths—your whole evolution, or at least your physiology has changed."

"Why do you say that?" Trakon asked.

"Because, women's breasts were created to feed and nurture the baby. Breast feeding is a common practice on Earth. It bonds the baby to the mother," D'laine explained.

Trakon's forehead creased as he considered what she said. He was quiet for a long time. "I want to explore this subject with the Visionary, and if necessary, the Egroms."

"Remember that book I found in the library? That might contain something about this subject. This business about the child growing for three years within the shell with none of the parents nurturing doesn't seem right," D'laine said.

Trakon frowned. "I would have disagreed with you a path ago, but now I understand what you are saying. I love to hold my children. It makes me feel connected to them. I have great love in my heart for them, and I would die protecting them, and you."

Pup lifted his head. His ears perked up. The door opened below. Soft footsteps climbed the stairs and murmurs were exchanged with the guards on the stairs. Kitry entered the turret room. Pup's tail thumped on the sofa in greeting.

Trakon's mother settled beside him on the sofa.

"Would you like to hold your future grandchild?" Trakon asked.

"No, you hold the egg," Kitry said.

"Mother, D'laine and I have been talking about our evolution," Trakon said.

"What about it?" Kitry said. Her brows crinkled in wonder.

"Did our people always pass eggs, or were there live births at one time?" Trakon asked.

"I'm not aware of live births," Kitry said. "Where did that subject come from?"

"Well, on Earth, women breastfeed their babies," D'laine said.

"I wondered why Tholian women even had breasts if they didn't use them for the purpose the creator gave them."

"Oh!" Kitry said.

D'laine wondered if Kitry considered the point she was making.

"I don't really know the answer to that," Kitry said. "My mother and grandmother never questioned these things, but they are valid questions. We should talk with the Visionary and perhaps search the library for answers."

She stayed a little while longer, then returned to her duty's downstairs.

"We made her very uncomfortable with our questions," Trakon said. He rubbed his hand down his face.

D'laine patted his arm. "Don't worry about it. We have every right to question the evolution and to find answers." She stroked the egg on her lap that rested in a little pile of gauze. "I'm convinced that our children will develop differently than a one-hundred percent Tholian child. The thought of waiting for three paths to greet our children seems preposterous to me."

Trakon had no reference in his heritage to continue the conversation on its present track.

CHAPTER NINETEEN

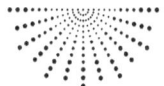

*K*ara happily discovered that she could read and translate from English to Tholian. She immediately began the task of converting several simple recipes for the chef. Tomato sauce, paste, diced tomatoes with herbs—for the creation of not only pizza, but for pasta dishes like spaghetti and lasagna. This also meant she had to provide recipes for the crust and noodles. She felt sure, after eating Tholian food, which included bread, that the chef would know how to improvise.

Next up was pecan pie. She had a wonderful recipe for a not so sweet pie that Victor, Darren and everyone back home loved. She planned to hand that off to the chef, and show him cookie and bread recipes that included nuts.

The whole creating documents and printing them where they dropped out of thin air, was mystifying, but she determined that she couldn't argue with a system that worked.

She wondered if there was an easier way to translate the recipes. Her two binders had personal favorites, but it would take forever, even with both she and D'laine translating them. She made a note to ask everyone about it.

With recipes in hand, she went to the enormous palace kitchen and sought out the chef. A tall, burly man dressed in a white long-sleeved tunic and matching pants approached her.

"Do you require special food?" he asked.

"Oh, no, I'm not hungry," Kara said. "I wanted to introduce myself. I'm Kara, one of the new Earthlings who immigrated here recently."

He grasped her forearm in greeting. "I am Grubio. How can I help you?"

Kara spied a tomato on a cutting board. "Have you tried our tomato?" She nodded to the fruit on the large central island.

"That's what it's called—tomato?" Grubio asked. "It is quite tasty and I've been thinking of different recipes I could use them in."

"I hope you don't mind, but I've translated a few Earth recipes you might find palatable," Kara said.

She handed the chef the recipes, and they had a long discussion about weights and measures. Kara mentioned she had sent for her measuring cups and spoons so he could see the difference between Earth measuring basics and Tholian. This way, he'd be able to make any required adjustments.

"Let me show you the garden, if you can get away for a little while. It's out the back gate," Kara said.

"I'd love to see this garden," Grubio said. He turned to his staff. "Does anyone want to see the vegetable garden with the Earth vegetables?"

There were several nods among the kitchen staff. Kara led everyone out of the palace, through the city to the rear gate. The guards on duty opened the gate, and they stepped into the wonderland of Ben's garden.

"Oh, my Thol!" Grubio said, as he stared at the sprawling tomato vines. "We should preserve some seeds in case anything disturbs the plants."

"This all grew from one small plant," Kara said. She turned

and pointed to the pecan tree. "This is the pecan tree. Those nuts from Earth. Have you tried them?"

"No, we haven't," the chef said.

Kara stomped on some nuts. "Just crack the shells and pull the nutmeat out and eat it. I'm positive you'll like it. Trakon and his parents liked them." She picked up the two cracked nuts and threw the shells on the ground, then held her hand out for Grubio and others to sample.

"Oh, these are delicious!" one of the staff members said. He went about stomping on a couple more nuts.

Kara pointed to the new cocoa bean trees. "These trees grow pods that produce cocoa, which, back home, gets turned into chocolate. Have you tried any chocolate from Earth?"

Grubio shook his head. "No, what is it?"

"It's to die for! Chocolate gets made into so many edible things," Kara said. She pressed her communicator and called Victor. "Is there any chocolate left? I wanted to let Grubio try some."

"Who's Grubio?" Victor asked.

"The palace chef," Kara said. She could hear Victor talking in the background.

"Ben has a stash. I'll bring a few pieces and we'll make sure Trakon doesn't confiscate them!"

"Your prince is obsessed with chocolate and pizza." Kara told Grubio. "When you get to where you can process the cocoa into chocolate desserts, make sure you hide the chocolate from him."

Grubio snickered. "The prince will imprison me!"

Victor, Lee and Stanley caught up with Kara in their suite. "Ben asked Al to buy more chocolate, and to look for a book about how to process the raw product into chocolate." He handed her a plastic bag of assorted bite-sized chocolates.

Stanley levitated the heavy box of books and binders. He settled the box on the coffee table. Lee handed over the measuring cups and spoons.

"This is great," Kara said. "Come to the kitchen with me and meet Chef Grubio. He loves the tomatoes and pecans. He'll love to sample the chocolate and see what he can create."

"I'll catch up with you later," Stanley said. He returned to his suite.

The Bennett's and Lee left the suite upstairs and went to the kitchen. They found Grubio sampling a pot of what looked like spaghetti sauce.

"Kara, would you like to sample my experiment with those tomatoes? I used your recipe," the chef said. He held out a spoon that contained some sauce.

Kara took a taste. Her eyes widened. "Oh, Grubio, this is delicious! What spices did you use? The taste is similar to what I made back home on Earth."

Grubio showed her where dried herbs hung in what she considered a spice closet.

Kara rubbed leaves between her fingers, sniffed them and licked her fingers. "This one is identical to oregano. And this one is similar to parsley."

"We brought some chocolate for you to try," Victor said.

"Grubio, this is my husband, Victor, and you probably already know Lee," Kara said.

Grubio and Victor grasped arms. "It's nice to meet you. I may have to request your wife's services while I'm experimenting with the tomatoes and nuts."

"Wait until you taste these chocolates," Lee said. "Then you'll understand why we had to grow the cocoa tree—which turned into a small forest just from one pod! The soil is so fertile here, and these trees require sun, rain and heat, all of which Thol provides plenty of."

Grubio stuck his hand in the bag and pulled out a chocolate.

He unwrapped the morsel, smelled it, then took a tiny bite. His eyes rolled up. "Oh, My Thol! Kara, help me convert a recipe for this delicacy."

"Well... we're looking for a book that tells us how to make chocolate from the raw product," Victor said. "We don't even know when the raw cocoa is ripe to use."

Grubio waved over one of the workers. "This is Hruk. He specializes in desserts and delicacies. Try one of these chocolates, Hruk."

Hruk pulled a chocolate out of the bag, unwrapped it and popped it in his mouth. He chewed for a second, then stopped. "OH, MY THOL! I have to create this!"

Everyone chuckled.

AL CAREFULLY WROTE OUT A NOTE AND SET IT IN THE SMALL SPARE room. He had to stop himself from checking the room every fifteen minutes to see if the note had gone over to Thol. He figured Stanley would call his cellphone as soon as he received the note from Ben.

After two hours of twiddling his fingers and not being productive at all, his cellphone rang.

"Hey, Stanley, I found some videos about making chocolate from the pods, but I don't know how to send them to you, or if you can even use them," Al said.

"I know this will sound weird," Stanley said, "but just send them to this phone account."

"There's no phone number showing on my cellphone," Al said. "Your name comes up, but when I look at the information, there's no phone number."

Stanley huffed. "Let me call you back. We've got to work something out."

"Okay. I've also found some articles that are PDFs with

pictures. I can print those out and put them in the other room," Al said. "But the videos show more detail. The whole process is a little complicated, but there're videos of people making chocolate at home."

Stanley disconnected the call. He went in search of Lee and Victor and found them still in the kitchen sampling Grubio's creations.

"Al has some videos and PDFs on how to process the cocoa pods, but I'm not sure how he can send them electronically," Stanley said. "A phone number doesn't show up on his phone when I call him."

"What about downloading them to a USB drive? Then Ben can bring them over," Victor said.

"I guess we could do that, but I'm determined to make my brain connection work both ways," Stanley said.

As they finished their discussion in the kitchen, Kara's communicator announced Jor-Dan calling. She tapped her communicator, but could not remember how to answer the call.

Victor walked over to her and tapped a button and brought up the menu. "Right here, hon."

Kara studied the menu, but the call ended. "Oh, no! How do I get Jor-Dan back?"

Victor showed her what to tap, and she connected to the king.

"I'm sorry, Jor-Dan. Victor was showing me how to answer your call, but I took a little while to figure it out," Kara explained.

"Don't worry about it, you're still learning our ways and technology," Jor-Dan said. "Would you be able to come to the room where we listen to petitions from the people? I would like you to listen to a complaint and let us know if this man is telling the truth before I grant or deny his petition."

"Oh! Certainly! I'll be right there. I'm in the kitchen with Grubio," Kara said. She tapped the menu to disconnect the call and turned to Victor. "This sounds serious! What if I don't know what I'm doing with these skills?"

Victor threw an arm across her shoulders. "Kara, this is your gift. Let's go see what this is all about."

"The king could really use your gift to keep the petitioners honest," Lee said.

They all walked out of the kitchen and went to the large throne room where the king and his advisors heard the petitions. Jor-Dan and Marrak were in a quiet discussion when they arrived in the room.

"Kara! Please join us," Jor-Dan said.

Kara nervously left Victor, Stanley and Lee. She cut through the line of petitioners to the other side of the table where the king, the documentarian, and the advisors sat.

"Thank you for coming," Jor-Dan said. He stood and patted her on the back for support. "This petitioner has told us his problem and we would like to verify the information."

Marrak leaned in and whispered in her ear. "Don't be afraid. The king explained your gift. There's no way you can make a mistake with your abilities."

"Tell your story to this Earthling," Marrak said to the petitioner.

A scruffy man stepped forward. He looked Kara over. "I told the king and the documentarian that my mother fell in the marketplace at a stall and broke her hip. I want the merchant to award me goods for this hardship."

Kara stared at the man. She barked out, "You are lying! Tell the correct story of what happened."

The man fidgeted. His eye developed a twitch. "Whatcha mean?"

Marrak pulled himself up straighter in his chair. "It means Kara caught you in a bold lie, and you need to rethink what happened. There is a just punishment for anyone who tries to scam someone. Would you like to amend your statement?"

The man realized he was in trouble. After several thoughtful minutes, he began again. "She tripped…"

"Lie," Kara barked out.

The man stared from one to another down the other side of the table.

"Did you push your mother?" Jor-Dan asked, not too gently. He was ready to throw the man in the dungeon for hurting his mother and trying to use her misfortune to collect goods.

The man huffed. "She was movin' so slow and I didn't want to wait all day to get what we needed."

Kara didn't refute what he said.

"So, you pushed your mother, and she fell?" Jor-Dan roared.

The man stepped back a couple of steps, but guards had moved in and prevented him from making a getaway.

"Lock him up," Jor-Dan said. He turned to Marrak. "Have someone go check on his mother. She may require medical attention, and it doesn't appear that her son is overly interested in her welfare." He turned to Kara. "I can't thank you enough for your service." He patted her hand.

Kara sucked in a huge breath. "I can't believe someone would hurt their mother because she wasn't moving fast enough. I wonder what else she's suffered? He should not walk free."

"We don't allow things like this, and when we find out about them, we take action to protect the weak," Marrak said.

The rest of the petitioners eyed Kara warily. They understood they would have to be one-hundred percent accurate with their requests from that point on. This was one rumor that would fly through Ebscalon, that would actually benefit the kingdom.

Kara returned to Victor, Lee and Stanley. Trakon had joined them at the doorway and had listened in on the petitioner.

"How do you do that? It's amazing," Trakon said.

Kara shrugged. "I have no idea. I just get this twinge at the base of my skull."

Stanley nodded in thought. "Your gift has something to do with the central nervous system."

Victor kissed her forehead. "The boys don't stand a chance now."

Lee smirked. "WE don't stand a chance. I suspect everyone will tiptoe around you from now on, Kara."

"I'm going to have to learn how to control my responses. A little white lie doesn't deserve full-blown retribution," Kara said. "What I mean is, say Darren snuck a dessert or something without permission. That's not as punishable as if he broke a window—never mind. There're no windows here."

"We get it," Victor said. "It's an awesome gift, Kara. And it looks like King Jor-Dan will have a great use for your skills."

They walked outside. Kara's dress, similar to a sari, flapped gently with the light breeze. They looked up and saw Ekka sailing through the air, returning to his tower.

"I'm so glad D'laine healed Ekka," Lee said.

CHAPTER TWENTY

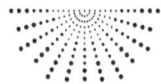

*L*ee, Brian and Jamie walked to Ethaderia's house. The blue, purple and green banners that flapped in the wind over the spires, also sported red, which meant that Ethaderia's mother was in residence. Lee was a little nervous about meeting his soon-to-be mother-in-law, and hoped she approved of him and the boys.

They stopped at her front door. Lee inspected his sons. Their uniforms were clean. Their faces weren't sweaty. They had combed their hair. He knocked on the door.

Ethaderia's manservant answered the door. "Hello, Mr. Jackson, boys. Won't you come in? The lady of the house and her elder mother are waiting for you in the main salon."

He stood aside while they entered the house, then escorted them to the room where the women waited.

Ethaderia jumped to her feet. Lee determined that she was as nervous as he was, because her mother was present. She rushed to him and clasped one of his hands, eyes wide. She turned him toward the regal woman on a sofa.

"Lee, Brian and Jamie, this is my mother, Augenta."

Ethaderia turned to her mother. "These are the Earthlings, Lee Jackson and his sons Brian and Jamie. Lee is my intended."

Lee detected a hint of force in the introduction. He wondered if Augenta had disapproved of the engagement. He put that out of his mind and approached the older woman, hand outstretched.

"It is a pleasure to meet you, Augenta. I've heard many nice things about you," Lee said. He was glad Kara wasn't present to call out the lie. Ethaderia didn't talk about her mother very much. He knew they had a sticky relationship.

Augenta allowed the arm-to-arm greeting. She looked Lee and the boys over.

Jamie, ever the friends-till-we-die type of boy, approached the woman. "You're just as beautiful as your daughter. I'm so glad she's going to be my mother, and you will be my grandmother!" He flung his arms around her neck and hugged her for all it was worth.

Augenta's eyes flew open wider than what Lee thought possible. She didn't thrust Jamie away; she patted his back in a stand-offish hug. "My dear child, you certainly know what you want in life, don't you?"

"He has always been a little over the top," Lee said.

After Jamie released himself from the woman, Brian approached her. He stuck his hand out in greeting.

The older woman appraised Brian. "You're a little more civilized than your brother."

Ethaderia clutched Lee and almost dragged him to a sofa. "Please, boys, sit and be comfortable." Once they settled on the sofa, she loosened up a bit. "Mother, as I've mentioned before, Brian is eleven paths and Jamie is seven. Lee was an engineer on Earth."

Augenta stared at her daughter. "I'm quite sure he can speak for himself."

Ethaderia bristled. "I don't understand your attitude,

mother. Lee and I will marry whether or not you approve of the union. Please explain your reluctance, or whatever it is that you don't approve."

"You are a wealthy woman," Augenta said, "and while you are attracted to this man, he is not Tholian. Your children would have tainted blood."

Ethaderia was about to explode, but Lee held up a hand to stop her.

"Augenta, on Earth I was a celebrated engineer who worked for the governmental space agency, with many inventions and patents—rights to my discoveries that companies paid me for. It was impossible to bring over my wealth to this world," Lee said. "However, I do not expect any woman to support me. I will speak to the king and queen about this situation and ask their guidance."

Lee stood. "Brian, Jamie, we need to go home."

"The palace is not your home!" Augenta said. "My niece, the queen, is simply being kind to you because your daughter is married to their son."

"That is not true, mother!" Ethaderia said. She stood and went to Lee's side. "Let me walk you back to the palace."

They left without another word.

Once outside, Lee and Ethaderia let loose deep sighs.

"Why doesn't she like us?" Jamie asked.

"It isn't that she doesn't like you," Ethaderia said. She fluffed Jamie's hair. "I think what she is upset about is that I chose your father over one of the men she presented to me."

"Why does it make a difference?" Brian asked. "You're the one marrying our dad. Not her."

"Son, this is no different from the way people act back on Earth. When someone with wealth marries below their station in life, others have problems with what they consider a socially unacceptable match." Lee pondered the problem. He turned to Ethaderia. "At this point, I don't think it would matter if I could somehow bring my wealth to Thol. Your mother seems to have a set mind on this."

Ethaderia squeezed his hand. "As Brian pointed out, she is not the one marrying you. Don't worry about anything. She can't stop us."

They arrived at the palace and went to the salon where the family met. Jor-Dan, Trakon, D'laine, Stanley and Victor were talking among themselves. Darren was on the floor patting the dogs.

"Where's Kitry?" Ethaderia asked. Her face was creased with stress.

"She's working on one of her weavings," D'laine said. "What's wrong?"

Without another word, Ethaderia rushed out of the room. Lee sat, uncomfortable with the whole situation.

"What happened?" Trakon asked.

Jor-Dan looked Lee over. "Something has disturbed you two. Unburden yourself. Maybe we could solve the problem."

"My future grandmother doesn't like us," Jamie blurted. "She wasn't nice to my father."

"She said mean things and accused our father of things," Brian said.

All eyes swung to face Lee. He covered his eyes for a minute. "I left all my wealth behind on Earth. She accused me of taking advantage of you, Jor-Dan, by living off you in the palace. Then she taunted her own daughter about any half-breed children we might have."

Jor-Dan shook his head. "That woman. She's done more harm to Ethaderia and her sister, Ilanda, than anyone could imagine. Kitry won't set foot in her cousin's house when her mother is in residence. The woman is bitter and takes it out on everyone."

"Someone needs to tell her that you and Stanley gifted Thol with the ability to make crestriders fly at night. That's no simple feat," Trakon said. He was livid. "I should go over there…"

D'laine pressed her hand on his thigh. "That won't solve anything. Your mother may come up with a solution."

Kara entered the salon. She felt the tension in the air and noticed that Brian and Jamie were unhappy, and Lee was very stressed. She crossed the room and settled beside Victor.

What's wrong? Kara sent to Victor.

Ethaderia's mother sounds like a witch. She has deeply disturbed Lee, the boys and Ethaderia with her wicked tongue, he sent.

Oh, no! Is Ethaderia talking to Kitry?

Yes.

I'll go see if I can help.

Kara stood and hurried from the room.

KITRY WAS INCENSED. AS THE STORY UNFOLDED, SHE LOST ALL ability to hold her temper.

Kara's head ping-ponged between Ethaderia and Kitry, listening to the angst pour out of the two women. She cleared her throat. The two women hesitated in the middle of a rant and looked her way.

"Kitry, you are the queen. Why don't you have Jor-Dan summon Augenta to the palace? He can be very imposing when he presents that regal, but fierce king." Kara remembered how he acted during petitions. "He can set her straight about what Lee has contributed to Thol."

Both Kitry and Ethaderia stared at Kara with wonder.

"That's an excellent idea!" Kitry stood. "Let's go to the salon and discuss this as a family."

They marched out of Kitry's domain like determined soldiers, down the hall, and around the corner to the main salon.

Jor-Dan's and Trakon's eyebrows rose. They recognized that look on Kitry's face, and knew they had to proceed delicately to avoid a situation that might backfire on them. They just had to wait until they heard what was to come.

"Jor-Dan, I want you to summon my aunt here in an official capacity, right this minute! You and Trakon can explain everything that Lee has brought to Thol. The ships, the Earth sport that has brought kingdoms together—and don't forget about our daughter-in-law—she saved Thol from the robot invasion! That woman needs to be taken down several pegs!"

Kitry's chest heaved from anger.

"Wife, that's an excellent idea."

Jor-Dan and Trakon both nodded.

"If she can't be proud of her daughter marrying a celebrated engineer, the father of a revered hero, and a beloved coach of baseball, then there's something radically wrong with her. That woman doesn't belong in this kingdom," Jor-Dan stated.

The king silently summoned two of the guard. They entered the room, each bumped a fist to his chest and waited for instructions.

"You are to go to Ethaderia's home and escort her mother here to the palace. This is not an invitation," Jor-Dan said.

The men saluted and left the room.

Ethaderia fidgeted as she sat beside Lee.

"Your mother needs to show you some respect, Ethaderia," Lee said. "She will not use you as a doormat, whether or not I am present. You are not a little girl who needs guidance from her parent. You're a grown woman with a mind of your own."

"Let us adjourn to the throne room," Kitry said.

The entire party left the main salon and walked down the hall to the throne room. Kitry and Jor-Dan took their places on their thrones. Trakon and D'laine sat on their lesser thrones. Everyone else stood behind the royals in their assigned places, boys included.

Brisk footsteps sounded the arrival of the guards and Augenta.

Augenta's eyes rounded the room and fell on Lee. "How dare you..."

Jor-Dan's voice boomed out as he rose to his feet. "Do not raise your voice in my presence. I am your king!" His intent was clear. "You have not respected me or your queen!"

Augenta startled. For a minute, her brain froze. She realized her mistake and humbly tapped her chest and lowered her head to the king and queen. "Please accept my apology, my king, my queen."

"You have assumed a great deal, Augenta. Not only have you disrespected your king and queen, you have insulted your own daughter and her intended, the revered man who gave the gift of night flight to our crestriders. That technology can now recover from the fifty paths of night flying disuse," Jor-Dan said. "You have an incorrect assumption that Lee Jackson is a loafer, taking advantage of his place in this kingdom."

Augenta sputtered to offer an explanation.

Jor-Dan boomed out. "Do not interrupt your king! D'laine Jackson, the daughter of this esteemed engineer and inventor, is Thol's savior. She rescued us from the robot invasion. Were you not aware that this devastating event could have turned every Tholian into a slave? And, your future son-in-law has brought the Earth sport of baseball to Thol. Just one game has united kingdoms! I suggest that you surrender your residence in Ebscalon and seek a place to live elsewhere. You are no longer welcomed at your daughter's residence. Vacate the premises immediately. These guards will accompany you to Ethaderia's residence and assist you with whatever preparations are required for your exit from her home. You will have thirty turns to leave Ebscalon."

Augenta appeared devastated. She bowed her head, tapped

her chest and retreated from the room with the guards. She never made eye contact with her daughter.

"Ethy, contact Ilanda and let her know what happened," Kitry said.

"Ilanda won't let her move into the palace," Ethaderia said. "Kensadora doesn't need another spiteful woman. Ilanda has her hands full with her mother-in-law."

"That was a very uncomfortable confrontation, but it needed to happen," Kara said. "Sometimes parents try to thwart the happiness of their children. I've seen it many times on Earth where a parent browbeats their child to where they have no self-esteem or confidence at all. I've never understood it."

"Bitter people want the company of other bitter people, so they try to create them," Trakon said. "Augenta has always undermined her daughters. I'm sure that's why Ilanda married the king of Kensadora and moved so far away."

"She was lucky to make a love match," Kitry said. "Her husband will not tolerate his mother-in-law's tricks. He recently had to displace his own mother so he and Ilanda could have their own happiness."

"In thirty turns, this chapter will be closed," Jor-Dan said.

CHAPTER TWENTY-ONE

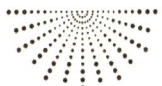

*T*he Egrom elders sat in debate around the fire. Swezek's passing prompted a serious discussion about his replacement. It had been three- or four-hundred years since the last elder had returned to the stars.

As Ghury looked around the circle, the only thing he thought about was the age of each elder. Bensol was the youngest, at six-hundred paths. Adrum was two paths Ghury's junior.

"There are several candidates ranging from two-hundred paths to six-hundred," Adrum said.

"Two hundred? That is too young to consider, "Drusta said.

"Not all the candidates are Egrom," Adrum reminded them. "There are others with qualifications we seek."

"Brian is too young. We might as well have Chacoodi in the running, for all the maturity the Earth boy would bring," Ditol said. "Just because his ability to sense portals is stronger than ours doesn't mean he would make wise decisions in other areas."

"We have all acknowledge that D'laine would be my replacement, so do not include her in the candidates," Ghury said.

"There are two strong Earthling choices: Greg and Stanley. For the Egrom choices, I would consider Wenk and Claggon. I would also consider Maldi Amadal."

The Egrom elders nodded, chirped and grunted in consideration.

Trabet chirped. "Excellent choices, Ghury. We must vote."

STANLEY, VICTOR AND THE VISIONARY STOOD AROUND THE domed table in the temple. Victor's eyes were closed, his hands outstretched to encompass the domed planet suspended off the surface. Clouds swirled around the replica that could be Earth or Thol, as he focused on the near future.

"There is much happiness approaching in less than a year," Victor said. "There will also be evolutionary changes." Victor opened his eyes and took a deep breath.

The Visionary nodded. He expected those things, but had been reluctant to verbalize anything. "We shall hold these things between the three of us. Our people may not welcome the changes you foresee. While they don't have a say so in evolutionary changes, Tholian humans would look at these things as a giant step backwards. So be it. We will witness how they react in the near future."

Stanley twitched. A hard startle poked him.

"What is it?" the Visionary asked.

"I'm being summoned by the Egroms," Stanley said.

"You'd better go then," Victor said.

Stanley stepped out of the temple and arrived in the middle of the Egrom village many miles away. "Did you summon me?"

The Egroms nodded. At first Stanley wasn't sure if they were nodding in the Egrom greeting, or nodding in confirmation.

"Greetings, Stanley," Ghury said. "Yes, we did summon you. As you witnessed, Swezek passed over into the light. It is our duty as elders to determine who the best candidate would be to replace him."

"We made a list that included more than just our kind," Drusta said.

All the Egroms nodded. Stanley waited for them to continue so he could figure out why they summoned him.

"We have chosen you to replace Swezek," Adrum said.

Stanley stepped back shocked. He wasn't sure if he heard Adrum correctly. "Me?"

They nodded.

"But, I'm not even Tholian," Stanley said. "I don't live in your village. How could I be one of your elders?"

"It is unnecessary to live here," Ghury said. "You are but a step away, and your powerful human brain has adapted to Thol. We will all be able to communicate as needed."

"Is this a big secret, or can I explain this to everyone back at the palace?"

"You'd best explain your new position so they understand when you have to be away," Adrum said.

"I'm honored," Stanley said. "Why didn't you choose D'laine?"

"It's not her time," Trabet said.

"You are no longer an Earthling. You might consider your kind, Eartholian," Ditol said.

"Eartholian," Stanley said. He nodded. "I like that. I will tell the others."

The Egroms nodded. Stanley stepped back to the temple.

"You have some news?" the Visionary asked.

Victor slapped Stanley on the back. "Congratulations!"

"You knew?" Stanley asked.

"I saw it, but didn't want to say anything," Victor said.

"Please share this news with me," the Visionary said.

"They chose me to replace Swezek," Stanley said.

The Visionary nodded. "A wise choice."

Stanley turned to Victor. "They suggested we no longer call ourselves Earthlings. We should consider ourselves Eartholians. I will inform the others at dinnertime."

BRIAN, JAMIE AND DARREN SAILED THROUGH THE SKY ON EKKA'S back. They landed in the Egrom village and went in search of Chacoodi. They found him on latrine duty, crushing rock.

"Can you come flying with us? We're going to Ta'Byu'Vohon to play with Cadj and Fazi," Brian said.

Kestrum approached the group. She looked them over. "Have you told your elders where you are?"

The boys squirmed.

"I thought so. Young boys should always seek parental approval before flying about on a borjo," Kestrum said. "What if you fell off the back of the beast? What if you were playing and a dangerous thing happened?"

The boys looked immensely guilty.

"Can Chacoodi come with us to Jakla's city… if we go back home and tell everyone where we're going?"

Kestrum looked them over with her stern facade.

They each stood straighter with serious faces.

"When will Chacoodi return to his home?" Kestrum asked.

"In a few hours," Jamie said.

"Make sure you keep everyone informed," Kestrum said. "If you are going to be late, tell your parents, otherwise they fear for their child's wellbeing."

"So, I can go?" Chacoodi asked, with a small voice.

Kestrum nodded.

Chacoodi and the boys' eyes widened with happiness. They raced through the village to where Ekka waited.

"Let's ask if Vila can come with us!" Brian said.

They raced over to the forest.

"Vila!" they called out.

The tiny Kudaja girl slid down an agrin vine and dropped to her feet, full-sized. "Hi!"

Brian explained where they were going and asked if she could come with them.

Vila mentally called out to her mother. "I promise!" She smiled wildly at the boys. "My mother said I have to be home in two hours."

They all ran back to Ekka and climbed aboard. The borjo lifted off the ground. The sound of five children happily screaming filled the air.

EKKA ZOOMED OVER EBSCALON. THREE OF THE BOYS SILENTLY contacted their parents to give their whereabouts. They didn't ask for permission for the play session away from home, they just informed where they were heading.

The borjo headed to the Plotal city and circled above. He began his descending flight near the construction site of a rather large building. Plotals scattered as the borjo swooped down to the ground. The beast landed and the boys and Vila scattered, running toward Jakla's residence. Moments later, Ekka took flight over the forest.

Cadj and Fazi flew out of their house and joined them. They all jumped in glee. Brian made introductions. Fazi and Vila took an instant liking to each other. They wandered around the Plotal city, talking and exploring. Cadj and Fazi showed the boys and Vila the transitions from the tent city to the homes.

"Want to see where our father works?" Cadj asked.

"Sure!" Jamie said.

They all followed Cadj and Fazi to the enormous building.

"This is the stronghold where our father meets with people, and where we are going to live," Fazi said. "Mother is supervising Bist, the architect, so everything in our living quarters is how she wants it."

Two huge Plotal guards nodded to the assortment of boys and girls. The children entered the building and meandered down a wide hallway to a large room.

Jakla sat on a huge, ornate chair. Several Plotals sat at a wide table, and a line of Plotals waited to present whatever it was they came to the council for.

Brian determined one Plotal was like Marrak, with writing tools and documents.

Cadj led them around the line of Plotals to where his father sat. "Father, I've brought my friends to show where you work."

Jakla looked over the group of boys and girls. He didn't know Chacoodi, although he had seen the Egrom boy before, and he had never met the Kudaja girl either. "Are you going to introduce your new friends? I have only met Brian, Darren and Jamie."

"Yes, father. This is Chacoodi, and this is Vila. They're from the Cember Forest," Cadj said.

"What do you do here?" Jamie asked.

"Basically, the same as Jor-Dan and other leaders," Jakla said. "I overlook my people and listen to their petitions. Sometimes they require help to solve a problem. Sometimes their dispute could lead to wrong actions. Things we, as a species, are trying to amend so we no longer are cast as a warring, bloodthirsty or cruel lot."

"I like your city," Darren said. "Your buildings are so big and spacious."

"We are large creatures, so our accommodations require adjustments from that which is normal for human Tholians," Jakla said.

Brian pointed to one of the Plotals at the table. "Is that your documentarian?"

"Yes, this is Anwak," Jakla said.

Anwak nodded at the children.

Brian walked up to Anwak. "Can I watch how you document things? I'm learning from King Jor-Dan and Marrak, his documentarian. Do you write in the same language as them?"

Anwak turned a petition around so Brian could read it, and pointed to the document. "Can you understand this? Our written language is universal, with a few nuances for Plotal terminology."

Brian looked over the document. "Oh, yes, I see what you mean. It's very interesting. Thank you for showing me. I'm very interested in what you and Marrak do. I like sitting in on the petitions in Ebscalon."

"Have your parents and your gifts developed yet?" Jakla asked Darren.

"Yes. My mother is a lie detector, my father sees the future, and I'm sort of a protector," Darren said.

"A lie detector?" Jakla asked. "How does that work?"

The boys fidgeted. Their recent experience with Kara was embarrassing.

"No one can lie around her," Jamie blurted, exasperated. "Not even a little fib!"

"Why would you lie? Don't you want to be an upstanding citizen?" Jakla asked.

"Come on, Jakla. You know how boys are. We go off on an adventure, but we don't want to tell our parents every single thing," Jamie said.

"So, how does Kara determine you're lying?" Jakla asked

"How do we know? She just does. And it's not just us. Jor-Dan called her into the room where he hears the petitions and she told him this man was lying about how his mother got hurt," Brian said.

Jakla stood. "I will pay the king a visit and learn more about this."

"Shall I cancel the rest of the petitions for today?" Anwak asked his leader.

"Delay the session. I will return in a few hours," Jakla said. He strode out of the room.

Brian, Jamie, Darren, Chacoodi, Cadj, Vila and Fazi followed Jakla out of the building over to the pakow holding area.

Jakla turned to the children. "Cadj, you and your sister are to remain here." He swung his focus to the others. "The rest of you should return to Ebscalon. How did you get here?"

"Ekka brought us," Jamie said.

Jakla stared down Chacoodi. "Did you tell your tribe where you are?"

Chacoodi gulped. "Yes! Kestrum granted me permission."

Jakla turned to Vila. "What about you?"

"My mother said I could come here with the boys."

Jakla nodded.

An attendant brought a pakow out of the pen. The beast was elaborately decorated with a large saddle, bridle and reins, along with braided hair with ribbons and gemstones. He handed Jakla a helmet which he settled on his head.

It thrilled Jamie to see the attendant talk to the pakow, and the pakow kneeled.

Jakla and a party of four guards rode out of Ta'Byu'Vohon toward Ebscalon.

"We'd better go," Brian said. "Thanks for showing us around. I hope next time you can come to Ebscalon!"

Cadj and Fazi liked that idea. "We will discuss that with our mother," Cadj said. "She will bring it up to our father—he should grant permission. He likes us to diversify our friendships."

Fazi and Vila clasped hands in a friend-forever sort of way.

"I'm so glad we met," Fazi said.

"Me too!" Vila said. "I will ask my mother if you can come for a visit. Have you ever been to the Cember Forest?"

"No! I want to see your city in the trees!" Fazi said.

"We should ask our parents to talk," Vila said.

Jamie silently called for Ekka. The great borjo spiraled down to the ground, and the kids climbed up on the borjo and they took off.

THE EBSCALON GATE GUARDS SENT A RUNNER TO THE PALACE TO alert them of the approaching Plotal party. Since there was peace between the Plotals and the human Tholian kingdoms, there was no escort to the palace.

Jakla and his party approached the plaza, dismounted, and handed their beasts over to the attendants to be cared for during the visit.

The head Ebscalon guard greeted the party with a thump to his chest. "Commander Bosakin! Welcome. The royal family and the Eartholians await you in the main salon."

He led the Plotal party through the entry of the palace to the large salon. "Commander Bosakin and party!" he announced to the group in the room.

Jor-Dan approached the Plotal. "Jakla, it is good to see you again."

"King Jor-Dan!" Jakla said. His fist hit his chest in greeting. He nodded to Kitry. "Queen Kitry!"

Jakla removed his helmet and fully entered the room, while his guard stayed at the entrance of the salon. He and Jor-Dan exchanged the Tholian arm grip.

"We had a visit from your young sons and their friends today," Jakla said. He nodded to Victor and Kara. "They told me of Kara's new skill and I wanted to verify this as fact."

Lee made a sour face. "Those boys of mine! They run wild all over the place."

Jakla let out a Plotal half roar which was the equivalent of a choking laugh. "Think of them as diplomats. They should visit more of the kingdoms to spread their goodwill."

"When you put it that way, I can't be angry with them," Lee said. "The problem is, they take off and then decide to tell us where they are."

Jor-Dan led Jakla to a large chair. The Plotal sat, wrapping his tail to the side of his hip and leg to accommodate his largess in the chair.

The majordomo brought a tray of large mugs of kahl. He served Jakla first, then his guard.

"I always appreciate your large drinking vessels," Jakla said. He turned to the king and queen. "Please tell me if this lie detector has helped you with petitions. Sometimes, when I listen to my people I am not sure if they are lying to me or not."

Kara cleared her throat to get everyone's attention. Since this subject was about her gift, she felt she should answer directly, not as a third party.

"Please explain everything," Kitry said.

"It started out at the dinner table," Kara said. She told Jakla the tale about the boys lying, what she felt and how it all played out.

Then Jor-Dan jumped in with the story about the petitioner who was trying to bilk a merchant. "After experiencing Kara's gift, I thought it best to have her listen to the petitioner. The man was lying and had to change his story more than once before the truth came out. He is being dealt with."

Ever the skeptic, Jakla needed proof. "Would it be appropriate to have an example of this lie detection skill?"

"Certainly," Jor-Dan said. "What do you think, Kara?"

Kara held her hands out with a shrug. "Tell me something that is the truth, then a lie, so you can see the results. You can tell as many fibs as you like."

Jakla's tail twitched. "We rode over on pakows."

Kara didn't do or say anything.

"A gagu bit my pakow," Jakla said.

"Lie!" Kara boomed out.

"This chair is very uncomfortable," Jakla said.

"Lie!" Kara smiled widely. "You're getting the hang of it."

"I don't like living here," Lee said.

"Big lie!" Kara said.

Jakla nodded. "You are highly skilled, Kara. I wonder if it will be okay to borrow you if the need ever arises in my dealings with petitioners?"

The boys and Vila entered the salon.

"Where have you been?" Lee asked.

"We rode Ekka over to the Cember Forest and picked up Chacoodi, then we asked Vila if she could come with us, then we flew to Jakla's city to see Cadj and Fazi," Jamie said.

"You didn't tell us until Kestrum made you," Lee said. "You knew she would contact us."

The boys squirmed.

"Come on, Dad, you know we don't get into trouble," Brian said.

"Oh, boy. That's a fib if I ever heard one," Kara said. "Not all your escapades are trouble-free. There have been some terrible consequences."

Brian's face turned beet red. "You know what I mean! We don't cause trouble with the residents, guards, animals or anything else. We just like to explore and play."

Kara nodded.

"I wanted to thank you for including Fazi in your playtime," Jakla said. "There are many times her brother excludes her when he is with friends."

"We like Fazi. She's a lot of fun," Darren said.

Vila squirmed. "Commander Bosakin, I would like to invite Fazi to our village, if it's okay with my mother."

Jakla looked the Kudaja girl over. "That's very thoughtful of you, Vila. I will discuss this with Neska, Fazi's mother, and we will speak with your parents."

Vila looked happy. She clasped her hands together. "I can't wait to tell my parents!"

Jakla turned his focus back to the adults. "We are planning a gathering in a few months. Most of the construction will be completed by that time, with the exclusion of additional housing in the far reaches of the city. We still have some tents, but those should be gone in another month or two."

"We would love to attend your gathering," Jor-Dan said.

"I can't wait to see the city," Kitry said. "Dreebo and Bist spent a lot of time discussing the plans and construction. Tell Neska to contact me if she needs any help."

"I will pass on your kind words and offer. There are a few of my people who do not want to give up the tents—it's all they have ever known. I hope they adapt to the permanent city I am creating," Jakla said.

"Sometimes change is difficult," Victor said. "Look how long it took us to decide whether to emigrate."

Jakla said his goodbyes; he and his party headed back home.

"Would it be okay if we took Chacoodi and Vila back home?" Brian asked. "Kestrum and Vila's mother expect them back right about now."

"I have to go to the village," Stanley said. "They can come with me."

Everyone clearly saw the disappointment on the boy's and Vila's faces.

"You've had enough flying around," Kara told Darren. "As a matter of fact, I have a need to visit the elders—to discuss how to convert the box of educational books into their movies."

The three Eartholian boys groaned. Freedom was slowly being taken away. They said goodbye to Chacoodi and Vila, then they were gone, along with Stanley and Kara.

CHAPTER TWENTY-TWO

They stepped into the Egrom village where the elders met around the cookfire. Chacoodi was about to run off, but Kestrum materialized.

"You can return to your previous duties," she told him.

Chacoodi's shoulders drooped as he realized he was back to latrine duty. He said goodbye to Vila and shuffled off in that direction. Vila took off running toward the trees.

"How can we help you, Kara?" Adrum asked.

Stanley took his place in the circle where Swezek used to sit.

"We have the school and educational books from Earth. Is it possible to take the contents of each book and create the movies you use for training?" Kara asked.

"A simple task," Adrum said. "Where are the books?"

"They're with Ben," Stanley said. "Want me to go get them?"

Adrum nodded.

Stanley stood, then he was gone. He returned minutes later with the box and Ben.

"Hello, Kara! Ready to get those wild boys educated?" Ben asked. He let his fingers trip over the spines of the books in the enormous box.

With the interdimensional mode of shipping, size and weight did not matter at all. The large box contained elementary, middle and high school books along with the basic college course books. Specialized subjects such as medical, science, physics, and botany were included in the box, and everything in between.

"I figured this was a good start. We can have Al send whatever we determine we're lacking," Kara said.

"It would be best to arrange these books according to how they are typically taught in your schools," Adrum said.

"Would you want us to put them in stacks on the moss, or stand them up on their spines, like these?" Ben asked.

Adrum looked into the box. "On their spines."

Kara, Ben and Stanley each grabbed some books and placed them in order of grade level. When the box was empty, each school grade was laid out on the moss.

"I think it would be best to have each school level a separate movie," Kara said. "So, these would be for elementary school. Then these would be middle school. This is high school, and these are college books," She pointed to each school level for Adrum. "Then there's the special interest books."

Adrum nodded. He started at the elementary school level and picked up a book. He held it in two of his hands for a minute, then set it back down. He made it through all the stacks of books, Egrom quick, for elementary school, then moved on to each of the other school levels. Within less than thirty minutes, Adrum created movies for each school level.

He sat Kara and Ben down and played a few levels for them to make sure everything was okay. All the text was verbalized. The teacher for elementary sounded like a young woman. She used inflections in her speech to emphasize things. Middle school was a male teacher. High school was a combination of teacher voices. College and special books were at a professorial level of communication with both male and female teachers, and sounded like higher education, but with value-added interest.

"This is wonderful!" Kara said. "If only learning was so easy back home. Everyone would have a higher education. Adrum, if it's okay with you, I would like to make a list of additional specialized books Al could send us. Things like languages, space exploration, and anything else that might be useful, or that could crossover to Tholian skills."

Adrum nodded. "There is no problem, Kara. We could take a full library and create educational training."

Ben's eyes glazed over at the mention of taking a full library. "I don't even have to guess what Lee, Stanley, Victor and I would enjoy!"

Kara nodded. "It's all set then. Now, how do I go about training the boys?"

STANLEY STEPPED KARA AND BEN BACK TO EBSCALON IN TIME FOR dinner.

"I hope you don't mind me barging in for dinner," Ben said.

A place setting lay in front of him.

"You are always welcome here, Ben!" Kitry said. "It is nice to see you again. How are you doing with the Kudaja?"

A serene expression crossed Ben's face. "I love the city in the forest. It is the most peaceful I have ever been in my life. And I have my own borjo, which makes life that much more fun."

Dinner was served. As Stanley stabbed a vegetable with his fork, he held the fork out in front of him. "The Egroms want us to stop calling ourselves Earthlings."

Lee and Victor's eyes darted to Stanley.

"Why? It's where we're from," Lee said.

"They said we are no longer Earthlings. We should consider ourselves Eartholians," Stanley said. "Makes sense."

The Eartholians weighed the word. Slowly, they nodded.

The Tholians nodded as well.

"Yes, I understand how that makes a difference," Jor-Dan said.

Victor nudged Stanley.

Stanley's eyebrow quirked up in question.

"Stanley has an announcement," Victor said.

The lightbulb blinked in Stanley's head. "Oh. I almost forgot. They chose me to replace Swezek, the Egrom elder who passed away."

It stunned everyone into silence. Forks stayed hanging in the air, mouths open.

Trakon and Jor-Dan made eye contact, then Trakon and D'laine. They were clearly shocked.

"The Egroms chose someone not of Thol? Not even their own race?" Trakon asked.

Stanley shrugged. "If they were going to choose anyone among us, I would have thought they'd choose D'laine, Brian or Victor."

"Why me?" Brian asked.

"Because you can detect the portals better than the Egroms," Stanley said.

"Why me?" Victor asked. "I've barely just arrived and don't know my way around."

"You can see the future," D'laine said. "I'm glad they didn't choose me. That seems like a big responsibility."

"It will mean a lot of stepping back and forth. I hope I can get to the bottom of this business with them not answering questions, or answering so esoterically we can't understand them," Stanley said.

"That would be very helpful," Kitry said, "especially about the prophecy. Maybe you can find out more information."

"I'm not sure what the rules are to being an Egrom elder," Stanley said. "It seems as if there are some restrictions between what the world knows and what the Egroms pass along to us." He stabbed another bite, chewed and swallowed. "There may be an initiation ceremony, some kind of swearing in. You know how mysterious they can be."

"If anyone is suited for this, you're the right person," Ben said.

They talked about the educational movies; the comment Adrum made about a full library.

Lee and Victor looked ecstatic.

"It took Adrum less than thirty minutes to convert all the books into movies," Kara exclaimed. "All grades! I'll bet these Egroms could take the entire Library of Congress and convert them in a single month!"

Lee, Victor, Ben and Stanley smiled gleefully. They looked like a bunch of boys in a candy shop with fifty bucks.

"We need to make a list," Lee said.

"Can't we go to specific libraries when they're closed for the day, grab the books and return them when they've been converted?" Victor asked. "I think it would be too much to ask Al to do this."

The Tholians' heads ping-ponged back and forth following the speakers.

"We could have Al look up the physical addresses," Stanley said. "I could go there, stack the books, then Ben could bring them over."

All the adults nodded, even if they didn't understand exactly how it worked.

The boys followed the adult conversations as best they could.

"What if you get caught?" Brian asked.

"Yeah, what if there're cameras in those places," Darren asked.

Jamie kept out of it. All he knew was that school was back

on. He visualized his days of running wild and flying off on Ekka's back shrinking.

"We don't have to make any decisions right now," Kara said. "You can think about these things for the time being."

After dinner finished, the Eartholian men climbed the stairs to Lee's suite. The rest of the group went to the main salon.

THE NEXT MORNING, JAMIE WAS WANDERING EBSCALON. HE ended up in the garden and stomped on some pecans. He picked through the shells and ate the meat. After several nuts, he filled his pockets with pecans.

A bird-beast landed on the ground in front of him and stared intently at his face. The critter had a purple flat bill instead of a beak. It had bright blue, orange and purple furry-fuzzy feathers on its head and body, stubby orange legs and clawed feet.

"Hello there," Jamie said. He looked up at the top of the pecan tree. "Your nest is up there?" He listened some more. "Okay, I'm probably going to need some help."

Jamie tapped his communicator and pulled up his contacts. "Stanley? I need your help in the garden."

Within a blink, Stanley was beside him.

"What's going on?" Stanley looked at the strange bird. "Who's this?"

"I don't think she has a name, but her nest is way up at the top of the pecan tree. She said a large predator bird keeps attacking her. She doesn't know where her mate is. He's been gone a long time."

Stanley covered his eyes with one hand and peered to the top of the tree. "No problem. You ready?"

"Yeah," Jamie said.

Stanley levitated Jamie to the top of the tree. He latched onto a branch and looked into the nest. Four colorful eggs lay in a bed of moss in the woven stick nest. They looked like dyed Easter eggs from back home.

Jamie looked over the eggs in the nest. As he turned to talk to Stanley, a floff flew at Jamie. The Cocker Spaniel-like bird snapped at Jamie.

"Go! This isn't your nest. Leave these eggs alone!" Jamie yelled into the floff's head, and verbally.

Stanley levitated to Jamie's side. He batted at the floff, but it was in attack mode. "We're going to need your sister for this one, Jamie."

They both called out silently to D'laine. Within a few minutes, D'laine, Lee, Brian, Darren, Victor and Kara ran into the garden. Trakon pulled up the rear.

"What's wrong?" Trakon asked, chest heaving. He sprinted all the way from the workshop area.

"Why are you up in that tree, son?" Lee asked.

"Stanley?" D'laine asked.

"This floff is attacking this bird's nest. She doesn't know where her mate is and she can't take care of her eggs and hunt at the same time," Jamie said.

AWAY! D'laine used The Voice at the floff.

The floff flew off a way, but didn't leave the area. It barked out its annoyance.

COME TO ME! D'laine blasted out the command.

The floff fell to the ground. It shook its head.

D'laine walked over to the bird-dog and stood over it. She spoke deep with The Voice. *Leave this dooba bird and her nest alone. Go now. Do not return here!*

The floff took flight and left the area.

"Stubborn creature!" D'laine said.

"Can someone help find her mate? The floff might have attacked him while he was hunting for food," Jamie said.

"Where would we look?" Trakon asked.

"I think I see it," Victor said. He jogged into the chocolate tree forest, the others following. Way into the depth of the forest, they found the bird on the ground, one of its wings broken. The poor bird scrabbled in a circle, one wing flapping.

"Oh, that poor thing," Kara said.

"Can you fix him, D'laine?" Brian asked.

Jamie dropped to the forest floor. He petted the bird on the head. "He said the floff chased after him and he crashed into a tree."

D'laine dropped to her knees beside her brother and the bird. She cupped her hands over the bird and closed her eyes. Her hands glowed in the shadows of the forest. Moments later, the bird was on its feet. It tested its wing. It rubbed its head against D'laine, then Jamie.

"He's very thankful that you saved him, D'laine," Jamie said. "He's going home now to check on his mate and their eggs."

The dooba took flight and weaved its way through the trees to the pecan tree.

"That's a strange-looking bird," Darren said.

"They mate for life," Trakon said. "I've heard that when one of them dies, the other goes into mourning for as long as a year."

"Oh, my goodness!" Kara said. "What lovely creatures."

D'laine took hold of Trakon's hand. "Why don't we go visit our eggs?"

Lee thought for a minute. "You realize it's been the equivalent of nine months... kelds since you passed your eggs? That would be the complete gestation period back on Earth. I wonder where they are in the Tholian sense of growth inside those shells."

"Only time will tell," Stanley said.

Jamie grabbed Stanley's hand. "Thanks for your help! I really appreciate it."

Stanley fluffed Jamie's hair. "That's what it's all about, Jamie. Helping people and creatures."

D'LAINE AND TRAKON APPROACHED THE DOOR WHERE HALVID AND Amoroso guarded the entryway to the turret room. Halvid opened the door after greeting them, then the princess and prince of Ebscalon climbed the stairs to the turret room. Zedonia and Felid tapped their chests as D'laine and Trakon entered the room.

It was peaceful in the open turret room. The guards retreated to the stairwell, and the anxious parents stood before their growing children. D'laine gently pressed a hand on the darker egg. The shells were the size of extra-large pumpkins. She stayed still with her eyes closed for several long minutes. Then she ran a hand over the lighter-colored egg.

D'laine touched Trakon's arm. "I don't want you to panic, but I'm going to do something, okay?"

Trakon looked apprehensive. "What are you going to do? Why should I worry?"

She didn't answer him. She closed her eyes. When she opened them, there was a blankness to them, as if she were staring through a blind spot in the air. D'laine reached inside the darker shell and withdrew their daughter.

Trakon was so shocked he seemed mute for the longest time.

D'laine turned to him. "This is what an Earth baby looks like at the end of nine months, when they are born."

Trakon sucked in a breath. "She's so beautiful! So tiny. She looks like you with your golden hair."

D'laine studied the tiny infant in her arms. "She has your eyes, Trakon. Would you like to hold her?"

He appeared very nervous, then shook it off. "Yes!"

D'laine transferred their daughter to Trakon's waiting arms. He let out a swoosh of a breath when he looked down on the baby in his arms. "I promise to protect you." He kissed her fore-head, adoration practically glowing from him.

D'laine retrieved the baby and placed her back into the protective shell. Next, she reached into the lighter shell and extracted their son. He was slightly larger than his sister and had a shock of black hair and blue eyes.

"Oh, baby boy, you are so handsome, just like your father!" D'laine said.

Trakon ran his fingers through the baby's hair. His skin was almost the same shade of bronze.

D'laine transferred the baby to his father's arms.

Trakon held him with such emotion. "Oh, D'laine. Now I understand what Tholians are missing. To hold my son and daughter in my arms is the most fulfilling feeling I have ever experienced. Do they have to return to the shells?"

"I don't know," D'laine said. "We should ask the Visionary or the Egroms."

She took the baby from Trakon and held him up to her shoulder. "Oh, baby. I love you so much." She kissed the infant on the forehead then lowered him through the shell.

Trakon crushed her to him. "Oh, D'laine. I love you so much." He kissed her passionately.

CHAPTER TWENTY-THREE

*V*ictor woke from a deep sleep to the flashing sky. His stomach grumbled, letting him know it was breakfast time. The other side of the bed was empty. He pulled himself out of the bed and sauntered to the bathroom. Kara was washing her hair in the pool. He removed his sleeping clothes and walked down the stairs into the perfect temperature of water.

"Good morning. Did you sleep well?" Kara asked.

"I slept like a log," Victor said. He dove under the water, surfaced, then flung his hair back. It had been months since he had had a haircut, and his once-trimmed hair was now sitting on his shoulders. He liked it, and knew that Kara liked it even more.

Victor poured shampoo into his hand and washed his hair, then returned to the side of the pool for body wash.

Kara was already out of the pool and drying off, when she turned to say something to her husband. She stared, then jumped into action. Victor was standing stone-still, hands at his side, eyes wide, staring into space.

"Victor! Victor, can you hear me?" Kara yelled in panic. She jumped into the pool and was immediately at his side. She gently touched his arm. He was pale and shaking. "Oh, god! What's wrong? Can you hear me? Can you say something?"

Suddenly, he shivered and snapped out of his trance. He startled when he saw the stricken expression on his wife's face. "What's wrong?"

"What's wrong? You were in this trance, staring like a statue," Kara said, her voice hitched high from raw nerves. "Are you okay? What happened?"

Victor abruptly was in motion. He thrashed through the water to the edge of the pool, practically ran up the stairs and grabbed a towel. "There's a storm coming. A huge, devastating storm, Kara. I need to warn everyone!"

He had barely dried off, when he was climbing into a clean tunic, similar to what the Visionary wore.

Kara rushed to dry off and dress into her sari-type dress and sandals. She practically ran out the door, trying to keep up with Victor.

He headed to the dining salon where friendly morning chatter was heard as they approached the room. His rushed entrance forced all eyes onto his taut face.

Jor-Dan was on his feet immediately, as was Trakon. Kitry sat, her face frozen with fear, as she saw the expression on Victor's face.

"What's wrong?" Jor-Dan asked.

Victor sucked in a deep breath to steady himself. "A devastating storm is approaching!" His eyes jerked from Lee to Stanley to D'laine, then the boys. "This is worse than a cat five hurricane. It's like nothing we ever experienced on Earth."

The Visionary hurried into the dining salon.

"A churling!" Kitry belted out.

"We haven't had a churling in several years," Jor-Dan said.

The Visionary nodded to Victor. "Your prediction is correct."

He addressed Jor-Dan. "You are in good hands. I will return to the temple and keep watch."

"Very good, Alatheers," Jor-Dan said.

The Visionary retreated from the room, his hands tucked into the sleeves of his tunic.

"The storm is quite a distance away, but moving fast. There's less than a week to prepare," Victor said. He pulled up a map from his communicator. He circled an area far, far away. "This is where the storm is right now. It's raging like nothing I've ever seen before."

They all came closer to view the map. They saw the wide trajectory of the storm.

Trakon jumped into action. "We need to alert all our citizens, all the kingdoms, the Egroms, the Kudaja, and Jakla's city. The construction sites could prove deadly for the Plotals."

"I'll step to the Cember Forest people and the Egroms," Stanley said, then he was gone.

Trakon tapped his communicator. "Klaxor, we just found out a devastating churling is approaching. We have less than a week to prepare. Get everything battened down."

Jor-Dan was talking on his communicator, calling all the kingdoms to warn them.

"D'laine, we need to move the eggs," Trakon said. He was in complete control.

"Where should we move them to? Our suite?" D'laine asked.

Trakon shook his head. "No, there's a catacomb of rooms below the palace. We reinforced them as a safe place for all of us, plus the advisors. It can hold hundreds of people comfortably. We'll arrange for Stanley to move the eggs and their vessels when we have everything in place. Don't worry. We have time."

"You take care of that, I'm going to the communal hatching center to make sure our future generations are protected as well," Kitry said, as she sped out of the room.

The majordomo rushed to the kitchen to inform Grubio.

They should begin to move provisions downstairs. The chaos from one of these storms could wipe out the food storage.

"Bring breakfast to the dining salon and leave the dishes on the table," Grubio instructed his staff. "The royals will eat when they finish with the initial preparations."

The staff hurried to place the breakfast items on the table in the dining salon.

Jor-Dan nodded to the staff. "Thank you."

Trakon pressed his communicator again. He searched the menu for the alert button, then spoke with a strong voice. "This is your prince. A devastating churling is approaching Ebscalon. There is less than a week to prepare. Remove everything from the marketplace. Batten down anything outside that can't be moved. Help your neighbors. Store food and water where you plan to evacuate."

"Trakon, set that so it will repeat every hour or two," Jor-Dan said.

Stanley stepped back into the room. "The Egroms plan to evacuate to the forest. Ghury said that their mushrooms may not survive. The Kudaja are a little safer, even up in the trees, due to the way they built the city. They are taking precautions."

"Should we send help to Jakla?" Lee asked. "I keep thinking of all those building materials, plus the portion of the tent city that's still being used."

Jor-Dan and Trakon nodded.

"I can help with that," Stanley said. "I'll be able to move things faster than they can with manpower."

"First, let me send for Dreboo so that his team of engineers can assess the catacombs," Trakon said.

"You call him. I'll work with him," Lee said. "I'll make sure we'll be safe down there."

"Okay, Stanley, let's go to Ta'Byu'Vohon," Trakon said. They were gone as the words left his mouth.

STANLEY AND TRAKON APPEARED BEFORE A LARGE BUILDING, AND in front of four Plotals.

The Plotals hissed loudly in warning, the pods on their tails opening to show the deadly barbs. A squadron of guards surrounded Stanley and Trakon.

Trakon raised a hand in front of him. "We've come to alert you of the approaching churling, and to help move your building supplies and anything else you require help with."

Jakla's aide overheard the commotion. He ran to where the commander was and alerted him to the visitors.

Jakla strode over to the place his aide showed where the visitors were waiting. He took in the defensive postures of his workers and guards. "Don't you recognize the Prince of Ebscalon? Why wasn't I contacted when they arrived?"

The head guard pounded on his chest in greeting to his commander. "I was about to contact you when you arrived."

"A little too late," Jakla growled. He turned to his visitors. "My warriors have a long way to go to become more hospitable."

"There's no harm done," Trakon said. "There's a deadly churling approaching. There's less than a week to prepare." He explained the timeline and how Stanley would help.

Jakla looked around his city. Building materials were stacked everywhere that construction was taking place. "What is the best plan of action?"

"Which of the projects is the closest to completion?" Trakon asked.

Jakla pointed to a building with minimal construction materials around it. "This requires only two more turns to completion."

"Tell your men work on that. Maybe double the number of workers so they can finish in one turn. Move everything else into the forest where the trees will protect it. It's too dangerous out here in the open," Trakon said.

"Do your people have a safe place to get through the storm?" Stanley asked.

"We will ride out the storm in the densest part of the forest," Jakla said. "I've been through several of these and I know how treacherous they are."

"Show me what I can move into the forest," Stanley said.

Jakla summoned Bist, the city planner. Stanley left with Bist to begin the teleportation of materials. Then the commander summoned Bist's assistants.

"Tell the women to dismantle all the tents. Just stack and bind them, and the human will transport them to safety," Jakla said.

"Move the pakows to the forest," Trakon said. "You know how easily they panic. You don't want to try moving them when the storm hits, they'll bolt and run into danger."

Jakla pointed to the four guards. "Ride a mile or two into the forest and set up an area for the pakows."

The guards took off running to the pakow pens, mounted up and galloped toward the Ikley Forest.

Stanley and Bist materialized in front of Jakla and Trakon.

Bist tapped his chest. "Stanley moved a large portion of the materials. He has them wedged in between trees, so they will be more protected and will not fly around to endanger us or the beasts. We will protect them further by covering the stacks with tents."

Jakla turned to Trakon. "You should return to Ebscalon. You are a father now and must protect your family."

They gripped each other's arms in the common greeting.

"We owe a great debt to you for this warning and the help," Jakla said.

"I'll be back as soon as I get Trakon home," Stanley said. He stepped Trakon back to the palace, then returned to continue helping the Plotals.

T<small>RAKON RETURNED TO HIGH ACTIVITY THROUGHOUT</small> E<small>BSCALON</small>. Merchants were securing their wares in their buildings and homes. The marketplace was emptying all loose materials that would be dangerous if left to the elements.

The palace was a whirlwind of activity. He found D'laine in the turret with the eggs, and the women warriors. He pecked her on the lips. "Where is your father and Dreboo? Do you know if they finished the assessment of the catacombs?"

"They're still down there," D'laine said. Her nerves were stretched tight. She remembered too many hurricanes in Houston. All the flooding, damage to buildings and the environment year after year, kept a lot of people on edge.

"When the catacombs are determined safe for our children, Stanley will transport them down there," Trakon said. "He's helping the Plotals move all that building material into the Ikley Forest."

"That's the best way to transport the eggs without any danger," D'laine said.

Pup was stuck against D'laine's side. He felt the tension, but didn't know what was wrong. She scratched his head subconsciously.

The door downstairs opened, and the dog was on his feet, teeth clacking.

"It's me," Lee called out. Then he headed up the stairs. "Is it safe to enter the room?"

"Yes, come in, Dad," D'laine said. "Pup's on edge, not knowing what's going on."

Lee entered the room. His eyes zeroed in on the diwal dog at his daughter's side. "Dreboo and I finished going through the entire catacombs. Everything appears in good shape. We couldn't see any stress fractures or cracks. As soon as Stanley returns, he can transport barrels of water for drinking, and a manual flushing system for bathrooms."

"Do you know if anyone checked the periscope?" Trakon asked.

"Periscope?" Lee asked. "Where is it? I can check it out."

"Let's go, you'll never find it on your own," Trakon said. He turned to D'laine. "Sit tight. It's not time to panic yet." He pecked her a kiss on the lips, then he and her father took off down the stairs.

THE CATACOMBS WERE THREE FLIGHTS OF STAIRS UNDER THE palace. Lighting globes floated in designated areas. Trakon walked Lee through a maze of rooms to a central place where an outdated piece of equipment was on a table.

"This is a manual system of communications, in case our communicators don't function," Trakon said.

He walked across the room to what Lee considered a replica of an Earth periscope from a submarine.

Trakon pulled the viewer around, folded down two armrests, and rested his arms on them. He looked through the viewer. "I think the mirror topsides has fallen."

He stepped out of the way so that Lee could look through the device. "I think it's still there, but may have slipped. I can see a tiny, shiny spot. Let's go check it out and get it repaired."

Trakon repositioned the periscope. "Need to lower it a bit so we can inspect the mirror."

They climbed up the three flights of stairs, exited the palace and walked around to a ladder built into the exterior palace wall. Trakon took to the ladder first, with Lee following. They arrived at a high point on the roof, and walked to where the periscope pipe stuck through the roof at knee height.

He and Lee took turns inspecting the pipe and mirror.

"The mirror dislodged from its post," Lee said. "I don't see any cracks, so if we can grab it, we can reattach it."

Trakon stuck his fingers down the pipe. He couldn't reach the mirror.

"This is one of those times we could really use chewing gum," Lee said.

Trakon raised his eyebrows in question, but Lee shrugged him off.

"Maybe Brian can reach it. His hands and fingers are much smaller than ours," Lee said. He summoned Brian and mentally walked him to where they were on the roof.

Brian climbed up the ladder and saw his father and brother-in-law. "What's that?"

"A periscope, like in a submarine," Lee said. "See if you can stick your fingers in here and grab that little piece of mirror."

Brian looked into the pipe, stuck his fingers in and pulled the mirror out.

"Thanks, son," Lee said.

"Need me to stick around and put it back in place?" Brian asked.

"Nope, it's supposed to sit right here near the edge," Lee said.

"Okay. See ya!" Brian said. He walked back to the ladder and disappeared over the edge of the roof.

They inspected the piece of mirror.

Trakon tapped his communicator. "Dannin, bring a bead of agrin sap up on the roof. I have to reattach the mirror to the periscope."

"Be right there," Dannin said, then tapped off.

"Those agrin trees are something else. That sap is the most diverse byproduct I've ever encountered," Lee said.

A few minutes later, Dannin stepped onto the roof. He

presented a small container of a yellow, gooey substance to Trakon. "This should be more than enough."

Trakon nodded. "Thanks. This should do it."

Dannin climbed back down the ladder.

Trakon smeared the agrin sap to the surface where the mirror mounted. Then he unhooked his laser weapon from its holder and twisted it until a click sounded.

He pressed a button on his suit and a shielded, clear form raised to protect his eyes.

"Don't look into this light until your form is in place, or the beam will damage your vision," he said. He showed Lee which button to press on his suit. When he had eye protection in place, Trakon secured the mirror to its post inside the pipe with his laser.

"That will take a little while to cool down," Trakon said. "Lee, why don't you go back downstairs and let me know if I need to make any adjustments to the angle."

"Okay, give me a few minutes," Lee said. He climbed over the edge of the building and descended the ladder.

After several minutes, Trakon noticed the periscope raising to its full height. It twisted and turned in all directions. His communicator beeped an incoming call from Lee.

"Everything looks good from down here. I saw the layout of the entire city, so we'll be able to assess damage and any problems."

"Okay, thanks. I'll head your way," Trakon said.

LEE AND TRAKON WALKED THROUGH THE CATACOMBS, CHECKING out each area. There was a bathroom area divided into male and female.

"We better set up a bathroom area for the dogs here," Lee said. "We'll also need to provide them with a water bowl."

"We should haul in several squares of moss," Trakon said. "We'll have to find a place to dispose of it daily."

"How long do you think we'll be down here?" Lee asked.

"It might be several turns. These storms are unpredictable. I've only experienced one, but I know from the histories of our people, that they can cause severe damage. If I'm not mistaken, a terrible one came through Ebscalon before I was hatched, that was responsible for many deaths."

Trakon worked his communicator and ordered workers to prepare for the dogs. He and Lee walked upstairs to the main salon. Kara informed them that Victor was with the Visionary, Jor-Dan was with his advisors, Kitry hadn't returned from the hatching center, and the boys were running wild. She hadn't seen D'laine yet, so she assumed she was still upstairs in the tower.

Stanley popped into the room.

"Are the Plotals all set?" Trakon asked.

"They're well underway. I've moved all their building materials and most of the tents are dismantled. They'll be roughing it in the forest for a while," Stanley said. "I told Jakla I'd return tomorrow to move their tents to the forest, and anything else that would be too burdensome for them."

"There's a lot you can help with here," Lee said. "There're dozens of barrels of water you can move to the catacombs, and I'm sure Grubio could use your help with food stores."

"Where are the water barrels?" Stanley asked.

"Outside the kitchen exterior door," Trakon said. "Grubio can show you where to put them downstairs. After that, we want you to move our children downstairs."

"There's a periscope on the roof, Stan," Lee said. "You may have to move debris during the storm so it stay's functional."

"A periscope, huh? Wonder who borrowed from whom?" Stanley asked. He headed to the kitchen. He latched onto the barrels and mentally held onto Grubio. Since he had never transported the chef, or anything else to the catacombs, he wanted to make sure everything arrived where it was supposed to.

Grubio showed Stanley the kitchen area. Stanley set the barrels where the chef suggested.

"Shouldn't we place barrels of water throughout the catacombs for people to access water?" Stanley asked.

"When we determine how many people and where they will be, we can distribute barrels to those areas," Grubio said.

They beamed back to the kitchen for more barrels and other heavy things the kitchen people required help with. Then Stanley stepped into the turret room.

He found Trakon pacing the floor, while D'laine sat in front of the eggs. "Ready to move the nests?"

Trakon called the warrior women at the bottom of the stairs to come up top. "Would you be able to transport all of us at one time?"

"Sure. Everyone gather around the eggs. I'll even take Pup with us," Stanley said. As soon as he finished talking, they were in the catacombs. "Where did you set up the temporary nursery?"

Trakon escorted Stanley to the room set aside for his children. Stanley levitated the eggs in their nests. They all walked behind Trakon to the room where he, D'laine, and Pup would stay while the storm raged outside. The warrior women would take shifts. Half would be stationed outside the room when Trakon and D'laine slept. The other half would sleep. Then they would swap times being inside the room during the times Trakon had duties to perform.

BRIAN, JAMIE AND DARREN RETURNED TO THE PALACE AFTER spending time with Ekka. They cleaned up for dinner and went to the dining salon. They could feel the tension wafting through the room.

"Where were you?" Lee and Kara asked at the same time.

"We were talking to Ekka... rather, Jamie was talking to Ekka, and we listened and offered advice," Brian said.

"Ekka's going to fly to the mountains and stay in his old cave," Jamie said.

CHAPTER TWENTY-FOUR

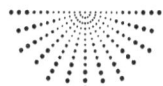

*E*verything that required being tied down in the city was secure. The boys lugged baskets of pecan nuts to the catacombs. They included tomato plant cuttings and chocolate pods for Grubio to preserve the newly cultivated Earth foods.

The marketplace was as quiet as a ghost town. The entire city was boarded up or locked down. All the ships were in their hangers. The palace staff, the royals and everyone who lived in the palace were down in the catacombs.

"What about the Visionary's temple?" Lee asked. "Will that dome-covered planet survive?"

"It's protected," Victor said.

"How?" Lee asked. He couldn't get his head around it. The replica of the planet hovered in air with clouds surrounding it, under the glass dome.

Victor pursed his lips. "Let's just say that the energy of Thol protects it."

Lee struggled with some of the concepts in his short time on the planet, but he understood Thol was radically different from Earth. In the sharing of space through the dimensional portals, these two realms were the equivalent of day and night. Earth was a tumultuous planet with warring nations. The people who strived to bring love, peace and change to the planet were gathering strength, but it would be eons before they succeeded.

Thol, while the most beautiful paradise Lee had ever seen, was a wild, dangerous place. But he loved it here and would never return to his former life. He hoped his sons would never want to return to that other place either.

He watched D'laine hover near her eggs. The shells were so large now, it was possible to guess at the size of the baby inside. When he touched the shells, he felt a response from inside. D'laine told him her children knew he was their grandfather and already loved him.

Lee made Ethaderia and her staff join him in the catacombs. While her house had a safe room underground, it was small and didn't have all the amenities that were required for what might be a lengthy stay underground.

Kara had become great friends with Kitry and her cousin. The three women spent a lot of time together weaving, discussing the education of the boys, the running of the palace and every subject in between.

"I hope we didn't overlook anything," Jor-Dan said. He fretted to Trakon, Stanley, Victor, Marrak, Lee and Dannin.

"Where are the pakows?" Trakon asked. "I can't believe I didn't think about them!"

"They're in the forest," Dannin said. "They should be okay. Hopefully, they will lie down on the forest floor. Maybe Jamie should talk to them!"

Trakon mentally searched the catacombs for Jamie and requested his presence.

The boys trotted into the room. Jamie saw the concern on the men's faces. "What's wrong? Did something happen?"

"Everything's okay, son," Lee said.

"Jamie, can you talk to Lulu and tell her to lay down on the forest floor? She needs to tell all the pakows to lie down so they are more protected," Trakon said.

"Sure, I can give it a try," Jamie said. His forehead wrinkled as he thought hard. "She said okay. She laid down, and she's sending me pictures of all the other pakows lying down. They're scared."

Jor-Dan fretted again. "When this is over, we need to consider building an underground place for the animals."

Jamie's face lit up. "Maybe Ekka…"

"Son, Ekka would think we gifted him a buffet," Lee said.

Jamie's face flushed. "Oh, yeah. I wasn't thinking."

Stanley was looking through the periscope. "Holy smokes! This must be the churling!"

The normally flashing, bright sky was ominously black. Huge clouds rolled over the city and settled. Wind and rain lashed at buildings. Stanley saw chunks of roofs hurled through the air and slamming into buildings and houses.

"My god! I hope we can survive this," he said.

Trakon looked at a gauge he had installed. It measured rain and wind. "The wind is 2.25 DPH."

Lee, Stanley and Victor did the translation in their heads.

"Two-hundred twenty-five miles per hour?" Victor gasped.

"And it seems to be hovering," Jor-Dan said. He looked through the periscope. "I suspect it will double that speed over the next few hours."

Brian wandered over. "Do you think the baseball stadium seats will be okay?"

Trakon and Lee shared a thoughtful glance.

"We engineered those seats for the weight of the Plotals and Egroms. Since they aren't solid… the air should pass through them. I don't think there will be major damage to them," Lee said.

D'laine joined the group. "I hope everyone took the storm warning seriously and prepared."

"We're in it now, and there's not much we can do about anyone who didn't prepare," Jor-Dan said.

"There are always those who think they can ride out one of these churlings," Dannin said. "We were lucky for an advance warning."

Everyone focused on Victor.

"You'd tell us if we were doomed, wouldn't you?" Stanley asked.

Victor huffed. "No one's doomed. Everything is going to be okay. As Dannin said, we had time to prepare."

FOUR MORE TENSE TURNS PASSED. EVERY ONCE IN A WHILE, A staticky communication would come through from someone in the city, letting them know what was happening in their area.

Trakon heard over his communicator that someone's house had blown apart, and that the Ciertron family was huddled in their exposed underground shelter, trying not to be blown away.

"Do you think it would be safe for me to go there and bring them here?" Stanley asked.

Everyone was tense as they thought about it.

Trakon walked over to the device that recorded the wind and rain. "Wind is 5.38 DPH."

The scientists gasped in shock. This was more than a superstorm.

"Do you need to go there, or can you bring them over from here?" Lee asked.

Stanley shook his head. "I don't know. I've never tried to do that from afar." He looked over to Victor. "You don't see me dead or hurt, do you?"

"No," Victor said. "You should be okay, but because of the

wind, you have to be quick—faster than you've ever been before."

"They're huddled together, so you should be able to step there and step back in a blink," Trakon said.

"Okay, here goes," Stanley said. He disappeared.

Several minutes passed. It was longer than they all expected and nerves were on edge.

Stanley materialized with the traumatized family. They were drenched, and the three children were crying and scared.

"I almost didn't make it," Stanley said. "My trajectory was a little off, and I landed in the open area. It took everything I had to not be blown away!"

"Thank you for saving us," the man said.

"Let me show you where you can clean up, dry off and get some food," Trakon said.

He led them out of the room to a different area. Kara approached them, concern clearly covering her face.

"Oh, my Thol! What happened?" Kara asked.

"These people almost got blown away when their roof detached," Trakon said. "Stanley rescued them."

Kara knelt in front of the children. "You're safe now. Let's get you dry and something to eat, shall we?"

The children and parents nodded, shocked into silence.

Kara led them away.

Trakon looked through the periscope. He noticed some shredded banners still flying on some nearby households. The wind was dying down; the storm dissipating.

Ghury appeared in the room.

D'laine rushed up to him. "You're safe! Was your village damaged? What of the Kudaja?"

"We lost quite a few of our homes, but our mushrooms grow

rapidly, so we will replant," Ghury said. "The Kudaja lost a boardwalk, but they will use a temporary rope bridge system when the storm passes."

"No lives lost?" Jor-Dan asked.

"No lives lost," Ghury confirmed.

"The storm should completely dissipate within the next ten hours," Trakon said. "Then we will assess the damage."

The three boys, along with the three rescued children, ran screeching down the hallway with the dogs romping with them.

Lee left the group and stepped into the hall.

"Stop running right this minute, or you're grounded!" Lee hollered.

The six kids screeched to a halt and regrouped. They snuck off to a small room in the catacombs with the dogs panting happily after them.

TRAKON LED AN ADVANCED TEAM OUT OF THE CATACOMBS TO THE palace above. Dreboo, the architect, and his team of engineers met Trakon, Jor-Dan, Lee, Victor and Stanley at the main entrance of the palace.

They split up to inspect every room and floor in the enormous building. Dreboo and two others headed to the kitchen. Trakon and Lee climbed the stairs to the turret room, the others split up to assigned quadrants.

They looked for stress fractures with the help of floating light globes to brighten dark corners. Until the clouds lifted, they required the lights to inspect all the walls, ceilings, floors, cabinets and closets.

Dreboo discovered a fracture inside the cold closet in the kitchen. He and one of his engineers assessed the damage. They determined they could repair it with their laser tools, which they went about quickly. They knew Grubio would be eager to put his kitchen back together again.

"Trace this fracture overhead," Dreboo instructed an engineer.

The engineer gathered a helper and headed up the main staircase. They traced the fracture to the roof and made repairs as they were discovered. Next, they left the palace and walked around to the back where the kitchen was. The outside wall contained damage as well. It was more severe than the inside fractures.

Dreboo was summoned to that location. He called Trakon, Lee, Stanley and Victor. He wanted all engineers to assess this heavy damage.

"We've repaired the fractures inside, all the way to the roof, but this exterior damage gives me cause to worry," Dreboo said.

Victor's eyes softened. No one realized anything was off until Stanley was about to talk to him.

"Victor?" Stanley called out.

Lee held up a hand. "He's getting something. He'll come back out of this when he has all the information."

Everyone watched as the Eartholian appeared to be sleeping on his feet. Suddenly, Victor shuddered and became alert.

"In four months, this fracture will deteriorate. It happens at a very busy time of the day. There will be a loss of life. To change the future, remove everything from the two interior walls. Then deconstruct this exterior corner and rebuild it with stronger material."

Trakon thought about it. He pulled up the building plans. There was an empty space that hadn't been used in several paths. It used to be a breakfast room. "We can tear down this wall and move the cooking equipment to that location."

"You'll have to re-route the ventilation." Lee pointed to the plans where the original ventilation over the cooking surfaces were. He traced the lines on the plans, which lit up and showed where the new ventilation should go.

The engineering team members checked in, one by one. No one detected any damage.

"The turret room is safe," Lee said. "We'll have to remove some debris, but there are no structural fractures."

"Father, we should alert the people it's safe to leave their places of shelter," Trakon said.

"Direct people to the throne room to report any damage," Jor-Dan said. "Marrak will compile a list of the worst of the damage, and we can have teams throughout the city helping with the cleanup."

"Stanley, we will need your help to move the kitchen appliances when the wall has been removed," Dreboo said.

"Just call me and I'll be there," Stanley said.

Trakon sent the alert. The city slowly began to come to life. Everyone left the catacombs and were assigned to outside cleanup.

The majordomo, Grubio and the rest of the kitchen staff groaned over the damage to the kitchen. They began by emptying cabinets of cooking and storage containers and moving them to the other room, while two engineers used laser cutters to open the room. They determined that the cold storage locker couldn't be moved.

Lee examined the locker, then the spice closet beside it. They sat on the wall of the exterior damaged area.

"Dreboo, it would be safe to cut out these two closets. Stanley could move them to the other wall, over there," Lee indicated.

The architect and city planner examined the plans, then studied the locker and closet. "Yes, I see what you mean. This will take a team cutting inside, and a team on the outside removing the building materials. It is much more efficient to move the locker and cabinet instead of rebuilding them."

Everyone agreed to the plan. Once everything else was removed from that wall, they hung a heavy-duty curtain from the ceiling to keep the restructuring dust restricted to the area of concern. With the laser tools, the work went quickly.

They called Stanley back to move the locker and closet. He studied the locker and the trajectory of where they wanted it. The locker was much heavier than the spice closet, so it was his biggest concern.

"Ben sure would be handy right about now," Stanley said. He stood about five feet in front of the locker and used both hands in a grabbing motion that latched onto the locker. He tugged with his mind. Something seemed stuck behind the locker.

"There's a section down the middle of the back of this thing that's still attached to the exterior," he said.

Dreboo rushed outside through the kitchen door. He and two engineers lasered the exterior debris away. They saw the problem right away and worked to release the one foot by five-foot length of hardened sandstone. They lasered through the material until it was free of any exterior material.

Dreboo tapped his communicator. "Can you hear me? Tell Stanley to give it another try."

They watched as the locker smoothly moved, leaving a gigantic gap in the wall. Dreboo rushed back inside through the opening and watched as the scientist slowly and carefully levitated the enormously heavy cold storage locker through the kitchen into the other room. Stanley settled the locker where Grubio wanted it.

Next, Stanley moved the spice cabinet. It was large, but was much lighter than the locker. Once they were in place, his next request was to move the cooking appliances.

CHAPTER TWENTY-FIVE

*M*arrak had his hands full. The throne room was filled to capacity with citizens reporting damage to their homes or businesses. Jor-Dan snagged Brian, Kara and D'laine to help. They had all watched the proceedings and understood how Marrak recorded incidents.

Brian surprised everyone with his insight in recording the damage. Marrak made Brian his second in command.

"Is the damage strictly on the roof, or have the exterior walls been affected as well?" Brian asked a man.

"The east side of the roof. There's also a crack down the wall," the man said.

"Okay," Brian said. "I hope you understand that we will assess all damage in the order of the direst, on down. Don't be discouraged, we won't ignore anyone. It will take time for the engineers to see to everyone's problems."

The man nodded and stepped out of line. He was replaced with someone else who needed to report damage.

Kara had just finished up with a report. The man had left the line when she looked up and called him back. "There was something else you didn't report."

The man looked at her, oddly. "No, I've reported all the damage."

Kara shook her head, adamant.

The man thought for a minute. "My intended's wedding attire was ruined."

Kara nodded. "Yes, that's it. I will note that on a different form."

"You would replace her wedding finery?" the man asked, astounded.

"This type of loss is a deep, heartfelt loss," Kara explained. "You go tell her not to worry."

Marrak stared at Kara. "How did you know that?"

Kara shrugged. "It came into my head. That's all I can tell you."

IT TOOK THE FOUR OF THEM A SOLID THREE TURNS TO LOG ALL the damage reports. There were two dire emergencies. A displaced roof was balancing precariously between two buildings, one edge sloping down. Engineers looked the problem over. The roof was in good shape. They requested that Stanley levitate it back to where it belonged, and they bolted it into place.

The dye vats inside the hosk building somehow moved across the floor which caused water to flood the room. The water started to seep into the room where the male hosks temporarily lived while creating silk thread. Crews were working on those problems amid the shrieking hosks who feared they would drown.

Jugdaak, the pakow handler, reported to Marrak that he was missing one pakow. "She may return to the pens, but I bet she'll return to the wild."

Power to the crestrider building had failed. They couldn't get the doors opened, so all crestriders were grounded.

"We're back to pakows," Trakon grumbled.

Lee and Victor headed over to the crestrider building to lend a hand. Stanley bowed out. He headed over to Ta'Byu'Vohon to move the building supplies and tents for the Plotals.

Jamie called Ekka back home. The giant borjo showed up with a lady friend. He had to explain the rules to her. She told Jamie her name was Foota.

"She needs to get used to being around people," D'laine told Jamie. "And how you and Ekka interact. Have her fly with you when you go somewhere. Once you trust her, have her take you on a short ride."

"Can we go to the Cember Forest? We want to make sure Chacoodi is okay," Jamie said.

"Okay, but don't stay away for a long time," D'laine said.

The three boys climbed up on Ekka's back and they took off to check on the Egroms and Kudaja. Foota flew beside Ekka.

They saw a pakow wandering around. Jamie pressed his communicator. "Jugdaak? I think we found your lost pakow." Jamie sent a mind picture to the pakow handler.

"Yeah, that's her! Thanks, pal," Jugdaak said.

Foota dove toward the pakow.

"No!" Jamie yelled. "You can't eat anything that's near the city. That pakow is not borjo food!"

Foota didn't want to obey, but Ekka took matters into his own wings and flew after his girlfriend. He nudged her—not gently. She changed her trajectory, and flew back up away from the now panicked pakow.

Jamie saw Jugdaak riding a pakow in the distance toward the lost cow. Ekka continued on to the Cember Forest, the boys clinging to him, with Foota following. They flew over the Egrom village. Several mushrooms were missing or toppled over. They saw Egroms on the ground gathering debris. Jamie aimed Ekka to the open field for a landing. Foota sailed beside him.

Chacoodi saw them and came running, happily yelling and waving to his friends.

Foota swooped in and grabbed Chacoodi and took to the air.

Jamie screamed in horror as the borjo flew off with his friend. Suddenly, Chacoodi was falling from the sky, flapping his hands.

An Egrom came running and stretched out his four hands toward the screaming Egrom boy. Chacoodi's fall slowed. The Egrom on the ground rotated him, and the boy gently landed on his feet.

Chacoodi dropped to the ground. He sprawled out, chest heaving from the fright. "Thank you for saving me!"

"You could have saved yourself. You require more training!" the Egrom said, then walked away.

Ekka landed nearby. Chacoodi scrambled away from Ekka's talons, looked around for the female borjo and ran toward the boys.

"Are you okay?" Brian yelled.

Chacoodi was breathing hard, his Egrom eyes wide as saucers. "Where did that new borjo come from?"

"Ekka brought her back after the storm," Jamie said. "I don't think she's going to be able to stay in Ebscalon. She tried to grab a pakow, then she almost killed you!"

"How'd you get loose?" Darren asked.

"I had to use my four hands to send shocks to her!" Chacoodi said. "I'm grateful for my uncle catching me. I would have gone splat on the ground."

"If D'laine and I can't make her understand the rules, she will have to return to the mountains," Jamie said. He patted Ekka. "I don't want to break Ekka's heart, but right now, Foota is too dangerous."

Ekka huffed some smoke through his nose. Jamie picked up

on his thoughts. The borjo was upset about what Foota did. He rose in the air and took off after his wayward girlfriend.

Jamie covered his eyes with his hand as he watched Ekka fly away. "I think he's going to explain things to her."

"I saw some mushrooms that fell over, and some that were missing," Darren said.

"Come look at the damage," Chacoodi said.

The boys ran across the moss through the village to the decimated area.

Brian looked around to get his bearings. "Was this Ghury's mushroom?"

"Yes! The storm tried to pull it out of the ground, but only tossed it over," Chacoodi said.

The boys looked at the gigantic fungi on its side, some of its roots still attached to the ground.

"I'm glad all of you stayed in the forest," Jamie said. "Was your house damaged?"

"No, my house survived," Chacoodi said. "Did you see the missing houses from the air?"

"Yeah, there's a whole circle of emptiness!" Darren said.

Brian bent and picked something off the ground. "Hey, here's a translator! I'll bet this came from Ghury's house."

The boys wandered around, snatching things off the ground. After a while their hands and pockets were full. Chacoodi brought them to where a table stood containing various items. They deposited their finds.

"Let's go see the Kudaja village," Brian said. "I heard the storm blew away a boardwalk!"

They ran toward the forest, Chacoodi leading the way. He stopped and pointed. The Kudaja were working to build another boardwalk, making modifications for heavy rain and wind.

"What are you boys doing here?" Herish called out from above.

Meeri ran down the stairs that wrapped around the side of an agrin tree. She presented them with the parental stink eye. "Does anyone know you're here?" She zeroed in on Chacoodi. "Did you ask Kestrum about leaving the village?"

Chacoodi's face lit up with fear. He rapidly shook his head.

"You'd better run back home," Meeri suggested.

Chacoodi turned to his friends. "I'll see you later!" He took off running.

Brian, Jamie and Darren wore expressions of innocence, although Brian was a little put off with Meeri's supervision. "D'laine said we could come here."

"Okay, at least someone knows you're not running wild," Meeri said. "How'd you get here?"

"Ekka flew us here," Jamie said.

"His girlfriend almost killed Chacoodi," Darren said.

Meeri's brows raised. "Girlfriend? Almost killed Chacoodi?"

The three boys took turns telling the story.

"A wild female borjo can't fly around here," Herish yelled. He talked to the workers, left them at the repairs and jogged down the stairs. "We have dozens of male borjos. They'd morph to full-size and fight, even though they've been neutered, they go crazy for a little while when a female is born or introduced."

"I don't think Ekka would like that at all," Jamie said. "We're not sure what we're going to do with Foota. She either has to follow the rules, or she has to go back to the mountains."

"Hi kids!" Ben waved from another boardwalk.

"Hi Ben!" they chorused.

Ben joined them on the ground. "I was heading over to the dining hall for lunch, want to join me?"

"Wow! This is like a cafeteria!" Brian said. "We don't have anything like this at Ebscalon, as far as I know."

Ben explained about the cooking and fire hazards and why no one had a kitchen in their house.

They ambled down the line and chose their food. With trays piled with plates of food, the boys followed Ben to a table and sat. They exchanged news while they ate.

"This churling storm was bigger than any storm Houston, or any other Gulf Coast location has ever experienced," Ben said. "I'm thankful they aren't seasonal every path."

"Did your house have any damage?" Darren asked.

Ben shook his head. "The way they secure houses and buildings in the trees, allows them to move with the trees. The boardwalk was the only damage that was significant."

"Ghury's mushroom house was knocked over!" Jamie blurted. "There's a bunch of mushrooms that got blown away."

"What about the palace? Did you have any significant damage?" Ben asked.

The boys took turns explaining about the kitchen and other problems they knew about.

"You'd better get going back home," Ben said. "You know what happens when you're gone too long."

"We'd better leave the forest so I can call Ekka," Jamie said.

Ben's face lit up. "Let me try to use my powers to send you home. Where do you want to end up?"

"Right outside the entrance to the palace," Brian said. "How will you know if we got there okay?"

"I have those coordinates and it shouldn't be any problem. I can materialize just about anything, anywhere," Ben said. "Ready?"

"Sure," Jamie said.

As Ben thought of the palace entryway, the boys disappeared.

THE BOYS MATERIALIZED AT THE PALACE ENTRANCE, BUMPING into Trakon, D'laine and the dogs, who had been leaving the palace.

"Oof! What the heck?" Trakon said.

"Sorry!" Brian said. "Ben sent us back from our visit."

"Where's Ekka?" D'laine asked. When she heard about the problems with the female borjo, her temper spiked. "Where's Foota now? We can't have a menace to the people, or our animals!"

"She may have flown back to the mountains," Jamie said. "I tried to talk to her about the rules, but she's stubborn! Ekka's going to explain things to her."

"That's not good enough!" Trakon said. "I can't believe she snatched up Chacoodi! Anyone travelling is now in danger!"

The boys were devastated over this new turn of events.

Jor-Dan emerged from the palace, followed by Marrak and Dannin. He zeroed in on the tension. "What's the matter? You all look very serious about something."

Lee wandered out of the palace.

Trakon ranted about Foota.

"She snatched Chacoodi?" Jor-Dan gasped.

"Call her here," D'laine said. "I'll deal with her and she WILL understand!"

Jamie called out silently to Foota.

Ekka and Foota circled the sky above Ebscalon.

"Call them down," D'laine told Jamie.

Ekka! Foota! Come down here!

Ekka gracefully landed in the plaza. Foota circled above, irritating D'laine.

"I need to teach this borjo some manners," D'laine said. *Foota! Down! Fly Down Now! Land here!*

The borjo ignored D'laine's request to land. D'laine summoned The Voice.

FOOTA—DOWN!

The female borjo almost dropped out of the sky. She landed with a slight thud in the plaza.

Ekka's shoulders were hunched up while he tried to get as close to the ground as possible. The dogs were all down on their bellies.

D'laine walked up to the female borjo. She forcefully spoke with The Voice. YOU WILL FOLLOW THE RULES! IF *YOU ARE TO LIVE HERE WITH EKKA, YOU WILL PROTECT EBSCALON! YOU WILL NOT EAT OUR PEOPLE, DOGS, PAKOWS, OR ANYONE HERE! YOU WILL NEVER EAT AN EGROM, KUDAJA OR A PLOTAL. YOU WILL FLY FAR AWAY FROM HERE TO HUNT AND EAT. DO YOU UNDERSTAND?*

Foota shivered with fear. She bowed her head to D'laine in understanding.

"We will care for you, Foota, for as long as you live here. Okay, fly away!" D'laine said.

Ekka and Foota took to the skies. Ekka headed toward his tower with Foota following.

"Will both of them fit in there?" Trakon asked.

"Yeah, Foota is smaller than Ekka," Lee said.

The dogs eyed D'laine warily and got up. She squatted down and patted each of them.

"It's okay. You're not the problem," she said.

CHAPTER TWENTY-SIX

*S*tanley moved all the Ta'Byu'Vohon building materials back to where Bist had showed him. He helped clear away materials from a collapsed framework, and then helped the female Plotals by depositing the tents in their designated areas.

"Your buildings are strong to remain standing through that churling," Stanley said.

"We learned long ago from our ancestors that if you're going to build anything, it must withstand the elements of Thol," Bist said.

"Back on Earth, we have storms called hurricanes and tornados. They are violent storms with great winds and flooding rains, but your churling is ten times more dangerous than anything I have ever experienced," Stanley said.

"We plan to excavate and build something similar to your catacombs," Bist said. "My team will have to meet with Dreboo to discuss that, but right now our main focus is to complete our build-out of the city and homes for our people."

Jakla approached. "Ebscalon is safe?"

Stanley told them about the kitchen problem, the dye vats in the hosk building, and the collapsed roof.

"Have you heard anything from the other kingdoms?" Jakla asked.

"I haven't, but I'm sure Jor-Dan or Trakon have heard reports," Stanley said. He told Jakla and Bist about the Egrom mushrooms and the Kudaja boardwalk.

A SINGLE MAN CRESTRIDER WITH THE PATROSYM FLAGS approached Ebscalon at a dangerous speed. The gate guards hailed the crestrider, and it hovered over the city gates.

"Hail, Patrosym flyer," the gate guard called out. "What is your business here?"

The ship's lieutenant tapped his chest in greeting. "We've come to solicit help from the Earthling with the big head."

"His head isn't big anymore, and they're called Eartholians now," the gate guard said. "What happened? Did the churling do great damage to Patrosym?"

"Part of the palace has collapsed, and the king is trapped under the debris! Can the Eartholian still move things?" the lieutenant asked. Panic edged his voice upon hearing Stanley's head was no longer big.

"Let me come aboard and I'll show you where to land," the gate guard said. He hopped down onto the deck of the ship.

The gate guard indicated where the ship should land in the plaza. They disembarked and ran to the entrance.

"There's an emergency," the gate guard told the palace guard.

They rushed into the palace to the throne room. The palace guard saluted and announced the two men.

"Your highness, a fleet lieutenant from Patrosym, along with one of our gate guards," the palace guard boomed out in a strong voice.

"Come, come," Jor-Dan said. He motioned with his fingers for them to approach.

Trakon stood by his father.

"King Jor-Dan; Prince Trakon, the king of Patrosym is trapped under the rubble of the palace! We request the help of your Earthling man," the lieutenant said.

"Emeric is trapped?" Jor-Dan gasped out. "What of the rest of the royal family?" He turned to Trakon. "Summon Stanley and the others. Dreboo as well."

"Princess Yalalore and the Queen were in the communal hatching building. They are safe," the lieutenant said. He let out a relieved sigh.

Stanley materialized in the throne room. "What happened?"

The lieutenant explained the emergency as D'laine, Lee and Victor entered the room. Dreboo and his team showed up next, followed by Kitry and Kara.

"We have to get the building doors open!" Trakon boomed. "We need our crestriders!"

"Let's not worry about that right now," Stanley said. "I can transport everyone. I just require a reliable sense of where to go because I've never been there before."

"I can guide you," Trakon said. He turned to the lieutenant. "Do you require anything?"

"Just your presence and help," the lieutenant said.

"Okay. We'll be there in a minute, so you can fly back," Trakon said.

The palace and gate guards escorted the lieutenant out of the palace.

"Lee, I'd like you to come along because you're an engineer," Trakon said. "Mother, I don't think it is a good idea for all the royal family to leave home. We're unaware of the extent of the devastation, and it could be dangerous."

Kitry nodded. "D'laine, Kara and Marrak will help me with

any issues that arise while you are gone. Be sure to communicate updates for us."

Jor-Dan nodded. "Are we ready?"

Stanley gathered those transporting to Patrosym in a tight group, away from everyone else. In a minute, Jor-Dan, Trakon, Lee, Victor, Dreboo and his associates vanished.

STANLEY USED TRAKON'S MIND VIEW FOR COORDINATES. THE group materialized inside the gates, but far from the palace. Rubble was everywhere. It was evident from the destruction that the buildings, which were much newer than the city of Ebscalon's architecture, were built with less than desirable materials and craftsmanship.

They all looked at the wreckage, gaping.

"How could this happen?" Lee asked. "Your building materials are stronger than the construction resources on Earth."

Dreboo shook his head. "When you cut corners, things tend to crumble."

They walked toward the palace. Many of the walls still stood, but the majority of the damage was at the rear of the building.

A duty of men in crimson and black Patrosym uniforms greeted them, along with Princess Yalalore.

"Thank you for coming to our aid," the princess said. "My father is trapped! It will take too much time for us to dig him out." She set her eyes on Stanley. "With your powers, you have the ability to save him."

She took in the group before her. Her eyes swayed to Lee and widened in interest.

Trakon recognized that look. "Yala, this is my father-in-law, Lee Jackson. Ethaderia, my cousin, and Lee's intended, couldn't come to your aid. She is helping my mother."

Lee controlled his face. He understood Trakon's meaning. *Just what I need, some princess with a mission.*

"Show us where the king was last seen," Jor-Dan said. He wanted to diffuse the situation—everyone was well aware that Princess Yalalore was husband hunting.

She led them around the side of the palace to where the structure had collapsed. "We're certain he was in the room hearing petitioners after the storm passed over. The collapse happened after the storm. The building just seemed to fall down!"

"How many people are there, trapped with the king?" Stanley asked.

"Several dozen—the room was filled with citizens reporting damage," one of the Patrosym men said.

"We aren't concerned with them, only my father!" Princess Yalalore said.

Everyone stared at her, shocked at her dismissal of her subjects. Trakon was aware that she was insensitive and shallow; but he didn't realize just how uncaring she was. He feared for the people of Patrosym. If the king died, Yalalore would try to push her mother out of the way to make herself the ruler.

Stanley looked over the deep pile of rubble. "Where should I move this debris?"

The Patrosym guard guided Stanley to where he should dispose of the building material. He returned to the palace and began to lift the top-most rubble. After several top-loads were offloaded, people swarmed through the building in search of the king and survivors.

They found King Emeric. Stanley had to remove a large block of material that trapped the king. Then a team rushed in ready to carry him out of the destroyed palace room.

"Let me move him," Stanley said.

The team stopped their grabbing of limbs to haul their king and let Stanley handle the matter.

Stanley levitated the king out of the way and settled him on the ground. He turned to Trakon. "Better get D'laine here. He's barely alive. I'll keep removing the rubble so they can search for the rest of the people that were in the room."

Trakon tapped his communicator. "D'laine, would you be able to come to Patrosym? The king is in bad shape. Stanley pulled him out of the building, but he needs help."

Yalalore was joined by her mother, the queen. They crouched by the king.

D'laine materialized, with the help of Ghury, who was by her side. They hurried to the side of the fallen king.

The Patrosym guard helped the queen and Yalalore to their feet, out of the way.

The queen implored D'laine and Ghury. "Can you save my husband?"

"She will try," Ghury said. He nodded to D'laine.

D'laine deflated and removed her boots. This healing would take massive power from Thol. She wished Greg Claymore were here.

You don't need Greg, Ghury sent. *You have undeniable power. Now is not the time to feel inferior.*

Both D'laine and Ghury did a body scan on the king. His life force was weak, but he was alive. That was more than D'laine had to work with when Marrak was attacked by the Fod.

D'laine removed her crystals from a pouch. She placed a crystal on the king's forehead, one by his heart and one on the ground by his heels. She held her largest crystal, closed her eyes and breathed in deeply. D'laine stood, feet spread shoulder width apart. She ran the crystal over the full length of the king's body.

"Trakon?"

He stepped forward to her side.

She held out her hand with the crystal. He placed his hand

under hers so their skin touched. D'laine dropped the crystal in his hand.

Trakon was familiar with her healing process. He stepped back until she called him again.

D'laine stood like a statue, feet planted in the soil.

Ghury gathered the people who watched. "This will be an extensive healing process that may take many hours. Do not disturb the princess. Don't talk to her. Don't touch her. She is in a deep trance, connected to both Thol and King Emeric."

The queen wrung her hands. "What should we do?"

"Help your people," Jor-Dan said. "They are in shock and could use food, water and comfort."

Stanley continued to remove destroyed material from the crumbled palace. A slew of people searched for citizens trapped under the rubble and dust. The Ciertrons and Eartholians helped the Patrosyms. They set up a triage area where the Patrosym healers could attend to those who were injured in the devastation.

Ghury helped the healers. There were so many wounded, the healers were overwhelmed and their energy dissipated rapidly.

Three hours passed. Stanley had moved to another building and was lifting the heaviest pieces of building materials and discarding them outside the city gates. There were so many piles of rubble, that he planned to speak with Ghury about having an Egrom come to disintegrate the mess.

Trakon stayed by D'laine's side. He didn't trust Yalalore, and wanted to make sure the conniving woman didn't disrupt the process to save her father. She was the type to take advantage of her mother's grief and displace her.

Trakon heard the word water in his head. He summoned Lee. "D'laine needs water. Can you ask one of the guards where you can get a glass of water?"

"I'll take care of it," Lee said. He hurried off and found the lieutenant he had been working beside. Several minutes later, he returned to Trakon with a glass of water.

Trakon held the glass to D'laine's lips.

She drained the glass. "Thank you."

"Whatever you need, my love," Trakon said.

The rumbling of pakows approaching the city caught everyone's attention. Jakla Bosakin and a large troop of Plotals rode into the crumbling city. They dismounted their beasts and Jakla approached the Patrosyms, Ciertrons and Eartholians.

Jakla nodded to Lee and Victor. "Your sons came to visit my children and told us of the catastrophic damage to Patrosym. We are here to help in any way we can."

Princess Yalalore stepped in front of the Plotal leader. Her lips curled in distaste. "We don't need your help, you slaver!"

Queen Egraphor grabbed her daughter's arm and yanked her back. "I apologize for my daughter. She is a narrow-minded, insensitive person and has no manners whatsoever."

"What do you think you're doing?" Princess Yalalore shouted.

"What I should have done paths ago," Queen Egraphor said. She nodded to a lieutenant of the guard. "Please escort my daughter to the temple. She is not to leave there until further notice. Do you understand?"

The lieutenant tapped his chest with a fist. "We will sequester the princess at the temple, my queen." He hauled the princess away as gently as possible, but it was obvious she struggled to free herself. The lieutenant called out to three more guards. They had no more trouble with the princess after that.

There were many surprised faces. The queen had a reputation of weakness in regards to her daughter. This new attitude made Jor-Dan and Trakon breathe a sigh of relief, along with many of the people of Patrosym who stood within earshot.

The queen turned to face Jakla. "Thank you for coming to our aid, Commander Bosakin. This storm has taught us a valuable lesson with a high price. My husband is in grave danger. I only pray that princess D'laine can save him."

Jakla nodded. "If anyone can save King Emeric, it is D'laine. Queen Egraphor, do not worry yourself about how your daughter addressed me. We Plotals understand that not everyone will embrace our new, peaceful ways."

The queen placed a hand on Jakla's arm. "While that may be true, there is such a thing as decency. When a neighbor offers help at a time of need, we should be gracious in our acceptance, not harangue them for their past."

Jakla nodded to the queen. The Patrosym citizens led the Plotals to where they required help.

Jor-Dan nodded to Trakon, then he joined the others lending help.

D'LAINE WAS DEEP INTO KING EMERIC'S HEALING. SHE KEPT HIM in a form of suspension so he would not feel his broken bones and organs being repaired. There were several minutes when she thought she'd lost him, but his spirit was strong. She sought Trakon with her mind. He lay a hand on her shoulder to let her know he was there for her.

Water.

Trakon held the glass to her lips, and she drained it. He looked her over and determined she was okay. He noticed a baby hosk between her feet and nudged it away from her. He didn't want the playful baby to distract her, and sure didn't want the hosk to call its friends to join in. He wondered what it was doing there, then he thought maybe the Patrosym hosk building was damaged. He shook his head, not thinking correctly. There were never baby hosks in the hosk buildings. Only adult males were ever in the hosk building.

He looked around and saw hosks aplenty. This was very

unusual. The females were extremely shy and scatted under the moss when humans were about. Baby hosks were more social, but to have them show up at a disaster site with so much activity was quite unusual.

Father! Trakon called out with his mind. He wasn't sure where his parent was amid the hundreds of people working the area.

What is it? Is everything okay? Is D'laine okay? Jor-Dan sent.

Something odd is going on. There are baby hosks and females all around D'laine.

Females are out?

Yes. I don't understand what's going on.

I'll be right there!

Jor-Dan walked over to Trakon. He looked at the hosks on the ground and scratched his beard. "What is going on? I've never seen such a thing!"

Trakon shrugged. "I have to keep nudging the babies away from D'laine so they don't distract her from healing Emeric."

Ghury materialized where Jor-Dan and Trakon stood. "The hosks are here to help D'laine keep her energy level up."

"Oh!" Trakon said. "They probably wonder why I keep pushing them away!"

"Let them gather. D'laine will feel their energy and it will strengthen her," Ghury said.

"I never knew hosks did this sort of thing," Jor-Dan said.

"They felt her call through her feet for energy," Ghury said.

Trakon and his father moved away from D'laine to allow the hosks to gather at her feet. As soon as they moved back, the hosks swarmed D'laine. There were dozens, then more showing up. They surrounded D'laine and the fallen king. Hosks were so thick on the ground, that they were standing on each other's heads and backs, making little purring noises.

"Are they going to be okay? Seems like they would suffocate on top of each other like that," Trakon said.

"They know their limitations," Ghury said.

FOUR MORE HOURS PASSED. EVERYONE WAS BEYOND TIRED. Stanley, Victor and Lee approached Trakon.

"I think it's time we quit for the turn," Lee said. "We're exhausted and won't be doing anyone any good at this point."

Lee saw all the hosks around D'laine. "What's with the hosks?"

Trakon explained what Ghury said.

"That's interesting," Stanley said. "I'm going to look for queen Egraphor and tell her we'll be leaving."

"Okay. I'm not sure how much longer this healing will take," Trakon said. He stared at his wife. "D'laine hasn't communicated with me in hours."

Stanley walked in the direction he had seen the queen last.

Lee thumped Trakon on the shoulder. "She's amazing, isn't she?"

Trakon's eyes softened. "Yes, she is."

D'laine stirred. Trakon could hear her breathing, whereas before, she didn't make a sound. He saw Emeric's chest rise and fall in a steady pattern.

"Look! King Emeric is coming around!" Victor said.

Stanley and the queen returned just when both D'laine and King Emeric's eyes fluttered open.

The queen dropped to her husband's side. "Emeric! Thank Thol you're alive!"

D'laine's knees turned to jelly. Trakon caught her before she crashed to the ground. The hosks went about their business, scurrying away from all the human activity to their mossy homes.

"Queen Egraphor, would you like me to transport the king somewhere before we depart for Ebscalon?" Stanley asked.

"Would you? The Plotals have brought and set up some of their tents. I will lead you there," the queen said.

Stanley levitated the king and followed the queen to a cleared space where several colorful tents stood.

One of the Patrosym guards pulled aside a tent flap, and they walked inside. It was furnished for royalty with rugs on the ground, chairs and sofas, and a partitioned off area where the bed stood.

Stanley gently levitated the king on the bed.

A healer immediately scanned the king and worked getting him comfortable.

The queen followed Stanley outside the tent. "I can't thank you and your fellow Eartholians enough for all you have done for us. Without D'laine, my husband would have died."

"We were happy to help," Stanley said. "Shall we return tomorrow?"

"I will have the lieutenant contact you in the morning," the queen said. "I must return to my husband's side now."

Stanley nodded, then stepped back to where the others were. "Ready to go home?"

"Yes. D'laine needs bed rest," Trakon said. "Has anyone seen my father?"

"He was with Jakla," Victor said. He tapped his communicator. "Jor-Dan, D'laine has finished healing the king. She's exhausted, and we need to go home."

"I'll be right there," Jor-Dan said.

Several long minutes later, Jor-Dan and Jakla walked up.

"King Emeric survived?" Jakla asked,

Trakon nodded. "He is with the healer in one of the tents you provided."

"My people are ready to return home as well," Jakla said. "We have rescued many people buried alive under this rubble. Ebscalon did not suffer this damage. Even Ta'Byu'Vohon in all the different phases of construction, didn't receive this amount of damage."

Jor-Dan shook his head. "Different people chided my kingdom for what they considered grandeur. Ebscalon was well-thought-out by great architectural minds only interested in building a city that would withstand weather and wars."

"This is why we came to you when we decided to build our city," Jakla said.

The Plotal warriors approached the group. Jakla's right-hand warrior thumped his chest. "Commander, we have finished for the night, and await your departure."

Jakla and Jor-Dan exchanged arm grasps. The Plotal nodded to the rest of the Ciertrons and Eartholians. "Until tomorrow."

When the Plotals stalked off toward their herd of pakows, Stanley gathered the group and he stepped them home to the palace.

CHAPTER TWENTY-SEVEN

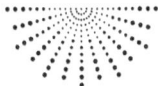

D'laine and Trakon rushed down the stairs to the catacombs where the women warriors and Pup protected the eggs. Now that they deemed the turret was safe, Stanley could levitate the eggs and the vessels to their rightful place.

Stanley trotted down the stairs and entered the temporary room where D'laine fussed over her unborn children, Pup half in her lap. "Ready to go up to the top?"

Trakon grabbed D'laine's hand and pulled her to her feet. "Yes, we're ready."

Stanley latched onto the nests, D'laine and Trakon and stepped them into the turret room.

Pup launched himself through the dog door in the corridor door, and up the stairs to the turret room. Moments later, Zedonia and Amoroso were in the room, and Cendi was in place on the stairs. Keeshi and Halvid were guarding the door entrance in the hallway.

D'laine looked around the cleaned room. "Trakon, one of the stools is missing."

Trakon took notice. The diwal dog liked his window perches.

"Why don't you build a bench that spans the walls under the windows. The dogs can use them to see out the windows, and people can use them to sit," D'laine said.

"Yeah, I can do that. Plus, if they are attached to the wall, we won't be worried about one blowing away," Trakon said.

D'laine noticed a new dog bed. "Pup, you're one lucky diwal dog, do you realize that? Someone brought you a new dog bed."

Amoroso's bright coppery face turned darker as she blushed. "He's such a good dog. I asked my friend in the weaving building if she could make a bed for him. It turned out great and he seems to like it."

"That's such a wonderful gesture. Pup is the number one protector. I find it very interesting that he has taken on this role. None of the other dogs seem to share his interest in the eggs," D'laine said.

"Let's go take a nap before dinner," Trakon said. He looked tired.

"You go rest up," Zedonia said.

Trakon grabbed D'laine's hand and they walked down the stairs, nodding to Cendi in the stairwell and to the other guards in the corridor. They stumbled into their suite and Trakon headed straight for the bathroom.

He deflated his suit and boots and stripped off his uniform. He walked down the stairs into the pool and let out a groan of pleasure. "This is just what I needed."

D'laine joined him. She ducked her head back and wet her hair completely. Trakon waded to the edge of the pool and pumped shampoo into his hand. He returned to his wife and lathered the top of her head. It took a lot of shampoo to wash her waist-long hair. It was thick and healthy, and he loved the feel of it in his hands.

She scrubbed his head. They both ducked their heads under

the water. D'laine paddled to the edge of the pool where she had discovered an almost invisible faucet with a sprayer in a little inset.

Trakon joined her, and taking the sprayer he rinsed her hair more thoroughly.

Once they finished cleaning up, they waded to the stairs and left the pool. They each grabbed a thick, fluffy gauze towel and dried off. It took much more effort to dry D'laine's hair, but once it was sufficiently dry, they returned to the bedroom, dressed in their nightwear and collapsed on the bed.

Two hours later, Trakon woke up with his stomach growling. He kissed D'laine on the forehead. "It must be dinnertime. My stomach is empty."

"Mine too," D'laine said, when her innards rumbled.

They rose, donned their robes and slippers and padded down the stairs to the dining room.

Eyebrows raised when they took their seats.

"Too tired to dress," Trakon said.

"We've had a very long, stressful day, so don't apologize," Jor-Dan said. "I don't believe I've seen you in your robe since you were twelve."

Ethaderia and Treikie joined them at the table by their prospective men.

"Jor-Dan, you were saying something about Egraphor?" Kitry asked.

Jor-Dan snorted a laugh. "Yalalore first looked to Stanley, then Lee. Trakon set her straight. We were all worried she would sabotage her mother when her father was gravely injured."

"Mother, you would not believe that girl! She's like a mruck or an og, for Thol's sake. She's so blatantly husband-hunting, not even the lieutenants are safe!" Trakon said. "If her mother hadn't stood up at that moment, when Jakla and his Plotals came to their aid, Yalalore would have thrown aside Egraphor and claimed the kingdom."

"The look on that girl's face when the queen had her removed to the temple!" Lee said. "She couldn't imagine her mother ordering her around like she did. Evidently, Yalalore was used to bullying Egraphor."

"I couldn't believe the things that came out of her mouth!" Victor said. "If Patrosym had her for a leader, they'd be doomed."

"Or, we'd be at war with them," Jor-Dan said, seriously. "Her thirst for power is dangerous." He looked around the table and his eyes rested on Trakon and D'laine. "She is a menace that requires watching in the event of her parents' demise."

"And to think you assumed she was a good match for me!" Trakon said. "Ebscalon dodged that lightning bolt."

D'laine's eyes jumped from one to another, following the conversation around the table. "There are other kingdoms across Thol, not just your neighbors. If Yalalore feels threatened, she may find a husband in a faraway land who matches her venom. As you said, Jor-Dan, we will have to watch her. We can't allow her to unhinge the peace."

"I still can't get over the destruction in Patrosym," Stanley said. "We sustained minimal damage here, and Ta'Byu'Vohon had minor damage, considering they were constructing buildings. The agrin sap is truly a remarkable product. When I make a mental list of all the things that sap is applied to, there's not much that doesn't benefit from the agrin tree sap. It forms an indestructible material. So, explain how the Patrosym buildings toppled."

"When I studied the material Stanley hauled away, and I examined some of the standing walls, it was clear that their builders did not use enough agrin sap. In many places there was none at all," Lee said. He turned to Victor and Stanley. "It seemed like they tried to use a tongue and groove method. That would have worked and made the walls strong, but the walls weren't reinforced with the sap."

"I would not want to be that builder when the dust settles," Trakon said. "He almost killed his king. And the remaining palace walls should be demolished so that they can rebuild the entire palace."

"That's for them to figure out," Jor-Dan said. "We'll see how everything looks tomorrow."

"Does anyone know if someone got the doors open in the crestrider buildings?" Trakon asked.

"Marrak said one of the men lifted the door enough for someone to crawl under, but the problem has not been solved yet," Kitry said.

"We can tackle that tomorrow," Lee said. "A switch could have been fried."

Trakon yawned loudly. He ran his hand down his face. "I'm going back to bed. This was a very long day."

D'laine's eyes were drooping. "See you in the morning."

The prince and princess sauntered off.

The men all exchanged looks.

Jor-Dan turned to Kitry. "Hosks came to D'laine's aid while she was healing Emeric."

"Hosks? What on Thol could they do to help?" Kitry asked.

"Ghury explained that they felt D'laine's need for more energy. Her feet were in the moss, down to the soil, and evidently the hosks took it upon themselves to gather and help support her," Jor-Dan said. He shared a mind vision of the little animals piled on top of each other around D'laine's feet and surrounding Emeric.

The women shared shocked expressions.

"I've never seen or heard of such a thing," Kitry exclaimed.

"She healed the king?" Ethaderia asked.

"The Plotals brought tents with them, and the king's men set one up for him," Victor said. "He will make a full recovery."

"What are they going to do about their daughter?" Treikie asked.

"It's a tenuous situation," Stanley said. "There are more wars on Earth because of family strife than I can recall. Many were long ago, but still, kingdoms fell due to treachery."

"From everything I heard," Kara said, as she looked around the table, "that girl had her sights set on Trakon. It seems to me that if she was stewing a resentment, Ebscalon would be a target."

Jor-Dan nodded. "We cannot let that happen, but the problem is, we don't know when that may happen. How would we prepare for such a thing?"

Victor smiled. "Luckily, you have me."

Everyone stood and left the dining salon.

IN THE PITCH BLACK OF THE NIGHT, PUP'S TEETH CLACKED THE death warning.

Amoroso sent a silent communication to Zedonia and the other women warriors on duty. *Pup detects danger! Keeshi, alert the prince and princess!*

A thump against the exterior turret wall suggested a crestrider had come alongside the building. One leg, then another slipped through the window opening. When the body was fully inside the turret, Pup attacked.

Futile screams arose from the man who came to harm the eggs. Trakon and D'laine thundered up the stairs. Amoroso and Zedonia flattened themselves against the wall to stay out of Pup's way. They were well aware of the dangers of being in the presence of a diwal aroused by blood.

D'laine squeezed around Trakon. "Pup, enough. Stop!"

Not much remained of the man. D'laine wanted some part of him to identify which kingdom he came from. Pup was in a complete frenzy.

PUP! STOP! D'laine shouted using The Voice. Then, *Good dog, Pup! Good dog.*

The diwal stepped back from his victim and dropped to the floor. His teeth clacked lightly when he spotted the women warriors. Then he sniffed, recognized their scents, and quieted his teeth.

The women visibly shuddered in relief.

Others thundered up the stairs.

D'laine dropped to her knees beside her two eggs. She splayed her fingers on each egg and rested her face on an arm. *You're safe. Everything is okay. Mommy loves you. Daddy loves you. Pup really loves you. The guards love you.*

Trakon approached the remains of the intruder. He met his father's eyes, then slid his eyes to Lee. "Patrosym."

Amoroso leaned out one of the open windows and spotted the crestrider hovering at the side of the turret.

Trakon's father and father-in-law stepped into the room to examine what remained of the man.

The uniform was definitely Patrosym. The man's head, neck and part of his chest and left arm were intact.

"I'm certain this was not the queen's doing," Jor-Dan said.

"Do we go there tonight, or wait until first light?" Lee asked. "And how do we want to approach? With warships to make them understand we mean business, or what?"

"Their crestrider is hovering outside," Amoroso said. "It has their colors and flags. They can't deny it's theirs."

"Can you get into it and fly it to the courtyard?" Trakon asked.

Amoroso tapped her heart in respect. "Yes." She climbed onto the ledge. She and Zedonia grabbed the edge of the ship to steady it. Amoroso climbed into the crestrider and took off toward the front of the palace.

Victor stepped into the room. "This was princess Yalalore. I suggest a warring approach for show. At this point, common sense should tell them we could wipe their entire civilization out with a blink from D'laine. However, the king and queen of Patrosym, and their entire kingdom don't deserve that."

"What do you see happening?" Trakon asked.

"There is a silencing helmet. I saw it in existence from long ago," Victor said. He looked to Jor-Dan. "Do you know what I am talking about?"

Jor-Dan looked thoughtful. "Yes. Yes, I do recall something to that effect. The Visionary may have one."

"What is this silencing helmet?" Lee asked. "How does it work?"

Kitry nodded. "Remember how Stanley's room was fortified with that material to absorb the dangerous frequency from his brain? The helmet was created so that no silent whispers or any communication can be received or made by the wearer."

"Does this mean whoever wears it can't talk, or they just can't communicate silently?" D'laine asked.

"We will have to find out exactly how communication works. I remember, once the helmet is secured to the head, it can't be removed without a cerebral key," Jor-Dan said. "It can't be cut off the head, even with a laser."

"We need to find one. I want to go there and rip Yalalore's head off, but I don't want to instigate war," Trakon said.

The downstairs door opened. Pup was on his feet chattering when the Visionary climbed to the top stair with the helmet in hand. The dog silenced his racket when he recognized the scent of a friend.

"Good dog!" the Visionary said. He handed the helmet to Jor-Dan. "Ekal and Rettu tested the helmet. It is viable. Who will own the key?"

"Me!" Trakon bellowed out.

D'laine stood. "I will own the key!" Her fierce gaze upon her husband didn't waver. "I am the mother, therefore I will be the one who administers the punishment!"

Trakon backed down. His hand grabbed one of hers. He squeezed slightly, then nodded. "Yes, being the mother, it is justified. We will all wear battle armor, understood?"

"To answer your question about communicating and how the helmet works, the silencing helmet cuts the ability to mind or verbally talk," the Visionary said.

They all examined the helmet. Two inches of a thick, clear agrin coating covered fine wires connected to crystals. Electrical elements stretched across the surface of the contraption. The inside of the helmet was smooth to the touch. A lip, or collar with two securing strips of agrin enforced material were woven around the base of the helmet to secure it in place on a head.

"Contact Dannin. Ask him to wrap these remains so we can present them to the queen," Jor-Dan said. "Kara, would you mind joining us tomorrow? We could use your skills dealing with this."

"Of course! I'd like to see the princess try to lie her way out of this," Kara said.

At first light, squadrons of Ebscalon warriors in battle armor stood outside the crestrider buildings, alongside those from the palace. The doors to the mothership buildings would not open.

Trakon bashed the panel on the building, his temper getting the best of him.

Stanley stepped forward. "May I?"

Trakon stepped aside, grumbling to himself.

Stanley sent a mental jolt to the mechanism, and the rooftop opened.

"Thanks," Trakon said, with an apologetic smile.

He pointed to two warriors. "Bring this aboard." The gauze sack was bloody, but not leaking through. He pointed to another warrior. "Return to the courtyard and fly the Patrosym crestrider. Wait for us, but you will lead the procession."

The warrior tapped his chest, nodded and ran off.

D'laine gripped the silencing helmet as she climbed the stairs.

Warriors rushed up the stairs to climb aboard the mother-ships, as others scrambled to the smaller crestriders. Three motherships rose, war flags flapping in the breeze. All the smaller crestriders flew war flags. They rose above the city, flew over the city gates, and headed to Patrosym.

CHAPTER TWENTY-EIGHT

*F*rom the sky, the Patrosym people and Plotals looked like tiny dolls. Plotal warriors pointed to the ships. War flags hadn't been flown on a Ciertron ship in over fifty years, since the big war that destroyed massive amounts of Tholian life and technology.

D'laine, Trakon, their fathers and everyone from the palace looked over the edge of the mothership they traveled on. They noticed fingers pointing to the air.

Jor-Dan's communicator announced an incoming query from Jakla Bosakin.

"Jor-Dan, why are you flying war flags?" Jakla asked. He kept his voice well-modulated not giving away he was nervous to be in the wrong place at the wrong time.

"We will meet with Queen Egraphor, and King Emeric, if he is back to health, about the attack we experienced last night," Jor-Dan said, in a formal voice.

"Attack?" Jakla gasped.

"We will see you on the ground, Jakla," Jor-Dan said. "You will see the evidence and hear the testimony. Where is the queen so we beam down our party at the right place?"

"The largest tent has been set up as the king and queen's quarters. The tent directly to the right is where meetings are taking place," Jakla said.

The ships sailed across the sky to the tents. The king made a full recovery. Emeric and Egraphor stood outside the tent Jakla mentioned, hands blocking the suns from their eyes, as they looked at the Ebscalon fleet led by one of their own crestriders.

"Let's wait until Jakla joins the king and queen," Trakon said. "He should be a witness to this."

"I agree. The Plotals are now good friends of ours, and I want to keep it that way," Jor-Dan said. He hailed the flight commander to take no action until further notice. Then Jor-Dan called his generals. "I want two platoons to beam down in conjunction with my party beaming to the surface. I want to show this is a serious offense and we are ready to decimate Patrosym."

"Acknowledged, sire! All is ready," one general responded.

They watched overboard as Jakla and several of his high-ranking guard ran toward the tents.

Once the Plotals were in place, a large party beamed down from one of the motherships. A platoon of warriors from each of the other two motherships arrived on the surface at the same time. The Patrosym crestrider landed close by.

Emeric came forward, confused. "Why are you running war flags, Jor-Dan?"

Jor-Dan nodded to the two men who held the bloody sack. They dropped the sack on the ground at the king's feet. "My daughter-in-law saved your life, Emeric. The rest of the Eartholians came to your kingdom's aid with their special skills. We did not expect your man to attack my grandchildren."

"Attack?" Emeric and Egraphor exchanged shocked glances.

Jor-Dan nodded to the bloody sack on the ground. "Here is evidence of what is left of your man."

Emeric called one of his men over. "Unwrap this."

The man knelt and unwrapped the gauze. The remains of the Patrosym soldier were displayed for all to see.

The queen pulled in a breath as she looked upon the bloody remains of one of her people. "Who is this?"

Emeric summoned his generals. "Can you identify this man? Is he truly one of ours?"

One of the generals stood over the head, arm and partial torso. "This is Lorand, one of Princess Yalalore's detail."

"What happened? This looks like a diwal attack," Emeric said.

"Princess D'laine has three trained diwal dogs that protect the kingdom of Ebscalon," Jakla said. "Besides a male borjo that has not been neutered."

The generals and Emeric exchanged questioning expressions.

"If the males are not neutered when young, they will breathe fire," Jakla explained.

"Your man Lorand flew this crestrider to the turret where my children grow in their shells," Trakon said. He was livid. "Fortunately, D'laine's dog is the protector of the eggs. Your man never stood a chance to harm my children."

"This was not our doing!" Queen Egraphor exclaimed. She was visibly upset at the accusations. "We would never harm a friend, and Ebscalon has always been our friend."

D'laine stepped forward. "We have the right to question your daughter."

Emeric nodded. "Yes, of course." He summoned a guard detail. "You will bring the princess here. No delays. Bind her, if necessary."

The head guard thumped his chest. "Yes, sire. As you wish." The guard detail headed over to the temple where the princess was detained under lock and key.

There was an uncomfortable silence while they waited on the guard detail to return with their prisoner.

"We brought with us today, Kara, wife of Victor," Jor-Dan stated. "Kara's Eartholian gifts are unique. She detects lies. We should have a demonstration before your daughter arrives so you will understand this gift and how it will apply to this situation."

"Detects lies?" Emeric asked. "How is that possible?"

"We have no idea, but Kara is infallible," Trakon said. "Shall we begin the demo? Tell a truth and tell a lie. Only Kara will determine which is which."

One of the generals stepped forward. He was a stern-looking fellow with a face that didn't know how to smile. "We believe our former building team cut corners to where our buildings collapsed."

Kara didn't respond.

The general raised an eyebrow. He cleared his throat. "A pakow has birthed a pink calf."

"Lie," Kara said. Her mouth quirked up at the absurd tale.

The others now understood. They blurted outrageous statements.

"Pakows can fly."

"Lie."

"A gagu adopted a bobboe chick."

No response.

"Really?" Stanley asked. "Isn't that unusual?"

"Yes, we do not understand what happened. Maybe the bobboe hen abandoned the chick for some reason," the general said.

More statements were made and Kara's gift was acknowledged as indisputable.

The guard detail returned with a struggling princess. She shot a venomous look at D'laine and Trakon. When her eyes fell to the bloody remains of her man on the ground, she attempted to step back, but the guard detail restrained her.

"Lorand?" the princess gasped. "What have you done with him?" Her face flushed with anger.

"We did nothing to him. D'laine's diwal dog gave sufficient warning through his teeth, but your man climbed into the turret where our eggs grow. He didn't stand a chance against Pup," Trakon said.

"You tamed a diwal dog?" Yalalore gasped.

"Three," Jakla said. "They are free to roam the palace and kingdom."

"They don't attack the citizens?" Emeric asked.

"Only when danger lurks," Jor-Dan said. He nodded toward the ground. "They give more than sufficient warning."

"Why did you send this man to harm my children?" D'laine asked.

"I don't understand what you're talking about," Yalalore said, affronted.

"Liar," Kara spouted.

"How dare you call me a liar!" Yalalore exclaimed.

"This is Kara, Yala. She has a unique Eartholian gift—she detects lies," Trakon said. "Your parents and generals tested her gift for accuracy. She never fails to recognize truths or lies."

Princess Yalalore's lip curled up into a snarl. "You have such a perfect life, don't you, Trakon? You spurned me for no reason whatsoever."

"Liar," Kara spat out.

"That's not true," Trakon said. "The conversations we had when we were together at functions were dismal. You only ever think of yourself. You never lifted a finger to better your people or your kingdom. All you were interested in was how you would live a life as a shallow little princess. I didn't want a trophy wife. I was already in love with D'laine, even though we had never met in person."

"Shall we begin a tribunal?" Jor-Dan asked of the audience.

The seriousness of the situation started to sink in. Princess

Yalalore glanced at her parents and the Patrosym generals. "Tribunal?"

"You may not have noticed the war flags on our ships," Jor-Dan pointed to the sky. "Your treachery was an act of war, princess."

Yalalore beseeched her parents with pleading eyes.

Queen Egraphor met her daughter's eyes with loathing. "You dishonor your father and I, and the entire kingdom with your actions, words and deeds."

King Emeric barely contained his contempt toward his only daughter. "You brought shame to Patrosym, daughter. Now we will decide what to do with you. Banishment is out of the question. We would not want you to align yourself with someone equally evil. You will no longer be heir to my throne."

Victor stepped forward. "King Emeric, Queen Egraphor, your son will be an admirable king. His sister will not influence him, so your kingdom is secure."

"We don't have a son," the queen said.

"Your son will hatch within the next three-path cycle," Victor said.

They stared at Victor in disbelief.

"Victor sees the future," Stanley said.

D'laine stepped forward with the silencing helmet in hand.

"What is that?" a general asked.

Trakon explained what it was and how it worked. "Someone would have to shave her head."

Yalalore gasped. She struggled to break free from the guards. "You're not shaving my head, or putting that thing on me!"

King Emeric silently called out to the royal barber. The man approached with his tools and a short stool.

"You will shave Princess Yalalore's head so we can secure the helmet in place," king Emeric said.

The barber tapped his chest. He set the stool on the ground.

The guards forced the princess onto the stool.

"No! Not my hair! Please, don't shave off my hair!" the princess wailed.

The barber extracted his laser light shaving blade from his tool pouch. He pressed a button and blue light emitted in the shape of a long, thin knife. He stood in front of the princess. "It would be best to sit still, or the blade may cut deeply into your scalp."

He pressed the light blade to the hair above her forehead. In one long sweep, the long, black hair came off in a wide strip.

Yalalore sobbed as sections of her hair fell to the ground, and nothing remained on her head.

D'laine stepped forward with the helmet. "Princess Yalalore of Patrosym, you shall wear the silencing helmet for the rest of your days on Thol. I hold the key. No one else can release you from this fate. Your king father and queen mother, along with the Patrosym tribunal will determine your future."

D'laine settled the helmet onto Yalalore's head. The collar settled into place around her neck and the ends fused themselves together as if living things.

"I would like help choosing the guard," Emeric said. He eyed Kara.

Kara nodded. "I would be glad to help."

"I want to make sure none of the guard favor my daughter. I can't have a conspiracy on top of this." Emeric turned to his generals. "Hand pick six men. They must be loyal to the crown, honest and trustworthy."

Jor-Dan whispered to Kara. "Go stand by Emeric."

Kara moved into position.

The generals conspired quietly, then began their calls. A detail of fifteen men came forward. They eyed Kara.

"You understand why you were chosen to stand here for selection?" Emeric asked.

A resounding Yes boomed out from the men.

"Are you loyal to your king and queen?" Emeric asked.

A resounding Yes boomed out from the men.

"Is there anyone among you who would conspire to harm Patrosym or its rulers?"

A forceful No boomed out from the men. The question shocked some of them.

Emeric's eyes swept over the men. "Are you loyal to princess Yalalore?"

There were two Yes responses.

"You two, please step aside," one of the generals said.

Kara held her hand up to oppose the general. "Rephrase the question before you pass a final judgment on these two."

The generals futzed amongst themselves, then looked askance to Emeric.

"What do you suggest?" Emeric asked.

"To begin with, they all should have pledged loyalty to the princess, as she is your daughter. But the question should be, would you conspire with the princess for her revenge?" Kara said.

There were nods from the generals and the king.

Emeric stood before the group of men. "Would you conspire with the princess for her revenge?"

A resounding No from the group, including the two soldiers set aside.

The questions continued about bribes, favors, and coercion. All the guards passed the test.

THE CIERTRONS AND EARTHOLIANS ARRIVED BACK AT THE PALACE a hour later. They headed to the family salon where they typically met. Kitry, Ethaderia and Treikie Soluveia stopped talking amongst themselves when the party returned.

Everyone flopped onto sofas and chairs, stressed from the trip.

"How were you received?" Kitry asked.

"It was satisfactory all the way around," Jor-Dan said. "Emeric and Egraphor didn't argue their daughter's role. They realize all too well how poisonous she is."

"Kara helped them choose the guards. It is imperative that we check on them periodically," Trakon said. "I want to make sure Yalalore is under lock and key and not wandering around."

D'laine stood. "I'll be back in a little while." She stood.

Trakon snatched her fingers and stood beside her. They left the room and approached the turret room. Amoroso, Cendi and Zedonia blocked the door at the bottom of the staircase.

Amoroso tapped her chest. "All is well, Prince Trakon and Princess D'laine." She grabbed the handle and opened the door for them.

Felid stepped aside on the stairs to let them pass.

Keeshi and Halvid were in the room, along with Pup, who was slumbering on his bed, one ear raised.

"Was your trip satisfactory?" Keeshi asked.

"Quite," Trakon said.

"Everything okay here?" D'laine asked. She sank to her knees on the floor and rested a hand on each growing shell as the guards retreated to the stairwell.

"It has been quiet," Halvid said.

"Good, that's the way we like it," Trakon said.

He joined D'laine on the floor and rubbed a hand over one shell, then the other. Trakon eased himself onto the sofa and pulled D'laine with him. "I don't know about you, but I'm beat."

"These past few hours have been nerve-wracking," D'laine said. "I hope Patrosym rebuilds a stronger palace, and they include a tower to hold your former girlfriend."

"She was not my former girlfriend!" Trakon stormed. "The woman has always been a mess, and for the life of me, I can't understand what my mother was thinking when she determined Yala was such a perfect match."

D'laine stretched up and kissed his chin. "She was probably running out of options and figured any royal wife would do."

Two tiny borjos buzzed around the window openings.

"Is it safe to come inside?" Herish called out.

Trakon turned and spotted the small version of his friend. He looked over to Pup, who had raised his head off his dog bed. "Yeah, it's safe."

Trakon and D'laine stood. Herish and Meeri climbed onto the windowsill and jumped to the floor before they morphed into full-sized Kudaja.

"I take it you heard what happened?" D'laine asked. She and Meeri hugged.

"Your brothers and Darren told us a wild story," Herish said. "What exactly happened? Did Pup actually leave anything of the Patrosym man?"

They all sank onto the sofa, and Trakon and D'laine got the entire story out, including several mind pictures.

"Oh, my Thol! What was that woman thinking?" Meeri trembled as she leaned forward and patted one of the eggs.

"If Queen Egraphor hadn't turned on her daughter, instead of letting her walk all over her, Patrosym would be our arch enemy right about now," Trakon said. "I feel we are in command here. We have the diwal dogs, the borjos, and Eartholian human weapons."

"Yeah, D'laine could stop them in their tracks," Meeri said.

"Actually, all Stanley would need to do is focus on them, think mass destruction and that would be that," D'laine said. "People seem to think since he doesn't wear the helmet any longer, he's just a normal man."

"And we've got Ben," Herish said. "That man is worth his weight in agrin sap!"

"Did you get that boardwalk replaced?" Trakon asked.

"That, and a few repairs. Your brothers said Patrosym was a pile of rubble. Is that true?" Meeri asked.

"Most of their buildings need to be rebuilt. No one has mentioned if the houses were affected. I'll ask Jakla. He brought a platoon of Plotals to help with the search for bodies," Trakon said.

"It's nice that the Plotals have really changed their ways," Meeri said. "Brian said Jakla's kids are their friends."

There was a loud sound from the sky outside, something unusual that was unidentifiable at first.

"What's that noise?" D'laine asked. She stood and turned toward the opening where the sound came from. She walked over to the window and was stunned with what she saw. An unmanned, full-sized borjo was approaching in a direct aim for the opening.

Trakon jumped to his feet, laser weapon drawn, followed by everyone else.

"D'laine, that's Foota! What is she doing?" Trakon yelled.

Before D'laine could order the borjo away, Foota flew into the turret room, opposite them. Pup didn't seem concerned. He never rose from his bed.

Trakon and D'laine stood their ground behind their eggs.

Herish and Meeri backed away from the female borjo, lasers in their hands, waiting for instructions.

They watched as Foota fluffed out her wings and lowered her chest over the two eggs, like a hen.

"What... what is she doing?" Trakon asked. His voice was garbled with shock.

D'laine was silent for a moment, taking in the whole thing.

They heard the running feet of guards from the hallway below. They yanked the door open, and many feet thundered up the stairs.

Trakon held up a hand to halt them from taking any action.

"It's like she's sitting on eggs, like a bobboe!" D'laine said. "I hope she doesn't decide that these are HER eggs!"

"Prince Trakon! What should we do?" the lead soldier asked.

Trakon shrugged. "I don't have a clue."

Family members rushed up the stairs and joined the crowd in the room.

"This is just too weird," Herish said.

"She's just helping," Jamie said. He approached Foota and rubbed her snout. "She's trying to make up for her bad behavior, and she was worried about your eggs after the attack."

"She can't hurt the shells?" Lee asked.

"No," D'laine said. "I'm getting the sense she has hatched her own eggs."

"Will the nests hold her weight?" Jor-Dan asked.

"I'm pretty sure we would have heard them collapse when she first lowered herself," Trakon said.

Jamie walked around Foota. "Her hind legs are on the floor, so she hasn't put her full weight on them. Come see."

D'laine and Trakon walked around the huge beast and saw what Jamie discovered. D'laine reached out a hand and laid it on the borjos folded wing.

"Good girl, Foota," D'laine said. She turned to the others. "Why don't we go downstairs to the salon?"

They tromped out of the room, down the stairs and through the hallways until they reached the main salon.

"Pup didn't even bat an eye," Trakon said. "Do you think they had some kind of conversation?"

"They must have. Normally, Pup would be in lunatic mode," D'laine said.

"You two have a security system no one else could ever get through," Herish said. He looked at Meeri, a question on his face. She nodded.

"Meeri and I are going to be parents!"

D'laine was on her feet and rushed in to capture Meeri in a bearhug. "Congratulations! I'm so happy for you!"

Hugs and thumps on the back went on for a little while until everyone calmed down.

"And, before anyone asks, no, we do not have twin eggs!" Meeri said.

Meeri and D'laine snickered together. They were joined by Ethaderia, Treikie Soluveia and Kara.

"You two are next," Meeri said, nodding to the two single women.

Ethaderia blushed. "We'd better get married first."

Treikie's skin flamed. "Oh, it's much too soon for that, isn't it?"

"Are there long engagements here on Thol?" D'laine asked. "I don't know all the customs yet."

"No, typically it's up to the families," Kitry said, as she joined the women. "But, remember, it takes time to plan for a wedding."

The men huddled in a group on the other side of the salon, talking among themselves.

"Oh, I can't wait to attend another Tholian wedding," Kara said. "Your rituals are so beautiful."

CHAPTER TWENTY-NINE

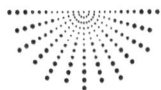

*A*fter a hour of lively conversation, Herish and Meeri headed home. Everyone else wandered into the dining salon for dinner. Pup trotted past everyone on his way to the kitchen. He stood, confused, trying to stick his head through a wall of gauze that held out construction dust.

The majordomo called to the diwal. "Pup! This way." He patted his thigh and made a waving motion. "Come, Pup!"

Pup heavily clacked his teeth once in frustration. He turned to the majordomo and followed him to the new entrance to the displaced kitchen.

"Grubio, feed the dog," the majordomo said. He gave the diwal a pat on the rump and returned to the dining room.

"How's the kitchen project coming along?" Jor-Dan asked.

"The chef is going to expand the facility, incorporating the temporary room," the majordomo said.

Jor-Dan laughed. "He probably wished for the damage to the wall just to expand!"

"I'm sure Grubio and Hruk will need the extra space for when they begin chocolate production," Lee said. "We all know Trakon can be demanding when it comes to his favorite foods!"

Trakon's eyes glazed over. "I can't wait! Chocolate and pizza!"

"You'd better not get fat!" D'laine poked him in the ribs.

"When everything is back in place, we will host a gala to announce your twin eggs," Kitry said.

"Trakon and I were talking about that before the storm hit," D'laine said. "Pup would never put up with any strangers near the eggs."

"Foota is now an additional guardian," Trakon said. "What are your thoughts, mother?"

"I believe it would be safe to present your eggs on a platform for the gala," Kitry said. "Your warrior guards would be present along with Pup. We wouldn't be able to take a chance with the borjo though."

"Let us think about it," D'laine said.

"There is plenty of time before we need to decide," Kitry said.

Stanley called Al from his suite and told him about the churling. "Al, you would not believe this storm. The Gulf of Mexico has never experienced anything even closely related to the size and strength of this storm."

After the weather update, Stanley got around to the reason for his call. "Would you be able to send us a USB drive with those videos of how to process chocolate?"

"Of course! I can do that after we finish talking," Al said.

Stanley also asked Al to send addresses for specific libraries. He explained Kara's experience with Adrum converting books to lessons.

"Wow! I'd love to experience that!" Al said. "I'll get those videos downloaded to the USB drive, and into the spare room."

They ended the call.

Stanley rubbed his hands together. "Chocolate! I know this will be great—no additives, no high fructose corn syrup, no GMO crap, no ingredients I can't pronounce—pure, wonderful chocolate! Trakon will be one of the happiest guys on the planet."

He continued to work on some design projects he was contemplating, and lost himself in the creative process. He felt a displacement and shook his head. He called Ben with his communicator.

"Ben, I talked with Al. I think he placed the USB drive in the spare room. Can you see if it's there? It has the chocolate videos for the palace chef," he said.

"Yup! I've got it. Hold on for a minute," Ben said. He popped into Stanley's suite, USB in hand. "You'd better share this! The Kudaja will want to get in on the chocolate making. Herish and Meeri love the stuff."

"Come on, let's go find the guys," Stanley said.

They left his suite and looked for Lee and Victor. Neither were in the palace. Victor was in the temple, and Lee was over in the workshop with Trakon and his crew. They walked over to the shop.

"Hey, Ben!" Lee said.

Stanley looked serious as he approached Trakon. "You're going to owe me big-time!"

Trakon studied the scientist. "What for now?"

Stanley held up the USB device. "See this? It contains video —mind movie instructions so Grubio and Hruk can make chocolate for you!"

Trakon's eyes widened. "Seriously?" He thumped Stanley on the back!

"Lee, can you get away for a few minutes? We're going to see what Al sent," Ben said.

"I'll be back," Lee told Trakon, Hexlon and the rest of the guys in the workshop.

Stanley, Ben and Lee returned to the palace and took the stairs to Lee's suite.

Lee inserted the USB into his laptop and opened the directory. There were three folders. One named Chocolate that contained four videos and a bunch of PDFs. The second folder was Libraries, and contained a Word document with addresses of the best-known scientific libraries from around the world. The third folder was entitled NOVEL in all caps. In that folder was one document, an outline.

The men were excited at the contents of the USB drive. Lee clicked on the first folder. They looked over the file names. One seemed to be a commercial video from a chocolate company. They looked at that first. The process seemed lengthy and complicated, plus the equipment was for a large quantity production.

Lee clicked on the next video, which showed a woman making chocolate from scratch at home. No fancy equipment.

"Kara can translate the voice-overs," Stanley said. "Shouldn't be any problem as far as I can tell."

"Lee, does your computer contain all the bells and whistles to produce videos and audios?" Ben asked.

"Yes, it does. I'd like to see if I could somehow update programs," Lee said.

"We could always send it to Al. He can download all the new features," Ben said. "We should send him our laptops periodically for those upgrades, until our technology is obsolete."

Stanley shook his head. "I'm working on something. We can get everything updated now, but in the near future, I will implement a solution. I don't want to go into details until I can test my theory."

Lee clicked on the last folder and they all read through Al's outline of the novel.

"This sounds great," Lee said. "I can't wait to read the chapters he produces."

"Where's Kara?" Ben asked.

"She's probably in the kitchen. She was helping Grubio with recipes for dishes that contained tomatoes," Lee said.

"I hope they share those with the Kudaja," Ben said. "The tomatoes were a big hit with the chefs. They're trying to grow a plant from the seeds. They want to know how to grow a pecan tree. Looks like they're rather fond of the nuts."

"Hmm," Lee said. "I'm sure there are instructions here somewhere. When D'laine was in junior high school, she was in a 4-H group, and one of their projects was to grow a pecan tree."

Lee searched for the file and found it in an archived folder. "Here it is. We can translate this into Tholian." He printed the English version.

- Choose nuts still attached to the tree. Cut around the hull to pry it open. Remove the nut.
- Store the pecan nuts for two to three months in a refrigerator, in a one-gallon sealable plastic bag filled with moistened perlite, to cold stratify them. Pour two or three tablespoons of water onto the perlite whenever it dries out.
- Choose a spot with light shade at midday.
- Bury the seeds at a depth equal to twice their width, which should be approximately two inches.
- Spread a one-inch layer of mulch over the loam mixture to help insulate the pecan seeds. Use acidic mulch such as pine needle compost or chipped oak leaves. Water to a five-inch depth to moisten the soil and settle the mulch.
- Water the pecan seeds whenever the loam mixture feels dry one inch below the surface.

- Watch for germination approximately one month after daytime temperatures stay reliably above 70 degrees Fahrenheit. Decrease watering by half after germination to promote root growth.
- Grow the pecan seedlings under bright conditions for their first summer. Provide one to two inches of water weekly.

They read over the instructions.

"Would you send me the file?" Ben asked. "I'll translate it and hand it over. I'm pretty sure it won't take long to grow a tree from a nut. Look at how quickly the plants I brought took off in this Tholian climate."

"Kara and Victor moved so fast, we never had the chance to get our coffee makers," Stanley said.

"Let's get Al working on the coffee plants," Lee said.

"We can ask him to research how coffee manufacturers create the different flavors. Are these plants bred for specific beans, or are flavors added during the roasting process?" Ben asked.

Lee made a list: coffee makers, bags of coffee, research for coffee bean roasting, etc. "We need to send the USB back to Al so he can provide the information."

"So, do we want Al to send ground or whole beans? I'll bet the chefs have something similar to a grinder, don't you think?" Ben asked.

Lee created a long list of coffee flavors for Al to purchase, along with coffee machines. They decided on the machines that used the reusable K-cup filters.

"Why don't we install one coffee maker in the dining salon for all of us here, and Ben can install one in the cafeteria? We'll need to order a couple of cases of those reusable filters," Stanley said.

"That's a good idea," Ben said. "I'll bet once Tholians get a taste of coffee, they will study the machines so they can create something even better."

Lee gave Al access to his bank account debit card for the large purchase amounts. There was plenty of money, and he knew the reporter wouldn't live high on the hog off his money.

Al was living for free in Victor's house. He had numerous vehicles at his disposal, and all the Eartholians had decided on a stipend from each of them while Al was writing the book. They were grateful to have someone there whom they could trust, and who could also fetch things for them.

Lee printed out a list and also included it on the USB drive in a folder called TO AL. Ben did his thing, sending the USB drive and note to the spare room in Victor's house.

THEY FIGURED THAT AL HAD JUMPED ON THEIR COFFEE REQUEST, immediately. Two days later, Ben delivered a coffeemaker, a dozen reusable K-cups, and several large bags of different flavored ground coffee beans to the palace in Ebscalon.

"Al's ordered us each a case of the filter cups. When they arrive, I'll let you know," Ben said. "I've translated the instructions and made cards to go over the machine, so people here can try for themselves. We'll need a sturdy trash can or something for the coffee grounds to be dumped into, so the cups can be rinsed and reused."

"Good thinking on those instructions," Lee said. He rubbed his hands together. "Let's go set this up. I can't wait for my first cup of coffee!"

Lee, Victor, Stanley and Ben tromped downstairs. First, they headed to the kitchen and found Kara and Grubio at the stove cooking something that smelled glorious.

"Hey, hon. Al sent the coffee machine and supplies," Victor said.

"Oh, coffee! Grubio, I can't wait for you to try our coffee!" Kara said. "We will need cups, a water source, and power."

"We've got the power source," Stanley said.

Grubio had a cook take over at the stove.

They all went to the dining salon to set up the coffee machine and supplies on the buffet table. When everything was in place, Lee made the first cup of coffee with his choice of roasted hazelnut. He slurped in a hot mouthful and let out a groan of happiness.

Kara had rounded up the Tholian equivalent of sugar, and pakow milk. She made the next cup and doctored her coffee with the sugar and milk, adding a little at a time until she had the flavor she desired.

"Oh, this is so good!" Kara said. "Grubio, try this flavor." She motioned to the bag of breakfast blend.

The chef hesitated, then made his cup. He took a sip, grimaced, then added sugar. He sipped again, his eyebrows rising. "This is interesting."

"When the chocolate is created, I'll be able to drink my café mocha!" Kara said. "Wait until you taste coffee and hot chocolate!"

Stanley and Victor made their coffee.

"I can't believe we finally have coffee! This is awesome!" Victor said. "I've started my day with coffee since I was sixteen, and this has been a hard withdrawal!"

Grubio examined the machine. "We need a water source here. A sink and a pitcher." He examined the coffee grounds. "Is this reusable for anything?"

"Back home on Earth, I mixed coffee grounds into my compost pile," Kara said.

"What is compost?" Grubio asked.

"Compost is made from vegetable and fruit peels and other parts we don't eat or use in cooking. I had a bin I put everything in and turned it every day so it would all get mixed up. Then when it all breaks down it turns into a nice dark soil that is highly nutritious for a vegetable garden," Kara explained.

"You added this coffee to the compost?" Grubio asked.

"Yes, most things from the kitchen are good for compost, except meat. You never want to use meat in compost," Lee said. "It rots and can ruin it. So, only use what Kara said."

CHAPTER THIRTY

*D*annin reported that Augenta had vacated her house. "We've been monitoring her, along with her communications."

"Who has taken her in?" Jor-Dan asked.

"Oddly, we're not sure," Dannin said.

"No one in the seven kingdoms has welcomed her?" Trakon asked.

Dannin shook his head. "No. We've even monitored all the Kudajara villages, Ta'Byu'Vohon, and the Egrom village."

"Where could she have gone?" Kitry asked.

"As you know, there are places on the other side of Thol that remain unexplored. It has been hundreds of paths since the last team was sent out to discover unknown lands," Jor-Dan said. "She most likely found an ally."

Ethaderia clenched Lee's hand. "You are positive she has left Ebscalon?"

"Her household is empty," Dannin said. "We think she left after the churling. Remember, there was chaos across the kingdoms, and no one was paying attention."

"How could she move her entire household with no one noticing transport of furniture?" Lee asked.

Dannin shrugged.

"She's gone. We can wipe our hands of her poisonous attitude," Kitry said. She reached across the sofa and patted Ethaderia's hand.

"I'll bet Stanley can find her," Lee said.

Stanley and Treikie walked into the salon. "I can find who?"

Everyone jumped into the conversation and explained the situation.

"I can give it a try," Stanley said. "I have her signature, for lack of a better word—what you would think of as an aura."

The scientist quieted and let his brain send out feelers for the hateful woman. After several minutes of silence, Stanley opened his eyes. "She's way, far away from here, with people I've never seen before. Their city holds a darkness. The common people live in fear of their leaders. I'll set up an alert, because this doesn't look like a good move to me. I'll ask the Egroms if they know of this place."

"It sounds like my mother found a place that fits her demeanor," Ethaderia said. "I'll tell my sister."

Jor-Dan, Trakon, Lee and Stanley flew to Ta'Byu'Vohon to see the progress the Plotals were making with their building.

Jakla and Bist gave them a tour. "We will be in the construction phase for the next two or three paths," Bist said. "But at least the main stronghold is almost complete."

They went inside the huge building. The visitors could see many examples of the Ebscalon palace in the stronghold's interior. The soft colors on the walls and the general layout were similar.

"Are you living here now, or are you still in your tent?" Lee asked.

"Neska has furnished our suites, and they are comfortable," Jakla said.

"Many paths ago before the Great War of Taylon, I had a Plotal friend named Orongo," Jor-Dan said. "Do you know if he is here among your people, or with another Plotal tribe?"

"One of my trusted advisor's is named Orongo," Jakla said. "Perhaps this is the same Plotal." Jakla tapped his communicator. He spoke to someone, then after several minutes, his communicator bleeped. "Orongo, come to the stronghold. There is someone who would like to speak to you."

After several minutes, a Plotal warrior entered the stronghold. He had a scar down the left side of his scaled face. His blue vest held several military decorations. He approached his commander, looked the group of humans over with little interest. Then his eyes zoomed back to Jor-Dan.

"Jor-Dan?" Orongo gasped, which, for a Plotal sounded like sandpaper on a jagged piece of metal.

"Orongo!" Jor-Dan let out a half-laugh.

Orongo and Jor-Dan grasped arms. They each barked out laughs of unbelief at their reunion.

"How are you, my friend?" Jor-Dan asked. "This is my son, Trakon."

"You found someone to marry you?" Orongo joked.

They picked up their friendship as if fifty years hadn't passed.

"Trakon's wife saved us from the robots," Jakla said.

"She's formidable," Orongo said. "I saw her on the battlefield. It is good we are a peaceful lot now; she would wipe us out for any discretion."

"Orongo, this is D'laine's father, Lee Jackson from the planet Earth," Jor-Dan said. "And this human is Stanley Daigle from Earth."

"There's a colony from Earth here?" Orongo asked. "I only knew about the healer with the Oolarooloo."

"There's just a small group of us," Lee said. "You'll most likely see my sons and their friends playing with Jakla's children."

"You are king now, Jor-Dan?" Orongo asked.

Jor-Dan nodded. "Yes, my father died shortly after the big war. My mother missed him so much, she only lingered a short while. It was a dark time for me."

Orongo's communicator beeped. "We will catch up later, Jor-Dan. Duty calls."

They grasped hands. Both of them seemed not ready to end their time together. Orongo left the building.

"It has been many, many paths since Orongo and I spent any time together," Jor-Dan said.

"I'm pleased that your friendship has survived the paths," Jakla said. "Would you like to continue the tour?"

"Yes. What you have accomplished in this short span of time is quite remarkable," Jor-Dan said.

Jakla led them down hallways and around corners, until a huge, carved double doorway appeared. He opened the door and escorted them inside. "This is where we live."

Extra-large furnishings were not so different from that at the palace of Ebscalon. Sofas and chairs with ottomans, side tables, floating globes, tapestries on the walls and rich rugs on the floor made a comfortable environment.

Neska entered the room. She tapped her chest to acknowledge both Jor-Dan and Trakon. "Welcome to our home. Please be comfortable." She held her hand out toward a setting for human-sized company.

Lee's eyes swept the room. "Your home is beautiful."

"My mate is giving you the grand tour?" Neska asked.

"Yes. I wanted to see if there was anything more I could do to help," Stanley said.

"You saved us hours with your help," Jakla said. "I'm sure we

308

would not have finished moving all the building materials or the tents before the churling hit."

They discussed the business at Patrosym, then the mystery of where Augenta disappeared to.

Jakla shook his head. "Let us hope she did not go to the Trangula!"

"I've never heard of them," Trakon said. "Who are they and where is their kingdom?"

"We came up against them many paths ago in the past, during our wanderings," Jakla said. His face turned fierce.

Two Plotal serving females entered the room with beverages and passed them out to the group.

"They are worse than we were before we mended our ways," Jakla said, apologetically.

"Are they humans?" Trakon asked.

Jakla thought about his reply. "They appear to be, but I suspect they are not a pure race. They are in the Valley of the Wailing Winds, and you should avoid them. If Augenta traveled there for shelter and they accepted her, you can bet they are scheming something."

Jor-Dan appeared uneasy.

"The Trangula killed my nepsa," Neska said. A fierce expression crossed her face.

Lee and Stanley raised eyebrows. They weren't familiar with that term.

Trakon saw their confusion. "Nepsa is the Plotal term for grandfather. Nepsi means grandmother."

"Oh, Neska. I'm sorry to hear about your nepsa. What happened?" Lee asked.

"It was ten paths after the big war. My nepsa was with a small scouting party looking for a safe location to settle for the night. They were attacked by the Trangula. They killed their entire party," Neska said.

"We retaliated, but when I look back on our actions, I realize now that revenge gains little comfort," Jakla said. "Still, be watchful, Jor-Dan."

They continued to talk for a half hour.

"We should get back to Ebscalon," Trakon said.

"Please join us tomorrow for dinner," Jor-Dan said. "My adopted grandchildren would like your children to come to the palace."

"They are well-behaved children," Neska told Lee. "You must be proud of them."

Lee laughed. "My sons love Thol, and the gifts bestowed on them. They enjoy coming to Ta'Byu'Vohon and playing with your children, so please bring Cadj and Fazi with you tomorrow."

"We will," Neska said. "Thank you for the invitation, Jor-Dan."

STANLEY STEPPED INTO THE EGROM VILLAGE AND JOINED THE elders around the cookfire.

"You wish to discuss things?" Ghury asked.

Stanley seemed thoughtful. "What do you know about the Trangula?"

"They are doski," Ditol said.

Stanley frowned. "I've never heard that term before. What does doski mean?"

"Two types of early humanoids in the evolutionary history of Thol mated. They are not what we would consider humans today," Ditol said. "Their arms are longer, similar to your apes when compared to humans."

"Luckily, they do not migrate out of the Valley of the Wailing Winds," Trabet said. "However, they have been known to travel many miles when they are seeking females to mate with."

"Jakla's mate, Neska said her nepsa was killed by the Trangula. We believe a woman from Ebscalon has gone there to live," Stanley said. "We're concerned because the woman is a vile person and could bring harm our way."

"Ebscalon is well-protected," Ghury said. "Victor and the Visionary will alert the king of any approaching war parties."

"When I searched for Augenta's aura, I found the Trangula kingdom. Their people are not happy. They seem beaten down. Why won't they band together to free themselves of this way of life?" Stanley said.

"They are not evolved enough to bring themselves out of the darkness," Adrum said.

Stanley nodded. "Thank you for this information. I will return to Ebscalon now and discuss this with everyone." Stanley stood and was gone.

THE NEXT AFTERNOON, JAKLA AND HIS FAMILY ARRIVED. KITRY and Kara took Neska on a tour of the palace, the hosk building, the weaving rooms, and the communal hatching center.

Jor-Dan, Trakon, Lee, Victor and Stanley brought Jakla to the catacombs and discussed their plans to create a bunker for the pakows.

The four boys and Fazi ran wild through the city, having fun. Then they ran to Ekka's tower and boarded the borjos. They flew all over the place.

The citizens raised eyebrows at seeing two Plotal children with the Eartholians.

Brian's alert sounded.

"We need to get back to the palace and washed up for dinner," Brian said.

They made a U-turn. Ekka and Foota flew over the city back to their tower.

"Wow! You're so lucky to have your own borjos!" Fazi said.

"We had a difficult time training Foota, the female," Jamie said. He explained what happened with Chacoodi.

"I'm so glad she didn't eat Chacoodi!" Cadj said.

"D'laine used The Voice to make her understand what she was not allowed to do," Brian said. "She can't eat any pakows, Plotals, Kudaja or Egroms."

Then they told what happened to Ekka when he ate the queper.

"Gross!" Fazi exclaimed. "D'laine put her hands inside the borjo's stomach?"

"Yeah, Trakon and my father had to pull it out the rest of the way," Darren said. "They were covered in this stinking goo. It was disgusting!"

They all ran to the palace, afraid they would be late.

"Fazi, there's the female's bathroom. We'll meet you out here in a few minutes," Brian said.

They entered their respective bathrooms.

Fazi washed her hands. Then she took a cloth and wet it. She wiped down the scales on her face, and through her little curly Mohawk. When she was satisfied that she would pass parental inspection, mainly her mother's, she left the bathroom.

She heard the boys inside their bathroom and shook her head. Four boys together was a little too much. They were noisy.

The boys exited their bathroom. The humans had cleaned up and combed their hair. Fazi inspected her brother. Cadj looked clean. They dashed to the dining salon where they discovered larger chairs and place settings for the Plotals.

All the women inspected the children nonverbally. Neska, Kara, Kitry, D'laine and Ethaderia nodded approval. Treikie suppressed a giggle. They grouped the kids at one end of the table and the adults at the other end.

When they were all seated, the majordomo and his staff brought platters of food around to each person.

"Take some vegetables, Cadj," Neska ordered.

Cadj scowled. The server repressed a smile as he returned to the Plotal boy with the platter. Cadj reluctantly scooped several vegetables onto his plate.

"And lower your tail!" Jakla said. He shook his head. "Boys!"

Cadj's tail was vertical, up the back of the chair. He quickly corrected the indiscretion and wrapped his tail down his side and around his lower legs.

Fazi giggled. At least she wasn't getting the parental grumbles.

"You should not find this funny, Fazi," Neska said. "I'm proud of your manners, but you are not perfect, so don't make your brother feel inferior."

"I'm sorry, mother," Fazi said.

"At least you have a boy and a girl," Lee said. "Try having two boys."

Jakla gruffed. "You have my sympathies."

"Trakon and D'laine will most likely have their hands full with their twin eggs," Kitry said.

"Twins?" Neska asked. "Isn't that rare for Tholian humans?" She leaned around Jakla slightly to catch D'laine's eyes. "Congratulations!"

"We were so worried through the churling," D'laine said. "Stanley transported them to the catacombs, but I had thoughts of disasters going through my head about the palace collapsing."

"We mothers live in fear about our children being hurt, or worse," Kitry said. "I'm sure it's a universal feeling with all females, regardless of species."

Neska nodded. "Yes, Jakla will tell you how crazy I was about our buried eggs. If anyone walked within five feet of the area, I would shriek."

Jakla let out a huff. "I ended up having to post guards at the perimeter of our egg hatching plot for the entire four months."

The Eartholians stared at the Plotals.

"On Earth, there are animals called alligators and crocodiles. On one hand, your forms are very much like theirs, but the resemblance stops there," Lee said. "They do not stand on their hind legs. They also lay eggs and they bury them in the ground."

Lee projected a picture of the animals.

Everyone stared at the alligator in Lee's projection.

"Do you think that is a relative of ours?" Neska asked her husband.

Jakla continued to study the projection. "It's possible we evolved from those creatures. I'm not sure how one of those creatures would have ended up on Thol, though."

"They have not changed in millions of years," Stanley said. "If you laid down on the floor beside one, you would be considered small. Some grow to twelve to fifteen foots long, and they move fast."

"I'm glad we don't crawl on our bellies," Cadj said.

After dinner, the adults retired to the family salon, while the kids headed up the stairs to one of their rooms, but not before they had to listen to mild warnings.

"No roughhousing," Lee said.

"Share your toys," Kara said.

"Remember, you are a guest," Neska said.

The boys and Fazi crept up the stairs on their best behavior.

The staff served Kahl as everyone settled in for conversation.

Stanley reiterated the conversation about the Trangula, and the information the Egroms passed along.

"Doski?" Kitry asked. She looked to Jor-Dan. "I don't recall learning about those creatures."

Jor-Dan shook his head. "I've never heard of them."

Treikie cleared her throat to get their attention. "Doskis originated during the Calming Age, when our world was going through a metamorphosis. This was between integrating humans and all the dominant species. The doski are not humans. They are a combination of the tree people, now extinct, and an early version of humans."

"If you look at them, you will notice their arms are longer than normal humans, and their noses are large and flat. There's a small hump between their shoulder blades which makes them look hunched over."

"By tree people, do you think those are like our apes?" Lee asked. He projected a picture of a gorilla.

"Yes, very similar," Treikie said. She studied the gorilla. "Your apes seem to have a thicker body, but the arms and noses are similar."

"This is very interesting," Jakla said. "It appears our worlds share similar species."

"It's interesting how different the evolutionary path is between the worlds," Jor-Dan commented.

"On Earth, there is an old saying," Victor said. "Which came first, the chicken or the egg. It's almost impossible to think that through. If the chicken came first, where did it come from? If the egg came first, how was it created?"

CHAPTER THIRTY-ONE

*E*thaderia, Kitry, Kara, D'laine and Treikie spent hours huddled in deep discussions. Changes were being made to Ethaderia's residence—all in secret.

Lee raised his eyebrows when he went to call on Ethaderia, and her manservant sent him away.

"The ladies are in a planning session and don't wish to be disturbed," the manservant said.

Lee stared at the man. "Eglabado, she honestly doesn't want to see me?"

"Mr. Lee, it isn't that she doesn't want to see you. She specifically told me to admit no one into the house while the ladies were in their planning session," Eglabado said. "Meaning you and the boys."

Lee huffed out a sliver of anger. He raised his hands. "Okay. I guess she'll let me know when she wants to talk." He turned and saw Jamie racing up to him. Lee held up one hand to his son. "Can't visit today. She's busy and can't be disturbed."

"What do you mean?" Jamie said, exasperated. He looked at Eglabado, who just shrugged his shoulders.

"Your father is correct," the manservant said. "She is busy planning something."

Seeing his father a little dejected, Jamie took his hand and pulled him in the direction to Ekka's tower. "Come on, let's go for a ride. That will cheer you up!"

Lee let Jamie tug him over to the borjos' tower house. They climbed the stairs to the large space where Ekka and Foota dozed.

"Ekka! Let's take daddy for a ride!" Jamie said. He turned to Lee. "Why don't you ride Ekka and I'll ride Foota?"

Lee made eye contact with Ekka. "Is that okay, Ekka?"

The male borjo huffed out a thin line of smoke.

"Yeah, he said that's okay," Jamie said. He climbed aboard Foota while Lee climbed up on Ekka's back.

The borjos stood. Ekka waddled to the opening and dropped out of the tower. He spread his wings and soared upward bringing a huge smile to Lee's face.

Foota followed with Jamie laughing.

The borjos sailed through the air over the city, then over the walls of the kingdom. They flew over miles and miles of moss, the Cember Forest, and way beyond where Jum, the worm-snake that once terrorized the kingdoms now lived.

Jamie directed the borjos to make a wide turn, and they flew toward Jakla's city. They passed above the kingdoms of Aveldon, Caradon, Jekorba, Kensadora, Lansobar, Mer and Patrosym. They headed back toward Ebscalon. Lee looked down and saw the garden, the pecan tree and the chocolate forest.

The borjos glided to their tower. Ekka entered first with a soft landing. He folded his wings, waddled several feet and settled down so that Lee could slide off to the floor. Foota came in a little faster.

"Slow down!" Jamie scolded her.

The female borjo landed delicately, folded in her wings and cuddled up to Ekka. Jamie jumped to the floor.

"Feel better, daddy?" Jamie asked.

"That was just what the doctor ordered," Lee said. "Good idea, son." He looked over the borjos. "I'm not sure I'm comfortable with you riding Foota. She still seems a little wild."

"It's okay," Jamie said. "She's getting used to our ways."

They made their way down the stairs and back to the palace.

JAMIE LED LEE TO THE KITCHEN TO HUNT UP A SNACK. THEY found Grubio and Hruk watching a translated video about the manufacturing of chocolate from the pods. Hruk was busy making notes and drawing sketches on a sheet of paper.

"Have you figured out how to make chocolate yet?" Lee asked.

"We've watched all the Earth videos. I'm ready to give it a try," Hruk said. "I can't get the taste of that chocolate confection out of my head!"

"A lot of Earthlings love chocolate, in all of its forms. D'laine loves café mocha, which is chocolate mixed into her morning coffee," Lee said. "What you have to do is make sure the ingredients are pure, which I'm sure they will be here on Thol. On Earth, the manufacturers add filler ingredients that aren't that good for people to consume, and they add a lot of sweeteners so people end up gaining weight."

"Yeah, you don't want to make Trakon fat," Jamie said. "D'laine wouldn't like that."

"We may have to insist on a daily limit for our prince," Grubio said, with a snarky laugh.

Grubio called to one of his helpers. "We have two hungry Eartholians here. Better get them something before they use their powers on us."

"I'm not sure our particular powers are anything to take down the kitchen," Lee said. "I can see your entire place in 3-D, and Jamie talks to animals, so unless you have animal brains in your heads, I think you're safe."

A young woman brought two small plates with slices of meat from last night's dinner, slices of tomato and bread.

"We need to teach them how to make a sandwich," Jamie said. He went about building his sandwich. "What can we use for mayo?"

Grubio stepped over to them. "What do you need?"

"Something to spread on the bread," Lee said.

Grubio whipped up several ingredients into what tasted like mayonnaise. "This should work. It's tangy."

Jamie dipped his knife into the bowl and spread some on his bread. He licked his fingers. "Tastes just like mayonnaise! Thanks, Grubio!"

Lee built his sandwich, cut his and Jamie's in half and they dug in. "Need to find something like romaine lettuce. There's got to be something close to it here on Thol."

"What do you call this?" Grubio asked as he watched Lee build his sandwich.

"When you place food between two slices of bread, it's called a sandwich," Lee said. "It was invented by a man on Earth hundreds of years ago."

"Sandwiches are very popular for when you want to eat when you're busy," Jamie said. "Or going on a picnic."

"What's a picnic?" Hruk asked.

"Say you and your girlfriend wanted to get away from the city and relax near an oasis, or just sit on a blanket on the moss and eat some food," Jamie said. "You could make some sandwiches and bring them with you."

"I like that idea," Hruk said.

JAMIE RAN OFF LOOKING FOR HIS BROTHER AND DARREN. LEE trudged up to Stanley's suite. He knocked on the open doorframe.

"What are you up to?" Lee asked.

"I'm mapping the Aguberro mountains and the Crest of Ingosaquille so we can get up there and look at the artifacts in that cave," Stanley said.

Lee strode over to where Stanley sat at his desk staring at his laptop screen. He grabbed a chair and plunked his butt down.

"How do we get in touch with Maldi Amadal when we're ready to go?" Lee asked.

"I'm not sure, but he's probably one of those beings that shows up when he's supposed to," Stanley said.

Lee nodded. That's the way it typically happened on Thol. "We will definitely need to strategize for this trip. I'll bet the Fod are all over the place, then there's the wild borjos. They may be protectors of the caves."

"If we flew there in crestriders, I'm not sure where we would land," Stanley said. He projected a vision of the mountain from when he returned the Fod. "I think the cave Maldi explored is up there." He pointed to the Crest of Ingosaquille where caves were numerous.

"Would the elevation cause a problem if we flew there?" Lee asked. "Remember when D'laine and Trakon flew to the Raagor Mountains, they had a problem with elevation sickness. That was much lower than this cave."

Stanley huffed out exasperation. "You're right. I wonder if I could step there with Maldi's guidance. Maybe I could try taking a scroll or something else and just step back here."

"Maybe you could grab the lot of the cave and bring it all back!" Lee's wild thought brought smiles to both their faces.

Stanley's alert sounded. "Dinnertime. Let's see if everyone wants to set a date for next week."

They left Stanley's quarters and trotted down the stairs to

the dining room. Trakon, Jor-Dan and Victor sat at the table, along with the boys. Lee and Stanley took their places.

"Where is everyone?" Lee asked.

The majordomo approached the table. "The ladies are not joining you tonight. They are at Ethaderia's home."

"They've been there all day," Lee said. "What's going on?"

All the men shrugged.

Lee turned to his sons. They shrugged.

Dinner was served. Lee and Stanley brought up the trip to the mountains, and they discussed Lee and Stanley's concerns.

After they finished dinner, the boys went back outdoors while the men retired to the family salon.

"Well, that was definitely a much quieter meal," Trakon said.

"Four women have a lot to say," Victor said.

"You'd better watch yourselves," Jor-Dan warned.

Just as the words flew out of his mouth, D'laine, Kitry, Treikie and Kara entered the salon.

"We balance the conversations," Kitry said. There was just a tad bit of emphasis on her statement.

Jor-Dan, ever the peace-keeper steered the conversation away from where he didn't want to go. "We were discussing plans to explore the cave on Mount Aguberro next week."

Ethaderia drilled her eyes into Lee. "You can't go next week."

"Why not?" Lee asked. He couldn't think of any one thing that would keep them from the trip.

"Because we are getting married next week!" Ethaderia said, elated.

"We are?" he asked. Lee made eye contact with the others to see if someone knew more than he did.

Trakon and Victor shrugged. Stanley looked over to Jor-Dan. He shrugged.

"We have it all planned out," Kitry said.

"It's not going to be elaborate, is it?" Lee asked.

"Thol, no! Ethaderia didn't want a big wedding with the rooms overflowing with people," Treikie said.

"We'll invite close friends, such as Ben, Herish, Meeri, Jakla and his family, Ghury, and anyone else you want there," D'laine said.

Lee stared at his daughter. "All I have to do is show up?"

The women smiled at him.

"Okay then," Lee said. "Just tell me when to show up and where to stand."

"This calls for a celebration!" Victor stated.

ETHADERIA WAS THE CLOSEST THING TO A PRINCESS D'LAINE HAD ever seen. She wore the traditional Tholian wedding dress that was similar to a decorated sari. The material was made of the finest hosk silk with bits of sparkling crystals and silver beads attached. The color of the material was difficult to describe, as it seemed to change colors anytime Ethaderia moved.

Lee was handsome in a white uniform with a silver and gold crestrider symbol. Without Lee and Stanley, the crestriders would still be thudding to the ground after the suns set.

Jamie fussed with the sleeves of his uniform. He had grown and the sleeves barely reached his wrists.

Brian was experiencing a similar problem, but with the legs of the uniform.

A tap sounded on the door, then D'laine let herself into the room. "Wow, daddy, you look so handsome!"

"You sure I have everything?" Lee asked. His nerves were not completely undone, but close.

D'laine looked him over. She noticed the symbols on his chest. "Everything is in place." She turned to her brothers and noticed their problems. She grabbed Jamie and turned him around to face her.

"Stay still. I'll fix your sleeves, okay?" she asked.

"It's too late to do anything," Jamie whined.

D'laine made him hold up his right arm. She found the button she needed and then straightened his arm out. She held the tiny button, and the material lengthened to the correct length. Then she repeated the procedure with the left arm.

"Wow! Will you look at this, daddy! This material makes adjustments!" This discovery thrilled Jamie.

D'laine turned to help Brian with the length of his uniform, but he already figured it out and stood straight, looking very smart in his outfit.

A tap sounded on the door and Jor-Dan, his dog La'gar'ish, and Trakon entered. They looked over Lee and the boys.

"I have more symbols for your uniform," Jor-Dan said. He held a gold symbol of the planet Earth. "This will identify you as an Eartholian." There was another symbol with the crown of the king. "This symbol identifies you as an advisor." Jor-Dan held them against the chest of Lee's uniform and they self-attached.

Trakon attached the Eartholian symbols to Brian and Jamie's uniforms.

"Is everyone ready?" D'laine asked.

"I'm ready to show up," Lee said, with a grin.

They left his suite and headed down the stairs to the throne room. Guests and dignitaries filled the room.

"So much for a small wedding," Lee said.

"We wisely allow the women to make these decisions," Jor-Dan said.

Lee and Trakon grunted.

The Visionary, dressed in a long, flowing white garment with a glittering multicolored cloth across the back of his neck that draped to his waist, motioned the wedding party forward.

Lee and Ethaderia were delivered to their places and faced each other. Brian and Jamie joined the rest of the family and friends.

Lee's eyes were filled with love as he gazed upon Ethaderia.
Ethaderia smiled back at Lee, tears spilling down her cheeks.
The Visionary tied one of Lee's hands to Ethaderia's hands with thin red threads.

"Eartholian Lee Jackson willingly receives Ethaderia Justalon of the Kingdom of Ebscalon as his wife and life partner. From this minute forward, your dreams of accomplishments are shared willingly between yourselves until one or both depart this life."

The Visionary repeated the same in reverse, with Ethaderia receiving Lee. After that, he painted a gold triangle symbol in the third eye area on each forehead.

He bent and whispered to both of them. Lee and Ethaderia rearranged their hair behind their right ears.

The Visionary painted the rim of their right ears with the same gold paint.

"You shall listen to each other and openly discuss the turns and future events, problems and successes, not dwelling on the past."

"As husband and wife life partners, you shall honor each other with truthfulness and loyalty, as equals. Your children will strengthen your bond to each other. May Thol bless you with as many children as you desire."

"You will protect one another, your kingdom, and Thol itself from danger. You will respect the elders of your kingdom, for one turn you, too, shall be an elder seeking the same respect you gave."

The Visionary turned and picked up a chalice that contained soil. He dipped his finger into the dirt and touched Lee at one temple, then the other. He repeated this on Ethaderia.

"This soil symbolizes the very ground of the planet Thol, which you stand upon. You are her stewards. Keep her safe for all inhabitants. May you bless her with your love and respect for all beings who share our space."

"May you have a wonderful celebration of your joining! From this minute on, Ethaderia Justalon shall officially be known as Ethaderia Jackson of the house of Eartholian of Ebscalon."

With that, Lee and Ethaderia held hands and turned to face the guests. They raised their bound hands together, and the guests cheered.

The kitchen staff, dressed in their finest, poured into the room with trays of abrajaii in crystal flutes, some of which were very large for the Egrom and Plotal guests. After around ten minutes, they seated guests at tables. The royal family and the newlyweds were seated at a table on a platform overlooking the room.

The staff delivered plates of food, while a Tholian band played dinner music on their unusual instruments.

Lee and Ethaderia did their best at eating their food. Lee's left hand was tied to Ethaderia's right hand, so with every forkful of food, Lee's hand raised with hers.

He leaned toward Jor-Dan. "This hand-tying is awkward."

"Wait until one of you has to relieve yourself," Jor-Dan chuckled.

Lee raised his eyebrows. He hadn't considered that.

Kitry elbowed Jor-Dan in the side.

"My wife has reproved me for my crass comment," the king said, still chuckling.

As they finished the main course, the kitchen staff served dessert. Brian stood and tapped his knife against his glass.

"Back on Earth, my father would have had a best man at his wedding, probably one of his colleagues. The best man always makes a speech and toasts the bride and groom," Brian said. "Since Tholian traditions are slightly different, I thought I'd take the place of the best man."

Brian smiled widely at his father and new stepmother. "Over the past seven paths, my father has been through a lot. He lost our mother in a terrible automobile crash on Earth. D'laine came close to dying in that accident. She was in a coma for a long time and dreamed about Trakon. Then I was hit in the chest by a baseball and almost died. The doctors discovered I had a tumor on my heart."

"After all that, D'laine was pulled through the portal to Thol. We didn't think we'd ever see her again, but she returned, cured me, and brought us back to Thol, along with Stanley." Brian took a breath. "My father is a strong man. He perseveres through whatever life throws his way. My brother and I are so happy to have a new mother. D'laine also, but she's sort of a mom herself, with her eggs." He raised his glass. "To my father and his bride. May they live a blissful life together!"

Glasses raised throughout the room.

"To Lee and Ethaderia," voices rang out.

Grubio and Hruk approached the table. The dessert chef held a covered plate and presented it to the newlyweds.

"To begin your new life together, Hruk has prepared a new delicacy in your honor," Grubio said.

With much fanfare, Grubio removed the lid to show small squares of a dark brown confection.

Lee gingerly took a piece and took a small bite. His eyes widened, his eyebrows rose and he shoved the last bit of the morsel in his mouth. He leaned across the table and glanced at Trakon. "Chocolate!"

CHAPTER THIRTY-TWO

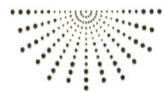

*D*ancing couples filled the floor of the large space. Brian spun Yucovia, his old dance partner, around the room. She had blossomed into a young lady and had moon eyes for her dance partner.

Jamie and Galgason were practically dance competition candidates. They slid across the floor with the adult dancers.

Even Jakla and Neska danced.

Who would have thought the Plotals danced the minuet—or even danced at all, D'laine thought. They're so graceful!

Stanley and Treikie were like Fred Astaire and Ginger Rogers going through the moves of the various dances.

The only ones who had any problems at all were Victor and Kara. Finally, after stumbling through the basic moves, Kara dragged Victor back to the table.

"We should have practiced more!" Kara whispered.

"I seriously doubt if anyone noticed," Victor said. "Besides, they'll chalk it up to us being the newbies."

After the dancing and all the ceremonial proceedings, the guests began to leave. Lee and Ethaderia approached Brian and Jamie.

"You'll be moving to Ethaderia's next week... notch," Lee said.

"How come we can't come with you?" Jamie asked.

"Your father and I have a lot to talk about for our new lives, and we have many things we still need to do, so it is better for us to take care of all those things before you move into your new living quarters," Ethaderia said. Her cheeks were turning a darker color.

"Son, we've talked about this. It's only one week," Lee said.

Brian poked Jamie in the ribs. "It's not like they're going across Thol. They're just down the street! We can get through one week without daddy!"

Jamie pouted. "Oh, okay."

"And you'd better make sure you behave," Lee said. He gave them that parental stink-eye of warning. "Don't cause anyone any trouble, understand?"

"We won't," they chorused.

LEE AND ETHADERIA DIDN'T PUBLICLY KISS AT EVERY OPPORTUNITY like D'laine and Trakon did. But they were always touching or holding hands, which didn't have the boys running.

The day of the official move out of the palace arrived. The boys marched down the road with their arms filled with their clothes and the few personal possessions they had collected.

Eglabado held the door open at Ethaderia's house, then he escorted them to their new rooms.

Jamie's eyes widened as he took in his new room. He dumped his clothes on the bed and stared at a crestrider model that hung from the ceiling and moved with the breeze. There was a shelf where carved toys of all Jamie's favorite creatures were lined up: Oggy, Ekka, Jum (the worm snake), some pakows, diwal dogs and hosks. A desk and bookcase were against one wall. There was a comfy sofa and chairs for company, and the big bed with a colorful assortment of bedding and pillows fit for a boy.

Brian's room was across the hall. His private space was similar, but they gave more space for his desk and shelving. He walked straight to the smart closet and hung his clothes. He noticed a game table and recognized a board game he had seen in Cadj's room at Ta'Byu'Vohon.

Lee and Ethaderia stood in the hallway between the two rooms.

"What do you think? Do you like your new rooms?" Lee asked.

Ethaderia held her breath, worried about her new role as stepmother.

"I love my room," Jamie yelled from his new space.

"This is really nice," Brian said.

"Jamie, hang your clothes in the closet," Ethaderia said. "They'll get all wrinkled in that pile on your bed."

Jamie scooped up the clothes and hung them in the closet.

"I know you've been here many times, but why don't we tour your new house," Ethaderia said.

They walked down the stairs and went to the large salon for entertaining guests, and a smaller salon for more intimate visits. Next was the kitchen. Ethaderia showed them where glasses, cups, plates and utensils were, so they could fend for themselves if the cook or another adult wasn't available.

"Perhaps I should show you and your father how we cook," Ethaderia said. "We could plan that one day this week."

"That's a good idea," Lee said. "I'd like to see how you prepare food here."

The front door chime sounded. After a few minutes, Eglabado escorted D'laine and Trakon to the kitchen.

"Hi, daddy. Hi Ethaderia," D'laine said. "Getting the boys settled in?"

"Do you have any chocolate here?" Trakon asked.

D'laine nudged him. "No, they don't have any chocolate!"

"I figured maybe Grubio gave them some for a wedding present," Trakon grumped.

"Daddy, I think we should chop down the chocolate forest!" D'laine said.

"That would most likely incite an uprising," Lee said. "Hruk is very keen on chocolate. Then there's Herish and the other Kudaja."

"I can't wait to sip a cup of hot chocolate," D'laine said.

"I just want to eat it by the handful," Trakon said.

"Honestly, Trakon," D'laine said.

The door chime sounded again. Moments later, Victor, Kara and Darren entered the kitchen. The boys took off running to show Darren their rooms.

The group settled in the smaller salon.

"Have you or your sister heard anything from your mother?" Kara asked.

Ethaderia shook her head. "Nothing, and I hope it stays that way."

"We've been out of the loop since the wedding," Lee said. "Is there a solid date when we're going to the caves?"

"Stanley thinks it would be better to have him step us there instead of flying," Trakon said. "I agree with his assessment. If we flew crestriders, it would take a week to get there, then there's the problem of where to settle the ships."

"If we flew Ekka and Foota, they might stir up trouble with the wild borjos," D'laine said. "So, it looks like it would be easier to proceed with Stanley's plan."

"That makes sense," Lee said. "Has anyone tried to contact the Plakado?"

"When we know for sure what turn we can leave, D'laine or the Visionary can contact him," Victor said.

The chime on the front door sounded again.

The following week, a group waited in the palace salon for the Visionary and Maldi Amadal. They decided Jor-Dan would stay behind due to the fact they didn't know what to expect on the trip, and they didn't want to place the king in jeopardy.

Trakon still wanted to recruit borjos, but the focus would be on the prophecy. They would search through the cave and see if there were any scrolls that specifically related to D'laine, Trakon, or their children's roles in the Prophecy of Thol.

The Visionary and the Plakado arrived. The Visionary held the ruby staff.

Maldi turned to Trakon. "If you are determined to bring some borjos back to Ebscalon, I suggest you bring Jamie with you. We will be able to fold a tunnel for him to fly a lead borjo with others following, back to Ebscalon."

"Father, what do you think? Can I bring back two or three?" Trakon asked.

"No more than three," Jor-Dan said. "And not until D'laine is here so she can control them."

"We definitely don't want them thinking they are being invited to dinner and we're the meal," Kitry said.

Lee pressed his communicator and called Jamie. "Do you want to go on this trip to the caves with us? Trakon is going to entice some borjos to come home with us, and will need you to communicate with them."

"Sure! I'll be right there!" Jamie said. He thundered into the palace and joined the others in the salon.

Stanley latched onto Maldi Amadal's aura signature. The group stepped forward and were gone.

STANLEY, LEE, TRAKON, D'LAINE, VICTOR, JAMIE, MALDI AND the Visionary found themselves in the cave.

"Jamie, you need to be careful when you leave the cave," D'laine said. "Remember, the Fod are all over the mountains and they protect the cave."

"Don't go anywhere without Trakon," Lee said.

Stanley and the others looked around at the artifacts and the shelves of ancient scrolls.

"Do you think it's possible for any of us to focus on the prophecy to identify the particular scrolls?" Stanley asked.

The Visionary, Maldi, D'laine and Victor made eye contact, thinking about Stanley's suggestion.

"Won't hurt to try," Victor said.

They each tried in their own way, but nothing happened.

"Trakon, why don't we try to hold the staff and see if we can find the scrolls that way?" D'laine asked.

"It's worth a try," Trakon said.

The Visionary handed the staff to Trakon. When D'laine placed her hand on the staff, nothing happened.

Maldi shook his head. "Remember, in that drawing on that scroll it showed both your hands on the staff. One of D'laine's hands first, then one of Trakon's, and so on."

"Okay. Let's try it," Trakon said.

D'laine placed one hand on the staff, then Trakon placed one of his. D'laine placed her other hand under Trakon's and he placed his second hand under hers.

The room lit up like the two suns were shining inside the cave. The staff vibrated at a high frequency.

"I hope this is safe!" Trakon said.

"I'll focus on the prophecy and the scrolls," D'laine said. She stared straight ahead, her eyes blanking somewhat.

Suddenly, scrolls were flying across the room and landing at her feet. Everyone else ducked and scooted out of the way. A pile of at least twenty scrolls sat at D'laine and Trakon's feet.

A large urn flew at Trakon. He ducked down. Lee caught the urn before it crashed to the ground.

The Visionary, Victor, Stanley and Maldi gathered around Lee. They studied the colorful images on the urn.

"D'laine, this has your and Trakon's pictures on it!" Lee said. "And, I think these are the twins!"

Jamie was exploring among the artifacts in a corner of the cave. He held a square container and stared at the images. "Uh, daddy. I think this is a picture of you!" He walked across the cave to where the group stood and showed them.

The container was decorated with images. The one prominent image looked like a King wearing a crown and flowing robes with gold braids.

"That looks like me," Lee said, bewildered. He looked at the Visionary. "Are you sure the rest of my family isn't involved with this prophecy?"

"What we have heard through the ages was only about D'laine and Trakon. This, however, looks like you!" The Visionary took the vessel from Jamie and turned it to see all sides. After he looked at the outside, he peered inside, which was empty, then turned it upside down to see the bottom. There wasn't anything inscribed on the bottom.

Lee took the container and walked it over to D'laine and Trakon. They stared at the picture, looked at Lee and back at the picture again.

D'laine attempted to remove one of her hands, but couldn't. "I can't remove my hands from this staff!"

Trakon tried with the same results. "This isn't good!"

The Visionary came forward. "Try removing your hands in the reverse order you started with."

Trakon removed his bottom hand, then D'laine removed her bottom hand. Then Trakon removed the top hand. D'laine held the staff out to the Visionary.

"All yours. Let's look at the scrolls," D'laine said.

"Jamie, keep looking around and see what else you find," Lee said.

After a hour of unrolling a few of the scrolls and reading passages, they gave up.

"Do you think we can try to bring these scrolls back with us?" Victor asked. "It's going to take a while to read through all of them."

"Let's experiment," Stanley said. He gathered up all the scrolls, stuck them in the container, along with the urn, then stepped forward. He disappeared—the scrolls and containers leaving the cave with him.

Maldi stared at the empty space. "I can't remember if I tried to step away. I only recall trying to leave through the cave opening."

A moment later, Stanley returned, empty-handed. "I left everything in the family room."

"Good! We can take our time reading through the scrolls," Trakon said.

"Trakon, let's find some borjos!" Jamie yelled.

Jamie raced to the cave opening. He looked outside to see if any of the Fod were close by. He stepped onto the ledge and gazed at the scene in front of him. Dozens of borjos sailed through the air, or lay settled in their nests.

"Oh, wow! Look at all the borjos!" he squealed.

Trakon joined him, his eyes wide with wonder. "How are we going to go about this?"

"I'll ask if any of them want to go home with us," Jamie said. "Ekka has always been straightforward with his answers. I'll bet these guys are too."

D'laine joined them. "How many more towers are in Ebscalon?"

Trakon thought a moment. He pressed his communicator. "Father, are there four or six more towers in the city?"

"Six," Jor-Dan yelled back. "But they haven't been inspected since the churling. And, we don't want that many of the creatures."

"You said I could bring back two or three," Trakon said.

"No more than three," Jor-Dan said. "They must follow the rules. We don't want citizens, pakows or anything else disappearing as midnight snacks."

Jamie called out silently to the borjos. *Who wants to live in the kingdom of Ebscalon where Ekka lives?*

Several borjos flew over to the cave ledge and glided through the sky.

"These borjos want to give it a try," Jamie said. "I'll tell them the rules and see if they agree."

If you live in Ebscalon, you will fly far away to hunt and eat. You cannot eat the humans, their pakows, Egroms, Plotals or Kudaja.

Four borjos flew away.

"Those don't like the rules," Jamie said. He turned to D'laine. "Why don't you say something to these three to make sure they want to come home with us."

D'laine gazed upon the three that were flying close by. She turned to Trakon and Jamie. "Go back into the cave. I'll call them down here but there's not enough room."

They joined the others inside the cave and watched as D'laine called upon The Voice.

Come Down! she called to the three borjos.

The beasts swooped down and landed on the ledge, one after the other. They folded in their wings and waddled forward.

D'laine looked at each borjo, making eye contact with each of them. *You will obey the rules at all times. Do you understand?*

They dipped their heads in submission.

You will fly far away to hunt and eat. You will do no harm. You will protect Ebscalon.

Again, they dipped their heads.

We will provide comfortable shelter and care for you.

D'laine rubbed each of their snouts.

Jamie and Trakon came out of the cave.

"When we get to Ebscalon, Ekka is in charge. He's the boss of the borjos," Jamie said. "His mate is Foota."

The borjos listened and didn't seem to have a problem with Ekka being in charge.

"Let's head back," Trakon said. "I don't want my parents thinking I've abandoned them to live in the caves."

"How are we going to do this?" Victor asked.

"We can do this in groups. I can take one borjo, Lee and Jamie. D'laine can take another borjo, Trakon and The Visionary. Maldi can take the last borjo, Victor and Lee."

"Okay, let's go back to Ebscalon!" Trakon said.

The groups of people stood by each borjo. Within a blink, the three borjos and the people were gone.

Everyone appeared in the courtyard, along with the three borjos. Ekka swooped over the courtyard. The wild borjos took to the air and followed respectfully behind Ekka.

Jor-Dan turned to Trakon. "You need to get those towers inspected."

"Don't forget we need to make them beds!" Jamie said.

"Okay," Trakon said. "Jamie, you go to the hosk building and start stuffing sacks. We'll need a lot of gauze for three beds." Trakon silently called for six soldiers. "Go with Jamie and fill sacks of gauze to make the three new borjos beds."

Next, he called Dreebo, the city planner and architect. "Dreebo, I need you to inspect the old towers for any problems from the churling." He explained what was going on.

"I'll find the three largest towers," Trakon told everyone.

Dreebo called his team together, and they split up.

Two hours later, Dreebo communicated with Trakon. "The

East tower has extensive damage. The southwest tower has a leak in the roof. All the others are in good condition."

Trakon went over to the hosk building. He found a mountain of sacks filled with gauze. He directed the soldiers to haul the sacks to the three biggest towers out of the remaining solid structures.

Jamie hauled a sack and tagged along with Trakon. Once the three towers had gauze on the floor, Jamie called to the borjos. They flew over the buildings and made their choices.

Trakon and Jamie climbed up the stairs of one tower. A borjo was creating a well in the middle of the gauze. He settled his large frame into the bed and huffed out what sounded like a sigh of pleasure.

Jamie stroked the borjo's snout. "What's your name?"

Grasko the borjo sent.

"Grasko?" Jamie asked.

The borjo snuffed out some smoke in acknowledgment.

"Hi Grasko. You can take a nap now. We're going to go see your friends," Jamie said.

"Remember the rules!" Trakon said.

They went over to the second tower and climbed the stairs. The borjo that sat on the nest looked rather regal the way he carried himself. He nudged Trakon.

"Oh! His name is Ehtuta, and he's your borjo, Trakon!" Jamie squealed.

Trakon's face lit up. "He's mine?"

"Yes, he's claimed you as his master," Jamie said.

Trakon stepped closer and rubbed the borjo's snout. "Welcome home, Ehtuta."

Jamie and Trakon visited the last tower. "This is Dundo. He's happy to be here. He said he'll protect Ebscalon."

They returned to the palace and joined the others in the family salon.

"Are all the borjos settled?" Jor-Dan asked.

"Yes. One has claimed me as his master! His name is Ehtuta!" Trakon sounded like a little boy with all his excitement showing. "Have you found anything interesting, or useful in the scrolls?"

"Not yet," D'laine said. "It's very dense reading because it's in an older language. I've just called out to Ghury to see if he can help me to read these."

Ghury stepped into the room. "You found scrolls about the prophecy?"

"Not only scrolls, wait until you see this container," Victor said. He didn't mention the likeness to Lee.

Ghury picked up the container and examined it. He studied the image then studied Lee's face. "One of your ancestors was a king."

Lee blanched. "Does that mean one of my relatives from Earth went through the portal?"

"It could also mean that someone from Thol deemed it necessary to hide someone from here, probably of royal birth, on Earth," The Visionary said.

Ghury held the container and became quiet. His eyes shut. Several minutes later his voice boomed out.

"You are a direct descendant of King Jangston," the Egrom said.

Everyone was filled with overflowing chatter at Ghury's proclamation that Lee was the direct descendant of the king of kings. Jor-Dan tasked a team to pour through the old scrolls and books for any inkling to King Jangston. He knew for a fact he had never learned about that king in his coming-up years.

CHAPTER THIRTY-THREE

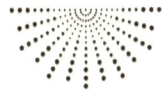

D'laine, Kitry and Ethaderia wandered through the marketplace to see what new baubles the craftspeople had for sale around Lee and Ethaderia's wedding theme.

As they strolled through the marketplace, D'laine stopped abruptly, grabbing Kitry and Ethaderia's hands, pulling them to a stop. She shushed them through mindtalk. Her eyes stared at a slightly hunched over man in a dark cloak.

Trakon! There's a Trangulan in the marketplace!

Stay back! He sent. *Don't let him know he has been spotted!*

D'laine ushered the women out of the marketplace and back to the palace.

Trakon and a squad of guards surreptitiously approached the Trangulan from different directions to make sure he did not escape. Once they were in position, they pounced on him. They hauled him to the palace, down the stairs to the cells.

They threw the infiltrator into a cell.

"What are you doing here, Trangulan?" Trakon asked.

The man threw off the cloak. It didn't conceal him as expected. His long arms reached to below his knees. He bared his teeth to Trakon and the guards, and made a sub-human noise.

"We are coming for you," he said.

The Adventure Continues

MAP OF THOL

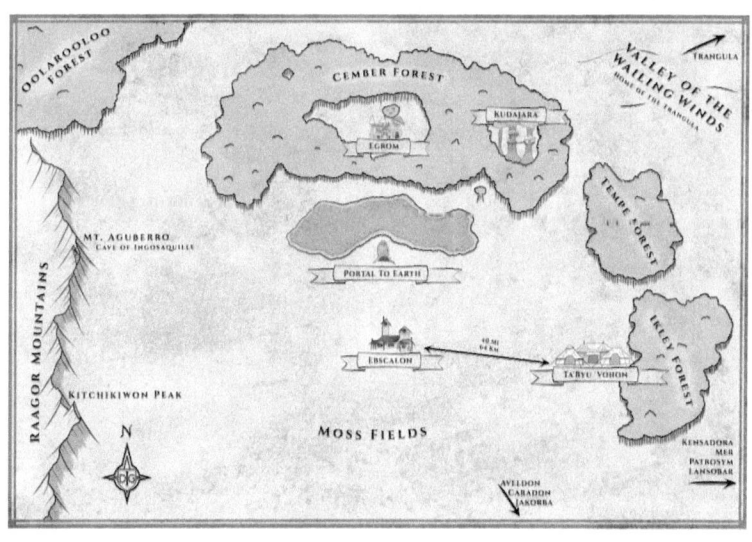

Creatures of Thol

Ghury
Egrom elder of the Cember Forest Tribe

Jakla Bosakin
Plotal Commander

Diwal Dog

Borjo

WANT MORE THOL?

THERE'S MORE THOL ON THE HORIZON! HERE'S A SNIPPET ABOUT BOOK 4 KING OF THOL:

Lee began having strange dreams shortly after the trip to the cave at the crest of Ingosaquille, on the Aguberro mountains. Ethaderia woke one morning to discover that Lee sported a trimmed beard. He didn't have one the night before.

Ghury proclaimed Lee was the direct descendant of King Jangstan. No one in the palace at Ebscalon had ever heard of him. Research uncovered that several hundred paths ago, King Jangstan ruled all of Thol—not just the Ciertrons of Ebscalon.

Everyone agreed something strange was going on with Lee.

Finally, after the eight kingdoms, along with Ta'Byu'Vohon and the Cember Forest villages recovered from the devastating churling, Ebscalon introduced D'laine and Trakon's twins: Jesslin and Kal-Dan.

D'laine shocked everyone at the event, including her family and friends, with the startling revelation about evolutionary and physiological changes to come. Not everyone is happy about that.

Foota sticks her head in Jamie's window. One of the twins needs help!

The boys discover things that look like cantaloupes. They bring one back to the palace and Trakon freaks out.

The Trangula storm the gates of Ebscalon. This is the first act of war since the Great War of Taylon.

The adventure continues
Book 4 ~ King of Thol
Book 5 ~ Earth Calling Thol

Did you miss Book 1? Prophecy of Thol
Book 2 ~ Gifts From Thol

Love of Thol: A Glossary

A * indicates a new character, creature, or thing introduced in
Love of Thol.

Characters

Absadul	One of the Egrom village elders.
Adrum	One of the Egrom village elders, he is tasked specifically with teaching D'laine the history of Thol.
Akubel	An ancient Egrom leader from long ago who received a prophecy.
Al Jordan	A junior staff member at Houston Daily News looking to make his big break, and a science fiction fan at heart. His plans to run a story on the anniversary of the Jackson family's disappearance turn into helping hide their existence on Thol.
Amoroso*	One of the women warriors assigned to guard D'laine and Trakon's unborn children.
Anwak*	The documentarian of the Plotals.
Aob*	One of the Kudaja's borjos, he chooses Ben as his rider.
Augenta*	Ethaderia's mother, she sorely disapproves of her daughter's match. After her exile from Ebscalon, she mysteriously vanishes.
Ben Joplin	The head of Rice University's physics department. He gets enlisted by Victor Bennett for a desperate plan to save the man's wife. The next to migrate to Thol after his retirement, he settles alongside the Kudaja and gains the gift of intertransport between Thol and Earth.
Bensol	One of the Egrom village elders tasked with helping and training D'laine to realize her destiny. He is the youngest of the Egrom elders.
Biggan	An Ebscalon guard assigned to D'laine and Trakon as the amorous couple's chaperone.
Bist	A city planner and one of several Plotals accompanying Jakla on his visit to Ebscalon.
Bok-Tor	A Safri prisoner D'laine saves from the Plotals.
Borg*	One of the Kudaja, he helps Ben adjust to Tholian life.
Brenda	D'laine's childhood friend since 3rd grade.
Brian Jackson	D'laine's younger brother; at 10 years old, he played in the Little League, but health complications put a stop to it. Traveling to Thol after being healed, he was the last to come into his powers: detecting the portals between the alternate earths. He develops an interest in learning how the kingdom of Ebscalon is run.
Buffy	The Jackson family's tan and white pit bull. Oddly, she seems to be getting younger on Thol despite her physical age.

Cadj*	Jakla's son, he and his sister befriend Brian, Jamie, Chacoodi, and Darren, often getting into trouble with them.
Cagmondoore*	King of the Kudaja; he is willing to let Ben settle in their village in Cember Forest.
Cendi*	One of the women warriors assigned to guard D'laine and Trakon's unborn children.
Chacoodi	A young Egrom from their village, he is quick to befriend both Brian and Jamie, becoming best friends with the former.
Chatter	Trakon's pet diwal dog.
Connor	Tall, dark-haired, and D'laine's ex-boyfriend.
Corl*	A furniture crafter; one of the Kudaja.
Dannin	One of Ebscalon's council members, he is in charge of livestock, food and water, and hosk gathering.
Darren Bennet	Victor Bennet's son, this 8-year-old is both space obsessed and loves a good story. Enamored by Thol, he has no objections once his parents are convinced to move there. His gift is revealed to be electricity.
Ditol	One of the Egrom village elders tasked with helping and training D'laine to realize her destiny.
D'laine Jackson	Smart and resourceful, D'laine was in for more than she could have ever imagined when her mysterious dream became reality. Now fully settled into Thol along with her family, learned advanced healing, and married to Trakon, the couple are in for a surprise when her body adapts to mimic Ciertron physiology.
Dreboo	Ebscalon's architect.
Drusta	One of the Egrom village elders tasked with helping and training D'laine to realize her destiny. He has a close connection to plants.
Dundo*	One of the borjos that come from Mt. Aguberro to live in Ebscalon.
Dupree	An inventor defensive about his achievements; he comes up with a device to pick up spectral images.
Eglabado*	The manservant at Ethaderia's home.
Egraphor*	Queen of Patrosym.
Ehtuta*	One of the borjos that come from Mt. Aguberro to live in Ebscalon; he becomes Trakon's mount.
Ekal	One of the Visionary's only two disciples.
Ekka	A full-sized borjo gifted to Jaime by a mysterious traveler. Made the protector of Ebscalon, he lives at the top of one of the kingdom's towers.
Emeric*	The king of Patrosym, his life is saved thanks to D'laine's healing.
Eric Villarreal	Rosa's husband.

Ethaderia Justalon	Cousin to Kitry, she found shared feelings with one of the newcomers from Earth, and is now finally joined in happy matrimony with Lee Jackson.
Fazi*	Jakla's daughter, she and her brother befriend Brian, Jamie, Chacoodi, and Darren, often getting into trouble with them.
Felid*	One of the women warriors assigned to guard D'laine and Trakon's unborn children.
Fod*	A mysterious figure and a member of the Fod race, a group of creatures who (due to a misunderstanding) intend to harm Marrak.
Foota*	Ekka's new borjo friend and mate
Forador	The agriculturist of Ebscalon.
Gafn*	A furniture crafter; one of the Kudaja.
Ghury	A key member of the Egrom village elders, Ghury becomes D'laine's mentor and guide for the path that lays ahead.
Grasko*	One of the borjos that come from Mt. Aguberro to live in Ebscalon.
Greg Claymore	An Eartholian sundered from his home and family many decades ago, Greg has come to terms with his new life on Thol; however, the newcomers to the planet find themselves suddenly in desperate need of his healing abilities.
Grubio*	One of the palace's chefs.
Hal-sa-Bin	A member of the Ebscalon council, he is in charge of security.
Halvid*	One of the women warriors assigned to guard D'laine and Trakon's unborn children.
Herish Cagmondoore	A Kudaja warrior of Cember Forest. Revealed to be the prince of his race, Herish tries to make amends with D'laine; all while getting into the occasional tussle with Trakon.
Hexlon	Usually seen working on the crestriders, Hexlon's various skills come in handy when he receives an unusual commission.
Hruk*	One of the palace chefs who specializes in desserts.
Ilanda*	Ethaderia's sister; she is already married to the king of Kensadora.
Jakla Bosakin	Once a pillaging warlord, Jakla has since turned to more peaceful ways, his goals switching from using D'laine's powers to rebuilding his people's kingdom.
Jamie Jackson	At only 6 years old, he's D'laine's youngest brother. Always having a special kinship with animals, Jamie's talent gets taken to new heights once his Tholian powers are realized; however, his innocence may mean learning the hard way that not all animals are perfectly friendly.

Characters, *Continued*

Ja-Toy-Anic	Despite being a citizen of Ebscalon, his loyalties may lie elsewhere.
Jawget	A Ciertron farmer infected by a mysterious ailment.
Jor-dan Bramstone	Despite his age of sixty years, the King of Ebscalon doesn't shy from being both venerable ruler and fearless warrior.
Jubulon	The ruler of Aveldon.
Jugdaak	The pakow handler of Ebscalon, he comes to verbal blows with Jamie over an injured og.
Jum	A young fhahadda saved and later relocated.
Kara Bennett	Victor Bennett's wife, and the receiver of a horrible medical diagnosis; the ripple effects of which will affect both Thol and Earth. Originally apprehensive about moving to Thol, she eventually agrees, gaining the gift of distinguishing lies and truth.
Keeshi*	One of the women warriors assigned to guard D'laine and Trakon's unborn children.
Kestrum	A female Egrom who lets D'laine stay at her mushroom house; the two quickly become fast friends.
Kitry Bramstone	The motherly Queen of Ebscalon, always looking to make those under her care as comfortable as possible.
Klaxjor*	One of Ebscalon's flight lieutenants.
Kyo*	Dannin's younger brother; he used to be Trakon's childhood friend before they grew apart.
Lansing	The widowed Queen of Jekorba.
Laoife	Mother to Ja-Toy-Anic, she shares both his leanings and vices.
Lee Jackson	Father of D'laine, Brian, and Jamie, this former NASA scientist's faith was tested when his eldest mysteriously vanished. Now reunited in a new world, Lee turns to using his career skills and his gift of holographic envisionings to help the Ciertrons with their technology. Though happily remarried and made an advisor to the king, there may be still more mysteries surrounding his ancestry.
Lorand*	A member of Princess Yalalore's guard detail, he is sent to either kidnap or kill the royal eggs.
Lori Jackson	Lee Jackson's late wife, and the victim to a tragic accident.
Lulu	A female pakow that becomes D'laine's mount.
Maldi Amadal	A Plakado traveler and wanderer, he has found several secrets on his journeys, including a mysterious staff.

Characters, *Continued*

Mark	Victor and Stanley's tech assistant.
Marrak	A member of Jor-Dan's council, his role is that of a documentarian, recording petitions made to the king, the decisions taken, and applying the royal seal to the finished documents. Victim of a mysterious attacker, he hovered between life and death.
Mayaar	Jor-Dan's manservant.
Meeri Glascombe	One of the Kudaja, she becomes Herish's betrothed and later his wife, befriending D'laine along the way. She is now with child.
Neska*	Jakla's mate.
Noona*	Tetonie's mate. She and her partner are the last of their race, and desperate for any help they can find.
Oggy	An injured og rescued and later adopted by Jamie.
Oogo	The leader of the Oolarooloo village who took in Greg Claymore.
Orongo*	Jor-Dan's old Plotal friend.
Pra-yor	One of several Plotals accompanying Jakla on his visit to Ebscalon.
Puando	A neutered borjo serving as Herish's mount.
Pup	D'laine's diwal dog. Took up the self-appointed role of fiercely guarding D'laine and Trakon's unhatched offspring.
Quag*	One of two farmers that come to Jor-Dan with a complaint over their shared well.
Quark Zerfre	One of Jor-Dan's advisors, he heads Ebscalon's crestrider fleet.
Rachel	D'laine's childhood friend since 3rd grade.
Rettu	The second disciple of the Visionary.
Rosa Villarreal	The Jackson family's housekeeper.
Scooby	One of the diwal dogs tamed by D'laine. Upon becoming King Jor-Dan's guard dog, he is given the Ciertron name of "La'gar'ish."
Sorgus Blaski	The leader of the Plakados and the one to discover Asbram.
Stanley Daigle	Victor Bennet's old friend and fellow physicist, this genius's enthusiasm with the alternate dimension theory is unmatched. With his head shape entirely restored and his gift of telekinesis and telepathy under control, Stanley is chosen for an important role; and might find love along the way too.
Swezek	One of the Egrom village elders tasked with helping and training D'laine to realize her destiny. Even Egroms can only live for so long; and Swezek is past his time.
Tetonie*	Noona's mate. The last of their race, Tetonie is willing to go to drastic measures to get help; though his horrendous social skills might hamper that.

Characters, *Continued*

The Visionary	Both healer and spiritual guide, the old Ciertron man is one of only three inhabiting Ebscalon's sacred temple.
Trabet	One of the Egrom village elders tasked with helping and training D'laine to realize her destiny.
Trakon Bramstone	The Prince of Ebscalon. Despite his hasty temper, Trakon is willing to befriend once adversaries; and maybe take his relationship with D'laine to the next level. He's recently developed an almost obsessive love for Earth food.
Treikie Soluvia*	Stanley's girlfriend, a scientist just as obsessed with the subject as he is.
Twum	D'laine's handmaiden assigned to her during her stay at Ebscalon's palace.
Ulavia	A Ciertron seamstress, she is hired to make D'laine's wedding dress.
Ulf*	One of two farmers that come to Jor-Dan with a complaint over their shared well, the problem lies with him, though in a way many might not think.
Uni*	One of the Kudaja, he helps Ben adjust to Tholian life.
Victor Bennet	An accomplished physicist and best friends with Stanley Daigle, he's one of few who found out what happened to D'laine Jackson. Later he moves along with his family to Thol, gaining the gift of foresight.
Vila*	A Kudaja girl who befriends and plays with Darren and Chacoodi.
Wegore	One of several Plotals accompanying Jakla on his visit to Ebscalon.
Yalalore*	The princess of Patrosym, she seems only concerned with herself, her father, and bettering her own social standing. Before D'laine's arrival to Thol, she was slated to be engaged to Trakon.
Youndon	The ruler of Lansobar.
Ystap Olu	One of several Plotals sent as diplomats, she is a city planner with her sights set on helping her people rebuild.
Yucovia*	A Ciertron girl who seems to be developing feelings for Brian.
Zandal	The cruel leader of the robotics forces of Zan, he aimed to conquer any and all who stood in his way; and an unknown anomaly provided just that opportunity.
Zedonia*	One of the women warriors assigned to guard D'laine and Trakon's unborn children.

Locations & Places

Asbram	Another separate realm, and the place to which the Plakados migrated to, vanishing from the surface of Thol.
Aveldon	One of Thol's city-kingdoms.
Caradon	A city-kingdom, and home to the Caradonians.
Cember Forest	Home to the Egroms and Kudaja, this giant, colorful forest is filled with massive, unknown flora and fauna.
Ebscalon	A Ciertron city of diamond-like roofs and colorful banners rebuilt in the wake of a devastating war, its name means "knowledge". Nests are being constructed on the city's towers to house the few full-sized borjos brought from Mt. Aguberro.
Egrom Village	Home of the Egroms of Cember Forest, visitors must be invited to it; else the village and inhabitants remain invisible to them.
Ikley Forest	A forest located nearby Ta'Byu'Vohon, the city-kingdom of the Plotals.
Ingosaquille	A crest on Mt. Aguberro, it is located one drok from the summit and hides a cave containing mysterious artifacts and scrolls from times lost.
Jekorba	A neighboring kingdom to Ebscalon.
Kensadora	A neighboring kingdom and the place where Ethaderia's sister lives.
Kitchikiwon	This mountain serves as home to the Raagor, the ice people living on the cold slopes and terrain.
Kudajara	The home of the Kudaja, it is located deep in Cember Forest. The village itself is made up of boardwalks, with its homes and structures built into the large trees.
Lansobar	A neighboring kingdom to Ebscalon.
Mer	Kingdom of the Mers.
Mount Aguberro	The least explored mountain on Thol, Mt. Aguberro is home to an impressive population of borjos, the untamed creatures able to reach their full-size without outside interference. It houses some form of ambient magic, allowing the Fod to assume different appearances as need be.
Oolarooloo Forest	Home to the Oolarooloo people's village. While this forest on the other side of Thol has no official name, it is certainly unforgettable, with lush flora and an abundance of fruits and vegetables like a garden.
Patrosym	A neighboring kingdom to Ebscalon.
Raagor Mountains	A large mountain range home to the Raagor Ice people.
Sagritol Valley	An unnamed valley hidden between the mountain ranges, it is odd by Tholian standards: grass instead of moss, small trees, and flora that appears to be Eartholian.
Ta'Byu'Vohon	The city-kingdom of the Plotals, it was destroyed in the Great War, leaving nothing behind. However, nothing states that it must remain that way.
The Visionary's Temple	The sacred Ciertron temple is set in the middle of Ebscalon.
Thol	An alternate Earth, Thol is the third planet in orbit; but this is where similarities end, with two suns, four large moons, vibrant landscapes, and a plethora of unique creatures and races.
Valley of Wailing Winds	Located on the opposite side of Thol, it is home to the Trangula people.
Zan	Another alternate Earth, this world has been reduced to a barren wasteland by its robotic inhabitants, humans made into slaves and prey.

Races

Caradonions	Another of the many races of Thol.
Ciertrons	Most resembling Earth's humans with their bronzed skin and dark hair, the Ciertrons are a technologically advanced society, defenders of justice who value honor despite their constant conflicts with Plotals. Their offspring are split between being born with childlike minds and those of adults. Ciertron women lay small eggs which slowly grow over several paths, reaching 2-3 feet in diameter before hatching.
Egroms	A wise, ancient race possessing wonderous abilities, the long-lived Egroms have since faded into myth and legend, isolating themselves in the Cember Forest while they continue to carry out their self-appointed duties. Recently, they have become more involved in the affairs of Thol's other races, interacting and aiding those they can. Egroms have an age limit of two thousand years; once it is reached they will pass on.
Fod	The sentinels of the cave on Mt. Aguberro. Resembling hunch-backed creatures covered in brown hair, they guard the cave's artifacts and treasures.
Kudaja	Described as tiny peoples who inhabit the Cember Forest, the Kudaja ride borjos as their mounts and wield wyres. Despite their stature, they possess a significant ability to morph to a larger form. However, not all Kudaja are able to do this.
Mer	A very similar race to the Ciertrons, Mers only differ by their square jaws and pronounced foreheads.
Oolarooloo	Distinctive by their tall and thin appearance, dark bronzed skin, oblong heads and long ears, and lengthy necks, the Oolarooloo a people living on the opposite side of the Thol, renown for being great healers and keepers of the knowledge of many mysterious of Thol.
Plakado	Long thought extinct, the Plakado are distant relatives of the Plotals, differing slightly with their lack of a snout, along with other features. Interestingly, they are physically incapable of entering places or past thresholds without first being invited in.
Plotals	Tall reptilian bipeds that appear both human and alligator with the addition of hidden barbs on the ends of their tails, their society was destroyed by the Great War, leaving the survivors to live a nomadic life of plundering and slavery across Thol. Recently, they have switched to a more peaceful way of living, trying to rebuild their old kingdom. Similar to Ciertrons, Plotals also lay eggs, burying them until they hatch.
Raagor	Living in the mountain range of their namesake, the Raagor wear little clothing without fear of the cold. Also known as the "ghost people" because of their hairless pale skin and blue veins, the Raagor avoid socializing with other races. They are capable of freezing a person with a single touch, but cannot withstand high temperatures, preferring to live high in the frigid mountains.
Safri	An intelligent race of Thol, the Safri have friendly relations with the Ciertrons and trade with them. Their appearance resembles a blend of human and goat, with horns, pointed ears, and cloven hooves; the small wings and three-fingered hands being an exception.
Sagritols	Appearing as dark humanoid with fine, fuzzy hair all over their bodies, and a butterfly's orange and black wings, Sagritols are fast and agile flyers, capable of withstanding cold temperatures. They have a pair of antennas on their heads which they can use to communicate, and unusually, arms located much further down their torsos.
Trangula	Inhabiting the Valley of Wailing Winds, the Trangula resemble humans with lengthy arms, large flat noses, and a small hump between their shoulder blades. They are seen as violent people, causing much problems and strife.
Triculated Cribustals	Tiny, parasitic organisms that feed off an individual's life force; they are foreign to Thol and come from another alternate Earth.
Zan Robots	These robots began as self-evolving technology built by the humans of the alternate Earth called Zan. Later, they took over the world and either enslaved or exterminated their creators.

Creatures

Augugal	A large spiked, hard-shelled animal, augugals are capable of blending into their environment, but these herbivores will prove to be both quick and dangerous when threatened.
Bobboes	Large, flightless birds raised by Ciertrons for their eggs, bobboes have large chests and a fluffy plumage of blue and purple.
Borjo	Resembling small dragons unable to breathe fire, the dragonfly-like borjo are used as mounts by the Kudaja. They are neutered upon hatching; otherwise, an unneutered borjo will grow to be large enough to ride by full-sized humans, capable of breathing fire with a wild temperament. These large borjos are unable to transform to a smaller size, unlike neutered ones. When ridden, they are steered using the fuzzy layers above their wings, but can also be communicated with using telepathic commands.
Diwal dogs	Roaming the sponge plains, diwal dogs are widely considered vicious carnivores, capable of stripping their prey in seconds with their layered, razor-sharp teeth. However, some find the gray-skinned, tufted canines to be misunderstood creatures.
Dooba	A bird-like beast with a bill instead of a beak, blue, orange, and purple feathers, short orange legs, and clawed feet. It lays colorful eggs and mates for life.
Fhahadda	A giant snake-like worm, the fhahadda burrows through the ground with the use of its many teeth. An odd creature, it is capable of both live births and egg-laying, with the number of offspring ranging widely in number. Despite this, no fhahadda has been sighted in over five centuries.
Floff	Despite its cute, wide-eyed appearance and fluffy limbs, this is a carnivore that hunts on the wing.
Gagu	Brightly colored feathers cover most of this flying creature, with its clawed membrane wings being the exception.
Grophie caterpillar	Living in the Cember Forest, its sting results in itchy purple spots that must be soothed with an Egrom antidote.
Hosk	This spider-creature's palm-sized, fluffy body varies in color, and contrasts its black legs and eyes. Living in colonies, it produces plenty of silken webbing from the moss-like sponges of the plains; a material widely used by both Egroms and Ciertrons alike.
Kumbora bear	While usually brown and green-furred, kumbora bears can change their colors to blend into their surroundings. Their long tails and flexible digits allow it to traverse the trees with ease.
Mruck	Appearing a mishmash of creatures with its lidless eyes, long trunk, split hooves, and short ears, mrucks are surprisingly edible and enjoy water.
Og	Large, lumbering animals with blue-tinged fur and nobbled heads that live on the sponge plains. Despite being prone to attacking other animals, ogs are in fact herbivores, their aggression stemming from being highly territorial.
Orich	A large flying creature with a heavily-built body and broad wings.
Pakow	The epitome of gentle giants, pakows are bulky, wooly beasts with six legs, wide faces, and compound eyes. They are used by several races as mounts, transportation, and labor.
Par	A type of scarlet-winged bird.
Queper	While they can be touched without any issue, the real problem is when a predator makes the fatal mistake of trying to eat a queper. This cloven hooved animal's flesh is highly toxic and poisonous.

Quokin	This draconic creature makes its home in water, recognizable by its green-tipped black scales and curious personality. It is said a person touched by a quokin will find their true love.
Ragapunga	Resembling an anteater, the ragapunga should never be startled, as it sprays a deadly acid when frightened to protect itself.
Saber-toothed chun	Large, saber-toothed felines the size of horses that inhabit the Raagor mountains, they serve as comfortable mounts for the Raagor people, their thick manes and paws suited for the cold environment.
Sidel	A rabbit-sized creature that lives on the sponge plains; its meat is an easy source of food.
Xidilot	Now extinct, the xidilot was the natural predator of the Sagritols, hunting their eggs. It resembled a large eagle, and the effects of its hunting habits was enough to force its prey to seek out increasingly desperate measures to hide their unborn offspring.

Measurements

Chack	A Tholian hour
Complete path	A Tholian year
Drok	Tholian unit of distance; equivalent to a mile
Dunct	A moment
Full turn	A Tholian day
Keld	A Tholian month
Notch	A Tholian week
Sepiks	Copper coins used by Ciertrons as currency.
Tuke	Tholian unit of distance; equivalent to a foot

Technology

Crestriders	Flying ships invented by the Ciertrons for travel and city-wide defense against intruders. They are capable of "beaming up" objects and people inside, can both fly and hover, and are controlled with a series of levers, switches, and a joystick. With the crystal solar tech improved by aligning the charging crystals, they can now operate at night.
GSB	Short for "gravitational synchronizing beam," crestriders use it to enable flight and store solar energy in crystal cells.
Jumpsuit	A Ciertron type of clothing made from breathable fabric and worn by its warriors. It has multiple different "forms", including an armored one for combat.
Light healer	A Ciertron invention that uses a beam of light to heal injuries.
Restorative chamber	A glassed-in multi-purpose chamber serving as wardrobe, washer, and restorer for clothing. Also known as a Smart Closet.
Silencing helmet	A helmet secured to the head with a "cerebral key", rendering it unremovable; it cuts off the wearer's ability to communicate both verbally and mentally.
Sonicate box	A Ciertron invention used to assess injuries.
Translator	A small metal clip placed behind the ear which then settles into the flesh and serves as an automatic language translator.
Wyre	Bows used by the Kudaja, they form an arrow made of pure energy when the glowing string is drawn. Arrows can be set to either stun or kill.

Miscellaneous

Abrajaii	A golden Ciertron drink resembling champagne; it is drunk during celebrations.
Agrin trees	These trees produce large amounts of sap, which is tapped and blended with hosk webbing to create many durable items like footwear and banners. Entire forests can grow from one seed, reaching heights tall enough to touch the clouds. Its hard and dense bark can be carved to make durable toys.
Bonding	The spiritual bond formed between partners in a Tholian marriage; once it has been broken, only time may heal it.
Churling	A devastating type of storm, with winds worse than a Category 5 hurricane.
Cribbage	A Plotal board game played with markers, octagonal dice, and dowels.
Eartholian	The term used to refer to those from Earth who moved to Thol and gained gifts.
Kahl	A thick, sweet alcoholic drink consumed by Ciertrons.
Lantern-wick plant	The exact name of this plant is unknown. It grows in large clusters among shaded areas of the Cember Forest, and its thick, oily blue stalks are used in lanterns due to their slow-burning nature.
Lightning stones	A special type of rock that produces a purple flame when gently tapped against itself. Banging them together creates an explosion.
Nepsa	Plotal term for grandfather.
Nepsi	Plotal term for grandmother.
The Great War of Taylon	A lengthy Ciertron-Plotal war that left both sides decimated.
The Staff	A sacred relic thought to have been destroyed centuries ago.
The Voice	A mysterious ability that allows one to control others with verbal commands.
Youngmen	Not all Ciertron children are the same; Youngmen are those that emerge from their eggs in child-like bodies but with the minds of fully functioning adults.

A NOTE FROM THE AUTHOR

If you discover a missing element that should be included in the
Glossary or Errors in the book, please let me know at
dawn@degreenfeld.com

ABOUT THE AUTHOR

D.E. Greenfield, aka Dawn Greenfield Ireland, is the award-winning author of 22 published novels which consists of 5 series: cozy mystery, sci-fi/fantasy, billionaire shapeshifters, and dystopian. There's also a stand-alone sci-fi romantic adventure. Currently 7 nonfiction books (1 hardcover) are under the Learning Smart book tab, and she adapted 4 of her screenplays into book format. She also has created over 50+ themed notebooks.

Two of her screenplays were optioned, and she worked on a screenwriter-for-hire project. Dawn has a certificate from the Professional Program in Screenwriting from UCLA (2002) and with ScreenwritingU.

D.E. Greenfield's business, Artistic Origins, has been around since 1995. Besides writing, she coaches writers, edits, formats and publishes clients' books.

Her former day job as an award-winning technical writer played a major role in her fiction writing. She is detailed-oriented, the organizational queen of the known universe, and never misses a deadline.

https://www.degreenfield.com

Sign up for the newsletter.

Actions Appreciated

Please leave a review on the website where you bought the book. Reviews help authors get recognized, get the word out and sell more books. I will love you forever if you leave a review!

HINT: don't regurgitate the synopsis for your review. Just tell people what you liked, didn't like – that's what people want – your opinion.

facebook.com/dawn.ireland.18
x.com/dawnireland
instagram.com/dawngreenfieldIreland
goodreads.com/dawnireland
linkedin.com/in/dawnireland